COCONUT LAYER CAKE MURDER

"Hannah!" Michelle answered on the first ring. "You have to come back to Lake Eden right away! It's an emergency!"

"Is something wrong with Moishe?"

"No, Hannah. Moishe's fine. Everybody's fine here, except . . ." Michelle's voice broke and she stopped speaking to clear her throat," . . . except Lonnie."

"What's wrong with Lonnie? Is he sick?"

"There's been a murder, a woman Lonnie knew from his high school class, Darcy Hicks. And Lonnie . . ." Michelle choked up again and then she began to sob.

"Calm down, honey," Hannah said, trying to make her voice as comforting as possible despite the alarm she was feeling. "Tell me what's wrong with Lonnie."

"It's awful, Hannah!"

"Whatever it is, it's going to be okay. I'll catch the first flight out and come right back to Lake Eden if you need me."

"I do! I need you, Hannah! There's nobody else who can help! And I'm too upset to do it alone!"

"Do what, Michelle?"

"Lonnie's classmate, Darcy Hicks, has been murdered. And Lonnie's thet . . ." Michelle took another breath and managed to choke out the words. "Lonnie's the main suspect!"

Books by Joanne Fluke

Hannah Swensen Mysteries

CHOCOLATE CHIP COOKIE MURDER
STRAWBERRY SHORTCAKE MURDER
BLUEBERRY MUFFIN MURDER
LEMON MERINGUE PIE MURDER
FUDGE CUPCAKE MURDER
SUGAR COOKIE MURDER
PEACH COBBLER MURDER
CHERRY CHEESECAKE MURDER
KEY LIME PIE MURDER
CANDY CANE MURDER
CARROT CAKE MURDER
CREAM PUFF MURDER
PLUM PUDDING MURDER
APPLE TURNOVER MURDER
DEVIL'S FOOD CAKE MURDER
GINGERBREAD COOKIE MURDER
CINNAMON ROLL MURDER
RED VELVET CUPCAKE MURDER
BLACKBERRY PIE MURDER
DOUBLE FUDGE BROWNIE MURDER
WEDDING CAKE MURDER
CHRISTMAS CARAMEL MURDER
BANANA CREAM PIE MURDER
RASPBERRY DANISH MURDER
CHRISTMAS CAKE MURDER
CHOCOLATE CREAM PIE MURDER
CHRISTMAS SWEETS
COCONUT LAYER CAKE MURDER
CHRISTMAS CUPCAKE MURDER
TRIPLE CHOCOLATE CHEESECAKE MURDER
JOANNE FLUKE'S LAKE EDEN COOKBOOK

Suspense Novels

VIDEO KILL
WINTER CHILL
DEAD GIVEAWAY
THE OTHER CHILD
COLD JUDGMENT
FATAL IDENTITY
FINAL APPEAL
VENGEANCE IS MINE
EYES
WICKED
DEADLY MEMORIES
THE STEPCHILD

Published by Kensington Publishing Corp.

COCONUT LAYER CAKE MURDER

JOANNE FLUKE

KENSINGTON
PUBLISHING CORP.

www.kensingtonbooks.com

This book is a work of fiction. Names, characters, businesses, organizations, places, events, and incidents either are the product of the author's imagination or are used fictitiously. Any resemblance to actual persons, living or dead, events, or locales is entirely coincidental.

To the extent that the image or images on the cover of this book depict a person or persons, such person or persons are merely models, and are not intended to portray any character or characters featured in the book.

KENSINGTON BOOKS are published by

Kensington Publishing Corp.
119 West 40th Street
New York, NY 10018

Copyright © 2020 by H.L. Swensen, Inc.

All rights reserved. No part of this book may be reproduced in any form or by any means without the prior written consent of the Publisher, excepting brief quotes used in reviews.

If you purchased this book without a cover, you should be aware that this book is stolen property. It was reported as "unsold and destroyed" to the Publisher and neither the Author nor the Publisher has received any payment for this "stripped book."

All Kensington Titles, Imprints, and Distributed Lines are available at special quantity discounts for bulk purchases for sales promotions, premiums, fund-raising, and educational or institutional use. Special book excerpts or customized printings can also be created to fit specific needs. For details, write or phone the office of the Kensington special sales manager: Kensington Publishing Corp119 West 40th Street, New York, NY 10018, attn: Special Sales Department, Phone: 1-800-221-2647.

The K logo is a trademark of Kensington Publishing Corp.

ISBN-13: 978-1-4967-1890-7
ISBN-10: 1-4967-1890-9
First Kensington Hardcover Edition: March 2020
First Kensington Mass Market Edition: February 2021

ISBN-13: 978-1-4967-1891-4 (ebook)
ISBN-10: 1-4967-1891-7 (ebook)

10 9 8 7 6 5 4 3 2 1

Printed in the United States of America

This book is for Megatronic.

Acknowledgments

Many thanks to my extended family for encouraging me to get back to writing when I bogged down.
I wish I had enough ovens to bake each of you a Coconut Layer Cake.

Hugs to Trudi Nash for recipe suggestions and for always being willing to talk about cooking and baking. And thanks to Trudi's husband, David, who encourages her to attend book events with me despite the fact that he has to cook for himself while she's gone.

Thank you to my friends and neighbors: Mel & Kurt, Lyn & Bill, Gina, Dee Appleton, Jay, Richard Jordan, Laura Levine, the real Nancy and Heiti, Dan, Mark & Mandy at Faux Library, Daryl and her staff at Groves Accountancy, Gene and Ron at SDSA, the crew at the Safari Room, and everyone at Homestreet Bank.

Hugs to my Minnesota friends: Lois & Neal, Bev & Jim, Val, Ruthann, Lowell, Dorothy & Sister Sue, and Mary & Jim.

A big hug for John Scognamiglio, the best editor I could possibly have.
There are times when you have the patience of a saint!

Hugs for Meg Ruley and the staff at the Jane Rotrosen Agency for their constant support and sage advice.

Thanks to all the wonderful folks at Kensington Books who keep Hannah sleuthing and baking yummy goodies.

Thanks to Robin in production, who catches my goofs and corrects them.
And thank you to Larissa for working on my behalf in publicity.

Thanks to Hiro Kimura for his incredibly delicious artwork.
I get hungry every time I glance at the cover of a Hannah book!

Thank you to Lou Malcangi at Kensington for designing all of Hannah's gorgeous book covers. They're simply delightful.

Thanks to John at *Placed4Success* for Hannah's movie and TV placements, his presence on Hannah's social media platforms, the countless hours he spends helping me, and for believing that it's what a son should do. *(If you meet John, please don't tell him that not all sons work as hard as he does for their mothers.)*

Thanks to Rudy for managing my website at **www.JoanneFluke.com** and for giving support to Hannah's social media.
And thanks to Tami for assisting with social media and helping to update the website.

Hugs to Kathy Allen for testing and tasting Hannah's recipes, and for never even mentioning that she wasn't fond of coconut!

And thanks to Kathy's friends and family for helping with events and for taste testing.

A big hug to JQ for helping Hannah and me for so many years.

Kudos to Beth and her phalanx of sewing machines for her gorgeous embroidery on our hats, visors, aprons, and tote bags.

Thank you to food stylist, friend, and media guide Lois Brown for her expertise with the launch parties at Poisoned Pen in Scottsdale, AZ, and baking for the TV food segments I do at KPNX in Phoenix.
Thanks also to Destry, the lovely, totally unflappable producer and host of *Arizona Midday*.

Hugs to Debbie Risinger and everyone else on Team Swensen.

Thank you to Dr. Rahhal, Dr. Josephson, Dr. and Cathy Line, Dr. Levy, Dr. Koslowski, and Drs. Ashley and Lee for answering my book-related medical and dental questions.

Hugs to all the Hannah fans who read the books, share their family recipes, post on my Facebook page, **Joanne Fluke Author**, and enjoy the photos of Sven, my *bear*-footed dessert chef.

Chapter One

Hannah Swensen was just taking the last pan of Cocoa Crisp Cookies out of her industrial oven when her partner, Lisa Beeseman, pushed open the swinging door that separated The Cookie Jar coffee shop from the kitchen. "There's a phone call for you, Hannah. It's Doc Knight, and he says he needs to talk to you."

"Thanks, Lisa." Hannah shoved the pan of cookies on a shelf in the bakers rack and hurried across the kitchen to grab the phone. Her heart was pounding hard, and it wasn't from her dash across the floor. She'd been waiting for Doc's call for two days now, and he was finally ready to give her the results of her test.

"Hello?" she said breathlessly.

"Hi, honey." Doc's voice was warm and Hannah wondered what that meant. "Can you come out to the hospital now? I need to see you."

"I . . . yes, of course I can. But . . ."

"I just got the results of your tests," Doc interrupted what was bound to be a question from his stepdaughter.

"I'll see you in a few minutes, then. When you get to the hospital, come straight to my office. I'll be waiting for you."

There was a click as Doc ended the call. It was clear he wouldn't answer any of her questions over the phone. Hannah was frowning as she replaced the receiver in the cradle. Couldn't Doc just tell her what she wanted to know? All she needed was a simple yes or no answer . . . unless there was something else wrong that he'd discovered from her lab test results.

You don't need any new worries, her rational mind told her.

Of course you don't, but that doesn't mean there's nothing else wrong, her suspicious mind insisted. *It could be anything. Hepatitis, a blood infection, an incurable disease that you picked up from traveling on your honeymoon . . .*

The only way she'd find out was to see Doc in person and Hannah knew it. She hurried across the kitchen and grabbed her parka from the rack by the back door. She didn't want to speculate about any more dire possibilities. They were endless. She'd just tell Lisa that she was leaving, get in her cookie truck, and drive to the hospital to hear what Doc had to tell her.

During her uneventful drive to Doc's Lake Eden Hospital, Hannah did her best to think positive thoughts. She pulled into the parking lot, parked in the visitors' section, and rushed in without taking advantage of the electric sockets on the posts in front of each parking spot to plug in the block heater in her truck.

"Hi, Hannah," the volunteer at the receptionist's desk greeted her as she came in. "Doc's waiting for you in his office."

"Thank you." Hannah signed the visitors book and hoped she didn't look as anxious as she felt as she walked down the hall. When she reached Doc's office, she took a deep breath for courage and opened the door.

"Hello, Hannah. He's in the inner office," Doc's secretary, Vonnie, told her. "Go right in."

Hannah thanked her and opened the door. She found Doc sitting at his desk, riffling through a stack of medical journals.

"Sit down, Hannah," Doc said, gesturing toward the chair in front of his desk. "No, you're not pregnant."

The news hit her like a blow between the eyes. "I'm not?" she managed a response.

"No, the sample we took was conclusive."

Hannah leaned back in the chair and grasped the arms tightly. "I . . . I don't know if I'm supposed to be devastated or relieved."

"Of course you don't. If I had to guess, I think you're a little bit of both."

"Yes," Hannah said past the lump that was forming in her throat. "But, Doc . . . *something's* wrong."

"Yes, it is. It's stress."

"Stress?" Hannah stared at him in shock.

"Yes, stress can take a toll on the human body, and you've been under extreme stress ever since Ross left Lake Eden. Stress throws off your body clock, plays havoc with your nervous system, and mimics symptoms of diseases you never believed you could contract. Every day someone comes in here believing that they're having a coronary event and it turns out to be a panic attack."

"But, Doc . . . I don't feel *that* stressed."

"Perhaps you don't think so, but believe me, you're stressed. And eventually, extreme stress will manifest itself in actual disease. That's why your mother and I have decided that you're going to take a little vacation."

"Vacation?" Hannah repeated the word. Her mind was spinning and she couldn't seem to think of anything else to say.

"That's right. Your mother got a call from Lynne Larchmont yesterday. Lynne made an offer on Tory Bascomb's condo, and the mayor and Stephanie accepted it."

Hannah blinked several times, trying to process this new, surprising information. "That's . . . great."

"Exactly what your mother said. And once she told me about it, I urged her to call Lynne back and tell her that you two will fly out to Los Angeles to help Lynne get things packed up for the movers."

"You mean . . . Mother and me?"

Doc nodded. "Precisely. I made the plane reservations for both of you last night. You'll be at Lynne's house by the end of the week."

"But . . ." Hannah stopped talking when Doc held up his hand.

"I know that Friday is Valentine's Day, but I've already talked to Marge and Nancy, and they'd promised to fill in for you at The Cookie Jar. Lisa assures me that they can handle anything that might come up, Michelle has agreed to stay at your condo with Moishe to oversee the work that's being done there, and Cyril will drive you to the airport in one of his limos."

Hannah just stared at him blankly. It seemed that Doc had thought of everything.

"Here," Doc said, handing her a prescription blank. "I've prescribed a vacation and you *will* go. I won't listen to any objections. You're my patient and you'll follow my recommendation. And besides, I love you, Hannah."

Tears sprang to Hannah's eyes. There was no doubt in her mind that Doc loved her. She gave a little nod, and then she managed a smile.

"Good!" Doc got up and walked around his desk to give her a hug. "There's another factor, too."

Hannah stared at him with some trepidation. "What's that?"

"You're not the only one who needs a vacation."

Hannah took a moment to digest that comment. "You mean . . . you're going to Los Angeles with us?"

"No, but your mother's going. And that means *I* get a vacation. You're doing me a big favor, Hannah."

Hannah couldn't help it. She burst into laughter. This wasn't the first time she'd been delighted that her mother had married Doc.

Doc smiled, and then his expression sobered. "You have no idea how worried your mother has been about you. It'll do her a world of good to spend some time in California with you and Lynne. And, to be perfectly honest, it's going to be a lot less stressful around here with both of you gone."

"Mother's been *that* worried?"

"Yes. You'll go, won't you, Hannah?"

"I . . ." Hannah dipped her head in a nod. "Yes, if you really think I should."

"I do. Helping Lynne pack will give you something else to think about, not to mention that your mother will be fascinated with the lifestyle in California. Lynne told her that she lives in a place called Brentwood and quite a few celebrities live there. Your mother doesn't think I know, but she has several subscriptions to those celebrity, tell-all magazines. And that's our secret, okay?"

"Okay," Hannah agreed. Perhaps it would be best to get away and gain a new perspective.

"Lynne's very excited about moving here to Lake Eden, Hannah. She said she's looking forward to being around real friends."

Hannah began to smile. "Well . . . in that case . . . What time do we leave?"

"On Friday morning. Get things settled with your crew at The Cookie Jar and then meet with Michelle. She can bring you whatever you need from the condo."

Quite unexpectedly, Hannah felt a surge of excitement. The world suddenly seemed less dreary, even though the skies were gray and overcast and snow was predicted. "Thank you, Doc," she said. "I'm going to drive over to Mother's and ask her advice on what I should pack."

Chapter Two

"Wake up, Hannah."

Hannah awoke with a jolt as she heard her mother's voice. "I'm too tired to go to school," she protested.

Delores laughed and so did someone else. And then a voice that Hannah didn't recognize said, "Your mother ordered coffee for you. Better wake up and drink it before it gets cold."

Hannah's eyes flew open and she focused on a tray table with a cup of coffee. She picked it up, took a sip, and saw the stewardess standing in the aisle of the plane. "Sorry," she apologized. "For a minute there, I didn't know where I was."

"Drink this and I'll bring you another cup before I close down the kitchen," the stewardess told her. "We'll be landing in less than half an hour."

"Landing in Los Angeles?" Hannah turned to address her mother, who was sitting in the window seat.

"That's right. You slept the entire way, Hannah. You must have been really tired."

"I must have been," Hannah agreed, finishing her coffee and handing the cup to the stewardess.

"I'll bring you two more cups," the stewardess decided, noticing that Hannah was having some difficulty keeping her eyes open.

Two more cups of coffee later, Hannah felt almost awake. She leaned forward to look out the window and smiled as she spotted what looked like miniature cars on the freeway below. The freeway disappeared a few moments later and there was nothing but blue below them. They must be circling over the Pacific Ocean, waiting for their turn to land.

There was a grinding noise and a jarring bump as the pilot lowered the landing gear. They were over land again now and the city streets were laid out in a grid below. As Hannah watched, the buildings grew larger and she knew that they were descending. And then the buildings disappeared and asphalt runways appeared. They flew over one of the runways, the ground came up toward the belly of the plane, and there was a jolt as the wheels touched down. They bounced up and then settled back down again, this time meeting the runway smoothly and taxiing toward the airport buildings.

Hannah reached for her seat belt, but her mother shook her head. "Wait until the sign goes off, dear. We have to stay seated until we reach the gate with the jetway in place."

"Yes, of course we do," Hannah chided herself for not remembering the protocol she'd learned on previous flights. "Until we reach a full and complete stop. Right, Mother?"

"That's right." Delores glanced at her watch. "We seem to be here right on time, dear. I hope Lynne got the schedule I sent her."

"I'm sure she did. Lynne's always been the type to be on time. I wonder if she's coming to meet us herself, or whether we should take a taxi?"

"When I talked to her last night, she said she'd be here. And if something unexpected happened, she'd send a car service for us."

It seemed to take forever to taxi up to the gate, and they had to wait for another few minutes for the jetway to be locked into position. At last the seat belt sign went off and Hannah stood up to open the shell above their heads to pull down their carry-on luggage. They joined the line in the aisle and soon they were walking down the jetway to the terminal.

"The stewardess said our luggage would be on carousel seven," Delores said, pointing to the sign that indicated the way to the baggage claim area.

As they walked inside the cavernous area filled with carousels that delivered luggage to the passengers waiting below, Delores stopped and gestured to a uniformed man standing next to carousel seven. "Lynne sent a car service. He has two signs, one with your name and one with mine."

"Ladies," the man greeted them. "I'm Robby, Mrs. Larchmont's driver. Did you have a pleasant flight?" When they assured him they had, he got a luggage cart, asked them to identify their luggage, and escorted them out of the building. He then led them across the street and into the limousine parking area. Once he had seated them in the car, he loaded their suitcases in the back, started the car, and drove out of the airport.

"This is nice," Hannah said, reaching for one of the bottles of water that had been placed in the console in front of them.

"Is water all right, or would you care for another beverage?" the driver asked her.

"Water is perfect," Hannah told him. And it was, but she couldn't help wondering what other beverages he might have offered.

"And for you, Ma'am?" the driver asked Delores.

"What other choices do I have?" Delores responded.

"I have several kinds of juice in the mini fridge between the seats in the back. And I also have a small bottle of Perrier Jouët. Mrs. Larchmont mentioned that it was your favorite champagne."

"How very sweet of her! Of course I'll have that."

"Very good, Ma'am. If you open the small refrigerator in front of you, you'll find champagne glasses and several individual bottles."

Once they had driven out of the parking garage, they turned onto a city street lined with shops and office buildings. They drove for several minutes in silence, and then Robby spoke again.

"Normally, I'd take the freeway to Mrs. Larchmont's home in Brentwood, but she asked me to give you a mini tour. Is that acceptable to you?"

Delores looked at Hannah, who nodded. "Yes, it is. We'd enjoy that."

"Good. We're about a mile from the airport now and if you look up, through the passenger compartment moon roof, you might see a jet flying overhead on approach to the airport. It will be low and it's startling when you see how big it looks when you're down here on the ground. I'll stop and park, and you'll see what I mean."

There was a parking spot in the block ahead and their driver parked at the curb. "We won't have to wait long," the driver told them. "Jets fly over here every five minutes or so."

Less than a minute later, Hannah heard a plane coming closer. The noise grew louder and louder, and both Hannah and Delores stared up at the glass in the moon roof. When the roar was almost loud enough to cause Hannah to cover her ears, she spotted a shadow and then a humongous plane passed directly over their limo.

"Good heavens!" Delores gasped, turning to Hannah. "Did you see that?"

"I saw it. I thought it was going to crash right into us!"

Their driver chuckled. "It was actually several hundred feet above us, but it does seem that way when you're down here on the street. It's always a thrill the first time you see it."

"Thank you for showing it to us," Hannah said as the driver put the car in gear and pulled away from the curb.

"There's more in store," the driver told her. "Mrs. Larchmont asked me to take you past the studio where she'll be working next week. She called ahead and got a pass for us so we can drive around the lot."

Hannah stared out the window. Los Angeles appeared to be a huge, sprawling city with more cars and traffic than she had ever seen before. It seemed as if everyone was in a hurry, and horns blared when there was the slightest delay.

"It's so green!" Delores commented as they drove down a street lined with palm trees.

"Actually, it's greener in the summer," Robby told her. "Right now it's winter green, and that's a pale imitation of the darker, more brilliant green we get in the spring."

"Maybe we're just used to winter in Minnesota," Hannah told him. "We live with a black and white landscape for four or five months every year. The only color we get is the blue of the sky, as long as it's not an overcast day."

"Quite a few people leave for a couple of months in the winter," Delores said, entering the conversation. "We call them *snowbirds* and when the snow starts to fly, they migrate to Florida or California. Winter can be very depressing because it's the same scene outside your window every morning. Snow, snow, and more snow."

"That sounds boring," Robby commented. "It must be a real treat for you to come here. Change is good."

"Yes, it is," Hannah agreed, and then she gasped as the driver pulled up in front of a pair of ornate gates. "Where are we?"

"Paramount Studios. It's one of the older studios in this area. Most of the others have changed names, but this one is still Paramount."

"And this is where all the movies are made?" Delores asked him.

"Not so much anymore. A lot of production companies have moved to other states, and some film in Canada. Toronto is a thriving film city now."

"Why did the companies move there?" Hannah asked.

"Taxes. California taxes are among the highest in the nation. There are lots of regulations, too. If you want to film a scene on a city street, you have to apply for a permit and pay to use it for a location. It's one of the reasons we're losing so much of our film and television industry."

"You seem to know a lot about it," Delores commented.

"I do. I haven't been a limo driver all my life, you know."

Hannah and Delores exchanged glances. Should they recognize Robby as an actor in a film or television program they'd seen? Would it be an insult if they asked him what he'd meant by his cryptic statement?

Hannah shook her head slightly, and Delores nodded agreement. Discretion was the better part of valor in this case. It might be insulting if they admitted that they didn't recognize him, especially if he'd been someone well-known. They could always ask Lynne about him later.

Once Robby had given their names to the guard at the studio gate and they were allowed to pass, the driver drove down a narrow street.

"Oh, look!" Hannah said, pointing to the empty parking lot. "Why is the parking lot painted blue?"

"That's the Pacific Ocean," Roby told them, "or at least it was the Pacific Ocean in several movies about the Second World War."

"But how could it be?" Delores asked him. "War movies have ships and submarines. That parking lot isn't big enough to hold ships and submarines!"

"It is if the ship or submarine is a miniature model," Robby explained. "And the cement is painted blue because they flood it when they want to film a water scene. It's been the Pacific Ocean, the Atlantic Ocean, even the China Sea. And let me tell you, the people who park there aren't any too happy about giving up their parking spot for a week or two every couple of months."

After a quick tour of the lot, Robby took them through Hollywood and down Rodeo Drive, where he pointed out stores with famous designer names. Delores was clearly fascinated, and Hannah watched as her mother took in every display in the shop windows.

"Do you want to stop and go into one of the shops?" Hannah asked her.

"No, dear. I might want to buy something and I'm not sure I could afford it. It's not like the Tri-County Mall, you know. I could buy something if I really wanted to, but . . ."

"But what?" Hannah asked.

"Look!"

Delores pointed and Hannah looked. There was a red patent leather bikini covered with a filmy, flowing float in a window filled with tote bags and sun hats. "You're not thinking of buying something like that, are you, Mother?"

"Good heavens, no! I was just trying to decide if I disliked anyone enough to give them something like that for a gift."

"Are you ready to go to Mrs. Larchmont's home yet?" Robby asked them.

"I'm ready," Hannah said, and then she turned to her mother. "How about you, Mother?"

"I'm definitely ready."

"All right, then." Robby turned onto another street and drove past homes that were set so far back from the street, Hannah could barely glimpse them. "What area of Los Angeles is this?" she asked.

"Brentwood."

"The houses are very large," Delores commented.

"Yes, I don't believe there are any houses, except for guest houses, of course, that have less than six bedrooms."

Hannah and Delores exchanged glances. "Is Lynne's house that large?" Hannah asked him.

"Yes, I believe it's an eight-bedroom, ten-bath home. Mrs. Larchmont lives on an estate that once belonged to Harlan Cornell."

Again, Hannah and Delores exchanged glances. Neither one of them recognized the name, but Harlan Cornell must be some sort of celebrity here in Los Angeles. Robby had spoken his name in an almost-reverent manner.

"My goodness," Delores commented.

"Yes, indeed," Hannah added, although she was clueless regarding Mr. Cornell's identity and she strongly suspected that her mother was, too.

"And here we are," Robby announced, turning into a circular driveway lined with flowering bushes in a variety of colors. "The house is right over this rise."

One glimpse of the house and Hannah reached out to squeeze her mother's hand. Lynne's home was a massive sparkling white house that was set in the midst of a perfectly manicured lawn that stretched back as far as they could see. The property was bordered by large trees which effectively hid it from the neighboring homes and gave the illusion of exclusivity. The house itself was built in the Colonial style with huge columns in front supporting a veranda with a second-story balcony above it.

"How beautiful!" Delores breathed, staring at the impressive structure.

Hannah simply nodded. She was a bit too awed by the sight of Lynne's home to speak. It was the largest home she'd ever seen. No wonder Lynne had told Delores that she had plenty of room and invited them to stay with her!

As the limo pulled up in front of the doorway, Lynne stepped out and hurried out to the car to greet them. She pulled open the door, not waiting for Robby, helped Delores out, and gave her a hug. "I'm so glad to see you two! Come in and let's get you settled. Don't worry about your luggage. Robby will bring it in."

Robby opened Hannah's door and extended his arm to help her out of the car while Lynne escorted Delores to the double doors at the front of the house. They crossed the wide veranda and Hannah followed them inside.

"Wow!" Hannah exclaimed, catching sight of the huge chandelier that hung in the foyer. "That's humongous, Lynne!"

"I know. Remember how I always said I wanted a house with a chandelier when we were in college?"

"I remember," Hannah told her, but she didn't mention the rest of the memory. Every time she'd been a guest in Lynne and Ross's small apartment, Lynne had voiced her wish for a chandelier. And Ross had draped his arm around Lynne's shoulder and promised that once they got married and bought their first house, he'd make sure that she had her chandelier.

"Is it very hard to keep clean?" Hannah asked, gazing up at the gleaming crystals.

"Yes, and I don't know what I'd do if I didn't have Maria to keep it clean and sparkling. Once every two months, Robby gets out the ladder and removes all the fobs, facets, and crystal pendants so Maria can put them through the dishwasher."

"Through the dishwasher?" Delores asked, looking positively shocked.

"Yes, she runs them through the wash cycle, but she uses the air-dry feature. Robby and Maria were part of Tom's staff when I married him, and Maria told me that she's been cleaning it that way for years. Once the crystals have gone through the air cycle, she wipes any moisture away with a soft cotton cloth."

Delores looked impressed, and Hannah wondered whether her mother would install a chandelier in the foyer of the penthouse that Doc had given to her as a wedding present. There was no question that Doc would indulge Delores if she truly wanted one.

"I think my ceiling is too low for something like that," Delores said, and Hannah gave a little smile. She'd accurately read her mother's envious expression.

Lynne turned to Robby, who had followed them in with the luggage. "I'll put Hannah in the Rose bedroom, Robby. And Delores will have the gold one."

"Very good, Mrs. Larchmont." Robby turned toward the wide staircase that led up to the second floor.

"I'll let them go up and get settled, and then we'll go out to a late lunch," Lynne told him. "Will you please make reservations at the French Room, Robby? Let's say for three-thirty?"

"Of course, Mrs. Larchmont," Robby said, and then he turned to Hannah and Delores. "If you ladies would care to come with me, I'll show you to your rooms."

Hannah and Delores followed Robby up the wide, carpeted staircase and down a lengthy hallway. They passed several doors and stopped at one near the end of the hallway. "This room is yours," he said to Hannah, opening the door and ushering her in.

"It's beautiful!" Hannah declared, entering the bedroom Lynne had chosen for her. The walls were painted a lovely shade of rose, and the curtains were a velvety shade of yellow.

"Your bathroom is right through here," Robby told her, opening another door and gesturing toward a large bathroom that was decorated in a reversal of colors with velvety yellow walls and lovely rose-colored curtains and towels. It was complete with a roomy shower stall and a huge bathtub with so many jets around the inside of the tub that Hannah was almost sure it also served as a Jacuzzi.

"And this is your closet," Robby said, opening another door to reveal a walk-in closet. "I'll set up the racks for your suitcases on the adjoining wall."

Hannah watched as Robby unfolded two luggage racks and positioned them on the far wall next to the closet. He lifted her luggage effortlessly onto the racks and turned back to her. "Would you like me to unpack for you?"

"Oh! Uh . . . no, thank you. I can do it myself," Hannah said quickly. There was no way she wanted Robby to see some of her favorite clothing, especially because she hadn't purchased anything new in several years, as well as several pairs of what Delores called *unmentionables*. Robby had obviously been trained as a butler, and the other guests that Lynne and Tom had entertained undoubtedly had undergarments that were much pricier and more stylish than the white cotton ones that Hannah purchased at CostMart.

"I'll get your mother settled, then," Robby told her, heading for the door.

"Wait!" Hannah said quickly. "Could you tell me a little about the French Room?"

"Of course. What would you like to know?"

"The name sounds very fancy," Hannah said choosing her words carefully. "Is it the type of restaurant where everyone dresses up?"

Robby shook his head. "Not really. Mrs. Larchmont often stops by the French Room for a bite after a day at the studio. And then she's usually wearing comfortable clothes."

"Yes, but Lynne's comfortable clothes probably cost more than everything in both of my suitcases!"

Robby chuckled. "You could be right, Ma'am. Mr. Larchmont always wanted her to dress in the height of fashion and she shopped at the finest boutiques."

Hannah took Robby's chuckle to heart. He'd been clearly amused by her comment. "Please call me Hannah, not Ma'am. I think my mother would like to be a Ma'am, but I'm just Lynne's friend from college."

Robby considered that for a moment. "Would it be all right if I called you *Miss Hannah*? I wouldn't want Mrs. Larchmont to think I was being too familiar."

"That's fine with me," Hannah said quickly. "I was hoping you could help me out, Robby. If I show you what I was planning to wear, would you tell me if it's appropriate? There's no way I want to embarrass Lynne by wearing something that's . . ."

"Too casual?" Robby asked.

"Yes."

"And I doubt you'd want to embarrass your mother, either," Robby said with a smile. "I probably shouldn't have said that."

"Why not? You're right." Hannah walked over to one of her suitcases and pulled out a forest green pantsuit that her mother had given to her as a present. "Do you think this would be all right to wear?"

"Yes, indeed. It would be perfect. It's a good color for you with your hair."

"Thank you." Hannah smiled at him. "You'd better go help my mother now. She's probably getting impatient."

Hannah waited as Robby crossed the room and went out the door, closing it behind him. Then she made quick work of unpacking and hanging what needed to be hung in her closet. Once her other clothing had been stashed in the dresser by the bed, she rolled her suitcases into the closet and went off to take a quick shower and change into the outfit that Robby had deemed appropriate.

 # Chapter Three

"**O**h, Hannah! You look absolutely lovely," Lynne complimented her as Hannah came down the stairs.

Hannah remembered what her mother had taught her about accepting compliments and gave Lynne a big smile. "Thanks, Lynne," she accepted the compliment gracefully. "Mother gave this to me for my birthday."

"It's perfect for you." Lynne took the cookie tin that Hannah handed to her. "Cookies?"

"No, I made Chocolate Peanut Butter Toffee for you."

A broad smile spread over Lynne's face as she pried off the lid and looked inside the round tin. "This is my very favorite candy! You used to make this for me every Christmas when we were in college."

"It's a little different this year because I couldn't find Nabisco Chocolate Wafers."

"But it looks like there's chocolate on top."

"There is. I melted chocolate and drizzled it on the top."

"It's pretty." Lynne took a small piece of toffee and bit into it. "It's just as good without the chocolate wafers, Hannah. Actually, it may be better. It tastes like there's more chocolate."

"That's because there *is* more chocolate. I used a layer of chocolate chips on top of the crackers."

"There's more salt, too. And I like it."

"I used Club Crackers and they're salted. The salt side is up and that adds more flavor to the chocolate."

"You're right. It's just wonderful!" Lynne reached for another piece and stopped herself just in time. "I'd better save this for later or I won't be hungry when we get to the restaurant."

Hannah motioned to the staircase as she spotted her mother. "There's Mother. It looks like she did something to her hair."

"My guess is Maria had something to do with that," Lynne told her. "She was a beautician before she married Robby."

Hannah didn't comment aloud, but she wondered if Maria could do something to improve her hairstyle. She'd often joked that she should start using a curry comb on her hair. Unlike Delores with her dark hair, her younger, light blond sister Andrea, and Michelle, the youngest of the Swensen sisters, whose nickname had been Jeanie with the light brown hair, Hannah had inherited her father's almost unmanageable curly red hair, along with his physique. Lars Swensen had been tall and burly with a tendency to put on weight. Hannah, unlike her mother and sisters, was quite tall and what her mother politely called *substantial*. Delores had declared once that Hannah could put on several pounds just walking past the candy store at the mall and staring at the display in the window.

"Am I late?" Delores asked, crossing the room to join them.

"Not at all," Lynne assured her.

"I'm here, Mrs. Larchmont." Robby appeared in the hallway. "I have the car out front if you ladies are ready to go."

"We are," Lynne said. "Perfect timing, Robby. I know that Hannah and Delores must be starving after having nothing but airplane food all day."

"Good heavens!" Delores gasped, catching sight of the woman who'd just walked into the French Room. "Is that . . ."

"Leslie Towers?" Lynne guessed.

"Yes! I saw her in *Peachtree Forever* and she was just wonderful! It's not polite to ask for an autograph, is it?"

Lynne shook her head. "No, but that's not Leslie Towers. Everyone always thinks that, but her name is Gloria Denning and she's my neighbor."

Delores looked disappointed, but then her expression changed to one Hannah could only classify as *cagey*. "I don't suppose she'd pose for a photo with me, would she?"

Lynne laughed. "Only if you promise to tell people she's Leslie Towers. Gloria loves to do that, but she draws the line at signing Leslie's name if people ask her for an autograph. Shall I ask her if she'd like to have lunch with us so that we can take a few photos?"

"That would be wonderful!"

Delores answered immediately and Hannah began to grin. Doc had been right. It was clear that her mother was starstruck.

"I'll be right back," Lynne said, rising from the table and hurrying to intercept her neighbor. After a short conversation, Gloria came back to the table with Lynne.

"Gloria won't be joining us for lunch," Lynne told them after she'd introduced them.

"It would have been fun, but I'm meeting someone in a few minutes," Gloria explained. "I'll be happy to pose for photos, though. It's fun to pretend to be someone famous."

Hannah watched as Lynne posed Gloria and her mother, and took the photos. She could tell that her mother was having the time of her life, and she wouldn't be surprised if Delores went straight down to Rod at the *Lake Eden Journal* when she got home and asked Rod Metcalf to put one of the photos in their hometown newspaper.

"How about you, Hannah?" Gloria asked when the photos with Delores had been taken. "Would you like to pose with me?"

For a moment, Hannah wasn't sure what to say. Would Gloria be insulted if she said that she really wasn't interested in having her photo taken with famous people, either look-alikes or real celebrities? Luckily, the perfect answer occurred to her.

"Thanks so much for offering, but I wouldn't want to spoil my mother's exciting moment. I'll be happy to let her have all the celebrity photo-ops for today."

Lunch had been wonderful, but Hannah noticed that her mother's eyes had closed several times during their trip back to Brentwood. "Are you tired, Mother?" she asked as they entered the house.

"Yes, I am," Delores admitted. "I was up late last night, waiting for Doc to come back from the hospital, and I didn't sleep well. If you girls don't mind, I think I'll go up to my room and take a nap."

"That's a good idea," Lynne said. "Traveling can be very tiring and it's been a long day for you."

"Then that's what I'll do as long as you don't need me," Delores declared, heading for the staircase.

"Are you tired, too?" Lynne asked Hannah.

"Not really. I think I got my second wind. Of course, sleeping all the way here on the plane might have something to do with it."

"As long as you're not as exhausted as your mother, stay and have another glass of champagne with me."

"That sounds nice, but just one glass," Hannah told her.

Lynne stood up and motioned to Hannah. "Let's go in the den. It's cozier. And we can have some of your Chocolate Peanut Butter Toffee for dessert. I carried it in there before we left the house and it'll go well with champagne."

Hannah followed Lynne down a long hallway. There was a door at the end and Lynne pushed it open. "Here's where I come to study my lines. Have a seat, Hannah. I'll get the champagne."

There were two leather chairs in front of the fireplace with a small table between them. Hannah took one and waited while Lynne opened a small refrigerator and took out a bottle of champagne. She opened it, poured two glasses, and carried them over to the small table. "It's Taittinger," she said. "That's my favorite champagne. If your mother had joined us, I would have opened a bottle of Perrier Jouët."

"Mother's favorite," Hannah confirmed it with a nod.

Lynne sat down in the second chair. "Do you have a favorite champagne?"

"Not really. I don't know that much about champagne. Norman's the expert when it comes to things like that."

"But Norman doesn't drink . . . does he?"

"No, but he's still an expert." Hannah didn't go into details about the reason that Norman didn't touch alcohol. He'd told her, but that was a confidence between the two of them and she wasn't about to break it. "Norman brought me a bottle of champagne called . . ." Hannah stopped, trying to remember. "It was French, and he said some people referred to it as *The Widow*."

Lynne nodded. "Veuve Clicquot. That nickname refers to a woman who inherited a winery from her husband and made their champagne into a success. Which champagne do you like best, Hannah? Norman's or mine?"

"I don't know. I think I'd need to have them side by side to compare them. I like your champagne very much, though."

"Good. I was hoping you would. Let's have a fire in the fireplace. It's a little chilly here today."

Hannah's eyebrows shot up in surprise. It seemed nice and warm to her, but perhaps Lynne had lost her tolerance for cold since she'd lived in California for so long.

"This is so handy," Lynne said, picking up the remote control that sat on the table, the one Hannah had assumed would operate the flat-screen television set on the wall. But Lynne didn't swivel in her leather chair to face the television set. "Are you going to turn on the television?" Hannah asked, thoroughly puzzled.

"No, just watch. I think you'll enjoy this," Lynne told her, aiming the control at the fireplace and pressing a button.

Hannah watched as the multicolored crystals in the bed of the fireplace began to glow. A moment later, small flames licked up between the crystals to make the colors even brighter.

Hannah knew she must have looked every bit as amazed as she felt. "That's beautiful!" she breathed.

"I know. This is the place I always sat when Tom was gone. And he wasn't here with me very often. He had a luxury apartment downtown in the financial district and when he wasn't traveling, he spent most nights there."

"Why?" Hannah asked, and then she wished she hadn't asked. Perhaps the reason was too personal for Lynne to divulge. "Sorry," she apologized. "If you don't want to tell me, I'll understand."

"That's okay. I can tell you." Lynne paused to take a deep breath. "I asked Tom why he bought the apartment and Tom told me that sometimes he was really tired after a late meeting with a client and it was exhausting to drive back here if the traffic was heavy."

Hannah was surprised. "The traffic here is *that* bad?"

"It can be, especially coming from downtown if there's a convention or a sports event."

"Did Tom ever take you to see the apartment?"

"Yes, it's on the top floor and it's completely renovated. The view is just breathtaking."

"And you helped him furnish it?"

Lynne shook her head. "No, he bought it completely furnished from a stockbroker he knew. Tom said the man made a fortune in hedge funds. He was moving to London and he planned to buy new furniture when he got there."

"I guess that makes sense. It probably costs a lot to move furniture to another country."

"Yes, it does. I believed the whole story until Tom showed me the bedroom." Lynne paused to take a sip of her champagne. "The first thing I noticed was the red velvet bedspread on the bed. Tom doesn't like red. It's his least favorite color. When we furnished this house, he told me not to buy anything red."

"Did you ask Tom about the red bedspread?"

"Yes, the second I saw it. He said he hadn't gotten around to replacing it yet, but this was a good three months after he'd bought the place. I found it hard to believe that someone like Tom, who hated the color red that much, would wait that long."

"Perhaps he was too busy with his clients?" Hannah suggested.

"That's the excuse he used. But then I noticed the bottle of perfume on the dresser. I'm almost certain that the stockbroker who'd owned the apartment wouldn't have worn Chanel."

"Oh, dear! Did you ask Tom about it?"

"No, I didn't mention it."

"Why?"

"I really didn't want to know, at least not for sure. Then, when Tom started spending more and more time at his apartment and less and less time with me at home, I knew our marriage was falling apart."

"And that's why you wanted Tom to come to Lake Eden with you?"

"Yes, I hoped that we could work things out, but . . .

that didn't happen. I'm just glad that Tom gave me this house when we got married. I'm working with a real-estate agent and she's going to sell it for me."

"But . . . will you need money to move?"

"No, I'm okay financially, Hannah. Most of the commercials I've done have gone nationwide and the residuals are good. I used the signing bonus that Gibson Girl Cosmetics gave me as a down payment on Tori Bascomb's condo."

"So you won't have to work?"

"Oh, I'll want to work eventually, but I have enough for this move. I'm not going to take any of the big furniture, just some small pieces that I don't want to leave behind. Everything else can be sold with the house."

"So we're just packing dishes and things like that?"

"Yes, and I'm going to take some of the artwork that I especially like. I have to remember that I'm downsizing and there's not room for everything in the condo. That's one of the reasons I asked you and Delores to come out here and help me. You and your mother have been in Tori Bascomb's condo, and you can help me judge what will fit and what won't."

Hannah thought about that for a moment. "Mother will be better at that than I will. She spent a lot of time at Tori's condo. They used to have coffee every morning."

"I know. She told me. But there's a second reason I wanted you to come out here, Hannah."

"What is it?"

"I need to find out if we can still be friends after what happened. I wouldn't blame you if you didn't want anything to do with me." Lynne took a deep breath and Hannah could see that she was upset. "After all, Hannah . . .

my husband, Tom, did some horrible things. And I was so immersed in my own problems, I didn't even suspect that Tom was involved!"

"Of course you didn't!" Hannah reached out to pat Lynne's arm. "I didn't suspect Tom, either. I had no idea it was Tom until I put all the pieces together that day at The Cookie Jar."

"Then you're not mad at me for failing to warn you? Or to tell you something that might have made you suspect that you were in danger?"

Hannah shook her head. "Of course not! I didn't suspect what Ross had done, either. It's almost impossible to suspect someone you love and trust enough to marry."

Lynne looked thoughtful. "I guess you're right. I'm sorry, Hannah. If I'd known, or if I'd had even the slightest suspicion, I would have told you."

"I know," Hannah said, and then she smiled. "So we're still good friends, right?"

"The best!" Lynne gave her a happy smile.

"Good, because I need to ask you for a favor."

"Of course. What is it?"

"Don't let Mother see your fireplace."

It was clear from her expression that she was puzzled. "Why not?"

"Because she'll want one just like it. And she'll needle Doc until he goes out and orders one for her."

CHOCOLATE PEANUT BUTTER TOFFEE

Preheat oven to 350°F., rack in the middle position.

16-ounce box Club Crackers *(mine were made by Keebler)*

1 cup milk chocolate chips *(you'll use a total of 2 cups—I used Nestlé)*

1 cup salted butter, softened to room temperature *(2 sticks, ½ pound)*

1 cup brown sugar *(pack it down in the cup when you measure it)*

1 cup milk chocolate chips *(this completes the milk chocolate chip total)*

2 cups peanut butter chips *(10-ounce bag will do—I used Reese's)*

½ cup chopped salted peanuts *(NOT dry roasted—measure AFTER chopping—I used Planters)*

Hannah's 1st Note: There are three packets in a 13-ounce box of Club Crackers. You'll use only one packet. You can buy a smaller box if you can find it, but you can always use extra crackers, right? If you can't find Club Crackers at your store, you can use any brand of salted soda crack-

ers. **Your goal is to cover the bottom of the pan as completely as you can with something both crispy and salty.**

Line a 10-inch by 15-inch cookie sheet with foil. If you have a jellyroll pan, that's perfect. If you don't, use a cookie sheet and turn up the edges of the foil to form sides.

Spray the foil with Pam or another nonstick cooking spray. *(You want to be able to peel the foil off later, after the toffee hardens.)*

Line the bottom of your pan completely with Club Crackers, salt side down. *(You can break the crackers in pieces to make them fit if you have to.)*

Sprinkle 1 (only ONE) cup of milk chocolate chips over the surface of the cracker-lined pan.

Set the jelly roll pan or cookie sheet aside on the kitchen counter while you cook the toffee mixture.

Hannah's 2nd Note: GOOD NEWS! You don't need a candy thermometer to make this toffee.

Combine the salted butter with the brown sugar in a medium-size saucepan. Stir until they are thoroughly mixed.

Hannah's 3rd Note: I use my Great-Grand-mother Elsa's wooden spoon to do this, but you can also use a heat-resistant rubber spatula if you wish.

Set the saucepan on the stovetop and turn the burner to MEDIUM-HIGH. STIRRING CONSTANTLY, bring the toffee mixture to a boil.

Boil for exactly 5 *(five)* minutes. Keep that spoon or spatula going! If you don't, your toffee will burn! If the toffee mixture sputters too much, you can reduce the heat a bit. If the mixture begins to lose the boil, you can increase the heat a bit. Just don't stop stirring until you've boiled it for 5 minutes.

At the end of 5 minutes, pull the saucepan over to a cold burner.

Pour the very hot toffee mixture over the crackers and milk chocolate chips as evenly as you can. Spread it out quickly with a heat-resistant spatula or a frosting knife.

Hannah's 4th Note: I start by pouring the mixture in lines from top to bottom over the length of the pan. Then I turn it and pour more lines

**over the width of the pan, until the whole pan is
crosshatched with the hot toffee mixture. If it
doesn't cover the crackers completely, don't
worry—it'll spread out quite a bit in the oven.**

Slide the pan into the oven and bake the toffee at
350°F. for 10 *(ten)* minutes.

Remove the pan from the oven, place it on a cold
stovetop burner or a wire rack, and sprinkle the
peanut butter chips over the top.

Cover the pan with a sheet of foil or an empty
cookie sheet. Let everything sit for 2 *(two)* full minutes. This will melt the peanut butter chips.

When 2 *(two)* minutes have passed, take off the
top cookie sheet or foil and spread the melted peanut butter chips as evenly as you can with a heat-
resistant spatula, a wooden paddle, or a frosting knife.

Using oven mitts or pot holders, place the pan in
the refrigerator to cool, uncovered, for at least 1
(one) hour.

Have a cup of coffee and relax while your toffee
is cooling and hardening in the refrigerator.

Remember that last cup of milk chocolate chips
and the chopped peanuts you haven't used yet?

Don't worry. They'll be used when your creation has cooled and hardened.

Once the hour is up, leave your pan in the refrigerator and pour the milk chocolate chips into a small-size microwave-safe bowl. *(I used a 2-cup Pyrex measuring cup—mine has a spout, which I find very helpful.)*

Melt your milk chocolate chips on HIGH heat in the microwave for 1 *(one)* minute. Then let the bowl sit in the microwave for another minute.

When the minute has passed, take the bowl out of the microwave and attempt to stir the chips smooth. If you can't and they're not completely melted, return them to the microwave and heat them in 30-second increments, followed by 30 seconds of standing time, until you can stir them smooth.

Take your hardened toffee out of the refrigerator and quickly drizzle the melted milk chocolate over the top of the cooled peanut butter chip layer. Be sure to let some of the peanut butter chip layer show through.

Sprinkle the chopped peanuts over the top of the chocolate drizzle and refrigerate the pan for another 2 hours.

When your Chocolate Peanut Butter Toffee has thoroughly chilled, peel it from the foil and break it into random-size pieces.

Hannah's 5th Note: Even though you have sprinkled chopped peanuts over the top of your toffee, it's still wise to warn everyone that this candy contains peanuts. Although peanut allergies are becoming less common, they can still be a dangerous problem!

Chapter Four

Lynne Larchmont's Home
Several days later

Lynne looked around at the boxes that were stacked in the living room, and groaned. "I'm taking way too much! There's never going to be room for all this in the condo."

"That's why we didn't tape the boxes closed," Delores told her. "Leaving them open gives you a chance to reassess and make a final decision."

"I guess I don't really need more than a dozen Waterford crystal champagne glasses," Lynne said with a sigh. "Unless . . ." She turned to Delores. "Would you like the other four dozen, Delores?"

"Oh, my!" Hannah recognized the amazed expression on her mother's face. "I . . . I'd love to have them, but I want to pay for them."

Lynne shook her head. "No, I'm giving them to you as a gift. They were a wedding present from one of Tom's clients and I won't be entertaining in Lake Eden the way I did out here. I want you to have them, Delores. It's a small price to pay for all the help you've given me during the past five days."

"Well . . . if you're sure . . ." Delores gave a little nod. "If I take them, you have to promise to come to all my dinner parties. And I promise not to partner you with any unsuitable men."

Lynne laughed. "It's a deal. I love to go to dinner parties." She turned to Hannah. "When we've finished packing, I'd like you to look around at the things I'm leaving behind. If there's anything you want, just tell me and I'll arrange to have it trucked to Lake Eden for you."

"Thank you, Lynne!" Hannah was impressed with Lynne's generosity. "You're going to sell everything else, aren't you?"

"Yes, my real estate agent will check with the buyers. If they want anything, she'll set a fair price and add it to the sales price. Anything that's left will go to Robby and Maria. I've already promised that they can hold an estate sale and keep whatever money they make."

Lynne's cell phone rang and she picked it up and glanced at the display. "It's my agent," she told them. "I'd better answer this."

"What are you going to take, Hannah?" Delores asked as Lynne walked out of the room.

"I don't know. I don't really need anything, Mother."

"But Lynne has some beautiful things."

"Yes, she does." Hannah thought about that for a moment. "Maybe I'll just ask her to choose something for me. I know she'll choose something she really likes and if she has any regrets later about giving it to me, she can have it back."

"That's a marvelous idea!" Delores said, just as Lynne came back into the room.

"I'm really sorry, but we can't keep our lunch reservation today. I have to go to the studio for a final commercial. Gibson Girl Cosmetics decided that they need one more for their flight of commercials to be shown next month."

"That's all right," Hannah said quickly. "Work comes first, Lynne."

Delores nodded. "Yes, and I'm not really hungry after three pieces of that marvelous coffee cake Hannah made for breakfast."

"Thanks for understanding. And I do have a little surprise for you. The director agreed to let the two of you come on the set when we're filming the commercial. Would you like to go with me?"

"Oh, yes!" Delores responded immediately. "I'd love to go!"

"Hannah?" Lynne turned to her. "And if you go, would you bring a couple of pieces of that coffee cake for the director? He's wild about home-baked goodies."

"I'll go. And of course I'll bring some coffee cake with me," Hannah said, but she added another sentence in her mind. *I have to go so I can keep Mother in line. She's so starstruck that I may have to tie her up to keep her from asking everyone there for an autograph.*

Hannah was surprised as she followed Lynne and her mother into the building that contained the sound stage. It was a huge warehouse, seemingly empty except for the section at the far end containing a set that duplicated a cosmetic counter in an upscale department store, complete with stocked shelves and makeup chairs in front of the counters.

"I thought it would be more glamorous than this," Delores confided to Lynne.

"It's a working set," Lynne explained. "Gibson Girl Cosmetics rents out this part of the building and this is where they shoot all their commercials."

Hannah noticed that Delores still looked puzzled. "But . . . I thought there'd be people with clapboards and all sorts of costumed actors and actresses running around."

Lynne shook her head. "Not here. This sound stage is set aside for filming commercials, and the production company moves in their own sets. They just rent the space, that's all."

"Oh," Delores said, looking very disappointed.

"Before we leave, we'll have lunch in the studio commissary. I have a pass to the executive dining room. It's on the second floor and we'll ask for a table on the balcony that overlooks the commissary. There'll be all sorts of actors in full makeup and costume down there."

"That would be wonderful!" Delores looked excited at the prospect. "But do the stars actually come to eat in their makeup and costumes?"

"Yes, if they only have a short lunch break and they'll be filming again when it's over. It takes a long time to put on makeup, especially if it's elaborate. Even some of the minor characters in science fiction or fantasy movies have to come in hours before they start shooting."

"Lynne!" a voice called out. Hannah turned to see a tall, thin man with dark hair hurrying toward them. "You're here early!"

"Yes, I wanted to introduce you to two of my friends from Lake Eden, Minnesota." She gestured toward Hannah. "This is Hannah Swensen. You've heard me mention her. And this is Hannah's mother, Delores Knight. I'd like you two to meet our director, David-Paul."

"Hannah," the director acknowledged her, "and De-lores. Lynne's mentioned both of you. Would you like to watch while we shoot the commercial?"

"We'd just *love* to!" Delores answered for both of them. "It's so exciting being in a real movie studio!"

"Not if you work here every day," David-Paul said with a laugh. "It's just a giant warehouse, and even with air-conditioning, it can get hot under the lights." Just then his cell phone rang and he pulled it out of his pocket to answer it. "Excuse me for just a moment, will you?"

"It's late notice, Harry," Hannah heard him say as he walked away. "Our lead is here already."

Lynne and Delores began to talk about the upcoming commercial. Hannah listened with mild interest, but she was much more interested in watching David-Paul's face. The conversation he was having with the person named Harry must have been irritating because he was begin-ning to scowl.

"She'll never work for me again!" Hannah heard him say, and then he jammed the phone back in his pocket and walked back to them.

"Cynthia can't make it," he said to Lynne. "Something about her husband being in the emergency room. Sorry, Lynne. Looks like I got you all the way out here for . . ." He stopped and moved a step closer to Delores. "How old are you?" he asked her.

"Excuse me?" Delores just stared at him. "A lady never tells her age!"

As Hannah and Lynne watched, David-Paul began to smile. "Perfect!" he said. "You'll do just fine."

"I'll do what?" Delores asked him, bristling slightly.

"You'll play Lynne's mother in the commercial."

Delores's mouth fell open and she looked as if someone could knock her over with a feather. "Me?"

"You. Yes, you'll be perfect." David-Paul stopped short and began to frown. "You're SAG, aren't you?"

"Delores isn't an actress," Lynne said quickly, since Delores seemed to be incapable of speech.

"That's okay. We'll work that out later. She looks the part and I'll rewrite the script. Just take her to the makeup trailer, will you, Lynne? And tell Julia that she needs bags under her eyes and a couple of grey streaks in her hair. The way she looks now doesn't look natural for her age."

Hannah gave a little gulp. She had to say something fast or she'd be forced to spend the remainder of the day assuring Delores that her hair looked perfectly natural and no one could possibly guess that she had it colored.

"Grey streaks would work," Hannah said with a nod. "Mother's supposed to look older in the commercial, isn't she?"

"That's right," David-Paul agreed quickly. "Nobody will believe she's Lynne's mother if we don't age her up a bit."

"Of course," Delores said, obviously pleased. "I didn't think of that."

Hannah breathed a sigh of relief as her mother began to smile. She watched as Lynne led Delores out of the building, and then she turned to David-Paul. "That worked," she said. "Nice recovery on your part."

David-Paul laughed. "Thanks! And thank you for cueing me in. I tend to say what I think and that's not always a good thing. I'm going to have some coffee. You want some?"

"Coffee would be good," Hannah said, following him over to the corner of the building, where there was an alcove with a coffeepot and a long table with chairs. "Are you hungry? I brought half of an Apricot Coffee Cake."

"That sounds great! I was going to buy some doughnuts for breakfast, but I was running late and I didn't have time to stop off at the doughnut shop this morning. Where did you buy your coffee cake?"

"I didn't buy it. I baked it this morning and we had some for breakfast."

"You baked it *yourself*?"

Hannah came close to laughing out loud. David-Paul sounded shocked that she'd actually baked it. "Yes, I baked it. I own a bakery and coffee shop in Lake Eden, Minnesota." Hannah unwrapped the coffee cake and set it on the table. The she reached inside the tote bag she'd brought with her and took out paper plates, plastic forks, and a knife. "I'll cut a piece for you. I already had mine this morning."

David-Paul began to smile as Hannah cut a big piece for him. "Are you trying to fatten me up?" he asked her.

"No, but you said you hadn't had time for breakfast and everybody says it's the most important meal of the day. You're hungry, aren't you?"

"Yes, and I'm getting hungrier by the minute. Your coffee cake smells delicious, Hannah."

"It is. I got the recipe from my partner's aunt. Aunt Nancy collects recipes, and every one she's given me has been wonderful." Hannah reached into her tote bag again and pulled out a tub of softened, salted butter and a plastic knife. "Would you like butter on your coffee cake?"

"I don't usually eat . . ." David-Paul stopped in midsentence and began to smile. "Why not? I'll have some butter. I think that I've already blown my daily calorie count by just looking at the huge piece of coffee cake you cut for me."

Once David-Paul had eaten his slice of coffee cake, he leaned back in his chair and gave a satisfied sigh. "That was great! I wish I lived in . . . what was the name of your town again?"

"Lake Eden."

"Nice name. If I lived there, I'd come into your coffee shop every morning."

"That would be nice," Hannah said, but her mind had another response that she didn't voice. *If you moved to Lake Eden from a big city like this with glamorous parties, hectic schedules, and exciting things to do twenty-four hours a day, you'd probably be jumping on the first plane back here before the moving truck even came with your furniture!*

"Thanks again, Delores," David-Paul told her as he poured her a second glass of wine. "You really helped me out of a rough spot today."

"Me too," Lynne added. "I really don't know if I could have shoe-horned in the time to make that last commercial if we'd had to reschedule it."

"I'm glad that I could help," Delores told them, but Hannah noticed that she was glancing over the balcony rail to watch a group of actors who'd just come into the commissary below. "Isn't that the cast from *One More Time With Feeling*?"

"Yes." David-Paul smiled at Delores. "Would you like me to ask Troy to come up here so you can get his autograph?"

"That would be wonderful!" Delores began to smile so widely that Hannah wondered if the street makeup that Julia had applied to her mother's face before they'd left the studio would crack.

"I'll text him for you," David-Paul said, pulling out his cell phone.

As Hannah watched the handsome actor at the table only a few feet below them, he picked up his cell phone, glanced at the display, and pushed back his chair. A moment later, he was climbing the stairs to the executive dining room. His rapid response reminded Hannah that she'd turned off her cell phone during the filming of the commercial and she hadn't turned it back on again. She did so immediately and when she glanced at the display, she saw that Michelle had called her three times in the past hour and she'd left messages each time. All three calls were marked URGENT, and Hannah knew that there must be something drastically wrong back home in Lake Eden.

"I'll be right back," she told them, slipping her phone back into her pocket and rising from her chair. "I have to return a phone call."

"Is there something wrong?" Delores asked immediately.

Not wanting to spoil her mother's obvious delight at meeting a big television star, Hannah cracked a joke. "Yes, they ran out of sugar at The Cookie Jar."

Delores looked at her blankly for a second, and then she began to laugh. "You're joking, aren't you, dear?"

"Yes, I'll be right back, Mother."

There was a directional sign at the back of the room and Hannah headed for the ladies' room. It would provide a quiet, private place for her to return Michelle's calls.

She pushed open the door to the ladies' room, stepped inside, and smiled as she realized that she was alone in an anteroom filled with chairs and a long makeup table with mirrors. She seated herself on one of the chairs, pulled out her cell phone, and punched in Michelle's cell phone number.

"Hannah!" Michelle answered on the first ring. "Thank God you got back to me! You have to come back to Lake Eden right away! It's an emergency!"

Hannah could feel her blood pressure rising. "Is something wrong with Moishe?"

"No, Hannah. Moishe's fine, but he's with Norman. I tried to bring him here to the condo, but he didn't want to go inside."

"Because I wasn't there?"

"That could have been part of it, but he yowled at the foot of the stairs and kept on yowling, even when I picked him up to carry him. I went up a couple of steps, but he was shaking so hard, I turned around and took him back to the car. Of course I'm not sure, but I think Moishe feels the same way you do about the condo. Something bad happened inside and he doesn't want me to go back there again."

Hannah wondered briefly if Michelle was anthropomorphizing, but her sister had a valid point. Perhaps it would be different if she'd been there to carry Moishe up the stairs, but they wouldn't know that until the renovation was finished and she tried it.

"So did you take him back to Mother and Doc's place?" Hannah asked.

"No, I thought he'd be lonely with Mother gone and Doc at the hospital all day. I called Norman and he said he'd come right out to get Moishe and take him to his house."

Hannah drew a sigh of relief. "Oh, good! Moishe loves playing with Cuddles. He's still there, isn't he?"

"Yes, and Norman told me that Moishe and Cuddles have been playing practically nonstop. Everybody's fine here, Hannah, except"—Michelle's voice broke and she stopped speaking to clear her throat"—except Lonnie."

"What's wrong with Lonnie? Is he sick?"

"No. There's been a murder, a woman Lonnie knew from his high school class, Darcy Hicks. And Lonnie . . ." Michelle choked up again, and then she began to sob.

"Calm down, honey," Hannah said, trying to make her voice as comforting as possible despite the alarm she was feeling. "Tell me what's wrong with Lonnie."

"It's awful, Hannah!"

"I understand," Hannah said, but of course she couldn't possibly understand if Michelle didn't tell her what was wrong. "Whatever it is, it's going to be okay. I'll catch the first flight out and come right back to Lake Eden if you need me."

"I do! I need you, Hannah! There's nobody else who can help! And I'm too upset to do it alone!"

"Do what, Michelle?"

"Help Lonnie!"

Hannah realized that her youngest sister was almost hysterical, but Michelle still hadn't told her what was wrong. Somehow she had to reassure Michelle so that Michelle would explain what had happened.

"All right, Michelle. I promise you that I'll help Lonnie. I'll come right back and do whatever I can for him. But first, honey, you have to tell me what's wrong."

"Oh!" Michelle sounded shocked. "Yes! Of course I do! I'm just so rattled, Hannah. Just give me a second . . . okay?"

"I'll give you as long as you need. Get a drink of water, try to calm down, and then tell me exactly what happened. Just put down the phone, go get some water, and I'll be right here when you come back."

Hannah heard Michelle put the phone down. There was the sound of a chair being pushed back. Then a cupboard door opened with a bang and there was the sound of water running. Michelle must have been in the kitchen at the condo when the phone rang. A chair creaked as Michelle sat down again, and Hannah heard her take a deep breath. Then she took another deep breath and picked up the phone.

"I'm back," she said, and her voice was steadier. "You're there, aren't you, Hannah?"

"I'm here. Now tell me."

"Lonnie's classmate, Darcy Hicks, has been murdered. And Lonnie's the . . ." Michelle swallowed audibly, took another breath, and managed to choke out the words. "Lonnie's the main suspect!"

 # Chapter
Five

It hadn't taken long for Hannah to pack. She'd pulled her clothes out of the closet, Maria had folded them and packed them in her suitcase, and now, less than a half-hour later, Robby was driving her to the airport. Hannah took a sip from the bottle of water that Robby had placed in the cup holder in front of her seat, and then she dialed Michelle's number.

Michelle answered immediately. "Are you coming, Hannah?"

"Yes, I'm on my way to the airport right now."

"Is Mother coming?"

"No, Lynne's travel agent explained that it was a family emergency. There was only one seat left and I got it. Mother's coming tomorrow afternoon. Are you okay, Michelle?"

"Yes, now that you're coming home. Lonnie's been a real basket case. Of course I don't blame him, but I'm finding it hard to be upbeat. Lonnie was so happy the night he went out to meet Brian and Cassie. They split up after their baby died, and both of them were miserable."

"Their baby died?"

"Yes, it was SIDS, sudden infant death syndrome." Michelle sighed deeply. "And to make things even worse, Cassie'd had two miscarriages before that. But little Meredith seemed to be strong and healthy. Lonnie went to the hospital to see the baby and told me that he'd never seen Cassie and Brian so happy."

"That's awful! How old was the baby when she died?"

"She was almost five weeks. Cassie told me she woke up one morning and Meredith was still sleeping so she got up and made the coffee. Then she came back to get the baby and . . . and Meredith was dead! It just about killed both of them, Hannah. They saw a family grief counselor for a month or so and it seemed to help Brian, but Cassie just couldn't get over the loss. She ended up leaving Brian and going to a new counselor, who seemed to help. Cassie made it through somehow, and she got back together with Brian. And now *there's a new tragedy.* And to make things even worse, their friend, Lonnie, could be charged with Darcy's murder!"

"Take it easy, Michelle. Mike's a good detective and so is Lonnie's brother, Rick. I'm sure they'll clear Lonnie and find Darcy's killer."

"But . . . you don't understand, Hannah! I didn't get a chance to tell you the whole story on the phone earlier, but there's a big problem with the sheriff's department."

"What's that?"

"There aren't any detectives left who can work on the case. And that's why we need *you.*"

"I don't understand. How about Mike? Isn't he handling the investigation?"

"He can't. Bill had to pull him from the case because Lonnie's his partner and the department has a rule about that. Bill says it's because partners have too much at stake and they're too emotionally involved to be objective."

Hannah thought about that for a moment. "I guess that makes sense. How about Rick? He's on the case, isn't he?"

"No, there's a rule about that, too. If someone in your immediate family is a murder suspect, no one in the family can be involved in the investigation."

"So . . . who's left?"

"A deputy that just made detective and Bill. That's it, Hannah. And that's another reason why I needed you to come back home."

"I understand, Michelle, and I'll be there tonight. We'll talk about it when I get there."

"Is there anything else you need to know right now?" Michelle asked her.

"Only one thing. Can somebody arrange for my transportation back to Lake Eden? My plane is supposed to land at six-ten tonight."

"We've already taken care of that. Norman's going to pick you up at the airport and bring you right back here to the condo. There's just one thing . . ." Michelle paused for a moment, and then she went on. "I'm not sure how to put this, but . . . do you think you'll be all right if you stay here at the condo? Your bedroom's not done yet, but you can have my room and I'll sleep on the couch."

Hannah drew a deep breath. She knew she really didn't want to go back to the condo, even though she wouldn't have to go into her bedroom. . . . "I'm not sure. Let's talk about that when I get there."

"Okay. I've got to go, Hannah. I have to do some shopping at the Red Owl."

"Will you call Norman and ask him to bring Moishe with him when he comes to pick me up?" Hannah asked her. "I really miss him."

"I would, but Norman's already left for the airport."

"So early? Unless there's a problem with traffic, he's going to have to wait for at least an hour and a half before my plane lands."

"He knows that, but he said he was driving down early so he could drop in to see Judy and Diana."

Hannah smiled. Norman was such a good man. Even though he knew now that Diana wasn't his daughter, he still kept in touch with her grandmother, Judy Thorndike. He even invited both of them to come to his house to stay whenever they wanted to visit him.

"It's okay, Michelle," Hannah said quickly. "I'm sure Norman will stop at his house to pick up Moishe before we come to the condo."

"Uh . . . okay."

Hannah caught the hesitation in Michelle's voice. "Why do you sound like that's not a good idea?"

Michelle sighed so loudly that Hannah could hear it over the phone. "That would be fine, but I'm really worried about Lonnie. He's on pins and needles about having you interview him. Once he gets here, I don't want to have him wait too long or he'll just get more and more nervous."

"No problem," Hannah said quickly. "I'll have Norman bring me straight to the condo. We can always pick up Moishe later. It's not that far from Mother's penthouse, and I'll probably stay there anyway."

"Oh . . . uh . . . you may not want to do that."

"Why not? I've been staying there ever since . . ."—Hannah stopped and took a deep, calming breath—"you know."

"I do, but Doc won't be there and you'll be all alone."

It was Hannah's turn to sigh. She was beginning to feel almost sorry that her mother hadn't taken the first flight home. She asked the obvious question. "Why won't Doc be there?"

"He has to stay at the hospital. There was a bad accident on the highway last night and he has three patients on life support."

"Oh, dear!" Hannah was immediately sympathetic. "Are they local? Someone I know?"

"No, it's a family from Michigan. It was a mother, father, and a three-year-old son."

"What happened?"

"A semi driver fell asleep, crossed the center line, and hit their SUV head-on. Doc's pretty sure the mother and son will make it, but the father's in bad shape."

"How about the driver of the semi?"

"He didn't make it, and they had to close down the freeway and divert traffic. Every deputy except Lonnie, Mike, and Rick drove out there to help. Andrea and I went out with coffee and cookies for people who got stranded in their cars."

"It sounds like it was a bad night on the highway."

"It was. We've had a huge wave of bad weather since you've been gone. You got out just in time. What's it like out there in California?"

"It's nice and warm, and the weather's perfect."

"Bring some of that weather with you when you fly

home." There was silence for several moments, and then Michelle spoke again. "Do you ever wish you lived there, Hannah?"

"Only when I hear about blizzards, tornados, and floods. I love Lake Eden, Michelle."

"Bad weather and all?"

"Yes, bad weather and all."

Michelle laughed. "Me too. It's going to be good to have you back, Hannah. I've missed you and it's been lonely here without you."

"It's kind of nice that you missed me, but . . ."

"I know. You're not sure you can stay here at the condo, but that's all right. I'll hold down the fort for you until you feel comfortable about coming home. I didn't see what you did, Hannah. That's probably why it doesn't bother me."

Hannah began to smile. "Thanks, Michelle. I *do* love the condo. It's just that the memories are . . ." Hannah paused, searching for the right word. "The memories are too fresh."

"I know. I mean, I *don't* know, but I can understand anyway."

Grateful tears came to Hannah's eyes. She truly appreciated her wonderful family, even with Delores and her fixation on Hollywood stars and looking younger than she actually was. Just wait until she told Michelle about the cosmetic commercial! They could have a good laugh over that.

"I have to go, Hannah. I'm putting up something for dinner and Lonnie's going to need some TLC. He's a strong guy, but right now he's . . . I'm not sure how to describe it, but . . ."

"Fragile?" Hannah supplied the word she thought her sister was searching for.

"Yes, fragile. This really devastated him, Hannah. I wouldn't have called you if it had been just some little thing."

"I know that. And I'll do everything I can to prove that Lonnie is innocent."

"I know you will. Bye, Hannah."

"Goodbye, Michelle. Give Lonnie a hug for me."

"Excuse me?"

Hannah awoke to a question from a pleasant female voice. She opened her eyes and blinked as she saw a young woman in a uniform leaning over her.

"Yes?"

"Sorry to wake you, but we're on approach. Could I get you a cup of coffee before we land?"

Hannah came back to awareness with a jolt. She was sitting in an airline seat, belted in with a magazine on her lap. She hadn't thought she'd sleep on the flight home, but it was perfectly obvious that she'd slept through the drink cart and the mixed nuts, or pretzels, or whatever this airline served with beverages. She'd also slept through any meal that had been offered, and now they were about to land.

"How long do we have before we land?" she asked.

"Long enough for you to have two cups of coffee and a snack if you'd like," the stewardess answered.

"Yes to the coffee. I think I need it."

The stewardess smiled. "I'd say that you do. You fell asleep before we taxied out of the gate, and you probably would have slept through the landing if I hadn't come over to wake you."

"Thank you for that!" Hannah said, and her gratitude was heartfelt. "Could I have the coffee right away, please?"

"Of course. I'll be right back."

The stewardess was true to her word. Once Hannah had made a hurried trip to the tiny closet that served as a bathroom and returned to her seat, the stewardess came down the aisle with a carafe of coffee and a cup. "How about a sweet roll to go with that?" she asked.

"Yes, thank you."

"Cinnamon or caramel?"

Hannah gave that a moment's thought. "The cinnamon, please," she said once she'd considered the fact that she might have to get up and go to the bathroom closet again to wash her hands if she got sticky caramel all over her fingers.

A few moments later, the stewardess delivered Hannah's cinnamon roll. Hannah took a sip of her coffee, picked up the roll, and bit into the perfectly round, perfectly frosted bun. She chewed, swallowed, and decided that she might have a new career baking cinnamon rolls for the airlines. The roll the stewardess had brought was perfectly formed, perfectly frosted, and perfectly spiced with cinnamon, but the end result was perfectly unremarkable. Given the choice a second time, Hannah might have gone for the caramel roll, but she had the sneaking suspicion that the end result might have been more of the same.

"Butter?" the stewardess appeared again, bearing a small plate of gold foil-wrapped butter.

"Thank you," Hanna accepted the plate gratefully. She slathered butter over the top of her cinnamon roll, took another bite, and frowned. Unsalted butter and no salt shaker or packet of salt in sight. Why did people from non-dairy states seem to think that unsalted butter was so elegant? And why did cooks and pastry chefs all over the world call for unsalted or "sweet" butter? They did that even if a generous measure of salt was called for in the recipe. It was one of Hannah's pet peeves. Why call for unsalted butter, especially if it was more expensive, when you were going to add salt to the recipe anyway? It just didn't make sense to her.

The stewardess came by Hannah's seat again and re-moved the butter plate and the dish that had contained Hannah's cinnamon roll. "Better drink the rest of that coffee fast," she advised. "You have only five minutes left before the captain turns on the seat belt sign and I have to collect everything from the tray tables."

"Thanks for the warning," Hannah said, smiling at the stewardess as she filled Hannah's cup with more coffee. "I'll gulp it, I promise."

The stewardess laughed and moved away, and Hannah leaned back in her seat with her coffee cup. The cinna-mon roll had been edible, the coffee was drinkable, and she surmised that the meal that had been served while she was sleeping had probably been perfectly prepared and adequate. Yes, indeed. There could be a new career for her in generating airplane food if she wished to pursue it. And she was very glad that she didn't have the slightest desire to do so.

The stewardess was approaching again, and Hannah made short work of gulping the rest of her coffee. She poured another half-cup, all that was left in the carafe, and managed to gulp that before the stewardess got to her seat.

"Here you are." Hannah handed her the coffee carafe and cup. "And thanks so much for waking me before we landed."

"That's quite all right. I'm glad I could help to make your journey pleasant," the stewardess responded with an answer that Hannah assumed had been taught to her in stewardess school. Then she smiled and leaned slightly closer. "You must have been hungry. You're the only person I've served today who ate every crumb of the cinnamon roll."

Hannah laughed and settled back to await the landing. The man next to her in the window seat had the shade on the window open and she watched as the plane flew through a layer of cloud and a very tiny version of the outskirts of Minneapolis appeared below. The houses and buildings seemed to grow larger as the plane began to descend rapidly and Hannah spotted the freeway, complete with miniature trucks and cars. Their headlights were gleaming in the darkness and looked like strings of illuminated pearls.

"Only a few more minutes," the man in the window seat said to her. "We should be right on time as long as we taxi straight to the gate."

"That's good," Hannah responded.

"You must have been tired. You slept almost all the way here," the man said.

Hannah smiled. "I guess I must have been."

The man turned to look out the window again and Hannah reached down to retrieve her cell phone from her carry-on that was stashed under the seat in front of her. As soon as they were on the ground, she'd call Norman to let him know that they'd landed.

Thoughts of Norman were pleasant and Hannah began to smile again. She'd missed him. She hadn't really realized it before, but she was very glad that Norman was coming to pick her up at the airport. Even though she'd been gone for only five days, it would be wonderful to see him again.

"Over here, Hannah!" Norman called out as Hannah approached the baggage carousel.

Hannah began to smile the moment she saw him, and her smile grew even wider as she approached.

"Hannah! You're home!"

He pulled her into his arms to hug her and a joyous feeling rushed through her. She really hadn't realized how much she'd missed Norman.

"Come with me," he said, grabbing her suitcases from the carousel and leading her out of the baggage area. "How tired are you?"

"I'm not very tired at all," she said as he loaded her suitcases in his trunk. "I slept on the plane. The stewardess had to wake me up right before we landed. Why do you ask?"

"Because Lonnie's waiting for you at the condo and if you're tired, I'll take you straight to my house and tell Michelle and Lonnie that I'll bring you out in the morning."

Hannah was grateful. "That's really considerate, but I'm okay. Besides . . . I really want to know what happened. I don't think I could sleep a wink without finding out tonight."

"Didn't Michelle tell you?"

"Not really. She was too upset to tell me anything except that Lonnie was the prime suspect in the murder of one of his high school classmates. She said that she needed me to come home because Bill had pulled Mike and Rick off the case, and Lonnie needed me to prove that he wasn't the killer."

"Okay, then." Norman gave a little nod. "You've got the bare bones and that's enough for now."

He started the car, drove toward the exit, and pulled up at the parking booth to pay for the parking. Once he'd done that, he exited the airport and took the on-ramp to the freeway. When he'd entered the flow of traffic and chosen the lane he wanted, he glanced over at her again. "Do you think you'll be all right staying at the condo?"

"I . . . I'm not sure," Hannah admitted. "I won't know until I get there."

"That makes sense. If you don't feel comfortable there, you can go home with me. My guest room's all ready and the cats will be really happy to see you."

Hannah felt a rush of gratitude. Norman always came through for her. "Thanks, Norman. It's good of you to offer and I think I'd like to take you up on that. I really don't want to stay at the condo. Michelle mentioned that Doc had to stay at the hospital tonight, and I don't really want to be all alone in the penthouse."

"That's understandable," Norman said, "I'm having some work done on the house, but there's plenty of room for you. And no strings attached, but you probably already know that."

"I do."

A mischievous grin appeared on Norman's face. "I

really like the sound of that phrase, Hannah. Maybe you should practice saying it."

For a moment she was puzzled, and then Hannah remembered that she'd said, *I do*. "And maybe I shouldn't practice it since I said it one too many times last year."

Norman reached out to take Hannah's hand and he gave it a gentle squeeze. "It wasn't your fault, Hannah. You had no way of knowing what was going to happen."

"That's true," Hannah acknowledged, but there was a slight catch in her voice. "Thanks, Norman."

Norman must have sensed that their conversation was becoming too serious and he cleared his throat. "When we're through at the condo, do you want to stop by the penthouse to pick up your cookie truck? Or would you rather ride to town with me in the morning?"

"I'd rather ride with you," Hannah told him, deciding immediately. "My truck hasn't been driven since I've been gone, and Michelle told me that it's been really cold here. I don't know if it'll start."

"Good point. Doc Bennett's filling in for me at the clinic tomorrow and after I drop you off at The Cookie Jar, I can drive to the penthouse and try to start your truck. That'll give me plenty of time to call Cyril and have one of his mechanics come out if there's a problem."

"That's perfect. Thanks, Norman." Hannah gave him a smile. "I'm really glad you picked me up at the airport. You just erased both of my worries about coming back tonight."

They rode in silence for several miles, and then Hannah turned to Norman again. "Do you know what happened on the night of the murder?"

"I know a few things about it, but I'd rather have you hear the whole story from Lonnie. He's the one who was there, and his account of what happened is the only one that counts."

"That makes sense."

"Why don't you lean back and get a little more rest," Norman advised. "It's going to be hectic when you get to the condo."

Hannah glanced at him in surprise. "Will *everyone* be there?"

"Not everyone. Doc's at the hospital and your mother's still in California with Lynne. I think it'll be just Michelle and Lonnie, but Andrea is driving out later. She's been helping Michelle cope with all this."

"But Bill won't be there, will he?"

Norman shook his head. "He *can't* be there. He's the lead investigator on the case. It's a position he doesn't want, but he's the only one left in the department who's not directly involved. There's a guy who just got promoted to detective, but he's never worked a murder case before. Technically, Bill isn't supposed to be working it, either, but he's the only one left with any experience. There aren't that many detectives on Mike's squad, you know."

"I know." Hannah nodded in agreement. "This is a really strange situation, Norman. This time they need us, but usually the sheriff's department hates it if we amateurs poke our noses into their murder cases."

Norman gave a little laugh. "That's true. It's ironic, in a way. Now they're all pulling for us to catch the real killer to clear one of their own. This whole thing is very unusual."

Hannah was silent for a moment, thinking about the circumstances of the case. Then she reached out to pat Norman's arm. "Do you want to help me with this case?"

"Yes, if you need me."

"Of *course* I need you! I always need you, Norman."

"Good to know. I like Lonnie and I want to see him cleared. I just can't believe that he could have killed anyone."

"I can't believe it, either," Hannah admitted. "Somebody else did it, Norman. And it's up to us to prove who it was!"

Even though she hadn't thought she was still tired, the sound of the purring motor and the smooth ride back to Lake Eden lulled Hannah into deep sleep. She didn't wake up until the wooden arm across the entrance road to her condo complex creaked up to let them in.

"We're here, Hannah," Norman said as he drove down the winding road that led to Hannah's building. "I'll let you off and park in the visitors' lot."

Hannah shook her head. "You don't have to do that, Norman, just park in Clara Hollenbeck's spot," she told him. "Marguerite and Clara went to a two-week church retreat and they took Clara's car."

"Okay." Norman drove down the ramp that led into the underground garage that served Hannah's condo building. "You're sure this is okay?"

"I'm positive. The day before I left with Mother, Marguerite dropped in at The Cookie Jar to pick up some cookies to take with them for the drive. Michelle was there and since she'd offered to stay at my condo, she promised to keep an eye on Marguerite and Clara's place."

"Okay," Norman said, pulling into Clara's parking spot. "Are you ready, Hannah?"

"Yes, come on, Norman. Let's go upstairs. We have to talk to Lonnie."

They hurried up the stairs and Hannah rang the doorbell. Michelle opened it almost immediately and hugged Hannah tightly. "Oh, Hannah! I'm so glad you're here!"

"How about me?" Norman asked, smiling to let Michelle know that he was teasing.

"Of course I'm glad to see you, too." Michelle gave a little laugh that sounded weak to Hannah's ears. "Come in! I've got soup to warm you up."

Michelle pulled Hannah inside and Norman followed. "Give me your parkas and sit down at the table. Lonnie will be here in about thirty minutes or so with the pizza and while we're waiting, we can have a bowl of Minestrone."

"You made Minestrone?" Hannah asked, slipping out of her parka and handing it to Michelle.

"Yes, in the crockpot. I made up the recipe when I was in college, and my roommates just loved it."

"Minestrone sounds good to me," Norman said, handing his parka to Michelle and sitting down next to Hannah. "I don't think I've ever had homemade Minestrone. Did it take a long time to make?"

Michelle shook her head. "It's a shortcut recipe, so a lot of the things in it are all ready to put in the crock. The only thing I added at the last minute are the green beans and the kidney beans. That's because if you add them when you start the soup, they turn into mush."

"And that's bad?"

"Yes, it tastes fine, but it ruins the texture. Minestrone is supposed to be chunky."

Hannah smiled. She was glad that Michelle was interested in cooking and baking, unlike their sister Andrea. But perhaps that wasn't a fair assessment on her part. It was true that when Andrea got married, her one culinary achievement had been making peanut butter and jelly sandwiches. Unfortunately, the one time Hannah had gone to Andrea's house for lunch, her sister had run out of fruit jelly and she'd made her trademark sandwiches with mint jelly.

Once Michelle had served her soup and both Hannah and Norman had complimented her shortcut recipe, Hannah decided to steer the conversation away from their current concern about Lonnie. "I know I've been gone less than a week, but did Andrea come up with another Whippersnapper cookie recipe?"

"Yes, she did! She baked them for Aunt Nancy and Lisa, and she's coming over later with another batch. I'm not supposed to tell you anything about them, but I tasted one and they're really good. I think they're her best so far."

"Which cake mix did she use this time?" Hannah asked, taking another spoonful of soup. It truly was delicious, the perfect blend of Italian spices and flavors.

"Funfetti"

"There's a Funfetti cake mix?" Hannah was surprised. She'd never seen it at the Lake Eden Red Owl store, but Florence didn't carry every single flavor of cake mix on the market. If you wanted something special, you had to ask her to order it.

"Yes, Florence ordered it especially for her. Anyway, Andrea added white chocolate chips and coconut to the mix and the cookies are wonderful. They're light and tender like all the Whippersnappers, but they have a tropical flavor."

Another question, one that had nothing to do with cookie recipes, occurred to Hannah. "You said that Andrea's coming later?"

"Yes, to bring her cookies. And there's another reason, too."

"What's that?" Norman asked.

"Andrea was going to try to get Doc's autopsy report from Bill's briefcase when he comes home for dinner. Bill always takes a little nap before he goes back to the station, and she's going to try to copy the report and put it back in his briefcase before he realizes that it's gone."

Hannah began to smile. "That's my middle sister!" she said in approval. "If anyone can sneak anything out of Bill's briefcase, it's Andrea."

Michelle turned to Norman. "Do you want more soup, Norman?"

"Yes, if there's enough."

"I made it in a slow cooker and there are five of us coming, counting Andrea. That's enough for a quart of soup apiece and there's no way we can eat *that* much soup."

"You convinced me," Norman told her.

"It's one of those recipes you can put up when you leave for work and it'll be ready when you come home for dinner. If you serve it with garlic bread, it makes a whole meal. I didn't do that tonight because we'd be too full to eat the pizza that Lonnie is bringing."

Hannah raised her napkin to her mouth to hide the smile that was turning up the corners of her lips. All she'd eaten at lunch was a small salad and she'd slept through the meal on the plane. She'd gotten up this morning at seven a.m. in California. Now it was almost nine in the evening here in Minnesota, and she'd missed dinner. And all she'd had to eat all day was one slice of coffee cake, a small salad that she hadn't even finished, and a tiny, not-so-tasty cinnamon roll on the plane. No wonder she was practically starving!

MEATY MINESTRONE SOUP

(A 5-Quart or 6-Quart Crockpot Recipe)

Hannah's 1st Note: If you want to make this into a vegetarian soup, simply leave out the meat and use vegetable stock instead of beef stock.

Ingredients:

>1 cup chopped onions *(2 small or 1 large)*
>1 cup chopped celery *(about 5 stalks)*
>3 or 4 uncooked Italian sausages *(I used the mild Italian sausages—if you like things spicy, feel free to use spicy Italian sausages)*
>1 medium-size yellow summer squash, chopped *(no need to peel)*
>1 small to medium zucchini, chopped *(no need to peel)*
>1 cup peeled carrot slices, chopped *(I used frozen crinkle-cut slices, thawed and chopped)*
>2-inch square Parmesan cheese
>1 to 2 teaspoons minced garlic *(jarred garlic is fine)*

2 cans *(14.5 ounces each)* beef broth *(I used Swanson)*

24-ounce jar of spaghetti sauce *(I used Prego with beef)*

1 cup water *(to swish around in the sauce jar and then add to the crock)*

2 cans *(6.5 ounces each)* of sliced mushrooms *(stems and pieces are okay)*

1 cup dry, uncooked corkscrew pasta *(or any other small dried pasta)*

Salt and pepper to taste

Additional Ingredients:

Hannah's 2nd Note: These are optional depending on how full your crock is and whether you have unexpected company and need to stretch the soup.

1 cup cut green beans *(I used frozen and let them thaw before I added them)*

15-ounce can white beans, drained

1 cup tomato juice

1 beef bouillon cube mixed with 1 cup water

Grated Parmesan cheese to sprinkle on top when serving

Spray the inside of a slow cooker with Pam or another nonstick cooking spray. ***This will make it much easier when you wash it!***

Peel and chop the onions into small pieces. Add them to the bottom of the crock. They will form part of the juice.

Wash and chop the celery into small pieces. Add them on top of the chopped onions.

Cut the Italian sausages into bite-size pieces. Add those to the crock on top of the celery.

Wash the yellow summer squash, cut it in half lengthwise, and then cut it in bite-size pieces. Add it to the crock on top of the Italian sausages.

Wash the zucchini, cut it in half lengthwise, and cut it into bite-size pieces. Add it to the crock on top of the yellow squash.

Place the carrot slices on a paper plate. Let them thaw a bit (if frozen) and then chop them into bite-size pieces.

Cut a 2-inch square of Parmesan cheese (or the equivalent) from a wedge of Parmesan cheese. Put it in the crock on top of the carrots.

Measure the minced garlic and add that to the crock on top of the Parmesan cheese.

With your impeccably clean fingers, toss the contents of the crock together, mixing it up by hand.

Open the cans of beef broth and pour it over the vegetable and sausage mixture in the slow cooker.

Open the jar of spaghetti sauce and pour that over the top. *There will be spaghetti sauce clinging to the bottom and the sides of the jar, but don't worry. We will take care of that next.*

Measure out one cup of water. Add it to the spaghetti sauce jar, put on the lid, and swish it around to get the clinging spaghetti sauce off the bottom and sides of the jar. Pour the contents of the jar on top of the mixture in the slow cooker.

Open the cans of sliced mushrooms and add them, juice and all, to the contents of the slow cooker.

Stir the contents of the crock with a spoon until everything is well mixed, put on the lid, then plug in the slow cooker and set it on LOW.

Hannah's 3rd Note: Be careful when setting the temperature on your slow cooker. I once failed to look and simply turned the dial one click, assuming that it was on LOW. When I came home, I discovered that the slow cooker was on WARM, not LOW. Now I check it twice to be sure I've selected the correct cooking temperature.

Cook your Meaty Minestrone Soup for 6 hours, or until the vegetables are tender. Give it a stir with a spoon and then add the uncooked pasta.

If you have room in the crock and you want to add any of the additional ingredients, do so now.

Stir to make sure everything is incorporated, replace the lid, and cook on LOW for another hour.

Your soup should be ready to serve in 60 minutes, but it can hold for two additional hours, or even longer if need be.

Before you serve, check the seasonings. If your soup needs salt or pepper, add it then.

To serve, ladle the Meaty Minestrone Soup into soup bowls and sprinkle with grated Parmesan cheese, if desired. If you add a small green salad and some crusty Italian bread or garlic bread, you will have an entire meal.

Chapter Six

"I'm sorry, Hannah," Lonnie apologized as he sat at the kitchen table with Hannah and Norman. "I told Michelle she didn't have to call you and ask you to come home right away. I didn't mean to spoil your vacation."

Hannah smiled at him. Poor Lonnie looked miserable. "You didn't spoil anything, Lonnie. I was ready to come home. Lynne only has a few things left to pack, and then she'll call the movers."

"When is your mother coming back?"

"Sometime tomorrow. We could only get one emergency plane ticket and I got it."

Hannah took a sip of her coffee, and then she turned to Norman. Dinner was over and all the pleasantries had been exchanged. It was time to get down to business. "Will you take notes, Norman?"

"Of course I will." Norman picked up the blank steno book and pen that Hannah had placed on the kitchen table. He flipped to the first page and said, "Okay. I'm ready, and I'll record it on my phone, too."

"I don't know what I can tell you, Hannah," Lonnie said, and then he gave a long sigh. "I just don't remember that much about what happened last night."

"It's okay. Let's start with the phone call you made to Michelle. What did you say to her?"

"I asked her if she wanted to go out to dinner and a movie."

"And she said . . ." Hannah prompted him.

"Michelle said she couldn't, that she had tryouts for the spring play, and then she had to go back to the condo to correct term papers. She invited me over for a night cap, and I told her I'd probably be there later."

"But you weren't," Norman said.

"No. Right after I hung up, my cell phone rang again and it was Brian Polinski. He said he was taking Cassie out for her birthday and she wanted me to meet them at the Double Eagle. I told him I'd catch a bite to eat first, and then I'd meet them there."

"Where did you go to eat?" Hannah asked him.

"I just went to Hal and Rose's Café for a Roast End sandwich."

"A Roast End sandwich?" Norman asked.

"That's what Rose calls it," Lonnie explained. "She makes a big beef roast and when she slices it for roast beef dinners, she cuts off the crispy part on the outside and leaves it in the pan. That's my favorite part and I always ask her to save it for me and give me a call when she's ready to make me a roast end sandwich. Those crispy parts are really good on rye bread with a little horseradish and ketchup."

"That does sound good," Hannah agreed. "What did you do after you finished your sandwich?"

"I called Michelle back and told her that I was going to

join Brian and Cassie for a birthday celebration. And she said I should stop by The Cookie Jar and pick up a birthday cake to take to Cassie."

"And that's what you did?" Norman asked.

"Yeah, I stopped by The Cookie Jar and bought a birthday cake right before I drove out to the Double Eagle. Lisa wrote Cassie's name on it and she even put birthday candles on top."

"What happened when you got out to the Double Eagle?" Hannah asked.

"I lucked out and parked three rows back from the door. Some guy in a pickup truck was just leaving and I got his spot. The parking lot was jammed and the band was playing. I could hear the music before I even opened the door."

It was cold when he got out of the car, and Lonnie zipped up his jacket before he picked up the cake box and headed for the door. He wasn't that fond of the Double Eagle, but he hadn't seen Brian and Cassie in a while. He decided he'd have only one beer, talk to them for an hour or so, and then he'd head on out to see Michelle at the condo.

Lonnie pulled open the door, stepped inside, and was immediately assaulted by the music. The band wasn't all that good, but they were loud. There were five or six couples on the dance floor in front of the elevated stage for the band, and Lonnie watched for a moment. Then he scanned the room for Brian and Cassie.

They weren't at the tables near the band. That was good. It would be deafening to sit that close to the music. He turned to look at the wooden bar that ran the length of the wall and he spotted Brian. Brian was easy to spot. He'd been a linebacker on their high school football team. Brian was well over six feet tall and weighed in at close to three hundred pounds. Brian was sitting next to two empty stools, and once Lonnie weaved his way through the crowd of people to get to the bar, he tapped Brian on the shoulder.

"Hey, Cap," Lonnie said, using the nickname Brian had earned by being chosen as the captain of their Jordan High football team.

Brian turned around with a smile on his face. "Hey, Lonnie," he said, patting the stool to his right. "Take a load off."

Lonnie slid onto the stool. A fairly tall, muscular man in his own right, Lonnie always felt like a little kid around Brian. He set the cake box on the bar and indicated the empty stool. "Where's Cassie?"

"She's catching a ride out with her sister." Brian pointed to the bakery box. "Is that what I think it is?"

"Sure is. I hope Cassie still likes Coconut Layer Cake."

"It's her favorite. Nice of you to bring her a birthday cake, Bro."

"No problem. I stopped at The Cookie Jar and Lisa wrote her name on the top with frosting and put some candles on it."

"I should've thought of that, but I didn't." Brian looked a little embarrassed. "All I gave her was a necklace and earrings. Her sister helped me pick them out."

"I bet Cassie liked that."

"I haven't given it to her yet. That's for when we get home." Brian picked up his drink and took a sip. "What do you want to drink, bro? I'm buying."

Lonnie thought about that for a minute. "Tap beer's fine," he said, and as he watched, Brian raised his hand, stuck up a finger in the air for the bartender, and yelled, "Tap one for Lonnie." Before he'd even walked in the door at the Double Eagle he'd set his limit at one beer only. After that, he'd switch to plain Coke. He wasn't officially on call tonight, but they could still ask him to come in if there was an emergency. The stretch of the interstate that ran past Lake Eden was icy tonight and there could be a multi-car pileup if someone got stupid on the road.

"Still going out with Michelle Swensen?" Brian asked when he sat back down on his stool.

"Yeah."

"It's been a while, huh?"

Lonnie nodded. "Couple of years."

"So it's serious?"

Lonnie shrugged. It was really none of Brian's business, but he didn't want to come right out and say that. "Maybe, maybe not."

Brian, who wasn't usually the sharpest knife in the drawer, began to smile. "In other words, butt out . . . right?"

Lonnie wasn't sure what to say, but he was saved from replying when Alvin Penske, one of the long-time bartenders at the Double Eagle, arrived with his beer.

"Hey, Lonnie," Alvin greeted him. "Haven't seen you around in a coon's age."

Most people used that old saying to mean a very long time and Lonnie bit back a grin, wondering what Alvin would say if he learned that raccoons in the wild only lived an average of two to three years. "You're right, Alvin," Lonnie responded. "It's been a while, that's for sure."

"Yeah. Don't think I've seen you since you got that cushy job at the sheriff's department."

Lonnie felt himself bristle, but he managed to keep the pleasant expression on his face as Alvin moved away. Alvin and his brother, Lenny, gave the sheriff's deputies lots of grief, serving one too many to their customers and sending them out to their cars impaired. The Double Eagle had been implicated in quite a few car accidents, fights, and episodes of general rowdiness. The owner had paid the fines and acted chastised in court, but it continued to be a trouble spot in Winnetka County.

"There's Cassie," Brian said, a broad smile spreading over his face. Lonnie was glad to see it. Even though Brian and Cassie had split up for a while, it was clear that Brian was just as crazy about his high school sweetheart as he'd been when they'd gotten married.

Lonnie put a smile on his face for Brian's benefit. He'd never liked Cassie all that much, but Brian was a good friend and you had to pretend to like your friends' girlfriends and wives, even if you didn't.

"Lonnie," Cassie called out, pushing her way to the bar. "Hey! Long time, no see. Don't you ever get out to our neck of the woods?"

"Not often," Lonnie said, giving her a chaste peck on the cheek. "You look great, Cassie."

"Thanks." Cassie turned to Brian. "Hey, honey. Get me a drink, will you? Tonight's a night for Tequila Sunrises, isn't it?"

Brian began to grin wider. "Sure is. Do you want me to order us a flight?"

"What's a flight?" Lonnie asked.

Cassie laughed. "Three drinks, silly. They call it a flight 'cuz after three of 'em you feel like your feet don't touch the floor." She moved closer to Lonnie, wrapped her arms around him, and gave him a little squeeze. "That's cute, huh?"

"Cute," Lonnie repeated, hoping his friends weren't going to get too drunk. He pushed the cake box over to Cassie. "This is for you, Cassie."

"For me?" Cassie lifted the lid on the box and began to smile. "How did you remember that it was my birthday?"

"I told him we were celebrating tonight," Brian said, before Lonnie could answer. "Lonnie picked up a Coconut Layer Cake for you."

"My favorite!" Cass was all smiles as she wrapped her arms around Lonnie and hugged him again. "And it's even got candles and my name on it!" She let Lonnie go and turned to Brian. "Light the candles, will you, Baby?"

"Sure." Brian took out his lighter, lifted the cake out of the box, and lit the candles. "Happy birthday, Cassie," he said. "I'm not going to sing, okay?"

"It's more than okay. It's a real present!" Cassie retorted with a laugh. "You're a lousy singer, Baby."

"I know. You keep telling me that."

There was a little edge to Brian's voice and Lonnie stepped in quickly.

"I promise you that I won't sing, either," Lonnie told Cassie. "I tried out for the men's chorus in high school and I didn't make it."

"I never tried out," Brian said with a laugh. "I knew better. I joined the band instead."

"You played drums, didn't you?" Lonnie asked him.

"Yes, and he was good," Cassie said quickly. "My baby's really great at banging things."

Brian looked slightly embarrassed at the double entendre, but he laughed anyway. So did Lonnie, mostly because it was expected, and Cassie leaned over so that she could kiss Brian.

Lonnie drew a breath of relief. Cassie always flirted outrageously with him and it made him more than a little uncomfortable. She'd always been a real flirt, and her marriage to Brian hadn't changed that.

"I was going to tell you to order two flights for us, but maybe we'd better split them three ways. We'll do two for me, two for you, and two for Lonnie."

"No can do," Lonnie said, shaking his head. "Thanks, but I can't drink hard booze when I might be called in."

"Okay, then you can have another couple of beers," Cassie decided for him.

"I'm switching to Coke after this one." Lonnie gestured toward his half-empty glass.

Cassie gave an exasperated sigh. "Party pooper!" She turned back to Brian. "Order Lonnie a Coke. And we'll split one flight of Tequila Sunrises."

"Two for you and one for me?" Brian asked with a grin.

"Nope. One for me and two for you. And if they total you out, I can drive." She turned back to Lonnie. "Is that okay, Mr. Deputy?"

"That's perfect." Lonnie gestured toward the cake. "Make a wish, Cassie. You'd better blow out the candles before they scorch the frosting."

Cassie closed her eyes and looked thoughtful. When she opened them again, she was smiling. "Okay. I made a wish. Let's see if it's going to come true."

Lonnie watched as Cassie bent closer to the top of the cake. She took a deep breath, blew it out, and managed to extinguish every one of the candles.

"Nice!" Lonnie complimented her. "What did you wish for?"

Cassie shook her head. "I can't tell you or it won't come true."

"I know what you wished for," Brian told her.

"Maybe you do and maybe you don't," Cassie said, slipping her arm around his waist and hugging him tightly before she straightened up again.

"I'd better sit over here, Baby," she said to Brian, taking the stool on the other side of him. "Lonnie doesn't have a girlfriend tonight and he might put the moves on me!"

"You're safe tonight, Cassie," Lonnie said quickly, knowing that Cassie was the type of woman who really believed she was irresistible to men.

"I am?" Cassie gave him a flirtatious look. "Why's that?"

"I'll probably get called in later," Lonnie answered quickly. "Were the roads still bad when you came out here?"

"They were awful! My sister almost slid off the road twice! And we were just crawling along." She turned to Brian. "We can't drink too much tonight, Baby. Lonnie's right. The roads are miserable."

"Don't worry. I'll only have two more drinks, that's it. And I'll do the driving. Before we start for home, I'll have a couple of cups of black coffee. You won't have to drive home, honey. And once we get there, we'll open that bottle of champagne we've been saving from the wedding."

"Perfect!" Cassie gave him a radiant smile and stood up again. "I'm going back to the kitchen to see if I can get us some plates and forks."

"Four plates?" Brian asked when Cassie came back and placed everything on the bar in front of them.

Cassie nodded. "I promised the cook I'd bring him a piece. And then Lonnie can take the rest of the cake home. These jeans are getting tight and I want to drop a couple of pounds."

"But this is your favorite," Brian argued.

Cassie laughed as she reached out to pat his stomach. "Yours too. I'm saving us from ourselves, Baby. If we take the rest of that cake home, it'll be crumbs by midnight."

Lonnie's slice of cake was almost gone when his cell phone rang. He glanced at the display, almost hoping that he was being called in to work, but the caller ID on the display read SUSPECTED SPAM. He answered anyway and got a recorded message that tried to sell him solar panels. Since he didn't own a house, he hung up and slipped the phone back into his pocket.

Since Cassie and Brian were talking to each other, Lonnie glanced around the cavernous interior of the Double Eagle. It was a huge barn of a place with tables on the floor and booths that were elevated two steps up on a riser. The booths were full, but there were still several empty tables on the ground level. He was scanning the tables when the couple sitting there caught his eye. The woman looked vaguely familiar, but it took a second and then a third glance before he recognized her. It was Darcy Hicks, another one of their former classmates.

"Isn't that Darcy?" he asked Brian and Cassie, gesturing toward the table.

"That's her," Cassie said.

"I thought so. Who's the guy with her? I don't recognize him."

"That's because he didn't go to school with us," Brian explained. "He's from Upsala and his name is Denny Jameson. He was on their football team."

"Okay, now I remember him," Lonnie said. "He was the quarterback, wasn't he?"

Cassie nodded. "Yes, and he was good. They beat us in the homecoming game."

"That's right. Everybody said he was going to go pro."

Brian shook his head. "He didn't. And I heard that just about killed him when he wasn't chosen in the draft. That's when he started drinking and put on weight. Booze'll do that to you if you're not careful, and he's a heavy drinker."

Cassie nodded. "I heard he had a slew of DUIs and he just got his license back last month." She turned to Lonnie. "You're not going to bust him, are you?"

Lonnie shook his head. "I'm off duty right now. I might tell Alvin he'd better eighty-six him, though."

Cassie looked relieved. "Okay. That wouldn't be a bad idea. I'd hate to see him busted when they just got engaged."

"Tonight?" Brian looked surprised.

"No, last week. A guy at work told me. I got a feeling it's going to be a really short engagement."

"You could be right," Lonnie told her. "They sure don't look very happy about it."

Brian nodded. "They're getting off to a bad start, that's for sure. He looks really mad and he just banged his fist on the table. And I can see that Darcy's been crying."

"Do you think I should go over there and see what's wrong?" Lonnie asked.

Cassie shook her head. "That's a bad idea. He looks too mad to be reasonable and he's bigger than you are."

Alvin came over with a tray of drinks and placed them in front of Cassie. "Here's your flight of Tequila Sunrises. Are you going to share them with Brian?"

Cassie nodded. "I'm only having one. The other two are Brian's. And Lonnie wants Coke after he finishes his beer."

"Figures," Alvin nodded, side-stepping to the soda gun behind the bar, filling a glass, and stepping back to set it in front of Lonnie. "You're being careful tonight, huh, Lonnie?"

"You bet. It's nasty out there on the highway and I could get called in at any time."

"You're right and the Coke's on the house. The boss likes to support our law enforcement officers."

Lonnie nodded, knowing that wasn't true. The last people the owner wanted in his establishment were law enforcement officers who might pick up the Double Eagle customers on their way home.

"It was bad when I came to work and that was at four this afternoon," Alvin told them.

"And it's still nasty," Lonnie agreed.

"I know. Everybody who comes in says that. All it takes is one idiot from out of state slamming on his brakes, and we've got a real . . . uh-oh!"

"What is it?" Lonnie asked, turning in the direction that Alvin was facing.

"Trouble on table six," Alvin said, and even though Lonnie didn't know the table numbers, he saw exactly what Alvin was seeing.

"Darcy," he said, cueing in Cassie and Brian, who also turned to look.

As they watched, Darcy had just picked up her drink and she took a big gulp. Denny was frowning and he looked as if he wanted to throw his own drink in her face. It didn't take a genius to recognize that Darcy and her fiancé's altercation had escalated.

Lonnie turned back to Alvin. "We see it."

"She hasn't had that much to drink," Alvin said. "This is her first drink and she asked the waitress to make sure that it was a light one, but I think I'd better eighty-six him. He's got more than a buzz on. Do you think I should go over and tell him that I'm cutting him off?"

Lonnie shook his head. "It's okay, Alvin. I know both of them. I'll take care of it for you."

"Thanks a lot, Lonnie!"

Alvin looked incredibly grateful and he wasted no time hurrying back to the waitress's station. Lonnie watched as Alvin had a brief conversation with his brother, Lenny, who was acting as the service bartender. Then both of them gave a thumbs-up in Lonnie's direction.

Lonnie returned the salute. He couldn't blame Alvin for not wanting to confront Denny. The Penske brothers were not large men, and Lonnie estimated that neither one weighed much more than a hundred and thirty pounds dripping wet. Denny probably outweighed either of them by more than a hundred plus pounds and he was still in fighting shape.

"Need some help?" Brian asked Lonnie, and it was obvious he'd overheard Lonnie's conversation with Alvin. "He's a lot bigger than you are, Lonnie."

"Thanks, but it's okay. Just keep an eye on things when I get there. If I give you the high sign, come and help."

Cassie slid off her bar stool. "I can help you, Lonnie."

"You?" Brian looked doubtful. "What can *you* do, Cassie?"

"I can go over there and ask Darcy if she wants to go

to the ladies' room with me. And I can make sure she stays there for a while. That'll take her out of the picture so you guys can deal with Denny."

"That's a pretty good idea," Brian complimented her. "Do you think she'll go with you?"

"Sure, she will. Women don't like to go to the ladies' room alone. Haven't you ever noticed that they always leave in pairs?"

Lonnie thought about that for a moment. "I just never thought about it before, but you're right, Cassie. Why do they go in pairs?"

"Because it gives them a chance to talk about their dates and compare notes."

Brian and Lonnie exchanged glances, and Lonnie suspected that they were thinking the same thing. They could live to be a hundred and they'd never really understand women.

"Give me a minute with Darcy," Cassie told Lonnie. "Right after she gets up and we leave, come on over and do what you're going to do with Denny."

Lonnie and Brian watched as Cassie walked over to the table and greeted Darcy and her fiancé. There was a short conversation, and then Darcy got to her feet and followed Cassie to the back of the building. They turned at the hallway where the restrooms were located and disappeared from sight.

"She did it," Brian said, looking surprised, but also quite proud.

"She sure did," Lonnie agreed.

Brian glanced at Lonnie's nearly-empty glass. "You must be thirsty. You finished that one in no time flat."

"I am. I think I put too much salt on the French fries I had with my sandwich."

"You ate food *here*?"

Brian sounded shocked and Lonnie laughed. "Heck, no! I know better than that. I stopped at Hal and Rose's Café to eat."

"That's good. At least I won't have to call the paramedics for you," Brian said with a grin. "On our way to Darcy's table, let's stop at the service bar and order you another Coke."

"Thanks. I'll just finish this one and then I'll go over and talk to Denny. Cassie did me a real favor. It'll be a lot easier to defuse the situation if Darcy's not there. Just keep an eye on Denny, will you?"

"Sure will. Don't worry about me, Bro. I'll be right there if you need me."

Lonnie stood up and was about to step away from the bar when Brian grabbed his arm. "Wait a second! Denny just got up. I hope he's not heading to the restrooms."

"If he is, I'll intercept him," Lonnie promised.

Both men watched as Denny headed toward the spot where the cocktail waitress was standing. There was a brief conversation, and then Denny got out his wallet and handed her some money. She nodded, walked up to the service bar, and turned the money over to Lenny Penske. Once she'd gotten change, she carried it back to Denny. Denny took some of it, handed the rest back to her, and headed for the door.

"He's leaving!" Brian sounded very surprised. "I wonder if he told Darcy that he was going."

"If he did, she'll probably tell Cassie." Lonnie watched the cocktail waitress as she put the tip money in her apron pocket, picked up the tray and the drink order that Denny had given her, and delivered them to Darcy and Denny's empty table.

"Denny paid for those drinks, but he didn't stick around long enough to drink his," Brian noted. "He must have told her to deliver them anyway."

"I think we should move over to Darcy's table," Lonnie suggested. "If Denny didn't tell Darcy that he was leaving, she'll be pretty upset if she comes back to an empty table."

Brian nodded. "You're right. Why don't you go over there and sit down? I'll catch the cocktail waitress, order a Coke for you, and ask her to bring these"—he gestured toward the flight of Tequila Sunrises—"over to Darcy's table. And don't forget the rest of the cake. Darcy might like to drown her sorrows in some of those great-tasting carbs."

HANNAH'S COCONUT LAYER CAKE

Preheat oven to 350°F., rack in the middle position.

8-ounce can crushed pineapple *(I used Dole)*

2 cups shredded coconut *(pack it down when you measure it)*

⅛ cup *(2 Tablespoons)* all-purpose flour

12-ounce *(by weight)* bag of white chocolate chips or vanilla baking chips *(11-ounce package will do, too—I used Nestlé)*

4 large eggs

½ cup vegetable oil

¼ cup cold whole milk

¼ cup rum *(I used Malibu Caribbean Rum with Coconut Liqueur)*

2 teaspoons coconut extract

8-ounce *(by weight)* tub of sour cream *(I used Knudsen)*

1 box of white cake mix with or without pudding in the mix, the kind that makes a 9-inch by 13-inch cake or a 2-layer cake *(I used Duncan Hines)*

5.1-ounce package of instant coconut pudding mix *(I used Jell-O, the kind that makes 6 half-cup servings)*

Prepare your cake pans. You'll need 2 round cake pans, 8 or 9 inches in diameter.

Spray the inside of your cake pans with Pam Baking Spray. Alternatively, you can spray them with Pam Cooking Spray and flour the inside of the pan, sides and all, knocking out the excess flour.

Hannah's 1st Note: To flour a baking pan, put some flour in the bottom, hold it over your kitchen wastebasket, and tap the pan to move the flour all over the inside of the pan. Continue this until all the inside surfaces of the pan, including the sides, have been covered with a light coating of flour.

Place a strainer over a bowl on the counter. Open the can of crushed pineapple and dump *(yes, that is a cooking term)* it into the strainer. Leave it there to drain while you continue to make the batter for your cake. *(You can save the juice to add to orange juice in the morning.)*

Put the coconut in the bowl of a food processor. Sprinkle on the 2 Tablespoons of flour. Process to chop the coconut into much smaller pieces by using the steel blade in an on-and-off motion.

Place the finely-chopped coconut in a bowl on the counter.

Put the white chocolate or vanilla baking chips in the bottom of the food processor bowl. In an on-and-off motion with the steel blade, chop the chips into small pieces.

Place the chopped chips in another bowl on the counter.

Hannah's 2nd Note: You can mix up this cake by hand, but it takes some muscle and you must make sure everything is well combined. It's a lot easier to do if you use an electric mixer.

Crack the eggs into the bowl of an electric mixer. Mix them up on LOW speed until they're a uniform color. The consistent color will tell you that the eggs are thoroughly mixed.

Pour the half-cup of vegetable oil over the eggs. Mix the two ingredients together on LOW speed.

Add the quarter-cup of cold milk to the bowl. Mix it in on LOW speed.

Add the quarter-cup of rum to the bowl. Mix that in on LOW speed.

Hannah's 3rd Note: If you do not want to use liquor in this cake, you can substitute another quarter-cup of cold milk for the rum.

Add the 2 teaspoons of coconut extract to the bowl. Mix that in on LOW speed.

Scoop out the 8-ounce container of sour cream and add it to your bowl. Mix that in on LOW speed.

When everything is well combined, open the box of dry cake mix and sprinkle HALF of it on top of the liquid ingredients in the bowl. (This doesn't have to be precisely half. Just use your best judgment.) If you add the cake mix all at once and then turn on your mixer, you risk having the dry cake mix fly all over your kitchen! (And please don't ask me how I know this.)

Mix in the first half of your cake mix on LOW speed.

Add the second half of your cake mix and mix that in. Continue to mix until everything is well combined.

Add the package of dry instant coconut pudding mix. Beat it in, again on LOW speed.

Finally, sprinkle in the chopped coconut and chopped white chocolate or vanilla chips. Mix them in thoroughly on LOW speed.

Remember the crushed pineapple that you set in the strainer on your counter? Now it's time to deal with that.

With the back of a mixing spoon, press down on the crushed pineapple in the strainer. Keep moving the spoon and pressing down until you've gotten as much liquid as possible from the pineapple.

Tear off several pieces of paper toweling and place it over the top of the pineapple in the strainer. Press down on that with your impeccably clean hand. Again, express as much liquid as you can. You want this pineapple as dry as you can get it.

Place the crushed pineapple in the bowl of the mixer and mix it in on LOW speed. Mix until it's thoroughly combined.

Shut off the mixer, scrape down the sides of the bowl, and give your batter a final stir by hand.

Use a rubber spatula to transfer the cake batter to the prepared cake pans. Do this as evenly as possible.

Smooth the tops of both pans with a rubber spatula and place them on the same shelf in the oven, leaving as much room between the pans as possible.

For two 8-inch rounds, bake your Coconut Layer Cake at 350°F. for 45 minutes, or until a cake tester inserted 1 inch from the center comes out clean.

For two 9-inch rounds, bake your Coconut Layer Cake at 350°F., for 35 minutes, or until a cake tester inserted 1 inch from the center comes out clean.

Before you take your cake out of the oven, test it for doneness by inserting a cake tester, thin wooden skewer, or long wooden toothpick one inch from the center of the cake pan. If the tester comes out clean, your cake is done. If there is still unbaked batter clinging to the tester, shut the oven door and bake your cakes in 5-minute increments, testing after each increment, until they test done.

Once your cakes have finished baking, take them out of the oven and set them on cold stovetop burners or wire racks. Let them cool in the pans for 15 minutes.

After the 15-minute cooling time is up, run a table knife from your silverware drawer around the sides of the pans to loosen the cakes.

Pick up each cake pan with oven mitts or pot-holders and tip the pan upside down on a cookie sheet lined with parchment paper. Gently tap the bottom of the pan to free the cake. Carefully lift off the cake pan so that the cake rests on the parchment paper.

Cover your cake layers loosely with foil and re-frigerate for at least one hour. Overnight is even better. You want the cake layers to firm up.

Frost your Coconut Layer Cake with Coconut Lemon Frosting. Alternatively, if you'd prefer a frosting that is not cooked on the stove, use the Coconut Lemon and Cream Cheese Frosting. *(Both frosting recipes and instructions for frosting your layer cake follow.)*

Yield: At least 8 pieces of incredibly good and very rich cake. This cake is wonderful with vanilla ice cream on top. Serve with tall glasses of ice-cold milk or cups of strong coffee.

COCONUT LEMON FROSTING

2 cups white chocolate or vanilla baking
　　chips *(11-ounce package)*
¼ teaspoon salt *(it brings out the flavor of
　　the chocolate)*
14-ounce can of sweetened condensed milk
1 teaspoon coconut extract
1 teaspoon lemon zest
1 Tablespoon *(⅛ stick)* salted butter
1 cup sweetened coconut flakes *(to pat on
　　top of the frosting you use)*

**Hannah's Note: If you use a double boiler for
this frosting, it's foolproof. You can also make it
in a heavy saucepan over low to medium heat on
the stovetop, but you'll have to stir it constantly
with a wooden spoon or a heat-resistant spatula
to keep it from scorching.**

Fill the bottom part of the double boiler with
water. Make sure the water doesn't touch the under-
side of the top.

Put the white chocolate or vanilla chips and the
salt in the top of the double boiler, set it over the
bottom, and place the double boiler on the stovetop

at MEDIUM heat. Stir occasionally until the white chocolate or vanilla chips are melted.

Stir in the can of sweetened condensed milk. Cook approximately 2 minutes, stirring constantly, until the frosting is shiny and of spreading consistency.

Shut off the heat, remove the top part of the double boiler, and set it on a cold stovetop burner. Quickly stir in the coconut extract and the lemon zest. *(It may sputter a bit, so be careful.)*

Add the salted butter and stir it in until it melts.

Keep stirring your frosting until it cools enough to reach proper spreading consistency.

The following frosting is the alternative to the cooked frosting.

COCONUT AND LEMON CREAM CHEESE FROSTING

½ cup softened salted butter *(1 stick, 4 ounces, ¼ pound)*
8-ounce package softened cream cheese *(the brick kind, NOT whipped)*
1 teaspoon coconut extract
Zest of 1 lemon
4 cups confectioners' *(powdered)* sugar *(no need to sift unless it's got big lumps)*

Mix the softened butter with the softened cream cheese

Add the coconut extract and the lemon zest. Mix well.

Hannah's Note: Do this next step at room temperature. If you heated the cream cheese or the butter to soften it, make sure it's cooled down before you continue.

Add the confectioners' sugar in half-cup increments until the frosting is of proper spreading consistency. *(You'll use all, or almost all, of the sugar.)*

To Frost Your Coconut Layer Cake:

Take your cake layers out of the refrigerator and put the first layer, upside down, on a cake plate.

Using a frosting knife, slather the top of the layer with the frosting you have chosen to use.

Put the other layer, right-side up, on top of the frosting you spread on the bottom layer.

Use your impeccably clean palms to press down on the top layer to make sure that it is securely in place.

Using a frosting knife, frost the sides of the cake. Use the edge of the frosting knife to smooth the frosting.

Slather the rest of the frosting on top of your cake and spread that out.

Smooth the frosting you placed on the top of your cake.

Quickly, before the frosting dries, pat sweetened coconut flakes all over the sides and the top of your cake.

If you wish, decorate the top of the cake with maraschino cherries cut in half vertically or use

whole maraschino cherries with stems pointing up in a circle around the circumference of your cake.

When you've finished frosting your cake, refrigerate it until it's time to serve it.

Serve this cake with plenty of strong, hot coffee or icy-cold glasses of milk.

Yield: At least 8 thick slices of rich, delicious Coconut Layer Cake.

Chapter Seven

Hannah reached out to refill Lonnie's coffee cup from the carafe on the table. It was obvious to her that he was reliving the night of the murder. His face was pale and his eyes were unfocused, almost as if he were in a trance.

"Lonnie?" Hannah said. "You want more coffee, don't you?"

"Huh?" Lonnie blinked a couple of times and then let out his breath in a huge sigh. "Sorry, Hannah. I was right back there at the Eagle, you know?"

"I know. Are you okay?"

It took Lonnie a minute to answer. He picked up his coffee cup, took a big sip, and then he nodded. "Yeah, I'm okay."

"Do you think you can go on for a while longer?" Norman asked him.

"I . . . yeah. You need to know everything, right?"

"Everything that you can remember," Hannah confirmed. "Tell us anything you noticed, even if you don't think it's important. Nothing's too small to mention, no matter what it is."

"You're doing great, Lonnie," Norman told him. "I almost felt like I was sitting right there with you and Brian and Cassie at the bar."

Lonnie smiled. "You're not the only one. It was like I was reliving it."

"And that's perfect." Hannah reached out to pat his shoulder. "Do you think you can go on, Lonnie?"

"Yes, just let me finish my coffee and then I'll tell you the rest."

Lonnie gulped the rest of his coffee and straightened up in his chair. "Okay," he said. "I was right at the point where Brian and I split up and I went over to Darcy's table. I remember that I was thirsty, really thirsty. And I remember wishing that I still had some Coke left. Brian was at the service bar and I could see him talking to Lenny Penske. Lenny laughed at something Brian said, and then he reached behind him to get another glass. That was when the cocktail waitress came up to Lenny with a tray. . . ."

There was a moment of silence while Lonnie closed his eyes. He was remembering how he'd felt that night, how loud the band was, and the din of voices getting louder and louder. And then he was there again, the night it all happened.

Lonnie slipped a bill under his empty Coke glass and stood up. It took a while to make his way through the room, dodging people on his way to Darcy's table. When he got there, he pulled out a chair, sat down, and watched as the cocktail waitress hurried to the place where they'd been sitting. She smiled when she saw the tip, picked it up and put it in her apron pocket, and loaded the flight of Tequila Sunrises on her tray. Then she went back to the service bar to pick up the Coke that Brian had ordered for Lonnie.

Lonnie swallowed hard. He really needed that Coke, and he hoped it wouldn't take her long to bring it to him. Then the front door banged open and Lonnie turned to see who was coming in. Would Denny have second thoughts and come back before Darcy got back from the ladies' room? And if he did, what should Lonnie say to explain why he had taken Denny's place at Darcy's table? Lonnie was still pondering these questions when the cocktail waitress arrived at the table with their drinks.

"Hi, Lonnie," she said. "I ran into Brian at the service bar and he asked me to deliver these drinks. One of those Cokes is for you."

"Thanks!" Lonnie grabbed it and took a huge swallow. Then he took another that drained half the glass.

"Here." The cocktail waitress set a large glass of water in front of him. "Help yourself, Lonnie."

Lonnie stared at her as she unloaded her tray. She looked vaguely familiar, but he couldn't quite place her.

The cocktail waitress noticed his stare and gave a little laugh. "You're thinking you know me . . . right?"

"Yeah," Lonnie admitted.

"But you can't quite place me?"

"You're right. I think I know you, though."

"You do. Think back, Lonnie. History class at Jordan High. I sat in the chair behind you."

Lonnie tried to visualize the classroom, but he couldn't quite remember who'd sat behind him. It was a girl, but who was she?

Lonnie wanted to lie and say he remembered her, but he curbed his impulse. Michelle always said his face was like an open book, and he figured the cocktail waitress would figure out that he still didn't recognize her. "Uh . . . actually . . ." he said, stalling for time.

"That's okay," the cocktail waitress said, arranging the drinks on the tabletop. "I look really different than I did back then. Let me give you a hint. I was class president and I played the flute in the band."

"Kay?!" Lonnie knew he probably sounded incredulous, but he couldn't help himself. "But you had brown hair. And you were . . ."

"Fat," Kay laughed as Lonnie hesitated. "I was fat," she said, finishing the sentence for him. "My hair's still brown, but now I have blond streaks."

Lonnie just stared at her. "You look great, Kay!" he said truthfully.

"Thanks. I'm married now. How about you? I heard you were dating Michelle Swensen."

"That's right. I am."

"I like Michelle. We used to always sit together at lunch. Are you serious about her?"

Lonnie nodded. "I'm serious, but we haven't talked about anything permanent yet." He felt a bit uncomfortable discussing Michelle with someone else, so he changed the subject. "Is your husband someone I know?"

"Yes, I married Joe Hollenkamp two years ago."

"Joe's a great guy, but he's . . . uh . . ."

"A lot older than I am?" Kay asked, obviously amused.

"Well . . . yeah."

"I know Joe's a lot older. He's twenty-five years older than we are. I'm good with that age difference, Lonnie.

Joe's the kindest, sweetest, most considerate man I've ever met. And I love him like crazy."

"You sound happy, Kay."

"I am." Kay looked slightly uncomfortable. "Darcy should be back any minute now. She went to the ladies' room with Cassie. What are you going to say if she asks you why you moved over here?"

"I'm going to tell her the truth, that I was sitting at the bar with Brian and Cassie and we noticed that she was fighting with Denny. When he left, Brian and I figured that she might need some moral support from her friends."

Kay smiled. "That's perfect."

"You don't think Denny's coming back inside, do you?" Lonnie asked the important question.

"I'm pretty sure he's not. He caught me right before I was going to deliver their drinks. He told me to go ahead and deliver them, and then he paid and left."

"And he didn't say anything about coming back?"

Kay shook her head. "Not a word. He was really steaming, Lonnie. And Denny's got a real temper. I don't know what they fought about, but it was really clear that Denny was furious with Darcy."

"Do you know if Darcy drove out here alone, or if she came with Denny?"

"She came with Denny. I had to run out to my car for something and Denny pulled in and parked right next to me. I walked back in with both of them."

"So Darcy doesn't have a ride home?"

Kay shook her head. "Not unless Denny cools off and comes back. And I think the chances of that are really slim. I know I wouldn't bet the farm on that happening."

"Okay. Thanks for the heads-up, Kay. I can always

drive Darcy home. I go right past her place on the way back to Lake Eden."

Kay looked pleased. "You're a good guy, Lonnie. I think Darcy must have been drinking before she got here because she looked pretty drunk when I delivered their last set of drinks. I wouldn't want her to go home with one of the guys that hang out here."

"Tell me about Denny. Was he drunk when he left?"

"Not that I could tell. He had a couple of Margaritas, but Denny's a big guy. And after two, he said that was his limit and switched to plain Coke." Kay gestured toward one of the drinks she'd placed on the table. "This Margarita's for Darcy. And the other drinks are part of the flight that Brian and Cassie ordered. The Cokes are for you and Denny, but since Denny's not here, you can have both of them."

"Okay, don't mind if I do. I'm really thirsty tonight." Lonnie reached for one of the Cokes and took a large sip. "Thanks for all the info, Kay."

"And thank you for taking care of Darcy. I can't help feeling sorry for her."

"Why's that?"

"Darcy's always had a real talent for picking the wrong men. Even back in high school, she was the one who dated what my mother used to call *bad boys*. I tried to talk to her about it once, when she was going out with a married guy. I told her she was worth more than that and he was just using her."

"What did she say?"

"She said it didn't matter, that he loved her and he'd promised her that he was going to divorce his wife so that they could get married."

"But that didn't happen, did it?"

"No, he ended up breaking it off with Darcy and going back to his wife."

Lonnie thought back to their high school days. "I don't remember him."

"You wouldn't. Darcy kept it a secret because she knew her dad would have killed her if he'd found out."

"But you like Darcy, even though you don't approve of her?"

Kay nodded. "I do. There's something about her that's childlike. Darcy trusts everybody and believes anything a guy tells her. I would have offered to take her home to keep her out of trouble, but I'm on clean-up tonight and I won't get off until after two."

"Well, you can stop worrying. I've got it covered." Lonnie glanced over at the service bar, noticed that Brian was no longer standing there, and began to frown. "Do you know where Brian went?"

"He said he was going to wait for Cassie and Darcy in the hallway outside the ladies' room. They must be sitting on the sofa in there, gabbing up a storm." Kay glanced at the service window and saw that Lenny was motioning to her. "I gotta run," she said, giving Lonnie a pat on the shoulder. "Thanks for taking care of Darcy for us, Lonnie."

"That's okay. I don't mind giving her a ride home. And besides, we have to stick together. Darcy's a classmate of ours."

Kay nodded. "You're right. And I wish everyone else felt the way you do, Lonnie."

After Kay left, Lonnie sat there for a while, watching the couples on the dance floor. None of them could have won a dance contest and, judging by the twists and twirls one couple was doing, it was amazing that they hadn't pulled a muscle yet. If there was any doubt in Lonnie's mind about the ability of ingesting alcohol to loosen inhibitions, the proof was right there in front of his eyes. It was clear that they thought they were descendants of Fred Astaire and Ginger Rogers and had inherited their talents tenfold.

The band finished up on a sour note that no one except Lonnie noticed or cared about, and left the stage to grab a quick drink before playing another set.

"Hey, Lonnie," a voice spoke close to his ear, and Lonnie whirled around. It was Lenny Penske and he slid into an empty chair. "Mind if I sit here for a couple of minutes? I'm on break."

"Make yourself comfortable, Lenny."

"Did you drink Denny's Coke?"

"Guilty. It was plain Coke, wasn't it?"

"Sure was. Didn't Kay tell you?"

"She told me. I was just checking, that's all. I'm not on call, but if anything happens tonight, I need to have a clear head."

"Like . . . you mean . . ." Lenny looked slightly embarrassed. "You mean if something happens with Darcy?"

"No! I mean if there's some kind of pileup on the road. They'll call me in and I want to have a clear head if I have to go."

"I got it. Sorry about that. I should have known better. You're still going out with Michelle Swensen, aren't you?"

Lonnie nodded. "Yes, and I'm going over there later tonight. I just want to give Darcy a ride home because Kay didn't think that Denny was coming back."

"Kay's right. Denny won't be back. I was watching the

fight they had and it'll take him at least a couple of days to cool off. He might even be gone for good. It's hard to predict those things, you know? You gotta feel sorry for Darcy, though, don't you? I think she really liked Denny. And except for his temper, he was an okay guy. Makes me wonder what they were fighting about."

"Whatever it was, it didn't look good."

"I know. That poor girl's got really bad luck with men." Lenny glanced toward the back of the room, pushed back his chair, and stood up. "And speaking of that, here she comes now. She doesn't look good, Lonnie. Better take her home soon and make sure she doesn't try to go out again."

Lonnie turned to see what Lenny had noticed. Brian, Cassie, and Darcy had emerged from the hallway and were making their way through the crowd. As he watched, Darcy stumbled and Brian grabbed her arm to steady her. Both Kay and Lenny thought that Darcy was already drunk when she came in the door, and this substantiated their suspicions. According to both of them, Darcy had ordered one drink, a light one, and there had been at least a third of it left in the glass when Kay had cleared it away. That wasn't enough alcohol to hit her that hard, and that meant that Kay and Lenny were probably right.

The longer Lonnie watched, the more convinced he became. It was time to cut this evening short and take Darcy home while she could still walk. He didn't relish the idea of carrying her across a snowy yard and into the house Darcy's father had left her. It was definitely time to leave.

"Hi, Lonnie, can I have a sip of your Coke?" Cassie smiled, as Brian helped Darcy into a chair at the table.

"Help yourself, Cassie," Lonnie said, handing his Coke over to her.

"Thanks," Cassie said, and then she turned to look at Darcy. "I think you'd better switch to something non-alcoholic, honey," she said, pushing a glass of water over to Darcy. "You've had enough for tonight!"

Lonnie reached out to reclaim his Coke, finished it, and stood up. "Hey, guys, order me another Coke for the road."

As he headed for the men's room, Lonnie was pleased. When he came back, he'd take Darcy home, and Brian and Cassie could help him get her in the car.

"Thank . . . you . . . Lonnie," Darcy said as he started the car. "Where's . . . Denny? Mad . . . at . . . me?"

Lonnie was puzzled. Most drunks slurred their words, but that wasn't the case with Darcy. She was speaking very slowly, and Lonnie wasn't sure why. Could drugs be involved? He'd never heard word one about Darcy and drugs.

"Where's . . . Denny?" Darcy asked again, settling back in the seat and letting Lonnie buckle her seat belt.

"He had to go, so I'm taking you home," Lonnie said, hoping she'd accept his explanation.

"Nice . . . of . . . you. What . . . is . . . that . . . box?"

For a moment, Lonnie was puzzled, but then he realized that Darcy was focusing on the cake box he'd placed on the dash. "It's a coconut cake from The Cookie Jar."

"Love . . . that . . . cake." Darcy tried to smile, but she couldn't quite manage it. "Can . . . I . . . have . . . cake?"

"I'll carry it in when we get to your place and you can have a piece," Lonnie promised. Then he buckled his own seat belt, started the car, backed out of his parking spot, and headed across the parking lot to the exit. "Just lean back and relax, Darcy. I'll take you straight home."

"Okay . . . Lonnie."

He had to stop behind another car that was waiting to exit and Lonnie glanced over at her. Darcy's eyes were closed and she looked as if she was about to pass out. He hoped she wouldn't. It would be much easier to walk her into the house than to carry her.

The drive to Darcy's house was fairly short, only a couple of miles. Earl Flensburg had been out with the snowplow, and the country roads weren't bad.

He pulled up in her driveway and was about to shut off the car when Darcy shook her head. "Wait," she said, opening her purse and fumbling around inside. She pulled out a garage door opener and held it out. "Press," she told him.

Lonnie pressed the button and the garage door slid up. Darcy's car wasn't there, so he pulled in. "Where's your car?" he asked her.

"Cyril," she said, leaving it at that.

Luckily, Lonnie knew exactly what she had tried to tell him. Cyril Murphy owned a gas station, car repair shop, and limousine service that was housed only a mile from Darcy's place. Her car must be there for servicing or repairs. He shut off his car and pressed the button on the garage door opener again to shut the door.

"I'll come around to your side and help you get out of the car," Lonnie said, reaching over to unbuckle Darcy's seat belt. "Do you think you can walk inside?"

"I . . . don't . . . know," Darcy said, and the monotone she'd been using shook slightly. "Don't . . . feel . . . good . . . Lonnie."

"I know. You had too much to drink. I'll help you inside and you can go to bed. If you get a good night's sleep, you'll feel better in the morning."

Darcy waited until Lonnie had opened the passenger door, and then she attempted to focus on the dashboard. "Cake," she said.

"I'll come back after it. And I'll put it on your kitchen counter. Then you can have some in the morning for breakfast."

"Yes."

There wasn't much emotion in Darcy's voice, but what little was there sounded pleased. Lonnie helped her out of the car, no easy task, and managed to pull her up the steps that led into the house. "Is the door locked?" he asked her.

"No. Lost . . . key."

Lonnie held Darcy with one arm and tried the doorknob. It opened immediately and he half-pulled, half-carried her inside. He walked her through the kitchen, careful not to let her trip on wastebaskets, mops, and other impediments on the floor, and took her through the living room doorway. "Where do you sleep?" he asked her.

"Hallway . . . first room . . . mine."

Her voice was no more than a whisper, and Lonnie knew he had to hurry and get her into her bedroom before she passed out. Her legs were like jelly as he walked her to the hallway and into the first bedroom.

"Here you go, Darcy," he said, pushing her onto the bed. "Can you get under the covers?"

"Nooooo."

"Then I'll cover you with a blanket," Lonnie told her,

grabbing the one at the foot of the bed and draping it over her. "Sleep, Darcy. You'll feel better in the morning."

"Caaaake."

Lonnie felt like laughing, but tears came to his eyes instead. Poor Darcy was really messed up. "I'll go get it and leave it right here on your dresser," he told her. "Just close your eyes and go to sleep. You can have some cake in the morning."

True to his word, Lonnie left the room and hurried through the house to the garage. He removed the cake box from the dashboard, carried it back to Darcy's room, and placed it on the dresser. As he did, the lid flipped open and he noticed a card taped to the inside, it had Cassie's name written on the front. He assumed it was a birthday card. Why hadn't Cassie opened it? And that was when it hit him, a lethargy so deep it bordered on paralysis.

"Whoa," he said, resisting the urge to fall on the mattress next to Darcy. He staggered from the room and down the hallway until he reached the living room. There was the couch, an overstuffed maroon monstrosity that looked so inviting, he couldn't resist. He told himself that there was no way he could drive home now. If he tried, he might fall asleep on the road. His feet, which suddenly seemed leaden, carried him to the sofa and he fell into its velvet depths, embracing the blackness that consumed his mind and carried him off to slumber.

 # Chapter
Eight

A bright light was shining in his eyes. Lonnie tried to turn over in bed to escape the morning sun, but something was in his way. He reached out with his hand and felt something padded, something soft, and something that felt like old velvet. There was nothing like that in his bedroom. Where was he?!

It hurt to open his eyes, but he did it. And the first thing he saw was his car keys on the coffee table in front of him, along with a garage door opener. But he didn't have a garage door opener. He had to get out of the car and open his garage door manually. He'd opened a garage to put his car inside, and the car keys on the coffee table were definitely his. The little metal tag with his initials proved that. He'd obviously driven here, but where was here?

He wanted to shut his eyes again, to sleep until his head stopped spinning, but the unanswered question plagued him. Since the garage door opener was next to his car keys, he must have managed to open a garage to pull in. He vaguely remembered the door sliding up. And he remembered helping someone out of his car. Who was it? And where were they now?

His mind seemed to be operating in slow motion and he did his best to concentrate. And very slowly, but eventually, the memory of the preceding night came flooding back.

Meeting Brian and Cassie at the Double Eagle and joining them for a beer. One beer. Not enough alcohol to account for his massive headache.

Eating the coconut cake he'd brought from The Cookie Jar with Brian and Cassie in honor of her birthday.

Watching Darcy and Denny fighting at their table. Getting a gut feeling that something bad was about to happen if someone didn't do something to defuse the situation.

Hearing Cassie's suggestion and seeing her hurry to Darcy's table to escort her to the ladies' room.

Spotting Denny paying the bill and leaving Darcy there at the Double Eagle.

Deciding to go to Darcy's table. Talking to his former classmate Kay and learning that Darcy had arrived with Denny and no longer had a ride home.

Driving Darcy home, Darcy who everyone had assumed was drunk. How she'd spoken very slowly, almost like a recording played at the wrong speed, but enunciating very clearly and not slurring her words.

It hit him like a bolt of lightning. Darcy! That's where he was! He was in Darcy's living room in the house she'd inherited from her father. He was on Darcy's couch, where he'd collapsed when he realized that he was in no shape to drive. And Darcy was in her bedroom, where he'd half-carried her before he'd fallen asleep for a short nap to clear his head, a short nap that had lengthened into the entire night.

Lonnie sat up and immediately grabbed both sides of his head. He had the mother of all headaches.

After a few minutes, Lonnie stood up. He was still slightly woozy, but his head was clearing. He had to check on Darcy to make sure that she was safely in her bed, asleep.

"That was when I went down the hall to her room and saw . . ."

Hannah gave a little gasp as she noticed that Lonnie's face had turned pale. His hand on his coffee cup was shaking so hard, the coffee would have sloshed out if he'd had any left. There was no way he could go on right now. He had to calm down first.

"Are you all right, Lonnie?" Hannah asked, patting his arm to rouse him.

"Wha . . ." Lonnie stopped speaking and blinked several times. "Oh! Hannah!"

"More coffee?" Hannah asked him, giving him the most natural smile she could muster. "You should take a little break, Lonnie."

"Yeah. And thanks, I'd like more coffee. I was feeling a little punky there."

"I'll get it," Norman offered, getting up from his chair and heading for the coffeepot. "How about another slice of pizza, Lonnie?"

Lonnie gave a nod. "Yeah, that would be good."

Norman carried the coffee carafe to Hannah to pour and heated a leftover piece of pizza in the microwave. He put it on a paper plate and carried it over to Lonnie. "Here you go," he said.

Lonnie wolfed down the pizza in several gulps, and Hannah guessed that he hadn't felt much like eating before. He'd been too nervous, knowing that he had to tell them about the night that had so drastically changed his life.

"Are you okay, Lonnie?" Norman asked.

"Better," Lonnie gave him a one-word answer. "I don't know what happened, but suddenly the words just wouldn't come out of my mouth."

"Just relax for a minute and drink your coffee. You're almost done with the story, Lonnie."

"I know. I wanted to keep going, but . . ."

"Chocolate," Hannah said, getting up from her chair. "You need chocolate, Lonnie. Your face is still really pale."

Lonnie looked doubtful. "But Doc says chocolate doesn't really do anything."

"I know, but it works anyway. There's nothing like chocolate to perk you up and get you going again. Just let me see what I've got in the cupboard and I'll fix something for you."

Hannah hurried to the cupboard and once she'd glanced inside, she started to smile. "This will only take a couple of minutes," she promised as she began to line up ingredients.

The first was all-purpose flour, followed by white granulated sugar, cocoa powder, baking powder, milk, vegetable oil, vanilla extract, Nutella, and powdered sugar.

"Do you want me to get out a mixing bowl?" Norman asked her.

"No, this is going to be my Chocolate Cake in a Mug. Just let me see if we have one more ingredient."

A moment later a package of mini chocolate chips joined the lineup on the counter, along with a twelve-ounce microwave-safe coffee mug.

"Okay, here goes," Hannah said, measuring out the dry ingredients and adding them to the mug. Then she made a little well in the center of the mug and poured in the wet ingredients. Once they had been stirred in, she added the Nutella and stirred that in.

All that was left was the finishing touch. Hannah scattered mini chocolate chips over the top, carried the mug to the microwave, and heated it on high for ninety seconds. Since it didn't look quite done, and her microwave wasn't the most powerful that was now on the market, she gave it another twenty seconds and then removed it from the microwave, using oven mitts.

"It smells fantastic!" Lonnie said, eyeing the mug with a smile. "I can hardly wait to . . ." He stopped speaking, realizing that Hannah had carried the mug over to the stovetop and set it on a cold burner. "What are you doing?"

"It has to cool for at least a minute and a half," she told him. "If you tried to eat it now, you'd burn your mouth."

"And it might be worth it," Michelle said, coming into the kitchen. "What did you make, Hannah? This whole condo smells like chocolate."

"Chocolate Cake in a Mug," Hannah told her.

"I've never had that!"

Hannah chuckled. Her sister sounded extremely envious. "I'd make one for you, but didn't you tell me that Andrea was coming over with her newest Whipper-snapper cookie?"

"Yes, but it's not *chocolate*!"

"I'm not having one, either. And neither is Norman."

Norman began to grin. "I wouldn't be too sure about that. I saw you make it and I remember exactly what you did. You'd better put away those ingredients before I decide to make one for myself."

"Sit down and have a cup of coffee with us," Hannah said, gesturing toward the empty chair at her soon-to-be-an-antique Formica kitchen table. "Lonnie's going to eat his chocolate cake before we continue with the interview."

Michelle exchanged glances with Hannah, and Hannah knew she'd caught the reference to chocolate. She sat down in the chair next to Lonnie and smiled at him. "I don't suppose you'd give me one bite of your cake, would you?"

Lonnie returned her smile. "You know I will. We always share good things. And . . . I guess . . . bad things, too."

"That's the way it should be," Michelle replied, slipping her arm around Lonnie's shoulders and giving him a little hug. Then she turned to Hannah. "Isn't that cake cool enough yet?"

"Yes, it is," Hannah said. She'd been keeping an eye on the clock and a bit over ninety seconds had gone by. She got up to touch the side of the mug and gave a little nod. "It's cool enough. I'll get a spoon."

"Two spoons," Michelle corrected her.

"Three spoons," Norman added to the spoon count.

"Okay, fine. Four spoons," Hannah said, reaching in

the silverware drawer and carrying four spoons to the table. "You start, Lonnie."

Lonnie dipped in his spoon, pulled it out loaded with the chocolate-laden cake, and handed it to Michelle. "You first," he said.

It was Hannah's turn to exchange glances with Norman. He'd caught Lonnie's selfless gesture, and both of them knew that Lonnie was truly in love with Michelle.

"Wonderful!" Michelle said, once she'd tasted the cake. "Your turn, Lonnie."

Lonnie took a spoonful, ate it, and sighed. "Oh, boy, that's good!" he commented.

"I'm next," Norman said, dipping in his spoon before Lonnie could get a second bite.

Hannah watched as Norman tasted the cake. Then she smiled as a rapturous expression appeared on his face. "Fantastic!" he said.

"I'm not going to take your comment at face value unless you notarize your tongue," Hannah told him, dipping her spoon into the mug and tasting the lightning-quick cake she'd just made.

"Well?" Norman prodded her.

"It's really, really good," Hannah replied, handing the mug back to Lonnie. "Eat the rest and have a little more coffee. And then we'll finish your interview."

Once Lonnie had made short work of the cake, Hannah rinsed out the cup, set it in the sink, and returned to the table. "Okay," she said, glancing at Michelle.

"I think I'll call Andrea and see what time she's going to get here," Michelle said, noticing the glance Hannah had given her and correctly interpreting the unspoken request. Michelle rose from the table, wrapped her arms around Lonnie to give him a little hug, and nodded at

Hannah. "Thanks for letting me have some of your cake, Lonnie," she said, straightening up and moving away from the table. "I'll be in the living room if you need me."

Hannah watched her youngest sister go and thought, again, how wonderful it was that sometimes a glance could speak volumes. Lonnie would tell Michelle everything about his night in Darcy's house eventually, but for right now, having Michelle at the table while they questioned Lonnie could be a distraction.

"Finish your coffee, Lonnie," she said, turning to him. "And then let's get back to work."

CHOCOLATE CAKE IN A MUG

This single-serving cake is made in a microwave.

Hannah's 1ˢᵗ Note: You will need a 12-ounce or larger microwave-safe coffee mug to make this cake.

4 Tablespoons *(¼ cup)* all-purpose flour
3 Tablespoons white *(granulated)* sugar
2 Tablespoons cocoa powder *(I used Hershey's)*
½ teaspoon baking powder
⅛ teaspoon salt
3 Tablespoons chocolate milk *(you can also use regular whole milk)*
1 Tablespoon vegetable oil
1 teaspoon vanilla extract
1 Tablespoon Nutella *(or any other chocolate hazelnut spread)*

---

more Nutella to spread on top BEFORE microwaving *(optional)*
15 to 20 mini chocolate chips to scatter on top BEFORE microwaving *(optional)*
powdered sugar to sprinkle on top AFTER microwaving *(optional)*

1 heaping Tablespoon of vanilla, chocolate,
or coffee ice cream to add on top AFTER
microwaving *(optional)*
1 dollop of sweetened whipped cream to add
on top AFTER microwaving *(optional)*

Hannah's 2nd Note: In place of Nutella, you can use peanut butter, cashew butter, or almond butter. You can even use a Tablespoon of marshmallow fluff if you poke it down in the center of the cup after mixing the batter with your fork. Or you can add one regular-size marshmallow and poke it down in the center after mixing. There's no limit to what you can add if there's room. Just use your imagination.

Lisa's Note: When I made this for Aunt Nancy, I didn't have Nutella so I used a Tablespoon of seedless raspberry jam and mixed it in with all the other ingredients. She loved it!

Spray a 12-ounce or larger mug with Pam or another non-stick cooking spray. You can also use baking spray, the kind with flour in it.

Spoon in the flour, sugar, cocoa powder, baking powder, and salt into your mug.

Using a fork from your silverware drawer, mix all of the dry ingredients together.

Add the milk, vegetable oil, vanilla extract, and Nutella. Mix them into the dry ingredients with your fork.

Once the ingredients are thoroughly combined, choose your toppings. If you use the Nutella or any other nut butter, spread it on top now. If you've chosen the mini chocolate chips, sprinkle those on top now.

Microwave on HIGH for 90 seconds to 2 minutes, watching carefully to make sure your cake doesn't overflow the top of the mug.

Use oven mitts to take the mug out of the microwave. It may be very hot, handle and all.

Set your Chocolate Cake in a Mug on a cold stovetop burner or a wire rack to cool for at least 1 minute. Then use any of the toppings you desire and serve it to your lucky guest.

Hannah's 3rd Note: It's easiest to bake one cake at a time. It doesn't take that long and the cake must cool before eating anyway. If you

bake more than one Chocolate Cake in a Mug at once, cooking time in the microwave will vary.

Michelle's Note: If I'm making more than one Chocolate Cake in a Mug, I mix them all up first and then microwave them one by one. The first cake will still be hot by the time the last one has been microwaved. They stay warm and deliciously gooey for a long time.

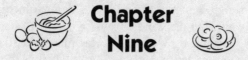

Chapter Nine

Lonnie drank the last of his coffee and gave a long sigh. "Okay," he said to Hannah and Norman, "I'm ready to go on. I remember that I was really dizzy when I stood up. I almost fell back on the couch, but I steadied myself on the coffee table. I don't know if it was or not, but the sun coming through the living room window seemed so bright, I wished I had my sunglasses. I squinted and went over to look out the window and everything was blinding white."

Lonnie stopped speaking and rubbed his eyes, and Hannah knew that even though it was dark outside now, he was back in the moment, back in Darcy's living room, and his eyes hurt.

It had snowed during the night and Lonnie turned away from the sparkling blanket of white that covered Darcy's front lawn. It was giving him a headache and, for just a moment, he considered walking out to the garage to get his sunglasses out of the glove compartment. He turned away from the window, took a couple of hesitant steps, and then gave a weary sigh. He didn't want to walk out to the garage twice. He'd just go to Darcy's room to check on her. If she was awake, he'd get her anything she wanted, and then he'd go out to his car and drive home.

Michelle! The thought occurred to him as he was making his way down the hallway and he stumbled slightly. He'd told Michelle that he'd meet her at the condo last night if it wasn't too late. He could say that it had been too late, but Lonnie didn't want to lie to the woman he loved. He'd drive to The Cookie Jar before she left for school and apologize for getting caught up in Darcy and Denny's problems and offering to drive Darcy home. Michelle would understand. She was the most understanding woman he'd ever known. All he had to do was explain what had happened and she'd be glad he'd stepped up and taken care of someone who couldn't get home by herself.

With only a tiny shred of worry left about how Michelle would react to his excuse for not driving out to the condo to see her, Lonnie continued down the hallway. The door to Darcy's bedroom was open and he stopped to glance in. There she was, stretched out in bed with a pillow over her face. She'd probably had the same reaction he'd had to the sun on the blinding-white snow and pulled it over her face so that she could sleep longer.

Lonnie tiptoed into the room and, very carefully, lifted the pillow from Darcy's face. He placed it on the bed and stood looking down at her for a moment. There was no movement, no flicker of her eyelids in response to the sunlight that was now hitting her face.

A sense of dread crept over him. This wasn't right.

This wasn't normal. Something was very wrong. He stood there for a minute or two, watching her, waiting for the movement of her chest as she breathed in and out.

There was no movement. Darcy was as still as the pillow on the bed next to her head, as frozen as the statue of Lake Eden founder, Ezekiel Jordan, that sat outside the double doors to their high school, as motionless as a person who was . . .

Dead. The word flashed through Lonnie's mind. He made a sound, a whimper of disbelief. No! Darcy couldn't be dead. She'd been drunk, or drugged, or something or other when he'd helped her to bed last night, but she couldn't be dead!

Even though he wanted to turn away, to hurry to the garage and drive home and pretend he hadn't seen what he had, Lonnie knew he couldn't leave. He swallowed once. Twice. And then he reached out for Darcy's wrist to check her pulse.

No pulse. He pressed a bit harder. No pulse. He bent down to place his palm in front of her mouth. It was open and he stood there for several moments, hoping to feel a slight breath, any movement of air at all that meant she was simply passed out and not dead.

He wasn't sure how long he stood there, looking down at her. It could have been only a few minutes, or it could have been much longer. He stayed there, staring, until her motionless image was burned into his mind. And then he backed up several steps and turned away, still not believing what his mind had concluded. Darcy was dead. She'd been alive when he'd helped her to the bedroom and now she was dead!

* * *

"Look around the room, Lonnie," Hannah said quietly, hoping that she wouldn't rouse him from his memory. "Tell me what you see."

Lonnie turned his head slightly, as if he were reliving the moment at her direction. "Yellow curtains. Pretty with sun coming through." He turned his head slightly more. "Green chair. Padded arms. Table and lamp." He turned his head yet again. "Dresser. Dark brown with old mirror. Silver lipstick, glass bottle, and . . ."

Lonnie's eyes flew open and he stared at Hannah with shock. "I forgot it before! I forgot to tell anyone!"

"What did you forget?" Hannah asked him.

"The cake!" Lonnie said loudly. "The Coconut Layer Cake we had for Cassie's birthday. Darcy asked me to carry it to her bedroom and I did. It was right there on her dresser. That's where I put it. But when I found Darcy, the box was gone! Somebody took it!"

It was a clue, of sorts, and Hannah was glad that Lonnie had remembered it. He gave them a few more facts before he slipped back in time to when it had all happened.

"I called Mike," he told them, and he shivered slightly. "I didn't know who else to call. It was better than it had been the night before, but I still couldn't seem to think clearly. All I knew was that Darcy wasn't breathing and I had to call someone. And I needed to tell Mike what had happened. So I called him."

"How long did it take for Mike to get there?" Norman asked him.

"I don't know. I don't remember looking at my watch.

Mike would know. He could check his phone to see when the call from me came in."

"And you could check your recent calls to see when you called him," Norman pointed out.

"I could, but . . . they took my phone." Lonnie pulled a phone out of his pocket. "This one's the replacement I got from Cliff at the hardware store."

"Did Mike come out to Darcy's house right away?" Hannah asked.

"Yes," Lonnie said. "I don't think it took him very long to get there. At least I don't think it did. Everything's a little hazy, you know?"

"That's okay," Norman reassured him. "What happened when Mike got there?"

"Mike told me that he was going to call Doc, and both of them arrived at the same time. And Mike told me to sit down on the couch and stay clear of Darcy's room, so that's what I did. I told Doc where she was and he went down the hallway with his bag. And Mike stayed with me."

"Did Mike ask you any questions?" Hannah asked.

"Yeah, he asked me what had happened and I told him all that I could remember. It wasn't a whole lot. It was like my brain was still asleep and I couldn't seem to recall very much. I'd just gotten to the part where I helped Darcy to bed when Doc came out of the bedroom."

"What did Doc say?" Norman asked. "Try to remember everything, Lonnie."

"He said that Darcy was dead. But instead of dying in her sleep, the way I thought, it was a homicide and Darcy had been murdered!"

"What did you say?" Norman asked.

"Or do when you heard that?" Hannah added.

"I . . . I felt really dizzy again and my knees buckled. I almost fell, but I managed to land on the couch. I couldn't believe what I was hearing. I'd been right there on the couch all night. Darcy had been murdered and I hadn't heard anything. I was so shocked, I couldn't say anything for a couple of seconds. It was like I couldn't seem to understand why I hadn't heard anything. I'm a detective. I've seen murder victims before. I really thought that Darcy had somehow died in her sleep. And I asked Doc if he was sure."

"And Doc said . . ." Norman prompted.

"Doc said he was sure, that she was smothered with a pillow in her sleep. And that was when Mike turned to me and asked me if I had been there all night."

"And you told him you had?" Hannah asked.

"Yeah, and I said I couldn't understand why I didn't hear anything. Darcy's bedroom wasn't that far away and I should have heard someone come into the house, walk to her bedroom, and . . . and . . ."

"Smother her?" Hannah finished for him when it was apparent that Lonnie couldn't go on.

"That's right. I was going to drive home, but I got so dizzy I didn't think I could drive and I decided to take a short nap. But I passed out and I didn't wake up until the sunlight came through the living room window. When Doc heard me say I'd been dizzy, he opened his bag and searched for something inside. And that's when Mike asked me if I'd been drinking."

"What did you say?" Norman asked.

"I said yes, but it was only one tap beer. That was all I had, that the roads were really bad and I thought they might call me in, so I switched to Coke after one beer. And that was when Mike and Doc exchanged glances and

Doc pulled a syringe and several vials from his bag. He said he needed samples of my blood and he filled a couple of the vials. Then he handed me a container and asked me to give him a urine sample."

"And you did all that?" Norman asked him.

"Sure. I knew everything would turn out all right, that I hadn't had any more to drink than that. And then Doc said that he didn't think one tap beer could have that effect on a guy my size unless I'd been drinking before that."

"And you told Doc that you hadn't?" Hannah asked.

"I did. I said all I'd had with dinner was coffee when I'd stopped at Hal and Rose's Café for a sandwich and fries."

"And this was before you met Brian and Cassie at the Double Eagle?" Norman asked.

"Yes, Brian was already at the Double Eagle when I got there. Cassie came a little later."

"What happened after Doc took your samples?" Hannah posed the question.

"There was a knock on the door and Mike answered it. It was two of Doc's paramedics. Doc said he wanted them to take me to the hospital for more tests. I asked why, and he told me that it was for my protection, that I wasn't functioning normally and my blood pressure was out of whack. He told me he wanted one of his interns to check me out and run some tests."

"So you went to the hospital with the paramedics?" Hannah asked.

"Yeah, I asked if I could drive there because I didn't want to leave my car. Doc said no, it wasn't a good idea for me to drive in my condition. Mike told me not to worry, that one of the other deputies would come out to drive my car back to my place. And . . ." Lonnie gave a little shrug. "I went with the paramedics and it's probably a good thing I did, because they put me on a cot in the back and I slept all the way to the hospital."

"How long were you in the hospital?" Hannah asked him.

"I got out that afternoon and the first thing I did was call Michelle at school. She picked me up and brought me here." Lonnie gave a heartfelt sigh. "I've never been so glad to see anyone in my whole life!"

The doorbell rang, startling all three of them, and Hannah gave Norman a nod before she turned to Lonnie. "That's enough for now," she told him. "I think we've got all the basics. Let's go in the living room and see who just came in."

Hannah led the way as all three of them left the kitchen. They found Andrea and Mike sitting on the couch with Michelle.

"Hi, Mike," Hannah greeted him.

"Hannah!" Mike jumped up to greet her. "Boy am I ever glad to see you!"

Hannah laughed. "You mean because you missed me so much?"

"Well . . ." Mike looked uncomfortable. "Sure, I did. And I'm really glad you realized we needed you here and you came right away."

"And so am I!" Andrea stood up to give Hannah a hug. "Sorry to cut your vacation short, but you're the only one who can get us out of this . . ." She turned to look at Lonnie. "I'm not sure what to call it, Lonnie."

"A real mess," Lonnie supplied the words.

"You're right, Lonnie," Andrea agreed. "It *is* a mess. And I realize that. And so does Mike, and that's why we're all here tonight. We have to put our heads together to figure out what to do."

"But not before we taste some of your new cookies," Hannah reminded her. "Michelle's been telling us how wonderful they are. You brought some, didn't you?"

Andrea pointed to the container she'd placed on Hannah's dining room table. "Of course I did. Do you have coffee?"

"We always have coffee," Hannah told her. "I put on a fresh pot before I left the kitchen. Let's take a couple of minutes to relax and have dessert. And then we can get down to the business of figuring out what we have to do to get Lonnie out of trouble."

CONFETTI BLIZZARD
WHIPPERSNAPPER COOKIES

Preheat oven to 350°F., rack in the middle position.

1 cup white chocolate or vanilla baking chips *(I used Nestlé)*

1 cup *(8 ounces)* sweetened coconut flakes *(pack it down in the cup when you measure it)*

1 box Pillsbury Funfetti cake mix *(the kind that makes a 9-inch by 13-inch cake)*

2 cups of original Cool Whip *(not low-fat Cool Whip)*

1 large egg, beaten *(just whip it up in a glass with a fork)*

½ cup powdered *(confectioners)* sugar *(for rolling the cookies—there's no need to sift unless it's got lumps)*

15 maraschino cherries cut in half lengthwise *(you can also use candied cherries, either red or green or a combination of both)*

30 minutes before you're ready to bake, stick a teaspoon from your silverware drawer in a large freezer-safe mixing bowl. Place the bowl with the spoon in the freezer to chill.

Measure out one cup of white chocolate or vanilla baking chips.

If you have a food processor, attach the steel blade. If you don't, you'll have to do your chopping with a knife.

Put the white chocolate or vanilla chips in the bottom of the food processor bowl.

Measure the sweetened coconut flakes. Make sure to press them down in the cup to fill it to the top.

Put the sweetened coconut flakes on top of the white chocolate or vanilla chips.

Process the chips and coconut in an on-and-off motion with the steel blade. Continue to process until they're in very small pieces.

Either spray a cookie sheet with Pam or another nonstick cooking spray, or line it with parchment paper and then spray that.

Hannah's 1st Note: When Andrea makes these cookies, she uses parchment paper, so all she has to do when she takes them out of the oven is pull

the parchment paper over on a wire cooling rack.

Remove the large mixing bowl from the freezer and add approximately half of the Funfetti cake mix from the box.

In a separate bowl, measure out 2 cups of original Cool Whip.

Add the beaten egg to the Cool Whip. Using a rubber spatula, fold the egg into the Cool Whip. Be careful not to stir too much. Keep as much air in this mixture as possible.

Return to the large mixing bowl, the one that you chilled and now holds half of the Funfetti cake mix.

Add the chopped white chocolate or vanilla chips and the chopped sweetened coconut flakes to the large bowl with the cake mix. Mix them in thoroughly.

Add the contents of the smaller bowl to the large bowl. Using the rubber spatula again, fold in the Cool Whip and egg mixture. Try to do this gently to keep the air in the mixture.

Sprinkle on the rest of the Funfetti cake mix on top, and fold it in gently with the rubber spatula. Continue to fold until everything is well mixed.

Open the packet with the multi-colored candy sprinkles and scatter them over the top of the mixture in the large bowl. Again, using the rubber spatula, fold them in.

Continue to fold until the multi-colored sprinkles begin to leave streaks of color in the cookie dough.

Place the half-cup of powdered sugar in a shallow bowl. Dust your impeccably clean hands with powdered sugar.

There are two ways to form dough balls with this sticky cookie dough. One is to scoop out dough with your chilled spoon and place it in the bowl of powdered sugar, rolling it around with your fingers until it forms a small ball. The other, easier way is to dust your hands with powdered sugar, pinch off a small amount of dough, place it in the bowl of powdered sugar, and shape it into a ball with your fingers.

Use your favorite method *(you may want to try both to see which one works best for you)* to form 12 dough balls for each cookie sheet.

If you don't have double ovens, place the remaining cookie dough in the refrigerator to wait until you have room to bake a second sheet of cookies. If you forget to do this and leave the bowl with the dough on the counter, it will be even stickier and more difficult to form into dough balls!

Place one-half of a maraschino cherry, cut side down, on top of each cookie ball on the sheet. Flatten the balls just a bit by pressing down on the cherry halves.

Bake your Confetti Blizzard Whippersnapper Cookies at 350°F. for 15 minutes.

Remove your cookies from the oven and let them cool for 2 minutes on a cold stovetop burner or a wire rack.

When 2 minutes have passed, remove the cookies from the sheet with a metal spatula and place them on the wire rack to complete cooling. If you used the parchment paper, this is simple. Simply pull the paper off of the cookie sheet and onto the

wire rack. The cookies can stay on the paper until they're cool.

Hannah's 2ⁿᵈ Note: Confetti Blizzard Whippersnapper Cookies are very pretty. Lisa and I are going to make them for Christmas parties using both red and green cherries on top.

Andrea's 1ˢᵗ Note: Bill always wants me to make these cookies so that he can take them to the sheriff's station. And now that Tracey's in school, she asks for these cookies every time there's a holiday and mothers bring refreshments for class parties.

Yield: 2 to 3 dozen very pretty and tasty cookies.

Andrea's 2ⁿᵈ Note: Tracey wants these cookies for her birthday party. She made me promise not to serve them to anyone except family until then.

Chapter Ten

When they'd eaten every single cookie that Andrea had brought, Hannah refilled coffee cups and gave Lonnie an assessing look. Lonnie's face was pale and he still looked as if he wished he were anywhere except here, discussing the fact that any day now, he could be charged with first-degree murder.

"Would you like to take a break, Lonnie?" Hannah suggested. "If you don't mind, we'll play your interview for Mike so we can bring him up to speed. You don't want to listen to it, do you?"

Lonnie shook his head. "No. If I do, it'll be like I'm . . . I'm back there again . . . you know?"

"I *do* know. Why don't you and Michelle put on your parkas and take a little stroll around the complex? And if you're interested, Michelle can show you the gym. There's a brand-new machine down there that nobody's ever touched. You use the gym at the sheriff's station, don't you, Lonnie?"

"Yeah, I work out a couple of times a week." Lonnie

gave a little sigh. "Of course, I haven't done that lately. The sheriff's station is off-limits for me now."

"I figured it might be. Check out our gym. You're welcome to use it if you'd like. And while you're there, maybe you two can figure out what that new machine does and how to use it. Norman and I looked at it and we didn't have a clue."

"I noticed that machine!" Michelle picked up on Hannah's idea and Hannah knew that her sister realized that she should keep Lonnie out of the condo until Mike had heard Lonnie's recorded interview.

"I can take a look at it," Lonnie told Hannah. "I know a lot about exercise machines. Between us, Michelle and I can probably figure out how to use it."

"There's a booklet on the machine," Norman told them. "I looked at it, but it was all Greek to me."

Lonnie smiled. Hannah wasn't sure if he knew that they were trying to keep him occupied for a reason, but if he did, he wasn't objecting. "Come on, Shelly," he said, grabbing Michelle's parka and handing it to her. "Let's go take a look."

Hannah, Norman, Andrea, and Mike sat at the table until Lonnie and Michelle had gone out the door. Then Andrea reached for the tote bag she'd brought with her.

Hannah watched as Andrea reached inside the tote and drew out a folder with papers inside. "Here," she said, handing it to Hannah.

"Doc's autopsy report?" Hannah guessed before she even opened the folder.

"Yes, it was in Bill's briefcase, but I had to wait until he went up to read Tracey and Bethie a bedtime story before I could copy it. There's another report in there, too. It has the results of Lonnie's blood test and all the other tests they did when he went to the hospital with the paramedics."

"Lonnie was drugged?" Norman guessed.

Andrea nodded. "The report says he was still under the effects of it when he got to the hospital. Doc told Mother he guessed it was some kind of sleeping pill that reacted with the alcohol." She turned to Hannah. "Do you think that'll help to clear Lonnie?"

Hannah exchanged glances with Mike, but he waited for her to answer. She wondered for a split second if this constituted a test of some sort, but quickly put that idea out of her head.

"Correct me if I'm wrong, but I think it could go either way," she said. "If Lonnie was drugged, for whatever reason, he might have acted out some resentment he had against Darcy and killed her without even realizing what he was doing. On the other hand, if Lonnie was drugged by a third person who wanted Lonnie to be at the scene when the killer murdered Darcy, the fact that Lonnie was drugged could exonerate him."

"Exactly right," Mike said. "Our first priority should be finding out how Lonnie got that drug in his system."

"Either Lonnie took that drug on purpose, or someone else gave it to him without his knowledge," Norman concluded.

"Do you think Lonnie took it on purpose?" Andrea asked, looking shocked at the thought.

Mike shook his head. "Of course not! But a good investigator has to consider all the possibilities."

"How can you prove that Lonnie didn't take the drug on purpose?" Norman asked Mike.

"We can't prove it unless we find the person who gave him the drug without Lonnie's knowledge to set him up for Darcy's murder, and that means our first order of business should be . . ."

"Making a list of everything Lonnie ingested that night," Hannah said quickly. "And once we know that, we can interview everyone who had the opportunity to add the drug to his food or his drinks."

Mike gave her a nod and a smile. "Exactly right." He turned to Norman. "Will you make a list for us?"

"Of course," Norman agreed, pulling a small notebook from his pocket. "Lonnie said he had coffee with his dinner at Hal and Rose's."

"Right." Hannah rushed to the drawer to take out one of the stenographer pads she used to keep notes when she was working on a murder case. She quickly jotted down the information, and then she gave Mike a curious look. "You usually take notes yourself, don't you, Mike?"

"Yes, but I'm not officially working on this murder case. I don't want to have anything in my handwriting that could taint the investigation by giving the prosecution any reason to throw out our conclusions."

"That makes sense," Hannah told him.

"Is everyone ready for my second piece of information?" Andrea asked. When all three of them nodded, she went on. "I'm going to show you Doc's autopsy report. It's a real shocker."

"You actually *read* it?" Hannah asked, knowing how squeamish Andrea was when it came to graphic descriptions of violence.

"Yes, and it made me sick to my stomach, but I wanted to know what it said. I didn't look at the crime scene photos, though."

"You put them face down on the glass and copied them, didn't you?" Hannah wanted to know.

"Of course I did. They're right here in this envelope." Andrea pulled a white envelope from her tote bag and handed it to Mike. "Some of them might be in here up-side down, though. I didn't check when I stuffed them in-side the envelope."

Hannah fully appreciated her sister's aversion to look-ing at crime scene photos. They didn't make her physi-cally ill, but she certainly didn't enjoy seeing the violence that a killer could inflict on a human being. She studied them carefully because she knew that something in the photos might provide a clue to the murder. And after Hannah had closed a murder case, she tried very hard to erase the images completely from her mind.

"You were at the scene, weren't you?" Hannah asked Mike.

"Yes, and I went into her bedroom, but I left after Doc confirmed that she was dead. I stayed with Lonnie until the paramedics took him to the hospital and that's when Bill told me to go home, that he was taking me off the case. He said he was taking Rick off, too, and he'd have to handle it himself with the new guy."

"And that's still the way it is?" Norman asked.

"Yeah." Mike paged through the photos, gave a little nod, and handed them to Norman. Then he turned to An-drea. "These aren't so bad. It just looks like she's sleep-ing."

"Maybe, but I know she's not and that makes them bad." Andrea swallowed hard and then she turned to Han-nah. "I don't have to look at them, do I?"

"Not if you don't want to." Hannah waited until Nor-man had finished paging through the photos, and then she took them from Norman. She studied every photo and gave a little shrug. "Nothing here is really helpful. Isn't that right, Mike?"

"Nothing that I can see. Give me the autopsy report, Andrea."

They all watched as Mike scanned Doc's report. When he finished reading, he gave a little sigh.

"What?" Norman asked him.

"There's one thing here that gives us a motive, and a whole new avenue of investigation."

"What?" Hannah asked, leaning forward.

"Read it for yourself." Mike handed over the report. "And pass the pages to Norman after you read them."

It's a test, Hannah's mind warned her. *He wants to see if you pick up on what he noticed.* She turned to look at Norman and realized that Norman had figured it out. They were on trial here so that Mike could see if they were good amateur detectives.

As Hannah reached the middle of the first page, she saw what had alerted Mike. She finished the page, handed it to Norman, and watched him as he read it. It took a minute or so, but then a startled expression crossed Norman's face.

"Oh, boy!" he said under his breath.

Hannah smiled. What had been obvious to Mike had also alerted them. It was another avenue of investigation, and it could very well be the reason that Darcy had been murdered. Darcy had been two months pregnant when someone had killed her.

Hannah read the second and final page, handed it to Norman, and looked over at Andrea. Andrea gave a little nod of acknowledgment, and Hannah knew that Andrea had also spotted the fact that Darcy had been pregnant.

No wonder she'd said that Doc's autopsy report was a shocker when she'd given it to them!

"Well?" Mike asked them. "What pitfalls do you see because of what you've discovered?"

Mike obviously regarded himself as their instructor in the art of investigating and for one brief moment, Hannah resented his attitude. Then she forced herself to think positively. Perhaps they didn't need Mike's guidance, but it couldn't hurt to let him play Professor Sherlock. Mike was understandably upset over the fact that the circumstantial evidence was stacked against Lonnie because Lonnie had been there when the murder was committed.

It was clear that Norman was waiting for her to respond to Mike's query, so Hannah hid the last shred of her resentment and jumped right in to answer Mike.

"Darcy's dead. So, it's obvious she won't be telling us who the baby's father is. That might be a pitfall!"

Andrea chimed in. "Maybe Darcy didn't tell anyone she was pregnant, including the baby's father."

Norman looked thoughtful "Then it wouldn't be a motive for murder, would it?"

"You're right," Mike said. "But what if Darcy confided in someone?"

"Then we'll have to talk to Darcy's friends and co-workers to find out if any of them knew," Hannah said.

"True," Mike said. "But you'll have to be careful that you don't alert Darcy's killer."

"And her killer could still be the baby's father," Andrea said.

"You're right," Noman said. "Nothing rules *that* out."

Hannah shook her head. "Well, Darcy was engaged to Denny Jameson, but he might not be the *father*."

"But why would Darcy get engaged to him if he

wasn't . . . ." Andrea stopped speaking and made a face. "I get it. If Darcy couldn't marry the father of her baby, she might have gotten engaged to Denny and pretended that the baby was his. That happens in movies all the time."

"Conjecture," Mike labeled it. "Let's get back on track here. What's the first thing you have to investigate?"

"The identity of the father," Andrea answered quickly.

"Norman?" Mike asked, turning to him.

"That'll be tricky. A baby doesn't come with a wrist-band with the name of the father printed on it."

Hannah couldn't help it. She started to laugh. The thought was so totally ridiculous. Andrea gave a little giggle even though she'd been the one to bring up that idea, Norman laughed, and Mike chuckled. They all felt better because of the levity.

Once the moment was over, Mike turned back to Norman. "So what can you do to attempt to find the father?"

Andrea thought about that for a moment. "We could start by finding out if she went to a doctor."

"How?" Mike asked.

"We could start with Doc," Andrea suggested. "And if he wasn't Darcy's doctor, he could ask around to find out who was."

"That's a possibility," Hannah said.

Mike shook his head. "That's the least helpful avenue to take. Doctors have issues with confidentiality. They're not going to tell you anything about their patients."

"But that doesn't matter, does it?" Andrea asked. "Darcy's dead."

"Believe me, it matters!" Norman disagreed. "The same rules apply to dentists. A medical professional can lose his or her license if he or she gives out information without the patient's consent."

"But that doesn't make sense if the patient is dead and can't object," Andrea pointed out.

"Maybe not, but it's still the rule," Mike told her. "Forget the doctors. You'll never get information from them directly."

"So, we start by interviewing Darcy's friends and coworkers," Hannah said.

"Right," Mike agreed. "You may luck out and find someone who can tell you something pertinent."

Andrea started to smile. "I can help you with that, can't I, Hannah?"

"Of course you can," Hannah answered quickly. When Andrea was first dating Bill, he bragged that she could get anyone to talk and it was true. Andrea was a great listener.

"And we'll ask Lisa, Marge, and Aunt Nancy to keep their ears open for any gossip they hear in the coffee shop," Hannah said.

"I can help you with that, too," Andrea offered. "I can do the invisible waitress trick and go around filling coffee cups."

"Perfect," Hannah told her. Andrea was excellent at identifying tables where customers were talking in hushed voices, and listening as she refilled their coffee cups.

"Okay. You've got a good game plan," Mike complimented them. "I just wish that . . ." He stopped speaking and gave a long sigh. "I feel so helpless. There's really nothing I can do to help."

"But there is!" Hannah said quickly. "You're already helping, Mike. I think . . ." She paused and wondered if she was going to regret what she was about to suggest, but it was too late to back out now.

"You think what?" Mike asked her.

"I think we all ought to meet at least a couple times a week to compare notes and talk about what to do next," Hannah told him. "We can meet at The Cookie Jar. That's convenient for everyone. We can talk in the kitchen when everyone else is working in the coffee shop. Let's meet there tomorrow morning."

"What time?" Andrea asked her.

"Seven. The baking's done by then, and that'll give us plenty of time to talk about what we need to do."

"Sounds good to me," Norman said. "Do you want me to bring something for breakfast? I could stop for dough-nuts, or sweet rolls, or . . ." He stopped talking and gave Hannah an apologetic look. "Sorry, Hannah. That's a lot like bringing pinecones to the North Woods."

"That's true," Hannah said with a smile. "There'll be plenty of coffee and sweet things to go with it, Norman. You don't have to worry about that. And, as an added bonus, I'll be able to try out our new recipes on all of you!"

Chapter Eleven

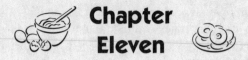

"We're here, Hannah," Norman said as he pulled up in his driveway.

Hannah laughed. "I'm awake," she told him.

"You were so quiet, I just assumed you were sleeping."

"No, I think I drank too much coffee to go to sleep. I'm wide awake and my mind is spinning around at high speed."

"Well, I can take care of that once we get inside," Norman said.

"How?"

"You'll see." Norman got out and walked around the car to open the passenger door. "Hop out, Hannah. I'll bring your suitcases."

Hannah got out of the car and took a deep gulp of the icy night air. The snow stretched out like a smooth sheet on the large circle of grass inside Norman's circular driveway, and the moonlight striking the surface of the snow made it glow with a pale, iridescent blue. As she walked toward the front door, Hannah gave a little gasp as she spotted a bulky figure standing by one of the windows. "Norman!" she whispered, grabbing his arm. "There's something . . ." She stopped in mid-sentence as she realized that the figure, a black bear, was as still as stone.

Of course it's as still as stone, her mind chided her. *That's because it's made of stone, or concrete, or something like that. It's a statue, just like the moose on the other side of Norman's house.*

Hannah began to laugh as she turned to Norman. "For a minute there, I thought it was real."

"Sorry about that," Norman said, slipping his arm around her shoulders. "I should have warned you, but I'm so used to it, I forgot you hadn't seen it yet. Meet Shag, the bear. I got him last month. It took three men to move him here, and I didn't have the heart to tell them that I really wanted him on the other side of the house."

"Shag is very realistic. He's probably a good deterrent for anyone who's thinking about breaking into your house at night."

"That's exactly what Mike said the first time he saw Shag! And he startled Michelle and Lonnie, too."

Hannah gave a little sigh. It seemed as if everyone had visited Norman at home except her. "Was Shag very expensive?"

"Yes, but the statuary place was going out of business and they were having a half-price sale if you bought two statues."

"Two? Where's the other statue?"

"In the butterfly garden. I'm not sure how long it'll be effective, but right now it scares the heck out of the winter birds that land there."

"I didn't know you had a butterfly garden! Where is it?"

"Right there." Norman pointed to the parklike area in the middle of his circular driveway.

"I see it," Hannah said, feeling foolish for not noticing the benches that Norman had placed at strategic spots.

"I should have noticed it at Christmas, but I didn't," Hannah apologized. "It's okay. They hadn't delivered it yet, plus you had a lot on your mind."

Hannah swallowed hard. Christmas had been difficult, to say the least. "What did you plant to attract the butter-flies?"

Norman looked pleased that she'd asked. "I started with phlox, but I didn't know it was spreadable."

"Do you mean like ground cover?"

"In a way. I had to limit my phlox to one area, or it would have taken over my other plants."

"Tell me about some of the others."

"I have pots of marigolds, another area with cone-flowers and lantana, an area of heliotrope, and a large patch of black-eyed Susans. It's relaxing in the summer, Hannah. Sometimes I just go out there when I get home from work and sit on one of the benches. And it's proba-bly silly, but I watch the butterflies and think about all the places they must have seen in their travels. The Monarchs migrate, you know. I drove down to the University of Minnesota Monarch lab to learn more about them."

"What did you find out?"

"They migrate to Mexico in the winter and they do it individually. They're beautiful, Hannah. This past August was great for me. That's Monarch season here and I had dozens feeding on nectar from my garden every day."

"That sounds wonderful. Will you let me come and sit in your butterfly garden when the flowers begin to bloom?"

"Of course!" A smile spread over Norman's face. "You're one of the reasons I planted a butterfly garden."

"I am?" Hannah was surprised.

"Yes! You said that if there really was a type of reincarnation, you wanted to come back as a butterfly."

"Did I tell you why?"

"You said butterflies were beautiful creatures and everyone who caught sight of them smiled."

"I don't remember saying that!"

"Well, you did. It was on our first date when I took you to the Woodley mansion for their annual party."

"Oh, dear! Did I have too much to drink?"

"No, we'd just arrived and the maid was hanging up our coats. You glanced in the mirror, gave a big sigh, and said you should have brought a curry comb to use on your hair. And right after that, you mentioned the butterflies."

"Okay. Now I remember." Hannah gave a big sigh. She remembered being very dissatisfied with her appearance, despite the lovely new outfit she'd bought at Claire's shop, Beau Monde Fashions. Even though both Claire and Lisa had told her that she looked wonderful when she'd tried on the dress, Hannah hadn't really believed them.

"You looked so beautiful that night," Norman said, almost as if he'd been reading her mind. "And you were wonderful about introducing me to everyone we met. I was really sorry when you had to leave the party with Andrea."

"Thanks, Norman," Hannah told him, and she meant it. But she couldn't help giving a little shiver as she remembered how she and Andrea had found the body in the old Cozy Cow Dairy building.

"You're shivering!" Norman said, slipping his arm around her shoulders again. "Let's go in and I'll light a fire in the den."

"Good idea!" Hannah said, smiling at him. "I'd love to sit in front of a fire and hold the cats in my lap. I know Moishe probably had a great time here with Cuddles, but I missed him a lot."

"Just like I missed Cuddles when you took care of her for me," Norman said, unlocking the front door and carrying her suitcase inside. "I'll take you upstairs and you can get into your robe and slippers. Just say hello to the cats and then follow me."

As Norman opened the door, Hannah assumed her usual position. If Moishe had heard them inside, he'd want to do his usual leap into her arms. She braced herself, feet slightly apart to maintain her balance, and prepared herself for the twenty-three pound onslaught. But there was no sound from running feet as the cats raced to the front door. Nothing, absolutely nothing happened.

Hannah felt a moment's panic. "Where are they?" she asked Norman.

"They're probably upstairs, sleeping. I left the television set on to mask any sounds from outside. They get upset when they hear the coyotes howling in the distance."

"Of course they do!" Hannah shivered again as she followed Norman up the carpeted staircase to the second floor. Even though she knew the cats were safely inside the house, she had visions of Moishe and Cuddles fleeing from the nocturnal predators. She knew that the coyotes had to eat to survive in the wild, but she would do everything in her power to make sure that feline wasn't on their menu.

"Here they are, Hannah," Norman announced, pointing to the king-size bed where Moishe and Cuddles were stretched out on feather pillows. "Wake up, Moishe. Your Mommy's here."

Moishe's ears flicked once, twice, and then he raised his head. He looked at Norman in what Hannah thought was surprise, and then he caught sight of her.

"Rrrooow!" he yowled, springing to his feet and racing to the foot of the bed. He stood there for a moment, just staring at her, and then he gave another yowl.

Hannah knew that familiar, welcoming yowl. It was the same cry Moishe gave every night when she came home from The Cookie Jar. She braced herself just in time as Moishe launched himself, went airborne, and landed in her arms.

"Sorry," Norman apologized. "I should have picked him up before he jumped."

Hannah laughed. "Impossible," she stated. "Once he yowls like that, it's too late." Since she needed both arms to hold him, Hannah leaned down and rubbed his head with her face. "Hello, Moishe. I missed you."

"Rrrrowww!"

"I think he's telling you he missed you, too," Norman interpreted as he reached out to pick up Cuddles. "Cuddles is glad to see you, too, but she's not quite so vocal about it."

"Hello, Cuddles," Hannah greeted her, sitting down on the edge of the bed with Moishe. She scratched him in his favorite spot behind his ears and reached out to give Norman's cat a pet. "I can see you took good care of Moishe while I was gone."

Cuddles began to purr, almost as if she'd understood Hannah's praise. All three of them watched as Norman went to the walk-in closet, flicked on the light, and came back with a suitcase stand.

"Here you go, Hannah," he said, lifting her suitcase onto the stand. "I'll leave you here and go start that fire in the den. Just take your time and come down when you're ready."

"But . . . this is your room," Hannah said, pointing out that obvious fact. "I thought you said the guest room was ready."

"It is. It's ready for me. I'm sleeping there tonight."

"But you don't have to give up your room for me," Hannah told him. "I can sleep in the guest room."

"No, you can't, not until I try out the new mattress. I know the mattress on my bed is good, but I'm not sure about the new one. You need a good night's sleep tonight because tomorrow is going to be a very long day for you."

"Because we're working on the murder case?" Hannah asked.

"That's one reason, and it's a big one, but there are a couple more tasks that'll take up your time."

"What other tasks?"

"Lonnie and Michelle are going to pull everything out of your bedroom at the condo. They'll pack it up in moving boxes and once you take out anything you think you'll need, I'll store them in my garage until the workmen are finished."

"But aren't you still enlarging the old garage and converting it into apartments?"

"Yes, it's a work in progress. I love it here, but it's a little lonely all by myself. My nearest neighbor is miles away."

Hannah thought about that for a moment. She knew she'd be lonely if she had a big house in the country and she lived alone. She'd felt lonely in her condo, even though she'd been surrounded by neighbors, when last month's blizzard had hit.

"It does make sense, Norman," she concluded aloud. "The old garage is at least a half-block from your door, and you won't be bothered by noise that far away. And since you're building it to be self-contained, there's no reason for your tenants to disrupt your lifestyle."

"Exactly!" Norman smiled at her. "It's a little cold in here, so let me start the fireplace for you. It vents into the room, so it should be nice and toasty by the time you're ready to go to bed."

Norman picked up a remote and handed it to her. "You'd better learn how to do this. You might get too warm and want to turn it down, or off."

"You got a remote!" Hannah said with a smile. "I used one of these in Lynne's house." She stood up and walked to the fireplace. "I'll open the glass doors."

"No need. They're fireproof glass."

"Are you sure? Lynne had to open her glass doors before she started the fireplace."

"That's California. In Minnesota, we have a choice, and I chose the fireproof glass. It has the added bonus of keeping Cuddles out of the fireplace in case she gets curious about the gas logs."

"Where do I point the remote?" Hannah asked him.

"See that squirrel?"

Norman pointed to a statue of a squirrel holding a nut that sat at the base of the fireplace. "Just aim it at the squirrel."

Hannah aimed the remote at the squirrel and pressed the On button. The remote clicked, the gas gave a slight hiss, and the gas logs started to glow. A second or two later, the flames licked up between the logs and a smile spread over Hannah's face. "It's wonderful, Norman."

"I know. I stash the remote in the bedside table so I can turn on the fireplace during the night if it gets really cold, or turn it down to low or off if I'm too warm."

Hannah looked down at the remote and saw that there were three buttons, one was marked On, the second one was marked Low, and the third one was marked Off. "What does low look like?" she asked.

"Try it and see."

Hannah aimed at the squirrel and pressed Low. The flames died down almost immediately and the gas logs glowed with radiant heat. It was the sort of glow one might expect from a large log that was almost consumed, and it was a beautiful sight.

"All set?" Norman asked, getting up and heading for the doorway. "I'll start a fire in the den."

"With a remote?" Hannah asked.

"No, with several real logs, some tinder, and a long wooden match. I had to have one fireplace that was wood-burning."

"In case a blizzard hit and your gas went off?"

"Exactly. I needed one room in the house that would be warm if the gas and the electricity went off. With the rustic furniture and the old-fashioned oak doors, it's like a log cabin down there in the den."

Except for the giant flat-screen television, Hannah's rational mind contradicted Norman. But Hannah didn't point that out. Instead, she gave Norman a little wave, went to her suitcase, and rummaged around for her pajamas, robe, and slippers.

Chapter Twelve

Hannah woke up with a smile on her face. She felt safe, secure, and well rested. The cats were sleeping next to her, each on their own feather pillow, and Moishe was snoring softly.

One glance at the window that overlooked the pine grove at the side of Norman's property, and Hannah saw that it was still dark. The moon was a sliver, low in the sky, and soon it would be daybreak.

Moving slowly and silently, Hannah got out of bed without waking the cats. She took a quick shower in Norman's huge bathroom, dried herself on a fluffy towel, and dressed in her favorite jeans and a warm, fleece sweatshirt. Then she left the bedroom, tiptoed down the stairs, and less than fifteen minutes after she'd first opened her eyes, she was downstairs in Norman's kitchen, assessing the contents of his refrigerator.

He had eggs and whipping cream. That was a start. And there was a package of pepper jack cheese. There wasn't any meat unless she counted a jar of herring and a ring of bologna, but there was a frozen, premade pie shell in the side-by-side freezer. Mentally, Hannah listed the ingredients she'd found. Eggs, cream, cheese, onion, and a pie shell. What could she make for breakfast with . . . "Quiche!" she said aloud. Perhaps there was something in Norman's pantry that she could add to her ingredients list.

Norman's pantry was filled with staples. The moment she turned on the light, she spotted flour, sugar, and shelves filled with jarred, tinned, and canned goods. She passed by the fruit, jams, olives, pickles, mushrooms, and sardines and reached for a can of corned beef hash. It had potatoes and meat, the perfect filling for a hearty breakfast quiche.

Flicking off the light, Hannah left the pantry and closed the door. She opened cupboard doors until she found a mixing bowl and then began to search for utensils. It took a while, but she managed to find a grater, a whisk, and a measuring cup. She couldn't find a quiche dish, but since the frozen shell was a deep-dish piecrust that came in its own disposable tin, she didn't really need one.

Hannah felt a tingle of excitement as she turned on Norman's oven and set the frozen piecrust on a drip pan. She'd never made a Corned Beef and Pepper Jack Quiche before. If it was good and both of them liked it, she'd write down the recipe and add it to her voluminous breakfast recipe file.

It didn't take long for the piecrust to thaw. Hannah began to prick it all over the bottom and the sides with the tines of a fork so that it wouldn't bubble up as she baked it. She'd almost finished when the oven beeped to tell her that it had reached the temperature she wanted. Hannah gave it another minute or two, to make sure she wouldn't lower the temperature too much when she opened and closed the oven door, and then she slipped the piecrust inside.

There was a pitcher on top of Norman's refrigerator and Hannah rinsed it out in the sink. Then she whipped up the eggs and the cream, and poured them into the pitcher. Once she'd stuck that in the refrigerator, she grated the cheese and opened the can of corned beef hash. Once the piecrust had come out of the oven, she let it cool enough so that it wouldn't melt the cheese she'd grated, and began to assemble her quiche.

Hannah put the grated cheese in the bottom of the piecrust. Then she spooned the corned beef hash in the same bowl she'd used to whisk the eggs and cream, and added a couple of squirts of hot sauce. She quickly chopped some onion and added that, followed by salt, black pepper, and a sprinkle of nutmeg. She mixed everything together, spread the mixture out in the piecrust on top of the cheese, and used the pitcher to fill the piecrust to the halfway mark. She would fill the piecrust the rest of the way once it was in the oven, and her quiche would be ready in less than an hour.

There was a delicious aroma in the air and Hannah turned to see that Norman's coffeepot was making coffee. A smile spread over her face as she realized that Norman must have set the timer before he went upstairs to bed. And that was when she also realized that she had made a quiche first thing in the morning without having a couple of wake-up cups of coffee!

"Uh-oh!" she said out loud. "I hope I didn't leave anything out!"

"Leave anything out of *what*?"

Hannah whirled around to see Norman in the doorway and she laughed. "The quiche I made for our breakfast. I assembled it without making coffee and that could be a clear and present danger."

It was Norman's turn to laugh. "Did you crack the eggs?" he asked her.

"Of course," Hannah answered quickly, and then she glanced at the kitchen wastebasket to make sure that there were eggshells in it. When she saw an eggshell peeking out, she felt like giving a huge smile, but she managed to keep a neutral expression so that Norman wouldn't notice how relieved she was.

"I'll get the coffee," Norman said, going to the cupboard and taking out two mugs. He filled both of them from the carafe that had come with the machine and walked back to hand one to Hannah. "Here's what you need, Hannah. I don't want you to fall asleep standing here. I had a friend who did that when we were studying for an exam in dental school."

"He studied standing up?"

"He said he had to, that it was the only way he could stay awake. He was afraid he'd fall asleep if he sat down in a chair because he'd be too comfortable, so he stood up in the middle of the room."

"And he fell asleep like that?"

"Oh, yes. And if I hadn't rushed across the room to catch him, he would have ended up on the floor." Norman looked surprised as he noticed that her coffee mug was empty. "Good heavens! Did you drink all that coffee already?"

Hannah glanced down at her mug. "I must have. There's nothing left. The only thing left in the bottom of the cup is your imprint for Rhodes Dental Clinic."

"I'll get you a refill. And then I'll put on another pot of coffee. We've got plenty of time before we have to leave for The Cookie Jar."

"What time is it? I didn't even look at the clock by the bed."

"Good for you! One of my patients in Seattle took part in a sleep study."

"The kind where they hook you up to all sorts of monitors for the whole night?"

"That's right. One of the technicians asked her if she had an alarm clock right next to the bed. And when she said she did, he told her to move it away to somewhere where she could still hear the alarm, but she couldn't see it."

Hannah was curious. "Why would that make a difference?"

"He told her that people get into the habit of waking up to check the clock to see how much time they have left to sleep, and they wake up more frequently than people who can't see what time it is."

"Interesting," Hannah said, wondering if she should move her alarm clock. She thought about it as Norman poured more coffee and decided that the clock was fine where it was. She was usually so tired when she went to bed, she didn't wake up in the middle of the night unless there was something wrong. And then, once she'd taken care of whatever it was, she climbed back in bed and went straight back to sleep again.

Norman placed the filled coffee mug in front of Hannah and walked over to check the oven timer. "Only five more minutes," he said. "How long does your quiche have to cool before we can eat it?"

"Fifteen minutes. It needs time to set up before slicing."

"Okay." Norman began to smile. "That means we have less than twenty minutes before Mike gets here."

Hannah was surprised. "You invited Mike for breakfast?"

"No, but he always shows up when we're about to put food on the table."

Hannah laughed. It was true. Mike seemed to sense whenever food was served. "Then I guess I'd better set three plates."

"I'll do it," Norman offered, walking to the cupboard and taking out three plates. "I think I have orange juice in the refrigerator."

"You do."

Norman began to grin. "So you scoped out my 'fridge?"

"Yes, I was looking for breakfast ingredients."

"How about my pantry?"

"I looked in there, too. That's where I found the can of corned beef hash."

"And my cupboards?"

Hannah sighed. "Yes, of course I checked out the cupboards. I had to find bowls, pans, and utensils. I couldn't make breakfast for you unless I . . ." Hannah stopped in mid-sentence as something occurred to her. *Does Norman think that you're a snoop?* Her rational mind posed the question.

"What?" Norman asked when she stopped speaking.

"Do you think I'm a snoop?" Hannah asked. "It just never occurred to me that you might mind if I came down here and looked for things for breakfast."

"Of course I don't," Norman told her, reaching out for her hand across the table. "And of course I don't mind. I was just teasing you, Hannah, and I'm grateful that you're making breakfast."

Hannah drew a relieved breath just as the stove timer started to ring. "I think it's done," she said, getting up from her chair, grabbing pot holders, and scurrying to the oven. She opened the oven door, peeked inside, and turned back to him. "Could you bring me a table knife from your silverware drawer?"

"Sure." Norman went to the counter, pulled out a drawer, and took out a table knife. He carried it to Hannah and stood there watching as she pulled out the oven rack and inserted the knife near the center of the quiche. When she pulled it out again, he asked, "Is it done?"

"It's done." Hannah showed him the clean knife blade. "If the knife had looked milky when I tested the quiche, I'd have given it another five minutes."

"So it's a lot like testing a cake."

"That's right." Hannah took the quiche from the oven and moved it to a cold stovetop burner. "I guess you were wrong about Mike. We can eat in about fifteen minutes and he's not here . . ." She stopped speaking as the doorbell rang, and laughed. "That's got to be Mike. You were right after all, Norman."

Hannah made quick work of setting the kitchen table and by the time Mike and Norman came into the kitchen, she was pouring orange juice and coffee.

"What smells so good?" Mike asked her.

"Breakfast." Hannah pointed to the quiche that was cooling on the stovetop burner.

"Is it a pie?" Mike asked.

"It's like a pie, but it's called a quiche. This one is a Corned Beef and Pepper Jack Quiche."

Mike looked surprised. "I've never had anything like that before! Is it good, Norman?"

Norman shrugged. "I don't know. Hannah's never made it for me before, but I'll bet it's great!"

Mike turned to Hannah. "Then I'll ask you if it's . . ." He paused for a second, and then he looked a bit sheepish. "Scratch that question, Hannah. I just realized that everything you make is good. Why should this be any different?"

"Thank you," Hannah said, accepting the compliment. "Would you like to have breakfast with Norman and me?"

Mike glanced over at the kitchen table. "You have three plates and everything. Were you expecting someone else?"

Norman shook his head. "Just you, Mike."

"But I didn't tell you that I was coming. "

No, but we know that you always seem to turn up when I'm ready to serve a meal, Hannah's mind prompted her to answer, but she didn't. They'd teased Mike too much about that in the past. Instead, she just smiled at him and said, "Both Norman and I were hoping that you might show up in time to try my quiche with us."

"Good." Mike seemed pleased with Hannah's response. He was smiling as he pulled out a chair and sat down next to Norman.

"We'll eat in about five minutes," Hannah told him. "The quiche has to cool enough for me to cut it. In the meantime, we'll have orange juice and coffee."

"Sounds great to me," Mike responded. "Will you sit down, Hannah? I've got some information for you."

Hannah sat down on the other side of Norman. "What is it, Mike?"

"I called Cyril at home last night to find out if Darcy's car was still out at his garage. He said it was."

"What's wrong with it?" Norman asked.

"Cyril didn't know, but he promised he'd have one of his mechanics look at it this morning."

"Is he going to call you and tell you what's wrong with it?" Hannah asked Mike.

Mike shook his head. "I told him not to call me because Bill had pulled me off Darcy's murder case. And I explained that any information he gave me couldn't be used as evidence."

"Good!" Hannah was clearly relieved. "I'd better call Cyril as soon as he opens the garage and tell him that I'll come out there."

Mike smiled. "I already did that. I told Cyril to take a look at the car himself and when he discovered what was wrong with it, to call you at The Cookie Jar and ask you to come out so he can tell you in person. Cyril promised me that he wouldn't let anyone else touch that car."

"I think I get it," Norman said. "You didn't want anyone but Cyril to touch it so if the killer sabotaged Darcy's car to make sure she was home the night of the murder, there wouldn't be so many fingerprints on it?"

"Very good, Norman! I just want to cover all the bases as far as the car is concerned. Maybe it's old and maybe it just broke down and it happened to be in the shop the night Darcy was murdered. Her car could have absolutely nothing to do with the murder case."

"Or it could be a clue to the killer," Hannah said quickly. "It might have *everything* to do with the case."

"Right," Mike said. "You have to treat everything that's out of the ordinary like it could be the clue that leads you to Darcy's killer." He raised his coffee cup and drained it, and then he leaned back in the chair. "Is that quiche cool enough to cut yet?"

Hannah glanced at Norman's kitchen clock. "I'll check."

"Thanks, Hannah. I was so hungry when I woke up this morning, I ate a big bowl of cereal, but that didn't seem to help. I even stopped for a frosted cinnamon roll and coffee at the Corner Tavern, but that didn't do it, either. My stomach's growling like crazy."

Hannah was grinning as she refilled Mike's coffee cup, and went to check her quiche. The cinnamon rolls at the Corner Tavern were the size of small dinner plates and if Mike said he'd eaten one, he'd also probably ordered one to go and inhaled it on the drive out to Norman's house. Mike's metabolism must be absolutely marvelous. It seemed that he could ingest huge quantities of food anytime he wanted and never gain an ounce of weight.

"Is it ready to cut, Hannah?" Mike asked.

"Yes," Hannah said, cupping her hands around the rim of the pan. "It's ready."

A smile spread over Mike's face and he gave a relieved sigh. "That's good because I'm practically starving over here!"

CORNED BEEF AND PEPPER
JACK QUICHE

Preheat the oven to 350°F., rack in the middle position.

The Quiche Shell:

You can mix up your favorite piecrust recipe and line a 10-inch deep-dish pie pan. Alternatively, you can buy pre-made, frozen piecrusts at the grocery store. *(If you decide to buy the frozen pie shells, make sure to buy 9-inch or 10-inch deep-dish pie shells.)*

Hannah's 1st Note: Pre-made frozen piecrusts are very good and they're a real timesaver. They generally come 2 pie shells to a package, and I always have a couple of packages in my freezer at the condo for emergencies. If you're embarrassed about using something "store-bought," just remove the shell while it's still frozen and place it in one of your pie pans of the same size before you make and bake your quiche.

Prepare your piecrust by cracking one egg and separating the yolk from the white. You can save

the white in a covered dish in the refrigerator to add to scrambled eggs in the morning.

Whip up the yolk with a fork and brush the bottom and insides of your piecrust with the yolk. When you're finished, prick the piecrust all over with the tines of a fork from your silverware drawer to keep it from puffing up in the oven.

Bake the empty piecrust in a 350°F. oven for 5 minutes. It won't be nice and golden brown, but you'll bake it again after you put in your quiche filling.

Take the piecrust out of the oven and set it on a wire rack or a cold stovetop burner. If "bubbles" have formed in the crust, immediately prick them with the fork to let out the steam. Let the piecrust cool while you mix up the quiche filling.

The Quiche Filling:

> 5 eggs
> 1 and ½ cups whipping cream *(also called heavy cream or manufacturing cream)*
> 5 ounces Pepper Jack cheese, shredded *(approximately 2 cups—measure AFTER grating)*

1 can *(15 ounces by weight)* corned beef
  hash *(I used Mary Kitchen hash by
  Hormel)*
¼ cup finely chopped onion *(measure
  AFTER chopping)*
Hot sauce to taste *(I used Slap Ya Mama hot
  sauce)*
½ teaspoon salt
¼ teaspoon freshly ground black pepper
¼ teaspoon ground nutmeg *(freshly grated is
  best, of course)*

**Hannah's 2ⁿᵈ Note: If you don't like Pepper
Jack cheese, you can use Monterey Jack, or pre-
grated Italian or Mexican cheese. Cheddar will
also do nicely. If you do this, you may want to
add additional black pepper for flavor.**

**Hannah's 3ʳᵈ Note: Nutmeg with corned beef
may sound a little strange, but it adds a nice
touch of sweetness to this quiche.**

Combine the eggs with the whipping cream and
whisk them *(or beat them at MEDIUM speed)*
until they're a uniform color. When they're thoroughly mixed, pour them into a pitcher and set it in
the refrigerator.

Sprinkle the grated cheese in the bottom of your cooled pie shell.

Open the can of corned beef hash and spread it over the top of the cheese.

Sprinkle on the onion, and add as many drops of hot sauce as your family would like.

Sprinkle the salt on top.

Sprinkle the ground black pepper over the salt.

Sprinkle the ground nutmeg over the pepper.

Put a drip pan under your pie pan.

Hannah's 4th Note: I line a jelly roll pan with foil and use that. You could also use parchment paper. If you line your drip pan, the liner will catch any spills and the drip pan will be easy to wash.

Take the egg and cream mixture out of the refrigerator and give it a good stir with a whisk or a mixing spoon.

Pour the mixture over the top of your Corned Beef and Pepper Jack Quiche until about half of the filling is covered.

Open your oven, pull out the rack, and set your pie tin and drip pan on it. Pour in more custard mixture, stopping a quarter-inch short of the rim. Carefully push in the rack, and shut the oven door.

Bake your Corned Beef and Pepper Jack Quiche at 350°F. for 60 minutes, or until the top is golden brown and a table knife inserted one inch from the center comes out clean.

When your quiche tests as done, remove it from the oven and set it, drip pan and all, on a cold stovetop burner or a wire rack. Let it cool for 15 to 30 minutes before you cut it into pie-shaped wedges and serve it.

This quiche is good warm, but it's also good at room temperature. If your family is crazy about bacon, sprinkle bacon bits over the top of the quiche before you bake it to add even more flavor. If there's any quiche left, which there probably won't be, cover and refrigerate it.

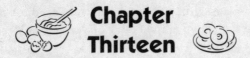

Chapter Thirteen

Hannah had just finished filling a plate with their latest creation, Butterscotch and Pretzel Cookies, when Andrea came in the back kitchen door of The Cookie Jar.

"Hi, Hannah," she said, hanging her black wool coat and silk scarf on the rack by the door. "Those cookies look great!"

"They are. I had one as soon as they were cool. You must be showing a house this morning."

Andrea looked at Hannah with the same expression that someone might use after watching a magician pull a rabbit out of a hat. "How did *you* know that?!"

"You were wearing your black dress coat with a silk scarf. That's what you always wear when you're showing a house to a prospective client."

Andrea laughed. "You're right! I do that because, if they don't know me, it's easy for them to spot me."

"Makes sense," Hannah said, going to the kitchen coffeepot to pour Andrea a mug of coffee. "The usual?"

"Yes, please. But one sugar, not two. This dress is getting a little tight on me and I think I've gained a pound or two."

"Really? You don't look like you've gained weight."

"Thanks, but I'd still better watch it. It's easy to gain weight if you come in here every morning. And I did that while you and Mother were gone."

Hannah was surprised. Andrea didn't usually come in every day. "Did you come in to see Michelle?" she asked.

"Yes, I came in to have coffee with Michelle, and Lisa and Aunt Nancy. I was lonely while you were gone."

Hannah was puzzled. "But you don't come in that often when I'm here."

"That's true, but I know you're here. And since I know that, I don't have to come in. That makes sense, doesn't it?"

"I guess," Hannah said, not adding that what she guessed was that Andrea must have suffered a blow to the head that had addled her brain. "Try a cookie and tell me how you like them."

"Okay," Andrea agreed, reaching for a cookie. She took a bite, made a sound of satisfaction, and finished it in record time. "Good," she said. "I love the salt and the sweet together."

"So do I. These are Lisa's brainchild. We make them with chocolate chips, but we never thought to try them with butterscotch chips."

"Well, they're just as good, maybe better," Andrea declared, reaching for another.

Hannah couldn't help smiling. Andrea had reduced the packets of sugar in her coffee, but she'd taken a second cookie. She almost pointed that out to her sister but decided to keep it to herself. Andrea was probably nervous about pleasing her client. "Tell me about your client," she suggested instead.

"He's very nice. Young. Married. Knows exactly what he wants. He also knows exactly what he wants to pay and he won't go over that amount. I've shown him ten houses so far and he won't budge from what he's willing to put down as a down payment."

"And most of your clients are flexible about that?"

"Yes, to a certain degree. I can usually get them to come up a little, but Roger simply won't budge."

"Don't worry," Hannah said quickly. It was clear that Andrea was stressed over her newest client. "You'll find the perfect house for him. You always do."

Andrea smiled. "Thanks, Hannah. You always know exactly what to say to make me feel better."

Hannah reached out to pat Andrea's shoulder. "Your client sounds very persnickety."

Andrea gave a little laugh. "I haven't heard anyone use that word since Great-Grandma Elsa died. I love that word. It describes my client perfectly. He's very demanding and he knows exactly what he wants."

"What *does* he want?"

"Three to four bedrooms, an attached garage, lots of vegetation including mature trees, a circular driveway, and no near neighbors."

"Sounds like he wants to live out in the country."

"Yes, but not *way* out in the country. The house has to be within a mile of town."

"Are there any houses like that?"

"A couple. I showed them to him, but he didn't like

them. One had an old barn about sixty yards from the house. When he said he didn't want a house with a barn, I told him it hadn't been used in years. I said that old barn wood was at a premium with antique dealers and he could probably have it torn down with no cost to him if he let whoever did it keep the wood."

"What did he say to that?"

"He told me he didn't want to bother doing that. He's a hard case, Hannah. He's not willing to budge an inch. Most people will haggle over the price, or demand that something be done to the house, but he's not even willing to go that far. He wants perfection, and he's depending on me to find it for him."

Andrea was getting frustrated again, and Hannah decided to change the subject. "It's too bad you don't like raisins. Aunt Nancy came up with a recipe for Cinnamon and Raisin Snaps that's been so popular, it outsells all the other cookies we bake."

"I'd like to try one of those," Andrea declared.

"But they're regular raisins, not golden raisins. And you told me you hate regular raisins."

Andrea shook her head. "Not anymore. I discovered the reason I didn't like them and I'm fine with them now."

Hannah looked at her sister curiously. "Okay. Tell me why you didn't like regular raisins before."

"Because Mother used to buy raisin bread and she'd give me raisin bread toast every time you weren't there to make me breakfast. She always left it in the toaster too long and the raisins got burned. That made them bitter and I don't like anything bitter. So it's not that I don't like raisins. I just don't like *burnt* raisins."

"I can understand that, and I can guarantee that our

Cinnamon and Raisin Snaps don't have any burned raisins."

"Then I'd really like to try one. You're not like Mother. You never burn anything."

Hannah was chuckling as she went off to get some of their newest cookies. Andrea had no idea that the first time she'd tried to make pancakes, she'd misread the recipe. Andrea was in preschool, Michelle hadn't been born at the time, Delores had been out at an estate sale, and Hannah had been alone in the house. She had been bored, all by herself, so she'd decided to page through her mother's cookbook and try to learn how to make something to eat. Since she wasn't sure how to use the oven, she decided to try pancakes.

Once she'd mixed up the pancake batter, she'd put butter in the frying pan and heated it up on the stovetop. The recipe said that when bubbles of water danced on the surface of the pan, it was ready for the pancake batter. Hannah had waited until the pan was hot enough, and then she'd poured in the pancake batter . . . *all* of the pancake batter. Somehow she'd managed to miss the line at the bottom of the recipe that stated the yield. If she'd read it, she would have known that the batter she'd mixed was enough to make eight pancakes.

Things had gone from bad to worse in a matter of minutes. Hannah had known she should flip her giant pancake over when bubbles appeared on the top surface. So she waited. And waited. And waited even when the frying pan began to smoke. Hannah figured that since she'd followed the directions to the letter, that must be perfectly natural. She'd opened the kitchen window to get rid of the smoke and continued to watch for the bubbles on top of her pancake.

The Swensens' next-door neighbor, who'd been working in her flower garden, had seen the smoke and had rushed over to knock on the kitchen door. When she'd seen the frying pan on the stovetop burned, she'd pulled it to a cold burner, shut off the heat, and pointed out Hannah's mistake. She had also helped Hannah wash the frying pan and air out the house. And even more importantly, she'd promised not to mention Hannah's cooking disaster to anyone.

"Where does your client live now?" Hannah asked her sister, carrying several Cinnamon and Raisin Snaps to Andrea.

"In St. Paul," Andrea told her. "He wants to get out of the city."

"Does he work there?"

"Yes, he's an urban planner, but he'd like to get out of the field."

Andrea took a bite of her cookie and smiled. "I like these, Hannah."

"Good."

There was a knock at the back kitchen door and Hannah went to answer it. Mike and Norman were standing there and she ushered them in. "Coffee?" she asked, once they'd seated themselves on stools at the stainless steel work station.

"Yeah," Mike said, giving her a smile and then turning to Andrea. "Hi, Andrea. I thought you'd be taking Tracey to school."

"Grandma McCann's doing the school run this morning," Andrea replied. "She drops Bethie off at Kiddie Korner first, and then she takes Tracey to school."

"Bethie's in preschool already?" Norman asked, looking surprised.

"Yes, but only two days a week. Janice Cox decided to let her in early because Bethie plays so well with Kevin."

"Phil Plotnik's son?" Mike asked.

"That's right. Sue's been working for Janice at Kiddie Korner for a while now. Janice lets her bring Kevin with her, and since Bethie and Kevin get along so well, Janice said Bethie could come, too."

"Here's your coffee," Hannah announced, setting hot mugs of coffee in front of Mike and Norman.

"Thanks," Norman said.

"Yeah, thanks, Hannah," Mike echoed.

"Why don't you tell Andrea the news you gave us at breakfast," Hannah suggested to Mike. "Since I've heard it, I'll go refill the cookie platter."

Andrea stared down at the empty platter in shock. "Did I just eat a whole platter of cookies?"

"There were only a few left," Hannah said in an attempt to wipe the horrified expression off her sister's face when, in actuality, there had been at least a half-dozen Butterscotch and Pretzel Cookies on the platter.

Andrea gave a relieved sigh. "Thank goodness for that!"

Hannah picked up the platter and half-listened as Mike told Andrea about Darcy's car and how Cyril had promised to check it out himself and not let any of his other mechanics touch it. He was just explaining why this could be important when Hannah carried a full platter back and set it down in front of them. "I'm going to call Cyril later to find out what's wrong with Darcy's car," Hannah told her.

"I could drive out there after I'm through with my client," Andrea offered.

"Bad idea," Mike told her. "You really shouldn't be

actively involved since your husband is the chief detective on the case. It might look bad if the case has to go to court."

Andrea sighed. "You're right, of course, but I'll come back in right after I show Roger the house to do my invisible waitress thing. This is going to be so much fun! Nobody will ever guess that I'm your undercover coffee shop spy."

BUTTERSCOTCH AND PRETZEL COOKIES

Preheat oven to 350°F., rack in the middle position.

1 cup softened, salted butter *(2 sticks, 8 ounces, ½ pound)*
2 cups white *(granulated)* sugar
3 Tablespoons molasses
2 teaspoons vanilla extract
1 teaspoon baking soda
2 beaten eggs *(just whip them up in a glass with a fork)*
2 cups crushed salted thin stick pretzels *(measure AFTER crushing) (I used Rold Gold, but Snyder's are fine, too)*
2 and ½ cups all-purpose flour *(pack it down in the cup when you measure it)*
1 and ½ cups butterscotch chips *(I used Nestlé)*

Hannah's 1st Note: If you can't find thin stick pretzels in your store, you can use the mini regular pretzels. Just make sure that any pretzels you use are SALTED. If they're low-salt or no-salt pretzel sticks, your cookies won't turn out right.

Hannah's 2nd Note: This dough gets really stiff—you might be better off using a mixer, or you may have to end up mixing this dough with your impeccably clean hands, almost like kneading bread.

Mix the softened butter with the sugar and the molasses. Beat until the mixture is light and fluffy, and the molasses is completely mixed in.

Add the vanilla and baking soda. Mix them in well.

Break the eggs into a glass and whip them up with a fork. Add them to your bowl and mix until they're thoroughly incorporated.

Put your pretzels in a Ziplock plastic bag. Seal it carefully *(you don't want crumbs all over your counter)* and place it on a flat surface. Get out your rolling pin and run it over the bag, crushing the pretzels inside. Do this until there are no large pieces and the largest is a quarter-inch long.

Measure out two cups of crushed pretzels and mix them into the dough in your bowl.

Add one cup of flour and mix it in. Then add the second cup and mix thoroughly. Add the final half-cup of flour and mix that in.

Measure out a cup and a half of butterscotch chips and add them to your cookie dough. If you're using an electric mixer, mix them in at the lowest speed. You can also put the mixer away and stir in the chips by hand.

Drop by rounded teaspoons onto greased *(or sprayed with Pam or another nonstick cooking spray)* cookie sheets. You can also line your cookie sheets with parchment paper, if you prefer. Place 12 cookies on each standard-size sheet.

Hannah's Note: I used a 2-teaspoon cookie disher to scoop out this dough at The Cookie Jar. It's faster than doing it with a spoon.

Bake the cookies at 350°F. for 10 to 12 minutes or until nicely browned. *(Mine took 11 minutes.)*

Let the cookies cool for two minutes and then remove them from the baking sheets. Transfer them to a wire rack to finish cooling.

Yield: Approximately 5 dozen chewy, salty, and sweet cookies that are sure to please everyone.

CINNAMON AND RAISIN SNAP COOKIES

DO NOT preheat your oven quite yet—this dough needs to chill before you bake it.

Ingredients:

> 1 cup raisins *(either brown or golden)*
> ¼ cup rum *(I used white Bacardi)*
> 2 cups salted, melted butter *(4 sticks)*
> 2 cups brown sugar *(pack it down in the cup when you measure it)*
> 1 cup white *(granulated)* sugar
> 2 large eggs, beaten *(just whip them up in a glass with a fork)*
> 2 teaspoons vanilla extract
> 2 teaspoons ground cinnamon
> 1 teaspoon baking soda
> 1 teaspoon cream of tartar *(critical!)*
> 1 teaspoon salt
> 4 and ¼ cups all-purpose flour *(pack it down in the cup when you measure it.)*

Dough ball rolling mixture:

¹/₂ cup white *(granulated)* sugar
1 teaspoon ground cinnamon
¹/₈ teaspoon ground nutmeg *(freshly grated is best)*

Hannah's 1ˢᵗ Note: If you're making these cookies for children or if you don't want to use rum, simply substitute water for the rum and add 1 teaspoon of vanilla extract for flavor.

Place the raisins in a microwave-safe bowl that will hold 2 cups.

Pour the quarter-cup rum over the top of the raisins.

Heat the raisin and rum mixture for 2 minutes on HIGH. Let it sit in the microwave for 1 minute and then take it out and remove it to a pot holder or towel on your kitchen counter.

Cover the bowl containing the raisins and rum with a sheet of foil to keep the heat in. The raisins will plump up while you're mixing up the rest of your cookie dough.

Place the 4 sticks of butter in another microwave-safe bowl. Melt the butter in the microwave for 2 minutes on HIGH. Let the melted butter sit in the microwave for another minute and then remove it to another pot holder or towel on your kitchen counter.

Add the sugars and mix. Let the mixture cool to room temperature while you beat the eggs and then stir them in. Add the vanilla, cinnamon, baking soda, cream of tartar, and salt. Mix well. Add flour in increments, mixing after each addition.

Add the raisin and rum mixture. Stir well so that the raisins are evenly distributed.

Use your hands to roll the dough in walnut-size balls. *(If dough is too sticky, chill for an hour before rolling.)*

Preheat the oven to 350°F. Combine the sugar and cinnamon in a small bowl to make the dough ball rolling mixture. *(Mixing it with a fork works nicely.)* Roll the dough balls in the mixture and place them on a greased cookie sheet, 12 to a standard sheet. Flatten the dough balls with a greased spatula.

Bake at 350°F. for 10–15 minutes. *(They should have a touch of gold around the edges.)* Cool on the cookie sheet for 2 minutes, then remove the cookies to a rack to finish cooling.

Yield: Approximately 8 dozen, depending on cookie size.

Chapter
Fourteen

Hannah took the last pan of Old-Fashioned Sugar Cookies out of the oven and placed it on one of the shelves in her baker's rack. She had just wheeled the baker's rack back to its spot against the wall, when there was a knock on the back kitchen door. It was a polite knock, a request to come in, and Hannah recognized it immediately. She hurried to the door, pulled it open, and said, even before she'd looked to see who was standing there, "Hi, Norman."

"Hi, Hannah. I brought your cookie truck back and parked it in your spot."

"Thank you, Norman! Did you have to use jumper cables to start it?"

Norman shook his head. "No, it started right up. Would you like me to drive it around to make sure the battery's fully charged?"

"That would be great, if you've got the time, but come in and have a cup of coffee first. It's cold out there."

"Not as cold as it was when you were gone. And that's

a comment on the temperature, not a reflection on how much I missed you."

Hannah smiled. "It's good to know you missed me. I missed you, too. I kept turning around to say something to you and then I'd realize that you weren't there."

"What were you going to say to me?" Norman asked, stepping in, shedding his parka, and hanging it on one of the hooks by the back door.

"Just things like, *Look at that gorgeous swimming pool*, or *Can you believe this house cost over three million dollars?* If you see something surprising, or amazing, or beautiful and you're by yourself and have no one to share it with, it feels really lonely."

"You're right," Norman said, walking to the work station and sliding onto his favorite stool. "What smells so good, Hannah?"

"Georgia Peach Cake. I'd give you a piece of it, but it's too hot to take out of the pan."

The phone rang once as Hannah was pouring coffee for both of them, but she didn't rush to answer it. Lisa, Marge, and Aunt Nancy were in the coffee shop and one of them would pick it up.

"Here's your coffee," Hannah said, placing it in front of Norman. Then she put her own coffee down on the stainless steel surface and sat down across from him. "Would you like a cookie, Norman?"

"Sure. What have you got?"

"Old-Fashioned Sugar Cookies, Molasses Crackles, Minty Dreams, and Cinnamon and Raisin Snaps."

"They're all good, but I can't have *that* many cookies. You choose."

Hannah took a sip of her coffee and got up again. "Okay, I'll be right back."

Hannah grabbed a plate, hurried to the baker's rack, and chose one of each variety. Then she came back to the work station and placed them in front of Norman. "I chose," she told him.

Norman laughed. "One of each. I should have guessed. Mothers aren't supposed to choose a favorite child, and I guess bakers aren't supposed to choose a favorite cookie."

"That's right."

The swinging door between the coffee shop and the kitchen pushed open and Aunt Nancy poked her head in. "You've got a call, Hannah. It's Cyril Murphy, from the garage. Do you want me to tell him you'll call him back?"

"No, I'll take it. Thanks. Are you busy out there?"

"Swamped," Aunt Nancy told her. "And everybody's asking Lisa if she's going to tell the story. She wants to know what she should tell them."

"Tell Lisa to say that I'm not sure yet, that we're considering it. And she can promise to let them know by later this afternoon."

"Will do." Aunt Nancy gave a nod and hurried back into the coffee shop.

"I'll be right back," Hannah told Norman as she got up and walked to the wall phone.

"Hi, Cyril," she said once she'd lifted the receiver from the hook. "Did you get a chance to look at the car yet?"

"I just finished with it. Can you come out here, Hannah?"

"Of course."

"I'll be in my office with the door shut, making notes on what I found. Just come on in when you get here."

"Did Cyril find anything?" Norman asked when Hannah got back to the work station.

"Yes, he wants me to come out to his office at the garage. Are you free to go with me?"

"I'm free. Doc Bennett is working full-time for a couple of weeks." Norman took another swallow of coffee.

"You don't have to rush," Hannah told him. "I'm going to pack up one of the Georgia Peach Cakes for Cyril and some cookies for his mechanics. It'll take me a couple of minutes."

Hannah made quick work of finishing her coffee and then hurried to the bakers rack. She was just feeling one of the cake pans to see if the cake was too hot to frost, when the timer on her oven rang.

"Perfect!" she said aloud.

"What's perfect?" Norman asked.

"It's time to frost my Georgia Peach Cakes. I'll do that first and let the frosting harden while I pack up the cookies."

Hannah chose a cake, moved it to the counter, and washed her hands thoroughly at the sink. Then she went to the stovetop and made quick work of making the frosting.

Once she'd frosted the cakes and carried them to the walk-in cooler, Hannah began to pack up the cookies for Cyril's mechanics. She chose six of each cookie on the baker's rack and dipped into the cookies that were waiting for Lisa or Aunt Nancy to use in the coffee shop for another dozen.

"I'm almost ready," she told Norman, who was just finishing his mug of coffee. "I'll just get a carry bag for these and we can go."

"Come finish your coffee first," Noman said, patting the stool next to him. "I've got something I need to discuss with you."

Hannah felt a moment's uneasiness. Norman sounded very serious. "Okay," she said, placing her cookies in a carry bag and then taking the stool next to Norman. "What is it, Norman?"

"It's this trip to Cyril's garage. I don't want to butt in, Hannah. That's the last thing I want to do. But sometimes I'm not sure if you want me to say anything in an interview with a suspect, or just be there when you're questioning someone. Sometimes I feel like I'm intruding on what you want to accomplish."

"But you're not!" Hannah's reaction was immediate. "You've never interfered, Norman."

"I'm glad to hear that, but I just need to make sure that you'll tell me if you don't want me to take part. That's all."

"I promise I'll tell you," Hannah said, reaching out for his hand. "And I appreciate that sometimes you ask questions that I wouldn't have thought to explore."

"Then I've never done anything to . . . to impede you? Because if I have, I promise you that I'll just sit there and listen."

"No! Don't change, Norman. I like what you're doing. We're a good team."

Norman smiled, and it was like the sun coming out after a stormy day. "Good! I just didn't want to assume, you know?"

Hannah picked up her coffee mug and drained it. "I'm glad we got that settled."

"So am I."

"Good, because I'm going to need you when we get

out to Cyril's. I don't know anything about cars, but you do. Ask any questions you can think of. It's my turn to listen and learn something."

Once they got to Cyril's Garage, Hannah parked her cookie truck and they hurried inside the building. Cyril's office was down the hall and Hannah led the way. The door was shut, and she gave a knock and then opened the door to find Cyril sitting behind his desk, paging through a stack of invoices.

"We're here," Hannah announced, walking to one of the chairs that flanked Cyril's desk.

"Make yourself comfortable," Cyril said, motioning to the chairs in front of his desk. "I appreciate what you're doing for my son, Hannah. You too, Norman. I know in my heart that Lonnie would never do such a thing, even if he was drunk, or drugged. It's just not in his nature."

"We know that, too," Norman said.

"It looks to us like somebody set Lonnie up," Hannah told him. "We're going to do our best to find out who."

"You'll do that. You always do." Cyril gave a nod. "Do you two want coffee?"

"No, thanks," Hannah answered for both of them. She'd had Cyril's coffee before and it was so strong, it could peel the paint off a new car. "It's nice of you to offer, Cyril, but we just had coffee."

"Hannah brought you something from The Cookie Jar," Norman announced, setting the large bag of cookies on Cyril's desk.

A big grin spread over Cyril's face as he looked at the size of the bag. "Thanks, darlin'," he said, and a bit of an Irish accent colored his words. "The guys love your cookies. I'll put this bag in the lunch room for their morning break." He eyed the cake pan Hannah was carrying. "What else did you bring?"

"Something special for you," Hannah told him, holding the cake up so he could see. "It's a Georgia Peach Cake and I baked it this morning. You'll need to put it in your refrigerator for a couple of hours before you slice it."

"Sounds good," Cyril said, taking the cake and peeking under the foil. "Smells good, too." He swiveled his desk chair, opened the small refrigerator behind his desk, and placed the cake inside. Then he swiveled back and gave Hannah another smile. "Bridget's crazy about your cakes. You know she's going to want the recipe, right?"

"I know and I printed it out for her." Hannah opened her saddlebag-size purse, took out several folded sheets of paper, and handed them to him. "Just to warn you, there's peach liqueur in this cake. Some of the alcohol evaporated when it was baked, but not all."

"Sounds fine to me," Cyril said. "Maybe I'll encourage Bridget to have two pieces tonight." He gave a devilish grin and waited for both Norman and Hannah to laugh. "And I'll make sure none of my mechanics go near it. We're really busy today and a couple of the cars need major work."

"Then I guess we'd better get down to business so you can get out there and supervise," Hannah suggested. "Thanks for personally diagnosing Darcy's car."

"No problem. I know why Mike asked me to do it, and I wore gloves when I lifted the hood. Tell him that, will you?"

"Of course we will," Norman promised.

"What did you find wrong with Darcy's car?" Hannah got back to the reason they'd come.

"It's simple, Hannah. There's nothing mechanical that's wrong with Darcy's car. Any mechanic in my shop could get it running again in less than two minutes."

Norman and Hannah exchanged startled glances. "What do you mean?" Hannah asked him.

"Darcy has . . ." Cyril stopped and frowned. "I should have said, Darcy *had* quick-release battery cables on her car."

"So someone released a battery cable to disable her car?" Norman guessed.

"Yes, both of them. If Darcy had raised the hood, she would have seen the loose battery cables right off the bat."

"What are the chances of those cables coming loose by accident?" Hannah asked.

"That would be zero. Somebody got under Darcy's hood and did it deliberately."

"So it couldn't have happened if Darcy drove over a curb? Or hit something with her car that bounced it up and down?" Norman pursued that line of questioning.

"Impossible," Cyril shook his head. "Those quick-release cables are pretty tight, and it takes some muscle to release them. You have to squeeze the sides together like a pair of pliers grasping something."

"It wasn't any kind of accident, then," Norman stated the obvious.

"No, it was deliberate. Somebody had to lift the hood and do it. But that wasn't the only thing wrong with Darcy's car. Someone who really *knew* this make and model of car did something to make sure Darcy wouldn't be able to drive it."

Cyril sat back in his desk chair and waited for them to react.

"What did this second person do?" Norman asked.

"Darcy's car has a fuse box under the hood. It's not clearly visible, so you have to know where it is to locate it. This person knew where it was, or looked for it until he located it, and then he removed one *particular* fuse."

"Wait a second," Norman said. "Those fuses control things like the airbags and the interior lights, don't they?"

"Right you are, boyo." Cyril lapsed back into his Irish accent. "That's the usual pattern for a fuse box under the hood. That was the case with Darcy's car, but her fuse box also included the fuse that controlled the fuel pump. Whoever did it knew which fuse that was, because that's the only one he pulled. You do know what effect that would have on a car, don't you?"

"I certainly do!" Norman said quickly. "A car that can't get fuel won't run."

"Right!" Cyril said, "Somebody opened the fuse box, took out *that* particular fuse, and closed it up again."

"So either battery cables or that fuse would disable Darcy's car," Hannah asked, and then she looked up at Cyril. "Am I right?"

"Yes."

"Do you think the same person would have done both of those things?" Norman asked him.

Cyril shook his head. "No, there was no need to do both, either one would have done the trick."

"Belt and suspenders?" Noman asked him.

Cyril chuckled. "My father used to say that! He used to also call it overkill, but I didn't want to say that in Darcy's case."

All three of them were quiet for a moment, and then Hannah broke the silence. "Is there any way of telling which action came first? The battery? Or the fuse box?"

"Not really," Cyril said. "I've got a theory about that, though."

"What's that?" Norman asked.

"I can't be positive, but I think two different people tried to disable Darcy's car."

"Why two?" Hannah asked him.

"Because whoever pulled that fuse knew something about cars and her car in particular. Maybe he has the same model of car, or he could have known which model she drove and researched it online. However he did it, he knew exactly which fuse to pull."

"And if he hadn't known which fuse, he would have pulled them all?" Norman asked.

"Yes, that's it, exactly."

"Is there any way of telling which came first, the chicken or the egg?" Hannah asked him.

Cyril threw back his head and laughed. "It could have happened either way."

"But if the battery cables were released first, would the second person have bothered to find the fuse fox and pull that particular fuse?" Norman asked.

Cyril shrugged. "Maybe. He might have been afraid that Darcy would spot the loose battery cables and hook them back up again. Taking out the fuse was sneakier, and most people wouldn't have thought to check that. Either that, or the person who pulled the fuse did it first. And another person, coming along after that first person, didn't realize that the car was already disabled and pulled the battery cables."

Hannah gave a dejected sigh. "It's possible either way. And that means we still don't know if there was one person, two people, or whether the battery cables or the fuse box came first."

"And that means we don't have any useful information," Norman concluded.

"Oh, yes, we do!" Hannah corrected him. "We know that someone who tampered with Darcy's car knew a lot about that particular make and model of car."

"It's a lead, even though it's very tenuous. It means that someone was angry enough to disable her car. And if they were angry enough to do this to her car, perhaps they were angry enough to kill her!"

They were all silent for a moment. It was a sobering thought. And then Norman turned to Cyril. "Did one of your mechanics tow Darcy's car here?"

"No, the auto club did it and I saw it come in. They used a flatbed tow truck. Darcy was driving her father's SUV, and it can't be towed by a regular tow truck."

"Did the person who towed it in look under the hood?"

Cyril shook his head. "Darcy told them to just bring it here, that I'd worked on it before and I'd know what was wrong."

"Do you know where the car was when the auto club picked it up?"

"Yes, the guy from the auto club was complaining about that. The car was in the employees' parking lot at DelRay Manufacturing. That's where Darcy worked."

Hannah and Norman exchanged glances. The first thing they had to do was find out if the employees' parking lot was accessible to the public. If it wasn't, whoever had disabled Darcy's car must have worked at DelRay.

"Do you know which shift Darcy worked?" Hannah asked Cyril.

"It must have been the day shift. The auto club towing service brought her car in at about six-thirty in the evening."

"Is there anything else you can tell us that might help in the investigation into Darcy's murder?" Norman followed up.

"Nothing that I can think of at the moment."

"If you think of anything . . . anything at all, please call us," Hannah told him.

"I will."

Hannah stood up. "We'll let you get back to work, then. Thanks for talking to us, Cyril."

"Will you keep me informed?" Cyril asked, standing up to shake Norman's hand. He turned to Hannah, gave her a hug, and sighed as if the weight of the world were on his shoulders. "*May the road rise up to meet you, and may the wind be always at your back.*"

It was almost like one of Reverend Bob's benedictions and Hannah felt tears come to her eyes.

"Thank you, Cyril," she managed to say.

Norman reached out to place his hand on Cyril's shoulder. "*May the sun shine warm upon your face, the rains fall soft upon your fields,*" he said, "*and until we meet again, may God hold you in the palm of his hand.*"

Cyril looked at Norman in surprise. "How did you know that? You're not Irish, are you?"

Norman shook his head. "Not me, but my best friend in Seattle was another dentist named Sean O'Connor. He told me his family was Shanty Irish."

"You say he was your best friend?"

Norman nodded. "We still get together every time we go to dental conventions. Sean knows the best Irish pubs in every city."

"Sounds like a fine fellow," Cyril said, beginning to smile. "I knew there was something about you I liked, besides the fact you fixed my teeth without hurting me."

GEORGIA PEACH CAKE

Preheat oven to 325°F., rack in the middle position.

Cake Batter Ingredients:

1 cup softened, salted butter *(2 sticks, 8 ounces, $\frac{1}{2}$ pound)*
2 cups white *(granulated)* sugar
4 large eggs
1 teaspoon salt
1 teaspoon baking powder
$\frac{1}{2}$ teaspoon baking soda
$\frac{1}{2}$ teaspoon cinnamon
$\frac{1}{4}$ teaspoon ground nutmeg *(freshly ground is best, of course)*
1 teaspoon vanilla extract
1 teaspoon almond extract
$\frac{1}{2}$ cup peach jam
3 cups all-purpose flour *(pack it down in the cup when you measure it)*
1 cup buttermilk *(or whipping cream)*

This cake is made in a 9-inch by 13-inch cake pan, either metal or glass. To prepare your cake pan, either spray it with Pam or another nonstick cooking or baking spray, or generously butter the bottom and sides of the pan.

Hannah's 1ˢᵗ Note: If Lisa and I are making this cake for catering, we use disposable foil cake pans. You can do this if you plan to give it to someone or take it to a potluck dinner. That way you won't have to ask for the cake pan back.

Hannah's 2ⁿᵈ Note: The following instructions are for an electric mixer. You can also mix this cake by hand in a large bowl, but it will take a strong beating arm to do it.

To Make the Cake Batter:

Place the softened butter in the bowl of an electric mixer. With the mixer running at MEDIUM speed, beat the butter for a minute or two.

With the mixer still running at MEDIUM speed, sprinkle in the white *(granulated)* sugar, beating as you sprinkle. Mix the butter and the sugar together until they form into a light, fluffy mixture.

Add the eggs, one at a time, beating after each addition.

Add the salt, baking powder, and baking soda, mixing until they are thoroughly combined.

Mix in the cinnamon and the nutmeg.

With the mixer still running, add the vanilla extract and the almond extract.

Add the peach jam and mix that in until everything is thoroughly combined.

Again, with the mixer running, add only one cup of the all-purpose flour. Beat it in thoroughly.

Mix in ½ cup of the buttermilk or whipping cream.

Add the second cup of all-purpose flour and mix well.

Mix in the remaining ½ cup of buttermilk or whipping cream. Mix that in thoroughly.

Add the remaining cup of all-purpose flour and beat on MEDIUM speed for 3 minutes, or until everything is thoroughly incorporated.

Take the bowl out of the mixer and set it on the counter.

If you haven't already prepared your cake pan, do it now.

Use a rubber spatula to transfer the cake batter to the cake pan.

Smooth out the top of the batter with the rubber spatula so that it's evenly distributed in the cake pan.

Bake the cake in a preheated 325°F. oven for 50 minutes, or until a cake tester, thin bamboo skewer, or long toothpick inserted in the middle of the cake comes out without batter clinging to it.

If there is gooey cake batter on the tester you used, bake your Georgia Peach Cake for another 5 minutes and test it again. Continue to bake your cake in 5-minute intervals until it tests done.

Take the cake out of the oven and set it on a cold stovetop burner or a wire rack to wait for its Butter Sauce.

Butter Sauce Ingredients:

$\frac{1}{2}$ cup salted butter *(1 stick, 4 ounces, $\frac{1}{4}$ pound)*
$\frac{1}{2}$ cup white *(granulated)* sugar
$\frac{1}{4}$ cup peach brandy or liqueur *(I used Drillaud Peach Brandy—you can use*

       peach juice if you don't want to use alcohol in this cake)
1 Tablespoon vanilla extract

To Make the Butter Sauce:

Take out a medium-size saucepan.

Hannah's 3rd Note: Don't use a saucepan that's black or brown on the inside. You'll be using it again later when you make the icing and you need to be able to see when the butter turns brown.

Place the ½ cup of salted butter in the bottom of the saucepan.

Add the ½ cup of white *(granulated)* sugar.

Stir in the ¼ cup of peach brandy, peach liqueur, or peach juice.

Do not add the vanilla extract yet. The mixture in the saucepan must cook first.

Heat the three ingredients in the saucepan on MEDIUM heat until the butter is melted and the sugar has dissolved, but DO NOT let the mixture come to a boil.

Hannah's 4th Note: You can do this in a microwave-safe bowl on HIGH for 90 seconds. (I used a 4-cup Pyrex measuring cup.)

Pull the saucepan over to a cold stovetop burner, shut off the burner you used, and add the Tablespoon of vanilla extract. *(Be careful—it could sputter a bit.)*

Use a food pick or a thin wooden skewer to poke holes all over the top of your cake. Don't be too gentle. You want the holes to go all the way down to the bottom of the cake. *(I used a thin wooden skewer and poked about 45 holes in mine.)*

Pour the warm butter sauce over the top of the cake as evenly as you can. If you used a saucepan, don't bother to wash it. You'll be using it again when you make the frosting.

Let the cake sit out on the wire rack or cold stovetop burner for at least 10 minutes so that the Butter Sauce has time to soak into the holes you poked and get all the way down to the bottom of your cake.

Cover your Georgia Peach Cake with foil and re-frigerate it for at least 2 hours. *Overnight is fine, too.*

When 2 hours have passed, leave the cake in the refrigerator and start making the Brown Butter Icing.

Brown Butter Icing Ingredients:

¼ cup salted butter *(½ stick, 2 ounces, ⅛ pound)*

2 cups powdered *(confectioners')* sugar *(pack it down in the cup when you measure it)*

1 teaspoon vanilla extract

2 Tablespoons heavy cream *(that's whipping cream, but you could also use half-and-half, which is light cream)*

½ cup sliced almonds *(optional—to sprinkle over the top of the cake after you frost it)*

Take your Georgia Peach Cake out of the refrig-erator and set it on the kitchen counter.

To Make the Brown Butter Icing:

If you used a saucepan to make the Butter Sauce, you already have a medium-size saucepan that you can use. *(It doesn't need to be washed first.)*

If you used the microwave instead, make sure that the saucepan you choose is not colored black or brown inside. *(I made that mistake once and I couldn't see when the butter had browned.)*

Put the ¼ cup *(half stick)* of salted butter into the medium-size saucepan.

Place the saucepan on the stovetop and heat it at MEDIUM-HIGH heat. The butter will melt and then it will brown. There's no need to stir until it begins to turn color.

When the butter is a nice caramel color *(this took about 5 minutes for me)*, slide the saucepan over to a cold stovetop burner and shut off the burner that you used.

Stir in the 2 cups of powdered *(confectioners')* sugar.

Put the 2 Tablespoons *(⅛ cup)* of heavy cream in a small cup and drizzle it in, stirring as you go until the frosting is smooth and spreadable.

This is another one of those wonderful no-fail icings. If it turns out to be too runny, add a bit more powdered sugar. If it turns out to be too thick and stiff, add a bit more cream. Continue to adjust these two ingredients until the frosting is the right consistency to frost your cake.

Using a frosting knife, spread your frosting all over the top of your cake. Make a smooth and even sheet of frosting.

If you decided to use the sliced almonds, place them on top of your cake before the frosting hardens.

Once your cake has been frosted and the frosting has hardened, cover it loosely with aluminum foil and place it in the refrigerator until you are ready to serve it.

To serve, cut squares of your cake and remove them from the cake pan with a metal spatula. Place them on dessert plates.

This cake is very rich and buttery. *(There's almost a whole pound of butter in it!)* Serve it with plenty of strong coffee or icy-cold glasses of milk. Anyone who likes peaches and almonds will love your Georgia Peach Cake.

Yield: Depending on how large you cut the squares of cake, your George Peach Cake will serve from 14 to 18 guests.

Hannah's 5th Note: Mother absolutely loves this cake. She's always been very fond of peaches and she loves things that are flavored with almond. If you bake it and invite Mother, you'd better plan on serving her at least two slices, perhaps three.

Hannah glanced at the kitchen clock. She'd worked almost nonstop since they'd left Cyril's garage. She'd dropped Norman off at his dental clinic so that he could finish his billing for the month, purchased two slow cookers at CostMart before she'd shopped for ingredients at Florence's Red Owl Grocery, and taken everything up to Doc and her mother's penthouse at the Albion Hotel. Once there, she started dinner for all of them and hurried back to The Cookie Jar to bake cookies for her customers and dessert for the dinner at the penthouse.

One glance at the kitchen clock told Hannah that it was almost time for Michelle to come in after her teachers' meeting at Jordan High. They'd both help out until time to lock up, and then they'd meet the rest of their extended family for dinner at the penthouse.

The phone rang and Hannah rushed to answer it. "The Cookie Jar. This is Hannah speaking," she greeted the caller.

"Hi, Hannah, it's Norman. I'm here and your mother's flight is about to land. Is there anything you want me to stop and buy before we get back to Lake Eden?"

"I don't think so. I shopped at the Red Owl this morning."

"What are we having for dinner?"

Hannah laughed. "You're beginning to sound like Mike. And when I tell him, he always says, *Good, that's my favorite!* Whether he's ever had it or not."

"Sorry about that, but what *are* we having for dinner?"

"Lemon Glazed Chicken Breasts over Tracey's favorite rice."

"That's my *favorite*!" Norman said quickly, and waited until Hannah rewarded him with a laugh. "Who's coming for dinner? When we get back to Lake Eden, I'll drop your mother off at the Albion, and then I'll pick up wine to have with dinner. If it's chicken, I guess it should be white wine?"

"That's traditional, but you'd better pick up a bottle of red, too. Lonnie likes red, and so does Doc. Mother will probably want champagne, but she's got at least three bottles in her office refrigerator and another in the refrigerator in the kitchen. I checked."

"Okay. That's all I need to know. I'm going straight down to baggage so I can meet your mother and carry her suitcases to the car."

"You're going to drop Mother off at the penthouse before you get the wine?"

"Yes, I thought she might want to freshen up and change clothes before everyone else arrives for dinner."

"You're right. Once you pick up the wine, you can

come back to the penthouse and keep me company while I do some last-minute things."

"I'll do that. Maybe I can help you."

"You certainly can. . . ." Hannah gave a little laugh. "You can take Mother to the garden, give her a glass of champagne, and keep her company."

"In other words, you want me to keep your mother out of the kitchen?"

"Exactly right. Michelle and I can handle things in there."

"Okay. I can entertain your mother with a PowerPoint presentation on gum disease."

Hannah laughed so hard, she sputtered. "Don't do that! You know how squeamish Mother is. She won't even look at raw beef liver."

"I thought your mother liked liver."

"She loves it, but she doesn't want to see it unless it's cooked with onions and bacon on top. And forget about clams or oysters on the half-shell. Just do me a favor and leave your laptop in the car. I want Mother to enjoy my Lemon Glazed Chicken Breasts."

Hannah had just seated herself on a stool at the work station with a final cup of coffee before she washed the kitchen coffeepot, when there was a knock at the back kitchen door. The minute she heard it, she began to smile. It was an authoritative knock, a no-nonsense summons that fairly screamed her visitor's identity. It was Mike, and he probably wanted a snack before he arrived at the penthouse for dinner.

"Hi, Mike," she said even before she opened the door.

"You forgot to check the peephole," Mike accused her as he walked into the kitchen.

"I didn't have to check the peephole. I knew it was you from your knock."

"Someone else could have heard my knock and duplicated it. Never assume, Hannah."

"You're right," Hannah said, even though she thought he was being more than a little too cautious. "Would you like coffee, Mike?"

"Sure. Do you have anything to go with it?"

"I bake for a living, Mike. Of course I have something to go with your coffee."

Mike gave her the sexy grin that always caused her mouth to go dry, her knees to turn weak, and her heart to beat faster. Even more dangerously, it brought forth memories of the first time he'd kissed her, and that made her blush.

"Just teasing, Hannah," Mike said. "I figured you had to have something good left. It's a long time since lunch, and I don't think I could make it to dinnertime without something to tide me over."

Hannah smiled. Mike's idea of *something to tide him over* was probably a thick ribeye steak with garlic bread and a banana split to finish things off. "I'll fix a plate of cookies for you," she promised, heading for the box with leftover cookies that she'd placed on the counter, lifting the lid and taking an inventory of what was inside.

"I've got Cherry Pineapple Drops, Fudge-Aroons, Cashew Crisps, Lemon Softies, Black and Whites, Rocky Road Bars, or Chips Galore."

"Sounds good," Mike said, giving her a nod. "No way I can choose, so I guess you can give me one of each, maybe two. You make the best cookies, Hannah."

Hannah grabbed a plate and kept her face turned away from Mike as she filled it with cookies. She had all she could do to keep from laughing. She should have known that Mike would want to taste them all.

"Wow!" Mike said, when Hannah arrived at the work station with a full plate of cookies. "These really look good! Did you go out to Cyril's to find out about Darcy's car?"

"Yes," Hannah answered, taking the stool across from him and picking up her coffee mug. "Norman went with me. Cyril told us he thought two separate people had tampered with Darcy's car and what he said made sense. I'll tell you all about his reasoning tonight. He also said that it wasn't permanently damaged and he could fix it in a couple of minutes."

"Did they tow it in from Darcy's house?"

Hannah shook her head. "No, from the DelRay employee parking lot. Darcy called the auto club and had them tow her car directly to Cyril's garage."

"So you're going to follow up at DelRay to see if anyone there had a grudge against Darcy?"

"Of course. I'm going to go out there tomorrow morning to talk to Darcy's co-workers."

"Good. No sense in wasting your time talking to the wrong people. What time is dinner, Hannah?"

"At seven-thirty. Michelle and I wanted to give Mother a little time to relax first, but you can come early, Mike," Hannah said quickly. "We'll be there."

Mike gave a little nod to confirm it. "I guess I could drink champagne, but . . . will there be any beer?"

"Cold Spring Export. I picked it up at Florence's this morning. It's in Mother's refrigerator, chilling."

"Great! That's my favorite beer, you know!"

"I *do* know and that's why I got it."

Mike reached for a Fudge-Aroon Cookie, finished it off in two big bites, and selected a Cashew Crisp. "You're really good to me, Hannah. Sometimes I wish you'd taken me up on my proposal. If we were married, I'd always have cookies."

"Ahh! That must be true love!" Hannah said, somehow managing to keep a straight face.

Mike stared at her for a second, and then he sighed. "All right. I get it. Maybe I should have phrased that a different way?"

"Yes. You could have said that if we were married, you'd always have love in your life."

Mike considered that for a moment or two, and then he shook his head. "That sounds like a Valentine card. Maybe it's true, but I wouldn't say anything like that."

"Then what would you say if I gave you another chance?"

Mike took a moment and then he smiled. He'd obviously thought of something. "How about this? I could say that if we were married, I'd love you forever."

Hannah studied his expression. No smile. No smirk. No glimmer of humor in his eyes. Mike was serious and he deserved a serious answer.

"I . . . I don't know *what* I'd say to that, but . . . I know I'd be grateful, and happy that you felt that way."

"And you'd love me forever, too?"

Hannah was silent. What could she say? This was getting too serious and she wanted to go back to their casual bantering before either one of them said something they'd regret later. It was time for a little light-hearted humor.

"If you said you'd love me forever, I'd probably ask you if you'd like another cookie," she answered, hoping that she could make Mike laugh, or at least stop being so serious.

Mike smiled. "And I'd probably take you up on it since my cookie plate is empty," he responded.

"Already?" Hannah asked, gazing down at the empty plate in shock. "You inhaled those cookies, Mike!"

"That's the test of a good cookie. Just give me half as many, Hannah. I don't want to spoil my dinner."

Hannah and Michelle were sitting at their mother's kitchen table, having yet another cup of coffee. Dinner was in the crockpot, and the table had been set with their mother's best china and silver. All preparations had been made, and all they had to do now was wait until Norman got back from the airport with their mother.

Hannah had just put on a fresh pot of coffee when the doorbell rang. She turned to look at Michelle and saw that her sister was already up and heading for the door.

"I'll get it," Michelle said, hurrying through the doorway. "It's got to be Mother and Norman."

Michelle came back into the kitchen. "They're here," she announced, stepping aside so that Hannah could see that Delores had someone with her.

"Lynne?" Hannah was shocked to see her friend. "I didn't realize that you were coming back here with Mother!"

Lynne exchanged conspiratorial glances with Delores. "We wanted to surprise you," she said.

"But how about the rest of the packing?"

"Robby and Maria are taking care of that," Delores explained. "There's not that much left, and they'll call the moving company when they're through. Lynne's things should be here in a week or two."

"And in the meantime, Delores was kind enough to offer to let me stay in one of her bedrooms, and since I'm staying here . . ." She stopped and turned to Delores.

"Lynne can help us with the investigation," Delores added.

"I'm glad you're back, Mother," Hannah told her, getting up to give her mother a hug.

"Me too, Mother," Michelle said, following Hannah's lead.

"And I'm glad to see you, too." Hannah turned to Lynne and gave her a hug. "Would either of you like coffee?"

"No, thank you," Delores responded immediately. "I had too many cups on the plane."

"Thanks, but no," Lynne said, shaking her head.

"Where's Doc?" Delores asked, and it was clear that she was eager to see her husband.

"In the garden," Michelle told her. "He's out there with the champagne bucket and he told me that he was going to pop the cork the minute he sees you."

"How lovely!" Delores said, a pleased smile spreading over her face. "I'm going out to have a glass of champagne with my husband. Take your time and freshen up, Lynne. Hannah will show you which bathroom to use. Then I want all of you to come out to the garden to join us."

"Mother?" Michelle called her back as Delores was about to go through the kitchen doorway. "I almost forgot. Doc told me that he put two interns and his best nurses on tonight so that he wouldn't have to go back to the hospital until tomorrow morning."

This news brought an even wider smile to their mother's face as she turned and hurried toward the entrance to the penthouse garden.

"She's happy to be home," Norman commented.

"Yes, she is," Michelle said. "And Doc's happy, too. He told me he hated coming home without Mother here."

"I'd call that smile she gave *rapturous*," Hannah commented. "It's nice to see Mother so much in love."

"Speaking of that"—Norman turned to Hannah—"I think you and Lynne should give them an evening alone tonight." He smiled at Lynne. "Hannah's staying over with me and I have a guest room, Lynne. Will you come out and stay at my house tonight with us?"

Lynne looked delighted at the suggestion. "Of course I will. That's a wonderful idea to leave those two lovebirds alone. Thank you for suggesting it, Norman."

Norman turned back to Hannah. "As a matter of fact, if you ladies don't mind, I'll take Lynne's suitcases out there right now and come back in time for dinner." He turned to Michelle. "Is there anything you'd like me to bring back for dinner?"

"Yes. Bring the cats, both of them. Mother loves to see them play in the garden, and I stopped by the garden center and picked up a bag of ladybugs."

"So we get to watch Moishe and Cuddles stalk the wild ladybug?" Norman asked.

Lynne gave a little shudder. "Do they . . . uh . . . eat them?"

Hannah laughed. "No! The reason it's so much fun to watch is that neither Moishe nor Cuddles is fast enough to catch them."

"I don't think they'd eat them anyway," Michelle said with a smile. "They have much more fun pawing at the branches and watching the ladybugs fly away."

"You're right," Hannah concurred. "Just wait until you see the expressions on Cuddle's and Moishe's faces. You can almost hear them thinking, *Why do they get to fly?*"

CHOCOLATE SALAMI

This is a no-bake recipe that is served chilled.

Ingredients:

> 1 and ½ boxes of vanilla wafers *(I used Nabisco Nilla Wafers)*
>
> 1 cup *(2 sticks, 8 ounces, ½ pound)* salted butter
>
> 1 Tablespoon cocoa powder *(unsweetened, I used Hershey's)*
>
> 14-ounce can sweetened condensed milk *(NOT evaporated milk) (I used Eagle Brand)*

Hannah's 1st Note: You can use any vanilla cookie that is tan or white and will resemble the fat particles in salami or Summer Sausage.

Hannah's 2nd Note: If you want to make your own vanilla cookies to crush, I'd suggest Old-Fashioned Sugar Cookies. They're delicious and very crushable.

Use a Ziploc plastic bag to crush your vanilla wafer cookies. Simply dump them into the bag, press the Ziploc strip at the top to lock it, and lay the

bag out on your counter. Either take out a rolling pin and crush them, or crush them by squeezing the bag in your hand. Your goal is to get cookie pieces approximately the size of coarse gravel.

Place the 2 sticks of salted butter in a microwave-safe bowl. *(I used a 4-cup Pyrex measuring cup.)*

Melt the butter on HIGH for 1 minute.

Let the butter sit in the microwave for 1 minute.

If the butter is melted, you're done. If not, melt it in additional 30-second increments with 30-second standing times in the microwave until it melts.

Pour the melted butter in a large mixing bowl.

Add the cocoa powder to the mixing bowl and stir it in.

Open the can of sweetened condensed milk and pour it into the mixing bowl. Mix it in thoroughly.

Add the crushed vanilla wafers *(or whichever cookie you chose to crush)* to the bowl. Mix it in thoroughly.

Place a sheet of parchment paper on your kitchen counter.

Scoop out roughly one-fifth of the mixture and place it on the parchment paper.

Spray your palms with Pam or another nonstick cooking spray and shape the salami "dough" on the parchment paper into a long roll the size of a salami.

Be sure to leave "ears" at the sides of your Chocolate Salami roll so that you can twist them to tighten the roll later.

Move your salami roll close to the bottom of the parchment paper and roll it up tightly. Press in the end of the roll with your palms.

Twist the loose paper on the sides of your roll so that your Chocolate Salami will stay tightly rolled.

Place the salami roll in a Ziploc freezer bag.

Take out one-fourth of the remaining mixture in the bowl and make another salami roll.

Place it in the Ziploc freezer bag.

Use one-third of the remaining mixture to make a third roll. Place that in the Ziploc bag.

Use half of the remaining mixture to make a fourth roll and place it in the Ziploc bag.

Roll the remaining mixture for the 5th Chocolate Salami and place it in the bag.

Now you have 2 choices.

You can place the Chocolate Salami rolls in the refrigerator for 2 hours before serving or you can place the Chocolate Salami rolls in your freezer.

Chocolate Salami rolls placed in the refrigerator will keep up to 1 week.

Chocolate Salami rolls placed in the freezer will keep for up to 6 months.

If you put the rolls in the freezer, thaw a roll by placing it in the refrigerator overnight.

Yield: 5 salami-size rolls or 3 rolls the size of summer sausage.

These Chocolate Salami rolls or Chocolate Summer Sausage rolls are a novelty, but they also taste wonderful. They're fun at parties that include children, even though it might mean getting dessert before dinner.

Wrap any leftovers and keep them in the refrigerator.

To serve, sprinkle powdered sugar over the rolls. Then slice with a sharp knife and arrange the slices on a platter.

Hannah's 3rd Note: I serve my Chocolate Salami or Chocolate Summer Sausage rolls by placing the slices on top of vanilla wafer or vanilla cookies.

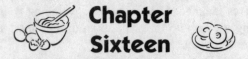

Chapter Sixteen

"I love this Chocolate Salami, Hannah," Andrea said. "Is it hard to bake?"

"It's not baked. It's simply a matter of mixing it up together and making it into rolls on parchment paper."

"Could I learn how to make it, Aunt Hannah?" Andrea's oldest daughter, Tracey, asked.

"Me too, Antanna?" Bethie echoed.

"No problem. I'll teach you some day after school. I have to make another batch for Bertie Straub anyway. She wants to serve them to her regulars down at the Cut 'n' Curl."

"These are dangerous, Hannah," Doc said, taking another slice of Chocolate Salami from the plate. "I've never had dessert before dinner before."

"Well, you'd better enjoy it because you may never have it again," Delores commented. "I have to watch your cholesterol."

"Don't worry, Lori. I'm watching my own cholesterol," Doc retorted, giving her a little hug.

Delores laughed. "I know you're watching it. You're watching it climb up the scale to an instant heart attack. No more Chocolate Salami for you!"

"Never?" Doc assumed a heart-broken expression.

"Well . . . not today." Delores turned to Hannah. "When are we eating, dear?"

"Now is a good time," Hannah said, rising from her chair. "Let's go into the dining room. Michelle set the table."

"And Lonnie brought flowers," Michelle added. "Shall I carry in your champagne, Mother?"

"That would be nice, dear," Delores said, handing Michelle her glass.

Doc got up and extended his hand to Delores, who took it and let him lead her into the dining room.

"The flowers are lovely," Delores said, as she took her place next to Doc at the table. "Thank you, Lonnie."

"Thank *you* for raising such a wonderful daughter," Lonnie told her. "I would have gone crazy by now without Shelly."

Hannah was secretly amused. Doc had called Delores *Lori*, and Lonnie had called Michelle *Shelly*. If Andrea and Bill were here, he'd probably be calling her *Andy*. Every Swensen female had a nickname except her. Why didn't she have a nickname?

As soon as her mind provided the answer, Hannah began to smile. There *were* no standard nicknames for Hannah. *Han* wasn't good and neither was *Nah*. Perhaps she was the lucky one in the family.

Then she thought of it and she shivered. *Cookie*. It was the nickname that Ross had called her. Should she be sad that she'd never hear him say it again? Or should she be grateful that he was gone for good?

"Why so serious?" Norman asked her.

"I was just thinking about something," she answered without going into detail. "And I'm hoping that Mother likes my Lemon Glazed Chicken Breasts."

"I'm sure she will."

"Uh-oh!" Michelle said, startling everyone at the table. "Feet up, everybody! I just heard the cats coming down the hallway."

Hannah was glad that her mother's dining room table and chairs were higher than hers at the condo, even Mike, who was taller than anyone there, had no problem tucking his feet up. She'd barely lifted her legs up to the second rung of the chair when the cats whizzed around the corner, claws skidding on the polished wooden floor, and raced into the dining room.

"Whoa!" Norman said, but of course it did no good. Cuddles was in the lead and she wasn't paying any attention to anyone except Moishe, who was chasing her.

"Stop it, Cuddles!" Norman said in an effort to gain control. But Cuddles simply made a land speed record lap around the dining room table and jumped up, landing squarely in Norman's lap.

"Oof!" Norman gasped, as his pet landed heavily.

And then, a split second later, it was Delores's turn to gasp as Moishe landed in her lap. "Moishe! Really!" Delores said, but there was a smile on her face. "I think he really missed me!"

Hannah couldn't keep the smile off her face. Moishe had just won all the points in the game of making Delores adore him.

"Well, that was interesting," Doc said, addressing Norman and Delores. "Do either of you need medical attention?"

"I'm fine, dear," Delores told him, despite the fact she was still a bit out of breath from the unexpected on-slaught.

"Me too," Norman concurred. "Cuddles settled right down and now she's purring."

Hannah glanced down at the cat in her mother's lap. "So is Moishe. As a matter of fact, I think he's so comfortable, he's fallen asleep."

"It was probably Moishe's idea," Norman said, smiling at Delores. "He missed you and Hannah so much, he convinced Cuddles to invade our dinner party."

Hannah laughed. "You're probably right. Either that, or Moishe is thanking Mother for the ladybugs."

"I bought those!" Michelle protested. "I made a special trip to the garden center to get them."

"And Moishe and I thank you, dear," Delores said, smiling at her.

"I'll pour the wine," Norman offered, reaching for the opener that Hannah had placed on the table and opening both bottles of wine. "Who wants red?" He looked around the table. Lonnie and Doc passed their glasses to Norman. He filled their glasses and passed them back. "How about white?"

"While Norman does that, I'll serve," Hannah said, reaching for the bowl with the rice. "This is Tracey's favorite rice. She calls it Mushy Roomy Room Rice. Will you pass the plates, Mother?"

Delores shook her head. "No, dear. I don't want to disturb Moishe."

"You're going to have to disturb him eventually." Doc looked down at Hannah's sleeping cat and frowned. "You just got home, Lori, and I'll be darned if I'll share our bed with Moishe tonight!"

Hannah laughed. "No problem, Doc. Moishe always sleeps in my bed with me."

"I've noticed," Mike said, giving a mournful sigh.

"So have I," Norman said, looking equally mournful.

That did it for Delores. She started to laugh so hard that she dislodged Moishe, who made a beeline for the garden under the dome. Cuddles saw him run and wasted no time in giving chase. In the space of a second or two, both cats were gone and everyone at the table, including Hannah, was laughing uproariously.

"I'll do the rice," Norman said, taking the bowl from Hannah's hands and motioning for Delores to pass her plate.

"And I'll dish up the Lemon Glazed Chicken Breasts," Michelle offered. "Just pass the plates with the rice and I'll do my part."

"What shall I do?" Hannah asked.

"Sit there and drink champagne with your mother and me," Lynne told her. "You've worked enough for one day."

"I don't know about you, but I'm absolutely stuffed," Delores declared, leaning back in her chair and smiling. "That was incredibly good chicken, dear."

"Thank you." Hannah accepted the compliment the way Delores had taught her, simply and sincerely.

"And the rice was perfect with it," Andrea commented.

"It's my rice, Mom," Tracey said proudly. "Aunt Hannah named it after me."

"That's right, honey," Hannah smiled at her oldest niece.

"Do I have a rice?" Bethie asked, looking slightly worried as she asked her aunt the question.

"Not tonight. Tonight you get to name the dessert."

"I do?" Bethie's smile was rapturous. "What is it, Antanna?"

"Some people call it a cake and some people call it a pudding. It has your favorite oranges in it, Bethie."

Bethie considered that for a moment, and then she nodded. "I thought of a name, Antanna."

"What is it?" Andrea asked her.

"It's Orange Pake."

Tracey looked slightly puzzled. "But, Bethie . . . there's no such thing as a pake."

"I know. But Antanna said that some people called it a pudding and some people called it a cake."

"Very clever, Bethie!" Hannah praised her. "From now on this dessert is called Orange Pake."

Bethie looked very proud of herself as Hannah went into the kitchen and brought out the cake platter. "Here it is, Bethie."

"It's pretty!" Bethie decided, smiling at her aunt.

"I think that since Bethie named the dessert, she should have the first piece," Lynne suggested.

"Absolutely right," Hannah agreed, cutting the first slice and putting it on a dessert plate. "Would you like sauce on it, Bethie?"

"Yes, please."

Hannah ladled on Soft Sauce, the topping without orange liqueur, and passed it to Bethie.

"Thank you," Bethie said politely, picking up her spoon and then putting it down again. "Grandma McCann says it's not polite to start your dessert until everyone else has been . . ." She stopped speaking and frowned. "I forget the word."

"Served?" Norman guessed.

"Yes! That's it, Uncle Norman! Hurry and cut more, Antanna. It smells really good!"

Once everyone had tasted Bethie's Orange Pake and finished their coffee or milk, Delores leaned back in her chair. "Would the girls like to stay overnight, Andrea?"

"Thank you, but not tonight," Andrea responded. "We have an early day tomorrow. Bethie is going to the mall with Grandma McCann right after they drop Tracey off at school. I'm showing another house to my client at seven-thirty, and then he's driving back to Minneapolis for a ten o'clock appointment."

"Is this the same man who wants a three-bedroom with an attached garage?" Hannah asked her.

"Yes." Andrea gave a deep sigh. "I've shown him every available house, and so far he hasn't even made an offer. This one fits his parameters, but the house he really wanted isn't on the market."

Hannah knew exactly which house Andrea's client had wanted. It was Darcy's house, and she was very glad that Andrea hadn't mentioned it in front of Lonnie. When she saw Andrea at The Cookie Jar in the morning, she'd ask her sister if Darcy's brother was planning to put the house on the market. It was a bit unlikely to wonder if Andrea's client had killed Darcy to get her house, but it was a motive. When she got to The Cookie Jar in the morning, she'd put the client's name on her suspect list.

Andrea gave a little nod. It was clear their sisterly radar was working. From the thoughtful expression on Andrea's face, Hannah knew that Andrea had thought of the very same thing.

LEMON GLAZED CHICKEN BREASTS
A Crockpot Recipe

Prepare a 4-quart crockpot by spraying the inside of the crock with Pam or another nonstick cooking spray.

Hannah's 1st Note: The recipe below is for a 4-quart crockpot. If your crockpot is a 5-quart model, increase the amounts for the ingredients by one-half. For instance, this recipe calls for six 6-ounce boneless, skinless chicken breast halves. If you want to make your Lemon Glazed Chicken in a 5-quart crockpot, use nine 6-ounce boneless, skinless chicken breast halves.

Ingredients:

> 6-ounce can frozen lemonade concentrate, undiluted
> ½ teaspoon ground ginger
> ¼ teaspoon ground black pepper
> 1 teaspoon dried parsley *(or fresh finely chopped if you have a kitchen herb garden)*
> 6 six-ounce boneless, skinless chicken breast halves

¼ cup water
2 Tablespoons cornstarch

Open the can of frozen lemonade concentrate and put the contents in a shallow bowl that's large enough to hold one of the chicken breast halves.

When the lemonade concentrate has thawed, stir in the half-teaspoon of ground ginger.

Stir in the quarter-teaspoon of ground black pepper.

Stir in the teaspoon of dried parsley *(or the fresh chopped parsley if you used that)*.

Dip each piece of chicken breast in the shallow bowl, coating both sides with the mixture.

Place the dipped chicken in the bottom of the crock.

Give the dipping mixture another stir and then pour it over the chicken breast halves in the crock.

Put the lid on the crockpot and plug it in. *(Don't laugh, I forgot to plug in my crockpot once and had to call out for pizza for dinner!)*

Turn the slow cooker on LOW and cook your chicken for 7 to 9 hours.

Hannah's 2nd Note: If you're in a hurry, you can cook your chicken breast halves on HIGH and it will take only 4 to 5 hours.

After your chicken has been cooked, lift it out of the glaze with a slotted spoon and remove it from the crock. Place it in a baking dish and cover the baking dish tightly with foil.

Turn your oven on the lowest possible temperature and place the chicken inside. This will keep it warm while you thicken the glaze so that your guests can use it as a sauce.

Turn the crockpot with the glaze inside to HIGH and replace the cover.

Mix the water and the cornstarch together in a small bowl.

Take the cover off the slow cooker, add the water and cornstarch mixture to the crock, and stir it in.

Replace the cover, but leave it slightly ajar.

Hannah's 3rd Note: Leaving the cover ajar will allow the steam to escape and cause your

glaze to thicken faster. It's just like making gravy. You don't cover it after you stir in the thickener.

Cook the glaze on HIGH for 15 to 30 minutes or until bubbly and thickened like gravy.

Serve the chicken over cooked rice or any kind of cooked pasta you wish to use.

Yield: If you serve Lemon Glazed Chicken Breasts with a mixed salad or vegetables of your choice, it will serve 4.

Hannah's 4th Note: I like to serve my Lemon Glazed Chicken Breasts over my variation of Holiday Rice. My niece Tracey calls it Mushy Roomy Room Rice. This rice is made in a casserole and baked in the oven for 2 hours. You can bake it in advance and simply reheat it before you're ready to serve your Lemon Glazed Chicken Breasts.

TRACEY'S MUSHY ROOMY ROOM RICE

Preheat oven to 350°F., rack in the middle position.

Ingredients:

> 1 cup long-grain brown rice, uncooked
> 1 cup wild rice, uncooked
> 2/3 cup brown Basmati rice, uncooked
> 3 and 1/3 cups chicken stock
> 3 chicken bouillon cubes
> 1/2 teaspoon ground black pepper
> 1/3 cup red onions, finely diced
> 2 cans *(13.25 ounces net weight)* button
>   mushrooms *(or any other kind of*
>   *mushrooms that you like)*
> 1/2 cup butter *(one stick, 4 ounces, 1/4 pound)*

Hannah's 1st Note: If you can't find one of the varieties of uncooked rice, just substitute any other variety that you like. Your goal is to come up with 2 and 2/3 cups of mixed, uncooked rice. If you can find a bag of uncooked mixed rice or uncooked rice medley that you like, you can use that as long as the total weight is 1 pound of uncooked rice.

Michelle's 1st Note: If you want a shortcut to this recipe, you can use those Uncle Ben pouches

of rice that you bake in the microwave. Just make enough pouches for your guests, dump them in a buttered casserole dish, mix in any seasonings you like, and cover the casserole with heavy-duty foil. Then all you have to do is stick the rice in your oven at a low temperature and serve it when your Lemon Glazed Chicken Breasts are ready.

Michelle's 2nd Note: If you make your rice this way, please don't tell Hannah.

Pour the uncooked rice in a strainer and rinse it off. Toss it a bit in the strainer to make sure to wash off any dust on the rice.

After you've rinsed your rice, pat it dry with paper towels. Leave it in the strainer in the sink.

Prepare a large round glass casserole dish by spraying the inside with Pam or another nonstick cooking spray.

Take out a saucepan big enough to hold the chicken broth and the rice. *(You won't add the uncooked rice to your saucepan until everything else has been cooked, so leave the rice in the strainer for now.)*

Measure out 3 and ⅓ cups of chicken broth and pour it into the saucepan.

Add the chicken bouillon cubes.

Heat the bouillon cubes and broth on HIGH heat on the stovetop until the mixture reaches the boiling point.

Turn the burner down to MEDIUM heat and stir until the bouillon cubes are dissolved.

Add the black pepper to the saucepan. Stir well.

Add the finely chopped red onions to the saucepan. Mix it in.

Open the cans of mushrooms, drain off the liquid, and add them to the saucepan. Stir them in and then turn off the burner and pull the saucepan over to a cold burner.

Add the rinsed rice to the saucepan and stir until the ingredients are thoroughly mixed. Give everything a final stir.

Transfer the rice mixture in the saucepan to the greased casserole dish.

Remember the butter you didn't use? Here's where it comes into play. Unwrap the stick of but-

ter, cut it into 8 pieces, and arrange the pieces on top of the rice mixture.

If the casserole dish has a cover, put it on. If it doesn't, cover the casserole dish with heavy-duty foil.

Bake your Mushy Roomy Room Rice at 350°F. for 2 hours.

When 2 hours have passed, take off the casserole lid or the foil and bake for another 20 to 30 minutes.

Hannah's 2nd Note: You can assemble this rice dish ahead of time and refrigerate it until you are ready to bake it. Then all you have to do is pop it into a preheated oven and bake it.

Yield: Enough Mushy Roomy Room Rice for 6 people.

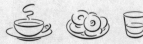

MANDARIN ORANGE BUNDT DESSERT
(Bethie's Orange Pake)

Do not preheat oven.
This dessert must "settle" for 30 minutes before baking.

> 2 twenty-ounce *(approximate weight)* loaves of sliced bread *(I used Oroweat white sandwich bread)*
> 2 fifteen-ounce net weight cans of Mandarin orange segments *(I used Dole brand)*
> 2 cups golden raisins *(I used Sun-Maid brand)*
> 1 and ½ cups white *(granulated)* sugar
> 2 teaspoons ground cinnamon
> 1 cup salted butter *(2 sticks, 8 ounces, ½ pound)*

> 7 large eggs
> 2 cups heavy *(whipping)* cream
> Sprinkling of grated nutmeg *(freshly grated is best, of course)*

Hannah's 1st Note: Lisa and I always use sandwich loaves of white bread because it's easier and faster to cut off the crusts. There are usu-

ally 22 slices per loaf, but you won't use the end pieces.

Prepare your baking pan before you begin by generously buttering and flouring the inside of a Bundt pan and dumping out the excess flour. Alternatively, you can use Pam Baking Spray, which contains flour. If you use the baking spray, spray the inside of the pan, let it sit for 5 minutes, and then spray it a second time.

Hannah's 2nd Note: Through experience, I've learned some tips for buttering and flouring a baking pan. You can make this task easier by buttering it *(don't forget to butter the middle part)*, dumping in a quarter-cup of flour, and sealing the open top of the pan with plastic wrap. Then you can shake it every which way to Sunday and your flour won't fall out on the floor. *(Just make sure the plastic wrap is on tightly, it certainly won't hurt to hold it over the sink or kitchen wastebasket as a precaution.)*

Divide your loaves of bread into thirds. *(I used 7 slices, 7 slices, and 6 slices per loaf.)* Stack the slices of bread on a cutting board and cut off the crusts. Then cut the slices into 4 triangles. *(Just make an*

"X" with your knife and that'll do it.) Repeat until all the slices, except the end pieces, are cut.

Arrange one-third of the crust-less bread triangles in the bottom of your Bundt pan, covering as much of the bottom as you can.

Open the two cans of Mandarin oranges and drain them in a strainer placed over a bowl. *(You will use some of the juice for the Orange Soft Sauce you'll make later.)*

Scatter HALF of the Mandarin orange sections in your strainer over the bread triangles in the Bundt pan. *(You'll use the other half of the orange sections later on in the recipe.)*

Measure out ONE cup of golden raisins and spread them out on top of the orange sections in the pan.

Sprinkle only ONE-HALF cup of the sugar on top of the raisins in your pan.

Sprinkle the sugar with 1 teaspoon of ground cinnamon. *(That's half of the cinnamon.)*

Unwrap ONE stick of butter *(½ cup)* and heat it in the microwave for 45 seconds on HIGH. Pour it over the ingredients in your Bundt pan.

Repeat the whole thing with the second part of the bread, placing the triangles on top of the ingredients in your Bundt pan.

Scatter the remaining Mandarin orange sections on top of the bread triangles.

Sprinkle the remaining golden raisins on top of the Mandarin orange sections.

Scatter a HALF-CUP of the sugar over the raisins and top it with ONE teaspoon of ground cinnamon.

Unwrap and melt the second stick of salted butter for 45 seconds in the microwave and pour that over the second layer in your Bundt pan.

It's time for the final third of the bread triangles. Place them on top of the ingredients that are already in the Bundt pan.

Press the bread down a little with your impeccably clean hands to make it fit in the pan.

Sprinkle the top with the remaining HALF-CUP of sugar.

Get out a mixing bowl large enough to hold 7 eggs and 2 cups of heavy cream.

Crack the eggs into the bowl and whip them up with a wire whisk *(or with an electric mixer)*. Be careful not to over-beat the eggs. You're making custard, not sponge cake.

Add the heavy cream to the bowl. Mix it in thoroughly.

Place your Bundt pan on a cookie sheet with sides, or another shallow pan that can hold any spills. This will be your drip pan.

Pour the egg and cream mixture SLOWLY over the ingredients in the Bundt pan. You may have to stop pouring several times so that the Bundt pan does not overflow.

Hannah's 3rd Note: It will take time for the custard mixture to soak into the bread, so don't hurry with the pouring. If the liquid threatens to spill over the top or run down the fluted tube in the middle of your Bundt pan, just wait a minute or two to let it soak in. When the liquid level goes down, add more custard mixture.

WARNING: You may not be able to add all of the custard mixture to the Bundt pan. That depends on

how much the kind of bread you bought will soak up. Don't overfill and risk spillage.

Hannah's 4th Note: I was able to use all of my custard mixture. The Oroweat white sandwich bread soaked it all up.

Once you've added all the custard mixture that you can, grate a little nutmeg over the top of your Bundt pan and let it sit on the kitchen counter for 30 minutes. ***This standing time is very important!***

When 30 minutes are up, preheat the oven to 350°F., rack in the middle position.

When your oven comes up to temperature, place your Bundt pan AND the pan you're using for spills in the oven. Bake at 350°F. for 70 *(that's seventy)* minutes.

Take your Mandarin Orange Bundt Dessert out of the oven and place it on a cold stovetop burner or a wire rack.

Let your dessert cool for 25 minutes and then place a cake platter over the top of your Bundt pan.

Using pot holder or oven mitts, flip the Bundt pan and the platter over so that the platter is on the bottom.

Give the Bundt pan and platter a gentle shake and set it on a towel on the counter.

Carefully lift the Bundt pan. The Mandarin Orange Bundt Dessert should fall right out of the pan and rest on the platter. If it does not, pick it up again and give it another little shake. Keep repeating until the dessert has loosened from the pan and is resting on the platter.

If you don't plan to serve your dessert until much later, or even the next day, let it cool completely on the platter.

When your dessert is cool, cover it with plastic wrap and refrigerate it. Mandarin Orange Bundt Dessert will keep in the refrigerator for 3 to 5 days.

To serve: Dust your Mandarin Orange Bundt Dessert with a sprinkling of powdered sugar and then pour a bit of Hard Sauce *(with alcohol)* or Soft Sauce *(without alcohol)* over the top and let it drizzle down the sides. You can decorate the top with more Mandarin orange slices if you wish, but it's pretty just as it is.

Carry your Mandarin Orange Bundt Dessert to the table so your guests can admire it. Then slice pieces, just as you would with a Bundt cake, place them on dessert plates, and pass the Hard Sauce and the Soft Sauce. Make sure your guests have cups of strong coffee or icy-cold glasses of milk to drink.

Hannah's 5th Note: This dessert is best served slightly warm or at room temperature. I pour my Mandarin Orange Hard Sauce and my Mandarin Orange Soft Sauce into separate gravy boats and tie a ribbon on the handle of the gravy boat with the Soft Sauce. I do this so that my nieces, Bethie and Tracey, know which sauce to use on their slices of dessert.

Recipes for the Mandarin Orange Hard Sauce and the Mandarin Orange Soft Sauce follow.

MANDARIN ORANGE HARD SAUCE

Ingredients:

> ½ cup *(1 stick, 4 ounces, ¼ pound)* salted butter, softened
> 2 cups powdered *(confectioners)* sugar *(there's no need to sift unless it's got lumps)*
> 2 Tablespoons *(⅛ cup)* Triple Sec or any other orange liqueur

Hannah's 1st Note: If you don't feel like going out to get orange liqueur, you can substitute regular brandy, or even rum.

Make sure the butter has softened to room temperature.

Place the butter in a medium-size mixing bowl or in the bowl of an electric mixer.

Beat the butter at LOW speed for 2 minutes.

Turn up the mixer speed to MEDIUM and beat the butter until it is light and fluffy *(approximately 2 additional minutes)*.

Turn down the mixer to LOW speed again and beat as you add one cup of the powdered sugar. Beat until it is combined with the butter.

With the mixer running on LOW, add one Tablespoon of the Triple Sec or orange liqueur and beat until it is combined.

With the mixer still running on LOW speed, add the final cup of powdered sugar. Beat until it is well combined.

Add the final Tablespoon of Triple Sec or orange liqueur and beat the mixture until it is smooth.

Check your Mandarin Orange Hard Sauce for consistency. It should be fairly thick, but still pourable. If it's too thin, beat in more powdered sugar. If it's too thick, add a bit more orange liqueur.

Store your Mandarin Orange Hard Sauce in a tightly-covered container in the refrigerator. Take it out thirty minutes or so before serving your Mandarin Orange Bundt Dessert.

Yield: Enough hard sauce to serve with your Mandarin Orange Bundt Dessert.

Hannah's 2nd Note: If you're in a hurry and you don't feel like making a hard sauce or a soft sauce, instant vanilla pudding made according to the package directions and thinned with a little additional Triple Sec or orange liqueur will do nicely.

MANDARIN ORANGE SOFT SAUCE

Ingredients for Soft Sauce:

> $\frac{1}{2}$ cup *(1 stick, 4 ounces, $\frac{1}{4}$ pound)* salted butter, softened
>
> 2 cups powdered *(confectioners)* sugar *(there's no need to sift unless it's got lumps)*
>
> 2 Tablespoons *($\frac{1}{8}$ cup)* Mandarin orange juice *(saved from when you drained your cans of Mandarin oranges)*

Hannah's 1st Note: If you didn't save the juice when you drained the cans of Mandarin oranges, you can use 2 Tablespoons of regular orange juice as a substitute. If you don't have any orange juice, use 2 Tablespoons of milk as a substitute.

Make sure the butter has softened to room temperature.

Place the butter in a medium-size mixing bowl or in the bowl of an electric mixer.

Beat the butter on LOW speed for 2 minutes.

Turn up the mixer speed to MEDIUM and beat the butter until it is light and fluffy *(approximately 2 additional minutes)*.

Turn down the mixer to LOW speed and beat as you add one cup of the powdered sugar. Beat until it is combined with the butter.

With the mixer running on LOW, add one Tablespoon of Mandarin orange juice *(or regular orange juice)*. Beat until it is well combined.

With the mixer still running on LOW speed, add the final cup of powdered sugar. Beat until it is well combined.

Add the final Tablespoon of Mandarin orange juice *(or regular orange juice)* and beat the mixture until it is smooth.

Check your Orange Soft Sauce for consistency. It should be fairly thick, but still pourable. If it's too thin, beat in more powdered sugar. If it's too thick, add a bit more orange juice.

Store your Orange Soft Sauce in a tightly-covered container in the refrigerator. Take it out thirty minutes or so before serving your Mandarin Orange Bundt Dessert.

Yield: Enough soft sauce to serve with your Mandarin Orange Bundt Dessert.

Hannah's 2nd Note: If you're in a hurry and you don't feel like making a Hard Sauce or a Soft Sauce, some instant vanilla pudding made according to the package directions and thinned with a little additional orange juice and/or Triple Sec will work fine.

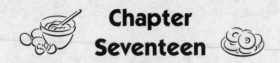

Chapter
Seventeen

Hannah woke up the next morning to find the winter sun peeking through Norman's master bedroom window, bathing the two cats sleeping on their respective pillows in a pale glow. She sat up quickly and turned to glance at the clock Norman had on his nightstand. Seven o'clock! She'd overslept and she'd planned to be at The Cookie Jar when Aunt Nancy and Lisa came in at six in the morning.

It only took a moment to pull on her slippers and a scant five minutes later, Hannah was in the shower, fully waking up as the multiple water jets relaxed her stiff muscles. Moishe had stolen her pillow again, a feline necessity since Cuddles had appropriated his.

Less than ten minutes later, fully awake and dressed, Hannah tiptoed past the guest room Norman was using and hurried downstairs to the kitchen. She pushed open the door, stepped inside, and was immediately seduced by her favorite morning aroma. "Coffee!" she breathed.

"Sit down. I'll pour you a cup," a voice said, and Hannah turned toward the booth in the corner of Norman's kitchen.

"Lynne!" Hannah exclaimed, obviously startled at the sight of her friend. "I thought you said you were going to sleep in this morning."

"I was, but I heard your shower running and I decided to come down here and make the coffee." Lynne patted the bench of the booth. "Slide in. You take it black . . . right?"

"Right. The coffee smells wonderful!"

"It should. I noticed that Norman had Blue Mountain beans from a place in New York and I used that. It's supposed to be the best coffee in the world."

"I believe it," Hannah said, inhaling the delicious scent.

"There was a note with my name on it next to the bag," Lynne told her, pouring a mug for Hannah and carrying it to the booth. "It said, *If you get up before I do, use this coffee for Hannah.* Norman loves you, you know."

Hannah knew she was smiling as she accepted the coffee from Lynne. "I know."

"Do you love him?"

"Yes, but not quite the way he wants me to."

"Give it time." She waited until Hannah had taken her first sip of coffee, and then she asked, "How do you like it?"

"It's wonderful!"

"I heard that," Norman said, appearing in the doorway. "I came in and shut off your alarm, Hannah. Lisa called and said she didn't need you early this morning. Lonnie was there and he filled Lisa in on the morning he found Darcy. He told her he wants her to tell the story because someone who hears it might come forward with new information."

"Good for him!" Hannah said, giving Norman a smile. "I was hoping he might do something like that, but I didn't want to ask him to do it. Lonnie's still a bit . . ."

"Fragile?" Norman suggested.

"That's it, exactly. He doesn't really want to talk about his experience and how he felt, but he will if he thinks it might possibly help to catch Darcy's killer."

"Is Lisa telling the story of the murder today?" Lynne asked.

"Yes," Norman answered. "She said she had it all worked out when she called here." He turned to Hannah. "That's one of the reasons she didn't want you to come in to help them bake this morning. Lisa said she wanted you to follow up any leads you already had. She assured me that she had plenty of help with Aunt Nancy, Marge, and Jack. And she said that Andrea called to find out what time she should come in to help wait on tables."

"I'll help, too," Lynne promised. "All I have to do this morning is rent or buy a car and drive out to the KCOW-TV station to talk to the owner about the Movies In Minnesota festival."

"They're still going to do it?" Norman asked her.

"Yes, but they're waiting until June. That way they won't run into big problems with the weather."

"Makes sense," Hannah commented. "But I need Andrea today."

"And I'll take Lynne out to Cyril's to ask about renting or buying a car," Norman promised.

Just then the stove timer dinged and Lynne got up from her chair. "Breakfast is almost ready," she told them. "I made Easy Cheesy Eggs Benedict."

"What's that?" Hannah asked her.

"You'll see," Lynne promised. "My mother always made

them on Christmas morning with my Aunt Daryl. I still remember helping them when I got older."

"What did you do?" Norman was curious.

"I buttered the English muffins before they went in the oven," Lynne told them. "I can hardly wait to see if you like them. I'm really hoping I made them right."

"I'm sure you did," Hannah said quickly. "Is there anything I can do to help?"

"Yes, get out three plates and put them on the counter, and I'll get the eggs and Canadian bacon out of the oven."

"I can help, too," Norman offered.

"Okay. Check the cheese sauce. It's in your microwave. If it's hot enough, take it out and you can ladle it over the eggs when I take them out of the muffin pan."

Hannah began to smile. This recipe sounded fascinating. "So, they're like Eggs Benedict without the Hollandaise Sauce?"

"Exactly. I could have made it from scratch, but it's quicker and easier with the cheese sauce."

All three of them got up to complete their assigned tasks and only scant minutes later, they were sitting down to eat Lynne's creation.

"Delicious!" Hannah pronounced. "Will you give me the recipe?"

"Of course."

"They're really great!" Norman agreed, turning to Lynne. "Is this why you wanted me to drop by the Quick Stop on the way to my house last night?"

"Yes, I haven't had these in years, but since I helped to make them every Christmas morning, I remembered how to do it. It's wonderful to have them this morning, almost like being home again."

"You can make this your Christmas tradition," Hannah told her, reacting to the wistful expression on Lynne's face. She knew Lynne's parents had died several years ago and since their house had been sold, it was impossible for Lynne to revisit the site of her childhood memories.

"Will you make these at my house this year?" Norman asked her. "I've had everyone here for breakfast on Christmas Day for two years in a row."

"I'd love to!" Lynne gave him a grateful smile. "I've really missed the friendships I had, growing up in a small town. Neighbors . . . friends . . . relatives . . . we all used to get together on Christmas morning."

"Then you'll just have to join us, especially since you'll be living here in Lake Eden," Norman told her. "Do you have any idea when your moving van will be here with your furniture?"

Lynne shook her head. "I'm not sure, but I didn't pack any big furniture. I didn't want much to remind me of my"—she stopped and gave a little sigh—"old life. I want to start fresh in Lake Eden, and that means buying my own furniture. That's another thing I'm going to check into today. Tori Bascomb's condo won't be mine for two weeks, but I'm hoping that Mayor Bascomb and his wife will let me in early." She turned to smile at Hannah. "Your mother already arranged to have Stephanie Bascomb and me over for coffee this afternoon in the penthouse garden. She says that all the furniture is still in the condo, and she thinks Mrs. Bascomb will let me use it until I replace it with mine."

"You do know that coffee in the penthouse garden won't have coffee, don't you?" Hannah asked her.

"Yes, your mother told me. She thought the second

bottle of Perrier Jouët might convince Stephanie to let me move in early."

Norman laughed. "Mrs. Bascomb will probably offer to let you use it if you buy some pieces from her."

"That would be good," Lynne said. "I especially like the furniture in the studio she used for acting lessons, and the living room furniture will do just fine for a while."

Hannah exchanged glances with Norman. From the look on Norman's face, it was clear he remembered hiding under Tori's bed when Al Percy had come into her apartment.

In response to Norman's raised eyebrows, Hannah gave a little shake of her head. Perhaps they'd tell Lynne about that later, but for right now, it should be their secret.

EASY CHEESY EGGS BENEDICT

Preheat oven to 350°F. degrees.
Place your oven rack in the middle position, and
position a second rack in the slot above it.

**Hannah's 1st Note: Before you start to preheat
your oven, make sure that a 12-cup muffin pan
will fit on the rack you put in the middle position. If it won't, move the rack you put above it
up another notch so that the muffin pan will fit.**

Ingredients:

> 6 English muffins
> ½ stick softened, salted butter *(2 ounces,
>   4 Tablespoons)*
> 12 slices Canadian bacon
> 12 large eggs
> Salt and pepper to taste

Cheese Sauce:

> 10.5-ounce *(net weight)* can of Campbell's
>   condensed Cheddar Cheese soup

Garnish:

Sprinkling of paprika on top of the cheese
sauce before serving *(fresh Hungarian
paprika is best)*

Directions:

Prepare a 12-cup muffin pan by spraying the inside of the cups with Pam, or another nonstick
cooking spray, or buttering them.

Take out a cookie sheet to use for the English
muffins. *(It does not need to be prepared by spraying or buttering since the English muffin halves
will be placed on it with the cut, buttered side up.)*

Separate the English muffins into 12 halves. *(You
can either cut them or pull them apart.)*

Spread the cut *(or torn)* side of the English
muffins with the softened, salted butter.

Place the English muffin halves, buttered side
up, on the cookie sheet and place the cookie sheet
on the kitchen counter.

**Hannah's 2nd Note: The Canadian bacon and
eggs that you will put in the muffin cups must go**

into the oven first because they will take longer to cook. You will put the cookie sheet with the English muffins into the oven when the eggs are halfway done.

Place a Canadian bacon slice in the bottom of each muffin cup. Press it down so it covers the bottom and goes a bit up the sides.

Crack an egg and tip the contents into one of the muffin cups on top of the Canadian bacon. Try not to break the yolks. Repeat this for all 12 muffin cups.

Slip the muffin tin into the preheated oven and set your stove timer for 7 minutes. *(The eggs won't be done, but that's when you'll put in the buttered English muffins.)*

Hannah's 3rd Note: The goal here is to have everything done at the same time.

While your eggs are baking, you will prepare your cheese sauce. This is really super easy, much easier than making a hollandaise sauce.

Open the can of Campbell's condensed Cheddar Cheese soup.

Spoon or use a small rubber spatula to remove the soup from the can and place it into a microwave-safe bowl.

Hannah's 4th Note: A word of caution! Do not add water or milk to the soup, even if you think it's too thick. The sauce should be thick and cheesy, and it will be spooned over hot baked eggs.

Heat the soup on HIGH in the microwave for 1 minute.

Let the bowl stand in the microwave for 1 minute.

Taste the cheese sauce. If it's not hot enough, heat it in 30-second increments with 30-second stand time until it is.

Leave the soup in the microwave until you're ready to take your Cheesy Eggs Benedict out of the oven. *Then, if it's not hot enough, you'll reheat it while you plate the Canadian bacon and eggs.*

When your stove timer rings and 7 minutes have passed, pick up your cookie sheet with the buttered English muffins and quickly place it on the rack

above the muffin tin. Shut the oven door and set the oven timer for another 7 minutes.

Get out 6 breakfast plates and place them on your kitchen counter. Once your Easy Cheesy Eggs Benedict come out of the oven, you'll want to serve them while they are hot.

When your oven timer rings, open the oven door and look at the eggs in the muffin cups. The whites should be cooked. If they aren't cooked, give them another minute or two in the oven. Most people like the whites of the eggs fully cooked and the yolks still a bit runny.

If the English muffins are beginning to get too brown on top, take them out of the oven now and set them on a cold stovetop burner. They will stay warm until the whites of your eggs are cooked.

Once the whites of the eggs are cooked to your satisfaction, take the muffin pan out of the oven and set it on a cold stovetop burner or a wire rack.

Set 2 English muffin halves, buttered side up, on each breakfast plate.

Carry the muffin tin over to the plates with the English muffins on them.

With a spoon or kitchen tongs, carefully transfer the contents of each muffin cup on top of each English muffin half.

Remove the cheddar cheese sauce from the microwave.

Spoon a helping of cheese sauce over each egg.

Hannah's 5th Note: If there is any cheese sauce left over, distribute it evenly over the eggs on the plate.

Sprinkle the paprika on top of the cheese sauce for a pretty garnish.

Serve your Easy Cheesy Eggs Benedict to your guests while they are still hot.

Hannah's 6th Note: If you like, you can accompany this brunch dish with slices of melon or other fruit.

Hannah's 7th Note: If you invite Mike for breakfast and serve Easy Cheesy Egg Benedict,

be sure to put a bottle of Slap Ya Mama hot sauce next to his plate.

Yield: This recipe serves 6 guests. If you have double ovens, the way Andrea does, you can make enough for a dozen guests at once.

Chapter Eighteen

Hannah had just finished taking a pan of Peanut Butter Sugar Cookies out of the oven, when her sister Andrea opened the back kitchen door, stepped inside, hung up her parka, and walked over to where Hannah was standing.

"Coffee?" Hannah asked, sliding the last pan of cookies onto the bakers rack.

"Sure. Why not?"

Hannah turned quickly and caught the dejected expression on Andrea's face. "Your client didn't like the house?" she guessed.

"He still insists he wants to wait to see if Darcy's brother puts her house up for sale. And the house I showed him fit every one of his requirements perfectly."

"Did he give you any reason for holding out for Darcy's house?"

"Yes, he said that he liked the view. I asked him what he meant because I don't think the view is anything special. It's just farmland, surrounded by some big, ugly rocks between Darcy's place and the next property. I just don't get it, Hannah."

"Maybe he's just one of those people who are impossible to satisfy," Hannah said, placing a cup of coffee in front of Andrea and filling a plate with fresh Peanut Butter Sugar Cookies.

"Those look good," Andrea said when Hannah carried them to the table, but she still looked disappointed. She reached for a cookie, took a bite, and smiled for the first time since she'd come in the door. "And they taste great, too."

"Thanks," Hannah said, and then she decided to cheer Andrea up even more. "Do you happen to know anyone who works the day shift at DelRay?"

Andrea gave a quick nod. "Sure. Glenn Rait works the day shift and so does Donnie Seifert."

"Do you know them well?"

Andrea thought about that for a moment. "It's not like we were close friends, but I know them."

"Do they know that you're married to Bill?"

Andrea began to frown. "I think so. Everybody in town knows I'm married to Bill."

"And they know that Bill's the sheriff?"

"Well . . . yes, I think so. They probably voted in the election. Why are you asking all these questions, Hannah?"

"Because I'd like you to go with me to talk to Glenn and Donnie."

It took a moment, but then Andrea understood. "You want to question them about something, and you want me to go along to introduce you?"

"That's right. Since you knew them back when, they may be more open with me if you're there."

"You're probably right. When do you want to go?"

"In an hour. I called earlier to find out when the day shift got a break and one of the secretaries told me."

"How long do they have?"

"Fifteen minutes, but that should be long enough. If we get there early, I can save a table and you can bring them over to introduce them to me."

"I can do that," Andrea said quickly. "Besides, it'll be fun to see them again."

"I thought I'd bring cookies."

"Good idea! That could help, especially if you give Glenn some of these peanut butter cookies. I used to give him half of my sandwich when we had peanut butter for lunch in the cafeteria. Glenn is crazy about peanut butter."

"How about Donnie?"

"I don't remember, but Donnie was always Glenn's best buddy. If Glenn starts to talk to you, Donnie will probably talk to you, too."

"Be careful of that car, Hannah," Andrea warned as they walked through the employee parking lot. "You're walking too close to the back of that car."

Hannah was surprised at the warning. "But I'm not going to bump into it or anything."

"It doesn't matter. That's the same car that Donna Summers has. Her husband bought it for her. And she was telling me all the problems she had with the alarm system."

"What problems did Donna have?" Hannah asked, moving away from the back of the car as she walked past.

"The alarm system turns on automatically when you

lock the doors with the remote control. And it's a really sensitive system. If anyone gets too close, the alarm goes off."

"Thanks for warning me!"

"I wouldn't have known, but Donna warned me. It went off for her once and it set off about a dozen other cars that were parked in the lot. Donna was embarrassed and worried that it might happen again. She took her car out to Cyril's garage so he could disable the alarm system."

"I think we go through this door," Hannah said, stopping at the interior exit.

"That's right. Just go to the center of the quad between the buildings and there are tables for the employees who bring their own lunches."

Hannah did as her sister instructed and they found their way to the area that was set aside for employees who wanted to eat their lunches outside. They took a seat at one of the tables, and a moment or two later, the door to the building opened and the workers began to stream out.

"Good thing we got here when we did," Hannah commented, watching the employees head for the tables like lemmings heading toward the edge of the cliff.

"You're right," Andrea said, standing up to wave. "Here they come, Hannah. You save the table. I'll go meet them and bring them over here."

"Hey, Hannah. You're lookin' good," Glenn said as Andrea brought the two men over to the table. "Sorry about all the trouble you had in the last couple a' months."

"Yeah, sorry about the trouble," Donnie echoed, but Hannah noticed that he was eyeing the bag of cookies she'd brought with her.

"Sit down, guys," Hannah said, opening the bag of cookies. "I brought something for your break."

"And I'll get coffee for you," Andrea offered. "Black? White? Sweet?"

"Black," Glenn told her.

"White and sweet," Donnie said. "I'll go with Andy and help her carry it."

Once Glenn and Hannah were left alone, he gave her an assessing look. "So you probably want to know about Darcy, huh?"

"That's why I'm here. She was your shift supervisor, wasn't she?"

"Yeah."

"I never knew her very well," Hannah told him. "Was she a good supervisor?"

"Uh . . ." Glen winced and shook his head. "Look, Hannah. This isn't going any further than you . . . right?"

"Right. So tell me how Darcy did as a supervisor."

"She lorded it over us. If we were two minutes and thirty seconds late to punch our time cards, she wrote us up."

"Two and a half minutes?" Hannah had trouble believing that anyone would quibble about less than five or ten minutes.

"That's right. And Donnie and I got docked an hour!"

"That must have made you very mad." Hannah passed the cookie plate to him.

"Oh, it did! Donnie and I depend on our paychecks to make the rent. We don't earn that much out here, and a couple of write-ups and you're not eligible for your yearly raise."

"And you and Donnie had a couple of write-ups?" Again, Hannah waited for Glenn to corroborate it.

"Yeah. One more after that last one and we would have lost our raises."

"I wouldn't blame you for being really mad at Darcy."

"Oh, we were mad, all right! And then . . ." Glenn hesitated and gave a little shudder.

"Then what?" Hannah prompted.

"Then we came in to work and heard she was murdered. That gave both of us the creeps."

Hannah gave what she hoped was an understanding nod and stifled her urge to ask another question. Mike had taught her that once a suspect began to talk, silence was a tool that could prod the suspect into even more revelations.

"I felt bad about how Donnie and I had hated her for that write-up," Glenn confessed. "That day at lunch everybody was talking about the murder, so Donnie and I went out to my car and ate our lunch there."

"Yeah," Donnie said, coming up to the table with their coffee. "Some people just shouldn't be line supervisors, you know?"

Glenn reached out for a cookie from Hannah's bag. "That's right. Some people get a little power and they just lord it over you like they're better than you are. Darcy was like that."

"And she took lots of breaks for herself," Donnie added. "She was always off flirting with the head shift supervisor. She used to slip him notes and stuff like that."

"That's right," Glenn confirmed it. "I don't think she ever hooked up with him, though."

Donnie gave a nod. "I don't think she did, either. He already had somebody a lot classier than Darcy."

"The main supervisor is Benton Woodley, isn't he?" Andrea asked him.

"Yeah," Glenn answered her. "Benton's a good guy. He can be tough, but he's fair. We talked to him right after we heard what happened to Darcy and he said not to worry about that bad write-up we got."

Donnie nodded. "Benton said that every write-up has to go through him, and he'd already thrown that one out."

"And that means we get our raise," Glenn said.

"Yeah, but I wish we'd known that right away. If we'd known that Benton was on our side, we never would have had to . . ." Donnie gave a little grunt and turned to look at Glenn. "Why did you kick me under the . . ." his voice trailed off and he swallowed hard. "Sorry," he said to Glenn, and then he clamped his mouth shut.

"Before what?" Hannah asked, honing in on the opening that Donnie had given her.

Glenn mumbled a word that Hannah would never have used in front of her nieces, and sighed loudly. "Cat's out of the bag, I guess. I'd better tell you before you think it's even worse than it is."

"Good idea," Hannah said, giving him an approving smile. "Tell us what happened, Glenn."

Glenn picked up his coffee cup and took a big swig, and Hannah had the suspicion that he wished it were something stronger. "Well . . . it was lunchtime on the last day of our shift and Donnie said I should get us something to eat and he'd run out to the car to get something he'd forgotten."

"And he caught me before I could put Darcy's hood down," Donnie said, looking very guilty. "It was just I was so mad, you know? I mean, I thought we'd lost our raise because of that witch and I wanted to get back at her somehow. I didn't think Glenn would go along with it, so I thought I'd do it myself. And then, if she asked him if he'd done it, he'd tell her that he didn't know anything about it."

Glenn went on with the confession. "But I caught him and I asked him what he thought he was doing. He told me it didn't make up for what she'd done, but he fixed her car so it wouldn't start when she came out of the supervisors' meeting after her shift."

"I was just so mad, I had to do something," Donnie said. "And . . . well . . . it was something."

Glenn gave a little laugh. "Donnie could never get a job as a mechanic. If I hadn't helped him, he would have flunked auto shop in high school."

Donnie grinned, his good humor restored. "He's right. All Darcy would've had to do was lift the hood and she could have seen what was wrong right away."

"What was wrong?" Hannah asked him.

"I unhooked her battery cables so her car wouldn't start," Donnie admitted. "I just wanted to bug her, you know?"

Hannah turned to Glenn. "Did you or Donnie hook the battery cables up again?"

Glenn shook his head. "Donnie was so proud of himself, I didn't want to spoil his fun. But I pointed out a way of making sure that even if Darcy or anyone else hooked up those cables again, her car still wouldn't start."

"What did you do?" Andrea asked him.

"I took a fuel pump fuse out of the fuse box." Glenn looked very proud of himself. "And with that fuse missing, Darcy's car wouldn't start even if she had the smarts to hook the battery back up."

"That sounds pretty sophisticated," Hannah commented. "Did you just pick a fuse at random? Or did you know which one to remove?"

Glenn gave a little smile. "I knew which one. My dad had this SUV, just like Darcy's, and I learned how to fix it when something went wrong. I kept it running my whole senior year. And that meant he let me borrow it anytime I wanted."

Andrea gave him an admiring look. "You must have passed your auto repair class with flying colors."

"Oh, I did. I got an A."

"The only one he ever got," Donnie told them. "Glenn was really proud of that A."

Now that the mystery of Darcy's car was solved, it was time to get down to some hard questions. Hannah took a deep breath and asked the first one that popped into her head. "Where were you guys the night that Darcy was murdered?"

"We had dates with two girls from Holdingford," Donnie said immediately. "It turned out pretty good."

Glenn smiled. "Sure did. We ended up going back to their place and . . . well . . . you don't really need to know any more than that, do you?"

Hannah shook her head. "Nothing except what time you got home that night?"

"It wasn't night," Donnie told them. "We got home just in time to change clothes and go to work."

"And we weren't late," Glenn added, and then he started to frown. "You don't think that we . . . I mean . . . we wouldn't have done anything to *really* hurt Darcy! We didn't hate her *that* much!"

"I'm sure you didn't." Hannah hurried to reassure them. "Have another cookie, both of you, and I'll tell you the real reason I'm here."

"You don't have to ask me twice," Glenn said, reaching into the bag. "You gotta try these, Donnie. They're peanut butter."

"Sounds good," Donnie said, getting a cookie for himself. He took a bite, began to smile, and then looked up at Hannah again. "You said you'd tell us the real reason you're here. What is it?"

"You worked with Darcy," Hannah told them. "And so did everybody else on your shift. You two strike me as being pretty good judges of people."

Glenn looked pleased at the compliment. "Yeah, we're pretty good at figuring people out."

"That's why I needed to see you. Can you think of anyone who worked here who might have hated Darcy enough to kill her?"

Hannah and Andrea were silent as the two men thought about Hannah's question. Finally, Glenn gave a big sigh. "A lot of people got irritated with her, especially when she was being a bit . . ." he stopped to search for another word, ". . . especially when she was being a pain in the neck. But I don't think any of them would actually hurt her." He turned to Donnie. "How about you? Can you think of anybody?"

Donnie thought about that for a minute, and then he shook his head. "A lot of people didn't like her, but nobody would have done something like that!"

"Did Darcy ever get anyone fired?" Andrea asked them.

"Yeah! There was one guy that got fired right after we started here, but Donnie and I ran into him a while ago. He told us that getting fired was the best thing that ever happened to him 'cause he got a new job that paid a lot better."

"So you can't think of anyone that might have killed Darcy?" Hannah asked her final question.

"No," Glenn answered. "Not unless it was someone she used to . . . uh . . . date."

"Yeah, Darcy ran around a lot, if you get what I mean," Donnie followed up. "I guess I can understand somebody killing her if they were in love with her and she ditched them for somebody else."

"Do you know anyone like that?" Andrea asked.

Both men shook their heads. "Not really," Glenn told them. "Darcy played the field and I don't think anybody was ever dumb enough to fall in love with her."

A bell sounded and Glenn and Donnie got up. "Time to get back to work," Glenn said.

"Take the cookies," Hannah told them. "I've got more where those came from."

Both men were wearing big smiles as they walked away with the bag of cookies and when they had left, Hannah gestured to Andrea.

"Did you get what you needed?" Andrea asked as they exited the building and headed back to Hannah's cookie truck.

"I think so. At least I got two new suspects to add to my list."

"Two?" Andrea asked as she climbed into the passenger seat. "Who are they?"

"Benton and Danielle." Hannah turned the key, put her cookie truck in gear, and headed out of the parking lot.

"I can understand Benton, especially if Darcy was trying to pick him up. But why do you suspect Danielle?"

"Because Danielle has been dating Benton for quite a while now. And Glenn and Donnie mentioned notes that

Darcy had written to Benton. What if Danielle read one of those notes?"

Andrea looked shocked. "Do you really think Danielle would be jealous enough to kill Darcy?"

Hannah shrugged. "I don't know, but I'm going to go to see Danielle this afternoon to find out where she was on the night of Darcy's murder."

CHIPS OFF THE OLD BLOCK COOKIES

Preheat oven to 350°F., rack in the middle position.

The following recipe can be doubled if you wish. Do not, however, double the baking soda. Use one and a half teaspoons if you double the recipe.

1 cup softened, salted butter *(2 sticks, ½ pound, 8 ounces)*
2 cups white *(granulated)* sugar
3 Tablespoons molasses
2 teaspoons vanilla
1 teaspoon baking soda
2 beaten eggs *(just whip them up in a glass with a fork)*
2 cups crushed salted potato chips *(measure AFTER crushing) (I used regular thin unflavored Lay's potato chips)*
2 and ½ cups all-purpose flour *(pack it down in the cup when you measure it)*
1 cup peanut butter chips *(I used Reese's Peanut Butter Chips)*
1 cup white chocolate chips or vanilla baking chips *(I used Nestlé Vanilla Baking Chips)*

Hannah's 1st Note: 5 to 6 cups of whole potato chips will *crush down* into about 2 cups. Crush them by hand in a plastic bag, not with a food processor. If you use a food processor, they will crush too much and end up being too fine. If you crush them by hand, they will end up being the size of coarse gravel.

Mix the softened butter with the white sugar and the molasses. Beat them until the mixture is light and fluffy, and the molasses is completely mixed in.

Add the vanilla and baking soda. Mix them in thoroughly.

If you haven't already done so, break the eggs into a glass and whip them up with a fork.

Add the whipped eggs to your bowl and mix them in until everything is thoroughly incorporated.

If you haven't yet crushed your potato chips, place them in a closeable plastic bag. Seal the bag carefully. *(You don't want crushed potato chips scattered all over your kitchen counter.)*

Hannah's 2nd Note: If you crush the potato chips too much, you won't have the right texture or crunch in your cookies.

Place the sealed bag on a flat surface and crush the chips inside with your fingers. Don't stop until the pieces are the size of coarse gravel.

Measure out 2 cups of crushed potato chips and mix them into the dough in your bowl.

Add one cup of flour and mix it in.

Add the second cup of flour and mix thoroughly.

Add the final half-cup of flour and mix that in.

Measure out one cup of peanut butter chips and add them to your cookie dough. If you're using an electric mixer, mix them in at the slowest speed. You can also take the bowl out of the mixer and stir in the chips by hand.

Measure out one cup of white chocolate chips or vanilla baking chips. Stir those into your dough.

Cover your mixing bowl with a clean towel or a sheet of plastic wrap. Let your cookie dough sit on the counter while you prepare your cookie sheets.

Spray your cookie sheets with Pam or another nonstick cooking spray. Alternatively, you can line the cookie sheets with parchment paper.

Hannah's 3rd Note: If you use the parchment paper, leave a little extra paper at the top and the bottom. That way, when your cookies are baked, you can pull the paper, baked cookies and all, over onto a wire rack to cool.

Drop the cookie dough by rounded teaspoons onto your cookie sheets. You can fit 12 cookies on each standard-size sheet.

Hannah's 4th Note: Lisa and I use a 2-teaspoon cookie scoop at The Cookie Jar. It's faster than doing it with a spoon.

Bake your Chips Off The Old Block Cookies at 350°F. for 10 to 12 minutes or until they are nicely browned. *(Mine took 11 minutes.)*

Let the cookies cool for 2 minutes on the cookie sheet and then remove them with a metal spatula.

Transfer the warm baked cookies to a wire rack to finish cooling.

Yield: Approximately 5 dozen crunchy, salty, and sweet cookies. Kids love these cookies.

Hannah's 5th Note: Be sure to tell your cookie-eating guests that there are peanut butter chips in these cookies.

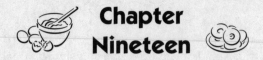

Chapter Nineteen

Hannah was sitting at the stainless steel work station in the kitchen of The Cookie Jar when there was a soft knock at the door. Since she didn't recognize the knock, she went to the door and looked through the peephole that Mike and Lonnie had installed. It only took one glance before she hurried to open the door.

"Lynne!" She greeted her guest with a smile. "Let me take your coat."

"Thanks, Hannah." Lynne shrugged out of her bright red parka and handed it to Hannah. "I'm so glad I finally found the right coat for this weather! It's freezing out there."

"I love your parka," Hannah said, admiring the lightweight garment as she hung it on a hook. "Did you buy it here?"

"No, your mother warned me that it would be cold when we got here, so I bought it in California. Do you have any idea how hard it is to find a parka in California?"

"Not really," Hannah said, motioning to a stool at the work station. "Sit down and I'll get you a cup of coffee."

"That would be great!" Lynne gave a little laugh. "I spent one whole afternoon shopping for that parka and I almost gave up when your mother suggested that I try a sporting goods store! Nobody in California needs a parka unless they go to a ski resort."

Hannah began to smile. "You're right, of course. California weather never really gets cold enough for parkas."

"I'm really glad your mother and Doc Knight have their climate-controlled garden. That's where we are having tea with Stephanie Bascom this afternoon. That's another reason I dropped by to see you. Your mother wondered if you could bake something for our tea."

"What does Mother want to serve?"

"Oh." Lynne giggled. "What does Stephanie like with her champagne glass of *tea*?"

"Any kind of appetizer will do just fine. Why don't I prepare a plate of cookies? That's good with champagne."

"Great!" Lynne began to smile. "I really love your cookies."

"Perfect. I'll have it ready to go at two-thirty for you. Did you get a rental car from Cyril this morning?"

"I did better than that. I bought a Land Rover, and I love it! I drove it out to KCOW-TV this morning and Chuck Wilson complimented me on my choice."

"What did you think of Chuck?"

"He's okay. He looks in the mirror a little too much for me, but a lot of people I've worked with are like that. He seems like a nice guy, though. And he promised to help me through my first couple of weeks on-air."

"First couple of weeks on-air?" Hannah set down her

coffee mug and stared at Lynne in confusion. "What do you mean?"

A happy smile crossed Lynne's face. "I got a job, Hannah! They gave me a tryout and they hired me to anchor the KCOW News with Chuck. We're going to be co-anchors."

"How about Dee-Dee Hughes? Did she get fired?"

Lynne shook her head. "No, she's moving. Chuck told me that she met some high-powered lawyer at a conference in Minneapolis, got engaged a couple of weeks later, and married him two weeks ago. She's moving to New York with him next week, and she told Chuck that her new husband doesn't want her to work. She didn't even bother to give notice. She just told everyone at the station that she was leaving and that was that."

Hannah was shocked. "You mean . . . she just quit with no notice or anything? And she left the rest of the news team in the lurch?"

"That's right. Believe me, Chuck wasn't happy about that! He told me he's been anchoring the news by himself for a week now while the producer looks for a replacement."

Hannah began to smile. "And you're Dee-Dee's replacement. Good for you, Lynne!"

"I'm really happy about it. The hours are fine and now that I have good transportation, I'm starting on Monday."

"That's wonderful!" Hannah was pleased for her friend. "You're really something, Lynne. You've been here less than twenty-four hours and you already have a place to live, a car, and a new career."

Lynne took a sip of her coffee and began to smile. "You're right. The only thing I'm missing is a cookie."

"Oh, no!" Hannah was thoroughly chagrined. "I'm sorry, Lynne. I was going to fill a plate with cookies and I got so excited for you, I forgot."

"That's okay. I was just teasing. But I really would like a cookie. What fantastic cookies do you have to celebrate my new job?"

"I know just the thing!" Hannah jumped up and headed for the baker's rack. "I just made these Snowflake and Ice Cookies. I haven't even tried them yet."

"Then we'll try them together," Lynne said, as Hannah filled a plate with her newest cookie.

"Not without me, you won't," Norman said, coming in from the coffee shop, just in time to hear Lynne's comment. "Those sound like interesting cookies."

"I'll get Norman a cup of coffee," Lynne offered, "and we will all try them."

Once Hannah set the cookie plate in front of them and they'd all tasted them and pronounced them excellent, Norman turned to Hannah.

"Lonnie's coming in with the cartons of things from your bedroom at the condo," he told her. "Do you want me to text him and tell him to take them to your mother's place?"

Hannah thought about that for a moment, and then she shook her head. "I don't want to store them there. I think it would be better if I got a storage unit. That way I could go through the boxes whenever I had any free time and decide which things I wanted to keep."

"I have some room in my garage," Norman offered.

Again, Hannah shook her head. "You're already storing all Ross's old film and video equipment. I'd rather take my things to that storage place out by the community college."

"Whatever you want," Norman agreed. "I've got a trailer hitch on my car and we can take them out there whenever you like."

Hannah glanced at the clock on the kitchen wall. "I can go at noon if that's okay with you. I've got Lisa, Aunt Nancy, Marge, and Andrea handling the coffee shop for the noon rush."

"That's fine with me," Norman agreed. "I'll give Lonnie a call and see if that's okay with him."

Norman got up and moved away so that they could talk while he called Lonnie.

"Norman's so considerate," Lynne commented.

"Yes, he is. That's one of the things I like best about him. Norman's a real gentleman and he always considers other people's feelings."

"Yes, especially yours. I've noticed that."

Lynne looked a bit concerned and Hannah wasn't sure why. "You look a little worried," she said. "Tell me why."

"Well . . . I really should offer to help you and Norman unload your things, but I arranged to meet your mother for lunch at Red Velvet Lounge at noon. If you need me, I can call and cancel."

"All set with Lonnie," Norman said, coming back to the work station just in time to hear Lynne's comment. "You don't have to cancel, Lynne. Lonnie told me that there's not that much, and Hannah and I can handle it."

"Whatever you say," Lynne said, and Hannah noticed that she looked relieved.

"Are you prepping for your tea with Stephanie Bascomb?" Hannah guessed.

"Actually, yes. When I told your mother that I was willing to pay rent if Stephanie would let me into the condo early, your mother told me not to offer that. And then she suggested that we ply Stephanie with . . ." Lynne stopped in mid-sentence and glanced at Norman.

"It's okay, Lynne," Norman reassured her. "Hannah told me about the type of *tea* that Delores serves when Stephanie Bascomb comes for a visit."

"Oh, good!" Lynne said, sounding very relieved. "I didn't want to give any secrets away." She turned to Hannah. "I'll run over to Granny's Attic to meet your mother, then. There might be something I can do to help her in the store before lunch."

"I'll walk you out," Noman offered, standing up so that he could help her into her parka and open the back door for her. When he came back, he sat down again and smiled at Hannah. "I told Lynne that if Stephanie wouldn't let her move in early, she was welcome to stay at my place. That's all right with you, isn't it?"

"It's fine with me."

"I thought so, but I really should have asked you first. My apologies, Hannah."

"No need for . . ." Hannah stopped speaking when she heard another knock on the back kitchen door.

"Mike?" Norman asked her.

"Yes, I'd recognize his knock anywhere."

Norman laughed. "Me too, now that you taught me to listen for it. Mike still does the *Let me in or I'll break the door down!* type of knock. If you get coffee for him, I'll go let him in."

"Deal," Hannah said, heading for the kitchen coffee-pot as Norman went in the opposite direction.

"Hi, Mike," Hannah heard Norman say as she poured a mug of coffee. When she turned around to carry the coffee back to the work station, Mike had already hung up his parka and was sitting on a stool.

"Hello, Mike," she greeted him. "Would you like to taste my new cookies? They're called Snowflake and Ice Cookies."

"Sure," Mike agreed immediately. "I'm always up for tasting new cookies."

Hannah went to the bakers rack, filled a plate with Snowflake and Ice Cookies, and brought them back to Mike. "Here you go," she said.

Mike grabbed a cookie and tasted it. "Good!" he said, swallowing hastily. Then he finished his first cookie, took a second, and asked, "Did you find out who disabled Darcy's car?"

Hannah came close to laughing. She should have known that Mike would ask her about her trip to DelRay this morning. "Yes, but they have alibis for Darcy's murder," she answered.

"Too bad," Mike said with a sigh. "Did you learn anything else?"

"Yes, Darcy flirted with Benton. She used to pass him notes when he came by to check the line."

"You're going to check into that, aren't you?" Mike asked.

"Of course I am, right after I go out to rent a storage locker for the things Michelle and Lonnie packed up from my bedroom."

"When are you going to do that?"

"At noon," Norman told him.

"Okay. I'll help you unload, it'll go faster that way." Mike plucked another cookie from the tray and took a bite. "I'm meeting someone out at the Corner Tavern for lunch today, but that isn't until one-thirty. That's pretty late for me. I'm practically starving."

Hannah knew she didn't dare glance at Norman or

she'd burst into laughter. Mike had just eaten four cookies and he was starving?

"I'm eating too much," Mike said, looking slightly guilty. "I think it's because I'm so frustrated with this situation with Lonnie. It's practically killing me that I can't help him. But if I start to investigate, it'll taint the whole murder case and nothing I discover can be used."

"I know," Hannah said, reaching out to pat Mike's hand.

Mike sighed and turned to Norman. "That's what happened when my wife was murdered. I was working for the Minneapolis Police Department at the time and I just couldn't leave it alone."

"I can understand that," Norman said. "You wanted to do something to help."

"Yeah, and I messed it up." Mike swallowed hard and took a deep breath. "Water over the dam, but it still gets to me. If I'd stayed hands off, we could have locked that little . . ." Mike stopped talking and blinked several times. "He was scum of the earth," he concluded.

All three of them were silent for a moment. Neither Hannah nor Norman knew exactly what to say to comfort Mike, and it was apparent to both of them that he was still grieving over his wife.

"All we can do is do our best," Norman said, reaching deeply into his bag of platitudes and squeezing Mike's shoulder. "I know that's what you thought you were doing. But this time, in Lonnie's case, you're restraining yourself. That's really hard to do. I know that. I spent a couple of years regretting my reaction when bad things happened to someone I cared for."

Mike gave a little smile. "I know. I checked into your background when you first started dating Hannah. Actually . . . if I'd been in your position, I might have done the same thing you did."

"And I probably would have reacted exactly the way that you did," Norman said.

This whole male-bonding thing between Norman and Mike was getting a bit too serious for Hannah and she rose from her stool. "I'm going to go tell Lisa that we'll be leaving at noon. You guys know where the cookies are if you want more."

On her way through the swinging door to the coffee shop, Hannah found she had mixed reactions. Her two former boyfriends were bonding and she supposed that was good. They were friends, she knew that. Did the fact that they were becoming even closer friends make her relationship with both of them even more of a triangle?

"Are you okay?" Lisa asked, noticing that Hannah was standing just inside the coffee shop, deep in thought.

"Oh! Yes, I'm fine. Do you have enough help for lunchtime? I have something I'd like to do, but I won't leave if it's a problem."

"No problem," Lisa said quickly. "Andrea just ran over to Al's office to drop off some paperwork, and then she's coming right back. Marge will be here in a minute for the noon rush, so I'll have plenty of help. Just go do whatever you need, Hannah. And, as a matter of fact, you don't have to come back in at all today. Everybody wants to free you up so you can find out who murdered Darcy."

Hannah began to smile. "I don't know what I'd do without you, Lisa."

"Well, you won't have to find out. Now, go and do whatever you have to do and don't worry about us."

Hannah reached out to pat Lisa's shoulder. "Thanks.

When Andrea comes in, would you ask her to stay until I get back? I should be back here by one at the latest."

"No problem."

"Tell her that I need her to help me with another interview this afternoon if she's free."

"Oh, I'm sure she'll be free. Andrea's so happy you're letting her help with this case. I . . . maybe I shouldn't say this, but I think she was feeling a little left out lately."

Hannah was taken entirely by surprise. "She was?"

"I think so. She used to help you with murder cases and lately you haven't needed her. She loves to help you, Hannah."

"That's good to hear, but . . . Andrea's really busy with her real estate business and her family. I didn't think I was right to take too much of her time away from those things."

"Andrea's like you. She doesn't know what to do with downtime. She told me once that she feels best when she stays busy."

"That's good to know. Well, I can certainly use her to help me this time. It's a hard case, Lisa."

"So you have a lot of suspects?"

"I have enough, but more crop up every time I talk to someone. It's complicated because Darcy was . . . well . . . there are quite a few people who didn't like her all that much."

"I know. Darcy wasn't in my class in high school, but I remember her. One of my sisters absolutely hated her because Darcy stole her boyfriend." Lisa read Hannah's *aha!* expression and gave a little laugh. "Forget it, Hannah. She was in Chicago the day Darcy was murdered and now she's on vacation with her husband in the Bahamas. There's no way she could have come back here and killed Darcy."

"That's good. There's no need for me to put her on my suspect list, then."

"That's right, but all of us here are keeping our ears open for any productive leads. If we're lucky, the invisible waitress trick will work in our favor again."

"Fingers crossed," Hannah said, turning to head back to the kitchen. "Thanks, Lisa. I'll check in with you when I get back."

SNOWFLAKE AND ICE COOKIES

Preheat oven to 375°F., rack in the middle position.

2 cups white *(granulated)* sugar

1 cup salted butter, softened to room temperature *(2 sticks, 8 ounces, 1/2 pound)*

3 large eggs, beaten *(just whip it up in a
glass with a fork)*

1 teaspoon baking powder

1 teaspoon baking soda

1/2 teaspoon salt

1/2 teaspoon ground cinnamon

1/2 teaspoon ground nutmeg *(freshly ground
is best of course)*

1/4 teaspoon ground cardamom *(if you don't
have it, substitute cinnamon)*

1 teaspoon vanilla extract

1/2 teaspoon coconut extract

1/2 cup milk

1/2 cup flaked coconut

2 cups rolled oats *(uncooked dry oatmeal—
use the old-fashioned kind that takes
5 minutes to cook, not the quick 1-minute
variety)*

2 cups all-purpose flour *(pack it down in the
cup when you measure it)*

1 cup white chocolate or vanilla baking chips
(I used Nestlé vanilla baking chips)

To Decorate:

¼ to ½ cup powdered *(confectioners)* sugar

Place the white sugar in the bowl of an electric mixer.

Place the softened butter on top of the sugar and mix at LOW speed for one minute or until the ingredients are blended.

Turn the mixer to MEDIUM speed and add the eggs. Continue to mix until the butter, sugar, and eggs form a light and fluffy mixture.

Turn the mixer down to LOW speed again and add the baking powder, baking soda, and salt. Beat until they are combined.

With the mixer still running on LOW speed, add the cinnamon, nutmeg, and cardamom. Mix until they are thoroughly combined.

Don't turn off the mixer and add the vanilla extract and the coconut extract. Mix well.

Then, with the mixer still on LOW speed, drizzle in the half-cup of milk.

Shut off the mixer and measure out a half-cup of flaked coconut. With the mixer OFF, add it to your bowl. Then turn the mixer back to LOW speed and mix in the coconut.

Leave the mixer running on LOW speed, and add the rolled oats. Mix them in thoroughly. Turn off the mixer.

It's time to add the flour. Measure out 2 cups of all-purpose flour, packing it down in the measuring cup. Place the flour you measure in a small bowl so that you won't have to keep count when you add it to the cookie dough mixture.

Turn the mixer on LOW again and add the flour in half-cup increments, beating for at least 30 seconds after each addition.

Hannah's 1st Note: You don't have to obsess about adding precisely half-cup increments of flour. Just eyeball it and be assured that the flour police will not be knocking on your door if you're a little under half-cup or a little over half-cup.

When the flour has been thoroughly incorporated, shut off your mixer, scrape down the insides of the bowl, and take the bowl out of the mixer.

Set the bowl on your counter and use a wooden spoon to give the cookie dough another stir by hand.

Measure out a cup of white chocolate chips and add them to your mixing bowl. Stir them in with the wooden spoon and once they're evenly distributed, prepare your cookie sheets for baking.

Prepare your cookie sheets by spraying them with Pam or another nonstick cooking spray. Alternatively, you can line the cookie sheets with parchment paper and spray that. I recommend using the parchment paper. These cookies tend to stick to the pan.

Drop your cookie dough by rounded teaspoonfuls onto your cookie sheet, no more than 12 cookies to a single sheet.

Hannah's 2nd Note: We use a 2-teaspoon disher when we make these cookies at The Cookie Jar.

Hannah's 3rd Note: You do not need to flatten these cookies. They will spread out all by themselves as they bake.

Bake your cookies at 375°F. for 12 to 15 minutes or until the tops are golden brown. My cookies were done in 12 minutes. Once they start to brown they do so rapidly. I usually set my timer for 10 minutes and watch them carefully for the last couple of minutes.

Remove your cookies from the oven and let them cool on wire racks or a cold stovetop burner for two minutes, then remove them from the cookie sheets and let them cool completely.

To decorate, if you wish, sprinkle them with powdered sugar.

Yield: 5 to 6 dozen delicious cookies that everyone will like.

Hannah's 4th Note: I've never met anyone who could eat only one of these cookies!

Chapter Twenty

Hannah could hear a bell tinkle as she walked into the Superior Storage office with Norman and Mike. Almost immediately, a woman emerged from the back room and hurried to the front counter.

"Welcome to Superior Storage," she said, smiling at them. "How can I help you today?"

"I'd like to rent a small storage unit," Hannah told her.

"I'll be glad to help you with that," the woman said. "My name is Cheryl and I'm the manager. Do you have photo identification that you can provide for me?"

"Yes, I do." Hannah took out her driver's license and handed it to Cheryl.

"Perfect, Miss Swensen. If you'll just wait a moment, I'll tell you what we have available."

Hannah watched while the manager clicked some keys on a computer keyboard, gave a little nod, and looked up. "I have one inside unit in the next building. And I have another outside unit next to the back wall."

"I'd like to rent the unit that's closest to the office," Hannah told her.

"That's a good choice." The manager smiled at her. "There are cameras inside the buildings and we're open twenty-four/seven. If you're nervous about coming here alone at night, you can come into the office and ask the person to keep an eye on you."

"And that's not the case with the outside units?" Mike asked her.

"No, even though this is a secure facility, that security only extends to the interior of the buildings. It hasn't happened, but it's possible that someone could be loitering outside, and the units by the back wall aren't lighted as well as the others. If you'd chosen the other unit I mentioned, I would have recommended that you bring someone with you if you came here after dark."

"That's wise," Mike said.

The manager smiled and began to enter Hannah's information on the computer. A few moments later, she looked up with a frown. "Are you sure you need a second unit, Miss Swensen? The unit you have doesn't have very much in it."

It was Hannah's turn to frown. "But . . . I don't have a storage unit here."

"Are you sure? I'm almost certain I saw your name on something in our three hundred building. Of course, I could be wrong, but please let me check." She clicked a few more keys and looked up with a triumphant smile. "Here it is! Didn't your fiancé tell you about the unit he rented in your name?"

Hannah looked at her blankly, and then she shook her head. "No . . . he . . . he didn't."

"Oh, dear! He told us he might have to leave on an urgent business trip and it must have slipped his mind. He came out here before we opened for business, arranged for a unit for you, and paid a year in advance."

Hannah was so shocked, she felt slightly dizzy. "No, he . . . he didn't tell me anything about it."

The manager sighed. "Well, I'm very glad you came out here today. You might never have known about it, and there are several things in that unit."

Suddenly the full ramifications of this storage unit occurred to Hannah and she opened her saddlebag-size purse. She pulled out her key ring and located the Superior Storage key she'd found in the safe deposit box that Ross had left for her.

"I think I understand," she said. "Are you talking about unit 312?"

The manager glanced down at her computer screen. "Yes, that's it," she said. "It's a medium-size unit, but he only had a few things for us to put in there."

"For *you* to put in there?" Mike asked, and Hannah noticed that he looked almost as surprised as she was.

"Yes. He came out here while we were still building and the units weren't ready for occupancy yet. It was too early for us to rent and I asked him if he could wait for a few weeks. He said he couldn't, that he had to leave any day on business and he wanted to get this taken care of before he left." The manager turned back to Hannah. "He said that all he wanted to store were several suitcases with papers and a few items that he might need you to come out and get to send to him."

"Then you rented to him, even though you didn't have any available units ready?" Norman asked her.

"It was all rather complicated. If I'd been here alone, I would have turned him down. After all, we do have rules about our rentals."

"But you weren't here alone?" Mike asked.

"No, the big boss was here for the day." She turned to Hannah again. "Your fiancé told us that he'd really appreciate it if we'd keep his suitcases secure until a unit was ready." The manager gave a little shrug and continued. "The big boss told him that if he rented the unit a year in advance, we would be happy to accommodate him."

"Were you comfortable with that?" Norman asked her.

"Not really, but there wasn't much I could do about it. When my boss said yes, I had to agree. The boss told me to keep everything in the office until the storage unit he'd rented became functional. And then I should move everything to unit 312 when it was ready."

"So that's what you did?" Hannah recovered enough to ask.

"Yes. Your fiancé filled out the necessary forms, brought his suitcases into the office, and that was that."

"Where did the key and padlock come from?" Mike asked her.

"When the big boss came to inspect the construction, he brought us some keys and padlocks from a facility that had closed. The building that was almost ready was the three-hundred building and so I gave your fiancé a key for unit 312."

"Are the suitcases in unit 312 now?" Mike asked her.

"Yes." The manager turned to Hannah. "I'll take you there and you can see how much room is left for your things. All I need is your signature since your name is the one that's listed."

Hannah took the form the woman pushed across the counter and signed on the dotted line. Her head was reeling from all this new information, but she managed to ask, "Can we go there now?"

"Certainly. I'll go with you to make sure your key fits." The woman came out from behind the counter and led the way out the door.

"This is nice," Norman commented as they walked past trees and landscaping. "Usually these places are fairly bare bones, aren't they?"

The woman laughed. "You're right. You should have seen the last place I worked. It was all asphalt, asphalt, and cinder block walls. There wasn't a tree or a bush in sight, and certainly not rose bushes like they planted at this one."

"You must be glad you left there and came here," Hannah commented.

"Oh, I am! Since we're just off-campus, I'm taking a couple of night classes at the community college. You can actually see the countryside here and the people are much friendlier. It's so much nicer than working in the industrial area of Detroit. When I look out the window here, I can see trees, and flowers, and grass. There, it was nothing but buildings."

Hannah was surprised that the manager liked the area so much in the winter. But Detroit had winter, too, and at least there were trees and birds here.

The manager opened the door to the three-hundred building and led them inside. She took them halfway down a corridor and stopped. "Here we are," she said, turning to Hannah. "Try your key and see if it fits."

Hannah took out her key and tried it in the padlock. It

slipped in easily and she turned it. Since everyone was silent, they all heard a click and the padlock snapped open.

The manager smiled. "All right, then. Just check everything out and let me know if you need any help unloading the items you want to store. If you do, I have two college students on call. They can help with lifting any boxes you have."

Once Hannah had thanked the manager and they were alone, she turned to Mike and Norman. "Ready?" she asked. "I don't know what Ross would have stored, but let's find out."

When both Norman and Mike nodded, Hannah pushed open the storage locker door and stepped inside. "The manager was right," she told them. "There's not much here."

"Nothing except those three suitcases," Mike said, spotting the stack in the storage locker. "Have you seen these suitcases before?"

Hannah shook her head. "I haven't. Ross must have bought them before he left. But I don't understand why he rented this locker for a year to store just these three suitcases. There was plenty of room in his closet at the condo."

"That's easy," Mike told her. "Ross didn't want you to see the suitcases and ask him what was inside."

"But why did he rent the storage for so long?" Norman asked.

"That's obvious, too," Mike answered. "He was planning to come back for the suitcases, but he didn't want anyone, including Hannah, to know they were here."

"And that's why he asked me for the key," Hannah

said, remembering what Ross had asked when he'd come back to Lake Eden before daybreak and confronted her at The Cookie Jar. "He wanted his money, but he also wanted the key to this storage locker."

"That makes sense," Norman said. "And that means there has to be something valuable inside those suit-cases."

Hannah's mind was spinning with unanswered ques-tions. "The only way to find out is to open them," she said reasonably, taking a step toward the stack of suit-cases.

"Wait!" Mike grabbed her arm and turned to Norman. "Do you have a clean handkerchief?"

"Sure." Norman reached into his pocket, pulled out a white handkerchief, and handed it to Mike. "Here you go."

"I need to open them, Hannah," he told her. "Do you have a problem with that?"

"Go ahead," Hannah said immediately. She assumed that Mike was attempting to preserve any fingerprints that might be on the suitcases, just in case there was something illegal inside.

"Stand back," Mike said, waving them away from the pile of suitcases. "Better yet, stand right outside the door."

Hannah and Norman exchanged glances as they moved toward the storage locker door. Hannah knew Norman had come to the same conclusion that she had. Mike was moving them away from the suitcases, just in case they contained any explosive devices.

"Okay. I'm going to open the first one," Mike said, using the handkerchief to push back the fasteners.

Hannah couldn't help it. She held her breath as Mike

prepared to lift the lid. It was eerily quiet in the corridor, almost as if the walls themselves were anticipating some kind of drastic result. She moved a bit closer to Norman, and he slipped his arm around her shoulders. Despite the comforting embrace, she could feel her legs begin to tremble.

"Oh, great! Not again!" Mike exclaimed, standing back so that they could see the contents of the first suitcase.

"Money," Hannah breathed the word. "*More* money!"

"Yes, but this is different," Mike said, motioning them back inside. "Nothing larger than twenties this time and they're mixed in with tens and fives."

"What do you think that means?" Norman asked him.

"Escape money. It's packed and ready to go. And no one will question the denominations. Hundreds would have been too risky to take with him. Someone might have questioned large bills and remembered more about him."

"I get it," Norman said quickly. "You can walk into a motel and pay with twenties. They're a common denomination. Paying for a room with hundreds might raise some eyebrows, especially if you get change back. Not that many people walk into a cheap hotel or motel and pay with hundreds."

"Exactly right," Mike said. He closed the first suitcase and set it aside on the floor. "Go back outside. It's time to check the next suitcase."

"But the first suitcase was okaȳ when you opened it," Hannah pointed out.

"True, but that doesn't mean the second one will be. Go out to the hallway, guys. I'm not going to open that suitcase with you two standing this close to me."

"Okay, if you insist," Norman agreed.

"I do. Now get out there and let me do it."

Mike sounded very definite and Hannah realized that it was pointless to argue with him. She gave a little nod and followed Norman out the door and into the hallway.

"He's just being really careful," Norman whispered.

"I know," Hannah responded in kind. "I guess we should probably be grateful he didn't call in the bomb squad."

"We don't have a bomb squad," Mike told them, startling them both. "And I wouldn't do this if I had any reason to suspect that there was anything explosive inside."

Hannah and Norman exchanged startled glances and Mike laughed. "I can hear you when you whisper. It's pretty empty in here and it's like a giant echo chamber."

"What would you do if you thought there were explosives?" Hannah asked him.

"I'd put in a call to the Minneapolis Police Department. They're big enough to have a bomb squad."

Norman and Hannah waited until Mike opened the second suitcase and beckoned them back inside.

Hannah stared down at the contents of the second suitcase. "Clothes?" she asked, looking up at Mike.

"Yes, all packed and ready to take with him. Do you recognize these things?"

Hannah shook her head. "I've never seen Ross wear shirts like this before," she said, pointing to several polo shirts in a variety of colors.

"But they don't look new," Norman noted. "And neither do those red and blue tennis shoes."

"He probably bought them and took them to the cleaners to wash," Mike speculated.

"But . . ." Hannah began to frown. "Ross never wore

polo shirts. And he told me once that he didn't like colored shoes. He said they were for kids. I never saw him wear anything but white tennis shoes."

"Ross packed these things to change his image," Mike explained. "That's clever. Most guys who are going on the run buy new clothes, but they don't generally think to change their style."

"Is that a Chicago Bears football jersey?" Hannah asked, moving closer to stare at the shirt.

"Looks like it," Mike agreed. "Was that Ross's favorite football team?"

"Ross didn't like football," Hannah told him. "He said that he'd never been big on sports, and the only thing he ever watched was college basketball."

"Looks like he had this all figured out," Mike said. "And since he changed his image, he was probably planning to use a fake name, too."

"Open the third suitcase, Mike," Hannah urged him. "I want to see what else he was planning to take with him."

Hannah and Norman stood outside while Mike opened the last suitcase. He gave a low whistle and they hurried back inside.

"I'd say he was definitely preparing to run," Mike commented, pointing to the array of ID cards, business cards, driver's licenses, and passports that were packed inside.

"Did he buy all those?" Norman asked, noticing that the driver's license on top had Ross's photo. "I know you can buy fake identification if you're willing to spend some money."

Mike picked up the license and glanced down at the name. "Rusty Bergen," he read aloud. "Ross could have bought this, but he also could have made it himself." He turned to Hannah. "He was a photography major in college, wasn't he?"

"Yes, still photography and video."

"And Ross had plenty of money when he was a student?"

"He was always treating us to dinner, or breakfast," Hannah said. "And he bought Lynne some beautiful jewelry."

"Then my guess is that forging fake identification cards paid for most of that. He didn't work, did he?"

"Not that I know of, but you can ask Lynne. She'd know." Hannah was silent for a moment, thinking about how drastically she'd misjudged the man she'd loved, and then she glanced at the ID card that Mike was holding. "Did Ross use his real name on that?"

"No."

"Which name did he use?" Norman asked.

"Roy Benson," Mike began to frown. "And that's unusual."

"Why?" Hannah asked him.

"Because one of the big mistakes that most criminals make is that they keep their initials."

"I think I know why he kept his initials," Hannah told them. "Ross really loved to change into his design sweat suits when he came home from work. They were made of velour, and he had a whole wardrobe of them. His initials were embroidered on the jackets in gold thread."

"So every jacket had the initials R.B. on the front?" Norman asked her.

"Yes, he told me he never went anywhere without them, and he even wore them to work sometimes."

"You could be right," Mike said, pulling the suitcase with the clothing over to him and going through the garments inside. He checked the stacks of shirts, pants, and jackets, and gave an affirmative nod. "He's got four colors of velour sweatshirts, pants, and jackets. And all of the jackets have R.B. embroidered on the front."

"Which other names did he use?" Norman asked.

Mike pulled the suitcase with the forged identification cards closer and picked up a stack of passports. "Ralph Black, Rudy Blaine, Roman Booker, Ronnie Barnes, and Robert Brown. There are some other names here with photos of other men."

"You mean they don't all have photos of Ross?" Hannah asked.

"No, and that makes me even more convinced that part of the money Ross made came from forging pieces of identification."

Hannah swallowed with difficulty. "That . . . that does make sense, I guess."

"I'm going to call Bill when we're through here, and have him pick up these suitcases. I want him to take them down to the station and put them in the evidence locker."

"But . . . why?" Hannah asked him.

"They could contain important evidence in several pending fraud cases. Do you mind if I do that, Hannah?"

"I . . . I . . . no, I don't mind," Hannah said, struggling to keep her equilibrium.

Norman reached out to take her arm. "I'm going to take you back to my car, Hannah. Just sit there for a while and try to relax. Mike and I will store your things in the locker."

"Right," Mike agreed immediately. "Drive Hannah

back to The Cookie Jar, Norman. Just drive the trailer down here and unhook it. When Bill gets here, we'll take care of the unloading, and we'll lock up the storage unit before we leave."

"But how about Lonnie's trailer?" Hannah asked.

"I've got a trailer hitch and I'll take the trailer back to Cyril's garage. That's where Lonnie got it. Just take care of Hannah, okay? It's been a rough day for her so far."

Chapter Twenty-one

"Thanks for asking me to come along, Hannah." Andrea was all smiles as they pulled up in front of Danielle Watson's dance studio.

"Thank you for coming with me," Hannah countered. "I need you on this one, Andrea. Danielle and I are friends, but you're much closer to her than I am."

"That might not be true after Danielle tastes your Pear and Apple Pie," Andrea said, but one glance at her sister's face told Hannah that Andrea was very pleased. "I just hope that Danielle will tell me if she can alibi Benton on the night that Darcy was killed."

"So do I!" Hannah picked up the pie she had baked and walked toward the door with Andrea. "This pie is heavy. Will you open the door for me?"

"No problem."

Andrea opened the door, and they both stepped in. Almost immediately, strains of music wafted down the staircase to meet them.

"Is that a waltz?" Andrea asked, starting to climb up the stairs to Danielle's dance studio.

Hannah listened for several seconds. "It sounds like it to me. I think it's the 'Anniversary Waltz.'"

"The only song that Dad would dance to?"

"That's right. Mother said the first time she danced with Dad was at his parents' silver wedding anniversary party. And they started dating right after that."

"Dad really didn't like to dance, did he."

It was a statement rather than a question and Hannah laughed. "He hated it. Mother said he was a pretty good dancer, but Dad was convinced that he had two left feet."

"Mother was wrong." Andrea said. "Dad danced with me once when I was learning how to waltz and he stepped on my toes."

As they climbed upward, the music increased in volume and Hannah could tell that the waltz was almost over. "Someone must be having an anniversary party," she commented.

"Right." Andrea reached the top of the stairs and entered the area Danielle had set aside for a waiting room. "Here we are," she said, taking a seat on one of the couches.

"Good," Hannah agreed, sitting down on the couch across from her sister and doing her best not to breathe heavily. If she was out of breath from climbing Danielle's staircase, perhaps it was time to consider that four-letter word she hated.

"I'm a little out of breath," Andrea confessed, breathing in deeply. "That's a really steep staircase."

"It certainly is!" Hannah responded, but her spirits lifted a notch. Andrea wasn't an ounce overweight and she kept herself in tip-top condition. It might not be time for a diet after all!

The two sisters didn't have long to wait. After less than five minutes, two older couples that Hannah didn't recognize came out of the interior. They smiled and nodded at Hannah and Andrea, walked through the waiting area, and left.

"Who were they?" Hannah asked, when she was sure that the couples were out of earshot.

"I don't know, and I thought I knew almost everyone around here." Andrea looked puzzled. "I'm almost certain I've never seen them before."

"You haven't," Danielle said, coming into the waiting room just in time to hear Andrea's comment. "They're the Landsdown twins and they're from Anoka."

"The men are twins?" Hannah guessed.

"Yes, and so are the women."

"You mean . . . two sets of twins married each other?"

"That's right. They met at a twins convention in Minneapolis and they just moved to Long Prairie. They're about to celebrate their wedding anniversaries and they wanted to learn how to dance for their joint anniversary party." Danielle stopped speaking and stared at the pie in Hannah's hands. "Something really smells great! What is it, Hannah?"

"Pear and Apple Pie. You know Charlie Jessup, don't you, Danielle?"

"Everybody knows Charlie and his sled dogs."

"Well, Charlie has a brother in California and his sister-in-law, Lyn Jessup, makes a really incredible pear crisp. Charlie brought me some the last time they flew out to visit. Lisa's Aunt Nancy tasted it and we came up with this recipe for Pear and Apple Pie. The crumble on top is almost the same as the one on Lyn's pear crisp."

"I love apple crisp!" Danielle said with a smile. "And I bet I'd like pear crisp, too. I can hardly wait to taste this pie, Hannah."

"Well, you won't have to wait for long." Hannah got up from the couch and handed the pie to Danielle. "Do you have a little time before your next class, Danielle?"

"Yes, fifteen minutes. Come in the back with me and I'll make you a cup of coffee."

Hannah and Andrea followed Danielle through the studio to the living quarters in the back. They waited at Danielle's small kitchen table while she made coffee for them.

"Shall I cut the pie for us?" she asked as she brought them cups of coffee.

Hannah shook her head. "Save it for tonight, so you can share it with Benton."

"Thanks. Benton's going to love it. He's always asking me when I'm going to learn to bake, but that's not going to happen anytime soon."

Once Danielle had seated herself at the table, she turned to Hannah with a smile. "I was wondering when you'd get around to interviewing me."

"You were?"

"Yes, I figured someone would tell you about Darcy and Benton, and I was prepared to call you tomorrow if they didn't."

"What about Benton and Darcy?" Andrea asked, leaning forward.

"You must have heard the gossip, Andrea." Danielle gave a little sigh. "Darcy was always trying to pick up on

Benton. She even left little notes in his pocket inviting him to come to her place."

"Did you see any of the notes?" Hannah asked her.

"I saw all of them. Benton showed them to me and we talked about what he could do to discourage Darcy without being mean."

"What did you decide?" Andrea asked her.

"We decided that nothing could discourage Darcy when she had her mind set on flirting with someone. We just . . ." Danielle stopped speaking and sighed again. "I kind of hate to say this, after what happened to Darcy, but it turned into a little joke between the two of us."

"But weren't you jealous?" Andrea asked. "I don't know how I'd feel if someone like Darcy came after Bill."

"If you were smart, you'd laugh about it. And that's exactly what we did. To tell the truth, I was a little jealous at first, until I was convinced that Benton wasn't interested in Darcy. You'd probably react the same way I did."

"Maybe," Andrea said, but Hannah noticed that her sister didn't seem all that convinced. "Did you ever confront Darcy? Tell her to back off?"

Danielle shook her head. "No, I thought that might make her think she was making inroads."

"But she wasn't?" Hannah asked.

"Of course not. Benton spends every night he can over here with me."

"How about the night that Darcy was killed?" Hannah couldn't help but ask.

"Yes, and I'm really glad he did!" Danielle looked very relieved. "We were together all evening. We took Del with us to dinner at the Lake Eden Inn. We had six o'clock reservations and we were there until eight. Then we drove Del back to his place, and Benton came home with me."

Andrea looked concerned. "Was Benton with you the entire night?"

"Yes. We had another glass of wine and watched a movie on television."

"Would you be willing to swear to that in a court of law?" Hannah asked her.

"Yes, I would," Danielle said quickly, "but I won't have to."

It was clear that Andrea was puzzled. "Why not?"

"Simple logic," Danielle said, beginning to smile. "It's because Hannah always catches the killer. And I know that Benton didn't do it."

A few moments later, Andrea and Hannah took their leave so that Danielle would have a few minutes to herself before her next dance class. They climbed down the staircase and Andrea turned back to Hannah as she opened the street door. "That's an awesome responsibility, Hannah."

Hannah was puzzled. "*What's* an awesome responsibility?"

"Danielle's counting on you to catch the killer to clear Benton, Lonnie's counting on you to do it to clear him, Michelle's counting on you to save Lonnie, Cyril's counting on you to save his son, Rick's counting on you to save his brother, Mike's counting on you to save his partner, and Bill's counting on you to solve the case because he can't use any of his detectives except the new guy."

Hannah gave a deep sigh. "You're right, Andrea. It *is* an awesome responsibility."

"What are you going to do if you can't find Darcy's killer?"

Hannah thought about that for a moment, and then she shrugged. "I think it's best if I put that possibility right out of my mind."

"How are you going to do that?"

"I'm just going to concentrate on doing what everyone expects of me and keep at it until I do."

PEAR AND APPLE PIE

Preheat oven to 350°F., rack in the middle position.

Hannah's Note: This pie was inspired by Lyn Jessup's Pear Crisp and Mom's Apple Pie.

The Crust:

One 8-inch or 9-inch frozen deep-dish piecrust *(I used Marie Callender's—you can also make your own if you wish)*

The Filling:

¾ cup white (granulated) sugar
¼ cup flour
¼ teaspoon ground nutmeg *(freshly ground is best, of course)*
½ teaspoon cinnamon *(if it's been sitting in your cupboard for years, buy fresh!)*
¼ teaspoon cardamom
¼ teaspoon salt
3 cups sliced, peeled apples *(I used a combination of Granny Smith and Fuji or Gala)*

3 cups sliced, pared pears *(I used fresh pears
   just barely ripe NOT overripe)*
1 teaspoon lemon juice
½ stick cold salted butter *(¼ cup, 2 ounces,
   ⅛ pound)*

If you use homemade piecrust, roll out enough
for a 9-inch round and place it in a pie pan.

If you are using a frozen piecrust, thaw it according to the package directions. Leave one right in its
pan.

To Make The Filling:

Mix the sugar, flour, spices, and salt together in a
small bowl.

Prepare the apples and pears by coring them,
peeling them, and slicing them into a large bowl.
When they're all done, toss them with the teaspoon
of lemon juice. *(Just sprinkle on the lemon juice
and use your impeccably clean fingers to toss the
apple and pear slices.)*

Dump the small bowl with the dry ingredients on
top of the apples and pears. Toss them to coat the
slices. *(Again, use your fingers.)*

Place the coated apple and pear slices in the pan with the piecrust. You can arrange them symmetrically if you like, or just dump them in as best you can. There will probably be some leftover dry ingredients at the bottom of the bowl. Just sprinkle it on top of the fruit slices in the pie pan.

Cut the cold butter into 4 pieces and then cut those pieces in half. Place the pieces on top of the apples just as if you were dotting the apples with butter.

Next, you will top your pie with a crumble very like the one that Lyn uses on her pear crisp.

Crumble Topping:

> 1 cup all-purpose flour, (*pack it down when you measure it*)
> ½ cup cold, salted butter (*4 ounces, ¼ pound*)
> ½ cup brown sugar (*pack it down in the cup when you measure it*)
> ½ teaspoon ground cinnamon

Put the flour into the bowl of a food processor with the steel blade attached. Cut the stick of butter

into 8 pieces and add them to the bowl. Cover with the ½ cup of firmly-packed brown sugar and sprinkle on the cinnamon.

Process with the steel blade in an on-and-off motion until the resulting mixture is in uniform small pieces.

Remove the mixture from the food processor and place it in a bowl.

Pat handfuls of the Crumble Topping in a mound over your pie. With a sharp knife, cut several slits near the top of the dome to let out the steam that develops when your pie bakes.

Choose a baking sheet with sides. Line the inside of the baking sheet, including the sides, with foil. *(This is in case any juice from the pie flows out of the top during baking and drips down onto the baking sheet.)*

Place your pie in the center of the baking sheet.

Bake your Pear and Apple Pie at 350°F. for 50 to 60 minutes or until the apples and pears are tender when pierced with the tip of a sharp knife and the Crumble Topping is golden brown.

To serve: This pie is yummy either warm, room temperature, or cold straight out of the refrigerator. If you serve it at room temperature or warm, it's wonderful topped with a scoop of vanilla or cinnamon ice cream. Make sure to accompany this pie with hot, strong coffee or tall glasses of milk.

Yield: 6 to 8 slices of delicious pie.

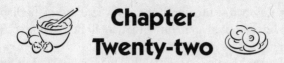

Chapter
Twenty-two

"Oh, good! You're back." Lisa greeted Hannah before she'd even had time to hang up her parka. "Kay Hollenkamp and her husband are out in the coffee shop and they say they really need to talk to you."

"Thanks, Lisa." Hannah hung her parka on a hook, poured three cups of coffee from the kitchen pot, and hurried to her favorite stool at the work station. "I'm ready. Please send them in."

"I'll get a plate of cookies for you." Lisa filled a plate with Strawberry and Vanilla Pinwheel Cookies and brought it over with the cream and sugar. "Aunt Nancy just made these. They're still a little warm."

Hannah reached out for a cookie, took a bite, and smiled in enjoyment. "They're wonderful!"

"I know. I had three. We took some out front, and I'll make sure that Andrea gets one. Are you ready to see the Hollenkamps?"

"I'm ready," Hannah said, remembering that Kay Hollenkamp was the waitress that Lonnie had told her about.

Since Kay had waited on Lonnie's whole group, perhaps she'd remembered something that could help the investigation into Darcy's murder.

"Hannah! Hello." An attractive woman walked in followed by an older man.

"Kay?" Hannah asked, wanting to be certain that this was Kay Hollenkamp.

"Yes, and this is my husband, Joe."

"Please sit down and have some coffee," Hannah offered, gesturing toward the empty stools at the work station. "You've been in before, Kay?"

"Many times," Kay admitted, glancing over at Joe. "But I hope Joe hasn't!"

It was a strange thing to say and Hannah was puzzled until Kay gave a laugh. "Joe's diabetic," she explained. "And he has to watch his sugar intake. Unfortunately, he loves all things sweet."

"I'm sorry," Hannah hurried to apologize. "Would you like me to remove the cookies?"

"I could have one, couldn't I, Kay?" Joe asked his wife. "I only had one piece of toast this morning."

"That's true," Kay responded, giving him a sweet smile. "I just don't want any repeats of the ice cream fiasco."

"Don't worry. I won't do *that* again," Joe promised. "It's just that I started thinking about ice cream and I lost all my willpower."

"I know, and I understand. I'm like that around Hannah's Salted Caramel Bar Cookies." Kay turned to Hannah. "I told Joe I needed to keep an eye on his sugar intake because I wanted us to celebrate our Golden Wedding Anniversary."

"Fat chance!" Joe retorted. "I'm already over fifty,

Kay. And not that many people live to celebrate their hundredth birthday."

"You will, if I have anything to say about it," Kay retorted, reaching out to pat his hand. "Have your cookie, Joe, and enjoy it. Because you're not going to have a second."

"I know." Joe gave a deep sigh and turned toward Hannah. "I don't know if I should love her for wanting to keep me healthy, or hate her for depriving me of almost all the foods I really like?"

"You should love me. And I know you do." Kay smiled at him fondly before she turned to Hannah. "Let me give you a little background while Joe's enjoying his treat. I work out at the Double Eagle as a cocktail waitress, and Joe usually takes me to work, sits there, listens to the music, and nurses a beer all night. Then we go home together."

"Unless she's on cleanup duty," Joe interjected. "Then both of us drive. It's a good job where Kay's tips are concerned, but it's not a very upscale place. I'd worry about her if she went there alone five days a week."

Kay smiled. "Joe's very protective. I do appreciate that. There are times when we get some rowdy customers at the Double Eagle."

"Like every weekend," Joe added.

"True." Kay gave a little nod. "Anyway . . . I waited on Darcy the night that she was killed."

"Tell me about it," Hannah urged.

"Well, she wasn't drinking all that much, but I think she must have taken some kind of drug, because by the end of the evening, she wasn't making much sense. And she had a huge fight with her fiancé. He got so mad, he left, and that's when Lonnie, Brian, and Cassie stepped in."

"That's right," Joe confirmed. "I was sitting at the bar and I saw the whole thing. Darcy and Denny were fighting like cats and dogs. I was afraid the fight would turn violent, and I was almost ready to go over there myself, when Denny stood up and left the table."

"He came up to me and asked for the check," Kay said. "Then he gave me some money, I got his change, and he stomped out of there. Unfortunately, Darcy had ridden with him that night."

"So Darcy was left with no ride home," Joe added.

"I was really glad when Lonnie told me that he was going to give Darcy a ride," Kay continued. "Brian gave her a ride a couple of times when he and Cassie were separated, but it might have caused a problem if he'd done it that night, being Cassie's birthday and all. And I was afraid that Darcy might leave with one of the other guys she'd dated. And a couple of them were . . . well . . ." Kay stopped and looked to Joe for assistance.

"She dated some guys who weren't exactly reputable," Joe said.

"You put it a lot nicer than I would have," Kay said with a smile. "Darcy wasn't known for her wonderful choices in male companions."

"Nice!" Joe said, complimenting her. "That was very descriptive, honey."

"Thank you. Anyway, once Lonnie stepped in, I knew that Darcy would get home safely. That was a relief. I knew Joe would have taken her home if I'd asked him to, but she wasn't walking very well and I didn't want Joe to have to carry her into her house. He slipped on the ice when he was ice fishing and he tore something in his arm."

"It was a ligament," Joe told Hannah. "It's healing, but

Doc Knight told me not to do any heavy lifting or stretching until it heals."

"That's right." Kay gave a nod. "Joe left right after we closed, and another waitress and I did the cleanup. It usually takes us an hour to an hour and a half to get everything done, so Joe left for home."

"Except I didn't go straight home," Joe explained. "I knew we were out of bacon and I like bacon and eggs for breakfast, so I drove out to the Quick Stop to buy what we needed."

"And while he was there, Joe bought something we definitely *didn't* need."

"Right." Joe gave a guilty sigh. "I was all set to check out at the register when I happened to notice they'd gotten in some Banana Blizzard ice cream. I'm crazy about Banana Blizzard ice cream and the Quick Stop doesn't carry it very often, but there it was in all its glory." He turned to Kay. "I had to buy it, Kay. It was practically screaming out my name."

Kay laughed. "I know. But Joe . . . *two* cartons?"

"I know. I guess I'm just lucky they didn't have three." Joe turned back to Hannah. "I got a spoon, too, a really nice, big measuring spoon. I didn't want to take the ice cream home because Kay might find the empty cartons, so I parked about a mile from our house and ate it in the car."

"All of it," Kay added. "Both cartons in one sitting."

"True. And it was *soooo* good!" Joe gave a sigh that sounded rapturous.

"And you were *soooo* sick later," Kay added.

"I know. Anyway . . . I sat there and ate that ice cream and stopped to put the cartons in the dumpster outside Darcy's house."

"Her house is a mile from us," Kay explained. "Since Darcy's driveway is past the town limit for garbage pickup, Darcy's father bought a dumpster and left it at the side of the road so the garbage men would pick it up there."

"When I got out of the car, I noticed another car parked in front of Darcy's garage," Joe went on. "I knew it wasn't her fiancé's car. Denny drove a dark blue Lincoln and this car was a really strange color."

"What color was it?" Hannah asked, beginning to see why Kay and Joe had come to tell her about this.

"It was a pinkish-orange, almost the same color as Kay used when she painted our kitchen. The car was a little lighter than that, but not a whole lot."

"They call that color melon," Kay told Hannah. "The man at the paint store said it was a cross between cantaloupe and watermelon."

"I've never seen a car that color before," Hannah said, frowning slightly.

"Neither have I," Joe agreed. "But just in case you're wondering, I only had one beer at the Double Eagle and I know what I saw. And right before I climbed back in the car, the front door of the house opened and someone came out."

"Could you see who it was?" Hannah asked him.

"No, I was too far away and some tree branches were in the way. But I didn't want whoever it was to think I was dumping trash in Darcy's dumpster, so I drove off before the other person could see me."

STRAWBERRY AND VANILLA
PINWHEEL COOKIES

DO NOT preheat oven. Cookie dough must chill before baking.

   1 cup white *(granulated)* sugar
   1 cup *(2 sticks, 8 ounces, ½ pound)* salted
      butter, softened
   1 large egg
   ½ teaspoon salt
   ½ teaspoon baking powder
   ½ teaspoon vanilla extract
   2 and ½ cups all-purpose flour *(scoop it up
      and level it off with a table knife—don't
      pack it down in the cup)*

   ———

   3 Tablespoons strawberry jam
   1 teaspoon strawberry extract
   1 teaspoon red food coloring
   ⅛ cup *(2 Tablespoons)* all-purpose flour
      *(that's in addition to the flour you used
      earlier)*

   ———

Confectioners' *(powdered)* sugar for rolling
out the dough

**Hannah's 1ˢᵗ Note: This recipe calls for liquid
food coloring. If you use gel food coloring, you
won't need as much because the color is much
more concentrated. Just watch the color of the
dough when you mix it and stop adding when
you think it's bright enough.**

**Hannah's 2ⁿᵈ Note: Mixing this dough is easy
with an electric mixer, but you can also do it by
hand.**

Place the sugar in a large mixing bowl.

Add the softened butter and mix until it's light
and fluffy.

Add the egg and beat until the resulting mixture
is a uniform color.

Sprinkle in the salt and the baking powder. Mix
until they're thoroughly incorporated.

Add the vanilla extract. Mix it in thoroughly.

Add the flour by half-cup increments, mixing
after each addition. Continue to beat for another min-

ute after the last half-cup of flour has been added and mixed in.

Scrape down the sides of the mixing bowl, take it out of the mixer, and set it on your kitchen counter.

Give the dough a final stir by hand with a mixing spoon.

Tear off a sheet of wax paper that's about 2 feet long.

Wet a kitchen sponge and wring it out in the sink.

Use the sponge to moisten the spot you've chosen to roll out your cookie dough.

Quickly spread out the wax paper, curled side down so it straightens out, on top of the moist spot on the counter.

Tear off another sheet of wax paper of the same size.

Moisten a strip about 2 inches into the bottom *(or top)* edge of the wax paper already on the counter.

You will need to use a second sheet of wax paper and overlap it on top of the first sheet.

Moisten the area of the bare counter where you want to place the second sheet.

Spread out the second sheet, curved side down, on your counter.

Hannah's 3rd Note: The reason for moistening the counter is to keep the wax paper from sliding around as your roll out your cookie dough. If you have a bread board in your kitchen, you can skip all the instructions for moistening the counter and using the wax paper. Simply get out your bread board and place it on the counter.

Dust the wax paper *(or the bread board)* with powdered sugar and spread it out evenly with the palm of your incredibly clean hand.

Remove HALF of the cookie dough from your mixing bowl and place it on the wax paper. *(Just guestimate half. No one will complain if it's not precisely half.)*

Form the cookie dough into a ball and then pat it out like piecrust with your hands.

Dust the top of your flattened cookie dough with more powdered sugar and spread it out with your hands.

With a rolling pin, roll the dough into a rectangle that is approximately ¼-inch thick.

Cover the vanilla cookie dough with wax paper.

Roll the dough up into a loose roll.

Place the loose roll in a Ziploc plastic bag, seal it, and put it in your refrigerator.

You're through with the vanilla part of your cookie dough for the present. Now it's time to mix up and roll out the strawberry part of your cookie dough.

Place approximately 3 Tablespoons of strawberry jam in a microwave-safe bowl. *(You don't have to be exact at this point.)*

Leave the jam jar on the counter.

Heat the bowl of jam on HIGH for 10 seconds.

Check the bowl with the jam. If there's 1 Tablespoon of liquid, you have enough. If there's not, add more jam to your bowl and melt that for 10 sec-

onds in the microwave. *(The object is to get 1 full Tablespoon of jam liquid.)*

Once the melted jam has produced 1 full Tablespoon of jam liquid, add it to the vanilla dough in your mixer bowl, put it back in the mixer, and turn the mixer on LOW speed.

There will be some solid parts of the jam left in the small bowl you used. Add them to the jar of strawberry jam, stir them in, put the lid on the jar, and put it in the refrigerator.

With the mixer running on LOW speed, add the strawberry extract to the bowl. Mix it in thoroughly.

Again, with the mixer still running on LOW, add the red food coloring to your bowl. Mix that in thoroughly.

Add the $\frac{1}{8}$ cup of all-purpose flour and mix that in.

Once the dough is thoroughly mixed, shut off the mixer, scrape down the sides of the bowl, and take it out of the mixer.

Give the strawberry dough a final stir by hand with a mixing spoon.

Repeat the instructions for preparing the counter for rolling out the dough.

Remove the strawberry cookie dough from the mixing bowl and form it into a ball.

Pat the dough ball down like piecrust, dust it with powdered sugar, and use the rolling pin to roll out another rectangle that is approximately ¼ inch thick.

Cover the strawberry dough with wax paper.

Roll the strawberry cookie dough into a loose roll, place the roll in a Ziploc plastic bag, seal the bag, and put it in the refrigerator next to the vanilla dough roll.

Chill both halves of your pinwheel cookie dough for at least 2 hours.

After your cookie dough has chilled for 2 hours, tear off another sheet of wax paper and spread it out on the counter. If you're using a bread board, spread the wax paper out on the bread board. You will use this piece of wax paper to wrap up your pinwheel dough roll once the vanilla and strawberry cookie dough are combined.

Dust the wax paper *(or the bread board)* with powdered sugar. This will hold the cookie roll you're about to make.

Carefully, try to unroll just a bit of the vanilla roll. If the dough breaks off, it's still too cold to unroll. Let it warm in your kitchen for another 10 or 15 minutes and then try again.

When the vanilla dough is warm enough to unroll, unroll it.

Carefully, peel off the top sheet of wax paper.

Now unroll the strawberry dough.

Peel the top sheet of wax paper from the strawberry roll.

Hannah's 4th Note: You will now have 2 unrolled sheets of cookie dough, the vanilla and the strawberry, stretched out side by side on your kitchen counter.

Here comes the tricky part:

Grasping the strawberry dough by the corners of its wax paper, carefully slide it so that the long side

of the strawberry dough rectangle is right next to the long side of the vanilla dough rectangle.

Still grasping the corners of the wax paper, flip the strawberry dough over on top of the vanilla dough so that the strawberry dough is nestled on top of the other with no wax paper between them.

Okay, THAT was the hard part. The rest is easy.

If the edges of the dough are uneven, trim them with a sharp knife. Use the pieces of dough you've trimmed for patches if there are any holes.

Working from the long side of the rectangle, use your impeccably clean hands to roll up the dough so that the dough forms a nice, tight log. This will create a spiral pattern when you slice the log into cookies.

When your cookie dough log is rolled, rub it with powdered sugar, turning it so the entire outside surface of the log is coated with the sugar.

Tear off another, longer sheet of wax paper. Roll your cookie log up in the wax paper. Twist the ends to keep the roll from coming undone.

Place the roll in a Ziploc plastic bag, seal the bag, and set it on a piece of cardboard or a flat tray. Then place it in the refrigerator for another 2 hours. *(Overnight is fine, too.)*

Hannah's 5th Note: At this point, you can even freeze the spiral cookie dough log. Just place it, wax paper and all, into a large Ziploc freezer bag. It will keep in the freezer for a month or two. The day before you're planning to bake your cookies, take the roll out of the freezer and thaw it in the refrigerator overnight. Then all you have to do is cut it into cookies and bake it.

When 2 hours have passed, preheat your oven to 350°F., rack in the middle position.

Line a cookie sheet with parchment paper or spray it with Pam or another nonstick cooking spray.

If your cookie log has flattened in the refrigerator, leave it in the wax paper and simply roll it around a bit on the counter to round it out.

Using a sharp knife, cut ¼-inch slices from the cookie dough log. Cut only as many cookies as you can bake at one time.

Place the Strawberry and Vanilla Pinwheel Cookies on the prepared cookie sheet, 12 to a standard-size sheet.

Once you've filled your cookie sheet, return the cookie dough log to the refrigerator.

Bake the cookies at 350°F. for 8 to 10 minutes or until the vanilla part of the cookie turns slightly golden.

Remove the cookies from the oven and cool them on the cookie sheet for 2 minutes, then remove them to a wire rack to cool completely.

Yield: 4 to 6 dozen pretty and tasty cookies that everyone will love.

Hannah's 6th Note: These are more work than most cookies, but they're well worth the effort. When you bring out a platter filled with Strawberry and Vanilla Pinwheel Cookies, your guests will love the way they look and taste.

Chapter Twenty-three

Hannah had just finished filling the bakers rack when Lisa came into the kitchen. "It smells good in here," she observed. "What did you bake?"

"Chocolate Cashew Marshmallow Bar Cookies."

"Great combination!" Lisa exclaimed, heading to the rack for a closer look. "They're just what we need, Hannah. We've been really busy today and these take less work than regular cookies . . . don't they?"

"Yes, and that's why I made them. Would you like a taste?"

"Yes! You get the bar cookies, I'll get the coffee," Lisa responded, heading for the kitchen coffeepot to pour them both a cup. "I think cashews are my favorite salted nut."

"Mine too . . . unless you count macadamia nuts."

"But those are so expensive."

"Yes, they are, unless you have a macadamia nut tree in your front yard."

"Macadamia nut trees don't grow here, do they?"

"Unfortunately not, but Lynne told me that a friend of hers in San Diego had one in her front yard."

"Really! What do they look like?"

"They're green pods about the size of a golf ball. You have to cut or break them open to get the nut out. And then you have to roast the nuts in the oven with oil and salt."

"That sounds like a lot of work."

"Lynne said it is, but if they grow in your front yard, they're free. And you can give a half-pound or even a whole pound of them for a gift and everyone thinks you're giving them something really expensive."

"Is that what Lynne's friend did?"

"Yes, and it backfired."

Lisa was clearly puzzled. "How? Almost everyone loves macadamia nuts, don't they?"

"I think so, but everyone knows how expensive they are. Lynne's friend gave a pound of salted, roasted nuts to her son to give to his algebra teacher for Christmas. And his teacher thought he was getting bribed for a higher grade."

Lisa laughed. "Oh, my goodness! What happened?"

"The friend's son brought the teacher home and showed him the tree, and then showed the teacher how to salt and roast them."

"Did the son get a good grade in algebra?"

"Yes, an A. But the teacher said the son deserved it with or without the macadamia nuts."

Lisa took a sip of her coffee and reached for a bar cookie. She took one bite, looked heavenward, and sighed. "Wonderful!" she declared. "I think we should bake these for Valentine's Day and pack them in pink satin, heart-shaped boxes. That would be bound to make anyone fall in love."

"You're probably right," Hannah told her, taking a bar cookie for herself. Even though this was the first time she'd made them and the recipe was a variation on a tried-and-true older recipe, Hannah totally agreed with Lisa's assessment. "These are dangerous," she said.

"Dangerous? But why?"

"Dangerous for anyone on a diet. I think they're addictive."

"You're probably right. The combination of chocolate and cashews is great. And the marshmallows enhance it perfectly."

There was a knock on the back door and Hannah began to smile. It was Norman.

"Norman?" Lisa asked.

"Yes. You're recognizing his knock now, too?"

"Yes, it's manly, but it's also polite. It's a great knock, Hannah."

Hannah was surprised by Lisa's insight. "You're right, Lisa. Manly, but polite. That describes Norman to a tee."

"Just sit here, Hannah. I'll go and let him in. Then I'll get coffee for him. Andrea should be back here soon. She just ran over to the real-estate office to make a couple of calls."

"Hi, Norman," Hannah greeted him as he walked toward the work station. "What have you been up to?"

"Not much." Norman sat down and thanked Lisa for the coffee she'd brought to him. "I'm surprised that Mike isn't here."

"Because I have some new bar cookies on a plate?"

"Have you ever noticed how Mike always seems to arrive every time you bake something new?"

"Yes," Hannah admitted with a laugh. "If I ate as much as Mike does, I'd weigh three hundred pounds."

"You and me both."

"Have a bar cookie, Norman," Hannah invited. "I want to know what you think of them."

Norman took a piece of Hannah's new creation and took a bite. He made a muffled sound of satisfaction and waited until he'd swallowed. "They're really good, Hannah . . . almost like a candy bar."

Before Hannah could thank him, there was an authoritative knock on the back kitchen door.

"There's Mike," Norman said. "We talked about his uncanny knack for arriving when you're serving something and here he is. Did you ever wonder if saying his name was a little like conjuring up the devil?"

Hannah was clearly shocked. "Don't say that, Norman!"

"I know. I was only joking, but it *was* pretty inappropriate. My apologies for even thinking that. I'll go let him in!"

"Apologies accepted, but you do have a point," Hannah admitted, getting up to fetch hot coffee for Mike and delivering it just as they returned and Mike was sitting down at the work station.

"Oh, boy!" Mike said, zeroing in on the plate of bar cookies. "Those look good!"

"They are," Norman told him.

"Have one." Hannah moved the plate closer to Mike. "Or two. Or maybe three."

"Don't mind if I do." Mike reached out to take two bar cookies. He took a bite of one and placed the second piece on the napkin Hannah had brought with his coffee. "Mmmmm!"

"Good, huh?" Norman asked him.

"Mmmmm!" Mike answered, finishing the first piece in one bite. He chewed, swallowed, and then asked, "What did you find out from Danielle?"

For a moment, Hannah wondered if Mike was a mind reader, but then she remembered that she'd told him her plan for the afternoon. "Benton has an alibi," she said.

"That's what I figured, but it never hurts to ask. Will she testify to that, if there's a court case?"

"Yes, but she'd rather not."

Mike picked up the second bar cookie, took a huge bite, chewed, swallowed, and nodded, all within the space of two or three seconds. "Then it's up to you to make sure she doesn't have to give a formal statement."

Hannah sighed. "I know. Andrea pointed that out."

"So what else did you uncover today?" Mike busied himself finishing the second bar cookie while Hannah gave an account of her afternoon. When she got to the part about meeting with Kay Hollenkamp and Joe and the strangely-colored car Joe had seen at Darcy's house, Mike actually stopped chewing for a moment.

"Interesting. I haven't seen a car that color around here." He turned to Norman. "Have you?"

"No, sounds to me like a custom paint job."

Mike turned back to Hannah. "Call Cyril and find out if he knows anyone with that color paint job."

"Andrea's doing that right now. She should be back here soon."

"Well, let me know," Mike said, rising to his feet. "Sorry I have to eat and run, but I've got some things I have to do before I get home. I've got to get cleaned up. I'm meeting a friend for dinner tonight."

"It doesn't have anything to do with the investigation, does it?" Hannah asked him.

"Nope, purely social." Mike walked over to get his parka. "See you guys later."

Once the door had closed behind Mike, Norman turned to Hannah. "I wonder what that was about."

"So do I, but he'll tell us eventually. And I don't think he's lying when he said it was purely social."

"I don't, either," Norman agreed. "Would you like to go out to dinner, Hannah?"

"Yes, thanks," Hannah answered immediately.

"How about Lynne?"

"I don't know. I would call to ask her, but she might still be at tea with Mother and Stephanie Bascomb."

"Then I'll text her. That won't disturb her. I just thought I'd take you ladies out for dinner before we went back to . . ." Norman stopped and began to frown.

"What is it?" Hannah asked.

"Something just occurred to me. You said the car that Joe Hollenkamp saw was parked in front of Darcy's garage?" He waited until Hannah nodded, and then he continued. "I wonder if she had an arc light outside the garage."

Hannah could feel her mouth drop open in surprise and she closed it quickly. "I never thought of that! Arc lights *do* have an orange glow."

"Yes, and if the car was painted a light tan, it would end up looking pinkish-orange if it was parked directly under the arc light."

Norman pulled out his phone, sent a quick text, and

laid his phone down on the work station. "We can drive past Darcy's place on our way back from dinner tonight. Most people have lights like that on a timer, and Darcy's father might have done that. If it's on when we go past, we'll see what color it is."

There was another knock at the back kitchen door, another knock that Hannah recognized. "It's Andrea," she said, getting up to let her sister in. "We can ask her if she knows about Darcy's light."

"And I can ask her to join us for dinner, if you don't mind," Norman suggested.

"Good idea!" Hannah said with a smile, walking quickly to the door. She was already planning to ask Andrea to bring the keys to Darcy's house, just in case the switch was inside and they had to turn on the arc light manually.

"Hi, Norman," Andrea greeted him as she sat down at the work station. "Oooooh! What are those?" She pointed to the plate.

"Chocolate Cashew Marshmallow Bar Cookies," Norman told her.

"Try one," Hannah said, delivering a cup of hot coffee for her sister and gesturing toward the plate of bar cookies.

"They smell great!" Andrea said, inhaling the scent that filled the kitchen.

"And they are great," Norman told her. "Go ahead, Andrea. Take a bite."

"Do I want to ask how many calories these are?" Andrea asked them.

"I wouldn't," Norman told her.

"I have no idea," Hannah added. "Besides . . . remember what Great-Grandma Elsa told us about cookies, pies, and cakes?"

Andrea looked at her blankly. "No, maybe I was too little to remember what she said."

Hannah smiled. "I guess you were, but I'll tell you. Great-Grandma Elsa said that all the calories baked off in the oven."

"I'm going to remember that," Andrea promised. "And I'm going to believe her. After all, would a great-grand-mother lie to you?"

Hannah and Norman watched as Andrea took a large bite. A blissful smile spread over her face as she chewed and swallowed. "Perfect!" she declared. "And it's so good to know that they don't have any calories." Andrea took another bite, and then she addressed Hannah. "Where's your murder book, Hannah?"

"Right here." Hannah retrieved the stenographer's notepad that rested on the vacant stool next to her. "I was just about to go over my suspect list."

"Well . . . you can knock off another two suspects," Andrea told her.

"Two suspects?" Hannah asked.

"Yes, Bill cleared Denny Jamison."

"Darcy's fiancé?" Norman asked her.

"Yes, when Denny left the Double Eagle that night, he went into a ditch several miles away. It was too far to walk back to the bar, so he called his sister to come and get him, and he spent the night at her house."

"So he couldn't have gone to Darcy's house with no transportation?" Norman surmised.

"That's right. And his sister wouldn't let him borrow her car because he'd had too much to drink. She didn't let him leave until he sobered up in the morning, and then she drove him back to his apartment."

"Good for her!" Hannah said. "She did him a big favor in more ways than one."

"And you're minus a suspect," Norman pointed out.

"I know." Hannah turned back to Andrea. "You said you cleared *two* suspects?"

"That's right. My client, the one who wanted to buy Darcy's house, was in North Carolina that night for his niece's wedding. He flew out at eight that morning and didn't get back until the following afternoon. And . . . in case you're wondering . . . he came back to Lake Eden today and bought Darcy's house from her brother."

"How many suspects do you have left?" Norman asked Hannah.

"Just three, counting Lonnie. And they're all long shots. This case is turning out to be the toughest I've ever worked on."

"You'll solve it," Andrea said, and Hannah noticed that she sounded very confident. "It's like Danielle said this morning. You always do."

CHOCOLATE CASHEW
MARSHMALLOW BAR COOKIES

Preheat oven to 350°F., rack in the middle position.

    2 one-ounce squares unsweetened chocolate
       (I used Baker's)
    ¾ cup all-purpose flour *(pack it down in the*
       cup when you measure it)
    ¾ cup white *(granulated)* sugar
    ½ teaspoon salt
    ½ cup *(1 stick, ¼ pound)* salted butter, soft-
       ened to room temperature
    2 large eggs
    1 teaspoon vanilla extract
    ½ cup chopped salted cashews *(I used*
       Planters—measure AFTER chopping)
    10.5-ounce package miniature marshmallows
       (you'll use ¾ of a package—I used Kraft
       Jet Puffed)
    2 cups chocolate chips *(I used Nestlé)*

**Hannah's 1ˢᵗ Note: This is a lot easier with an
electric mixer, but you can also make these bar
cookies by hand.**

Before you start, prepare a 9-inch by 13-inch cake pan by spraying the inside with Pam or another nonstick cooking spray. Alternatively, you can line the pan with aluminum foil and spray that.

Hannah's 2nd Note: If you decide to line your cake pan with foil, use the heavy-duty foil. Then, once your bar cookies are cool, you'll be able to lift the contents right out of the cake pan and your pan will still be clean.

Melt your chocolate first so that it has time to cool. Unwrap the 2 squares of unsweetened chocolate and place them in a microwave-safe bowl.

Heat the chocolate squares for one minute on HIGH. Then let them sit in the microwave for another minute.

Take the chocolate out of the microwave and try to stir it smooth with a heat-resistant spatula. If the chocolate has melted, you're through with this step.

If you can't stir the chocolate smooth, put it back in the microwave and heat on HIGH in 20-second increments with 20-second standing time until you can stir it smooth.

Set the bowl with the melted chocolate on the counter to cool while you mix up the rest of the recipe.

Combine the flour, sugar, and salt in the bowl of an electric mixer. Beat them together on SLOW speed until they're combined.

Add the softened butter to the bowl. Beat on SLOW speed until the butter is well incorporated.

Turn the mixer up to MEDIUM speed and beat the mixture until it is light and fluffy.

Crack the eggs and add them to the bowl one at a time, beating on MEDIUM speed after each addition. Again, make sure the resulting mixture is light and fluffy.

Cup your hands around the bowl with the melted chocolate squares. If it's warm to the touch but not so hot it might cook the eggs, add the chocolate to your mixture. Beat until everything is well combined.

Turn your mixer down to LOW speed and add the vanilla extract and the half-cup of chopped cashews. Mix everything in thoroughly.

Transfer the batter to your prepared 9-inch by 13-inch cake pan and smooth the top as evenly as you can with a rubber spatula.

Bake at 350°F. for 20 minutes.

Take the pan from the oven and immediately pour the miniature marshmallows in a single layer over the top. This should take about three-quarters of a 10.5-ounce bag. Work quickly to spread the marshmallows out as evenly as you can.

Cover the pan with heavy-duty foil crimped down tightly over the sides, or with a spare cookie sheet that entirely covers the top of the cake pan. Leave that in place for 20 minutes. You want the miniature marshmallows to melt on the bottom and attach themselves nicely to the top of your bar cookies.

When 20 minutes have passed, melt 2 cups of semisweet chocolate chips in the microwave on HIGH for 2 minutes. Let them cool in the microwave for another 2 minutes and try to stir the chips smooth. If you can't, microwave them again in increments of 30 seconds with 30 seconds of standing time in the microwave until you can stir them smooth.

Spread the melted chocolate over the marshmallows as evenly as you can with a heat-resistant rubber spatula. Then set the pan on a wire rack to cool.

When the bar cookies are cool and the chocolate on top has hardened, cut them into brownie-size pieces and serve. If you want to hasten the hardening of the chocolate, slip the pan into the refrigerator for thirty minutes or so, and then take it out to cut the bar cookies.

Arrange the bar cookies on a pretty platter and serve for a luscious treat. You can store any leftovers in a tightly-covered container, but Lisa and I bet there won't be any left!

Yield: Each pan makes approximately 24 bars.

"Thank you for dinner, Norman!" Andrea told him as she climbed into Grandma McCann's car. "I'll meet you at Darcy's house."

"See you there," Norman said, opening the back door for Lynne and the front passenger door for Hannah. He climbed into the driver's seat and followed Andrea out of the Lake Eden Inn parking lot and onto the highway.

"This is going to be interesting," Lynne said from the back seat. "I've noticed that arc lights play havoc with colors, but it never occurred to me that an arc light might turn some colors into pinkish-orange."

"Me neither," Hannah agreed.

"Don't count your chickens before they're hatched," Norman warned them. "I could be wrong about this."

"And that's why we're going out there to test it," Hannah said. "I'm just hoping that you're right, Norman. A light tan car is a lot easier to find than the pinkish-orange color that Joe Hollenkamp described."

"A lot of people drive light tan cars, don't they?" Lynne asked.

"Yes," Hannah answered. "I called Cyril and he said that light tan was almost as popular as white."

"But you said Lonnie's car was dark blue," Lynne reminded her. "Doesn't that clear him?"

"No. Lonnie parked his car inside Darcy's garage. The car that Joe Hollenkamp spotted was outside. It could have belonged to a couple of kids sharing a six-pack of beer in a place that was off the road. Or someone who needed to catch an hour's sleep before driving on."

"I guess that's true," Lynne admitted.

"And for all we know, Darcy was already dead when Joe spotted that car," Norman added.

"It's confusing," Lynne admitted, sighing deeply. "I read mysteries, but this one's got me stymied. There just aren't any good clues."

Norman pulled up next to Darcy's dumpster in the place where Joe had told them he'd parked. He gave a little polite tap on his horn to tell Andrea that they were in position, and all three of them got out of Norman's car to peer through the tree branches at Darcy's garage and Grandma McCann's light tan car that Andrea had parked here.

"It's pinkish-orange," Lynne said.

"It sure is!" Hannah reached out to pat Norman on the shoulder. "You were right about the color, Norman!"

All three of them hurried back to the car. Norman gave another polite beep of his horn, and they heard Andrea's car start. In a few moments, she pulled out of Darcy's driveway and took up a position next to them.

"Was it pinkish-orange from here?" she asked them.

"It was," Norman answered her. "Thanks for checking it out, Andrea. And thank Grandma McCann for letting you borrow her car."

Andrea waved and drove off, making a U-turn to go back to town. Norman put his car in gear and drove in the opposite direction.

"Did what we learned tonight help you in the investigation?" Lynne asked Hannah.

Hannah was silent for a moment, and then she nodded. "Yes, it eliminated several possibilities."

They were all silent as Norman drove down the country road. Hannah leaned back in the seat and closed her eyes. It was good to have people like Norman, Lynne, and Andrea in her life.

She was swimming in a pool of warm caramel, practicing her stroke for the competition. She knew she had to hurry because the air outside was cold, the caramel would begin to solidify soon and she'd have to get out of the pool.

She swam to the end of the huge mixing bowl, pushed off from the rim with the wooden spoon that had belonged to her great-grandmother, and switched to the breast stroke. That required a flutter kick with her legs, and she hoped that she'd be able to do it fast enough to keep her afloat.

The caramel was growing thicker and more viscous. Soon it would be sticky and gluey. When that happened, she wouldn't be able to move her legs, and she still had to do the backstroke.

Even though her body was losing the ability to move

through the cooling caramel, she somehow managed to cross the mixing bowl. A push off the rim brought her to the final lap in her competition, but she knew her arms and legs would not carry her much longer. She would be stuck here in the caramel just like a fly on a spiral of sticky flypaper. There would be no way she'd be able to pull herself out of the mixing bowl, and she would die here, her fate the fate of the fly.

"Noooo!" she moaned, and she could feel the tears run down her cheeks. "I have to get out! I have to win! Help me!"

"Hannah?" a voice called her name. "Hannah, wake up!"

"Wake?" she mumbled, the word unfamiliar to her. "I have to finish. They're depending on me!"

Strong arms wrapped around her and lifted her out of the caramel mixing bowl. Her eyes fluttered open and she blinked several times.

"Take it easy, Hannah. It was just a bad dream. You're okay now."

"Norman?" Her eyes focused on his face. "What . . . happened to my big mixing bowl?"

She felt his body shake with laughter and he reached out to stroke her hair. "Your mixing bowl?"

"I was swimming!" she tried to explain. "All I had to do was do one more lap. But I couldn't because . . . because it was too sticky."

"That must have been one heck of a nightmare!" Norman commented, pulling her a bit closer in his arms. He grabbed a tissue from the box on the bed table and wiped the tears from her eyes.

"Did you . . . hear me?" Hannah asked him, hoping she hadn't made too much noise.

"No, Moishe came in to wake me up. He led me up here and you were crying."

"Then Lynne's still sleeping?"

"I think so. I didn't hear her get up."

"Oh, good. What time is it?"

"A little after five in the morning."

Hannah sighed. She felt terrible for getting Norman up this early. "I'm sorry Moishe woke you," she apologized.

"I'm not. It's freezing in here, Hannah." He looked over at the window. "Did you open the window?"

"Yes. I was really warm when I went to bed and I needed to cool off."

"Well, I think you cooled off too much. It turned really cold around midnight or so and you're shivering. I'll start a fire to warm you up."

It didn't take long for the room to warm once a fire was burning in the fireplace, and the cheerful light seemed to chase away the last vestiges of her dream. "Thank you, Norman," she said, snuggling down under the covers. "I should probably get up, but it's so nice and warm in here, I'm getting sleepy again."

"Good. Sleep for another hour, Hannah. My alarm's set for six and I'll wake you then. And don't start anything for breakfast. I already told Lynne that I'm taking both of you out to the Corner Tavern for pancakes and sausages."

"Perfect," Hannah said, pulling the covers up to her chin. "Thank you, Norman. You're wonderful in the middle of the night."

"You'd better not say that to anyone else!" Norman teased her. Then he bent down, kissed the top of her head, and walked out of the room.

Hannah felt a thump as Moishe landed on the pillow next to her head. She was warm, the fire was cheery, and she was loved. She gave Moishe a pat, settled back on the pillow, and fell asleep with a smile on her face and Moishe purring beside her.

Chapter
Twenty-five

Hannah closed her shorthand notebook with a snap of pure frustration. She was getting nowhere with Darcy's murder investigation, and she had no idea who she should interview next.

"Hannah?" Andrea came in the swinging door from the coffee shop. "Lonnie's here and he'd like to see you, if you have the time."

"I have the time. Thanks, Andrea. Give me a couple of minutes to get some cookies for him and then send him back here."

As she prepared a plate of cookies, Hannah hoped that Lonnie hadn't come to ask her how she was progressing with the murder investigation. If he did ask, she wasn't sure what she should say. It would be cruel to tell the chief suspect, the man she was convinced was innocent, that she'd gotten nowhere despite the leads that various people had given her. She'd run into quite a few dead ends, but that was about it.

Once she'd poured coffee for both of them and set the

platter of cookies on the work station, Hannah sat down on her favorite stool. She paged through her murder book for the fourth time that day and gave a heartfelt sigh. Everyone, even Mike, said that she was a good investigator, but she didn't have much to show for it in this case.

"Hi, Hannah." Lonnie breezed through the swinging door and came straight to the work station. "Thanks for seeing me. I didn't want to interrupt your baking, but I remembered something that might possibly help . . . maybe. Anyway, I talked to Michelle, and she told me to get in here and tell it to you."

Hannah smiled at him and reached for her murder book. A possible clue? A new suspect? Any conversation overheard that might identify a motive for Darcy's murder?

"Michelle's right," she told him. "Anything you can remember about that night or the next morning could be very helpful."

"Remember the cake that the killer took? When I set it down on Darcy's dresser that night, the lid flipped up. There was an unopened birthday card with Cassie's name on it left in the box with the cake. I remember thinking that I'd give it to Cassie the next time I saw her, but I forgot to take it out."

"Then you think that the killer took Cassie's birthday card?" Hannah asked him.

"I guess so, I don't know what else to think."

When Lonnie left, Hannah tried to concentrate on the murder case, but everything she'd learned since she'd come back to Lake Eden was roiling around in her mind.

"I have to bake," Hannah said aloud. And almost immediately, she knew that baking was the right thing to do. Baking was structured, step after step, and it freed her mind for whatever thoughts might occur to her.

What should she bake? Hannah thought about cookies, pies, and breads. Any of those categories would do. But then she realized that what she really wanted to make was cookies, a kind that would organize her mind and set it free to make connections and piece together the facts she'd learned about Darcy's murder.

It was like arranging the pieces of a jigsaw puzzle into categories by color and shape, before starting to put it together. Perhaps, if she concentrated on arranging the clues in her investigation into categories, the bigger, more important puzzle of Darcy's murder would come together in her mind.

Hannah flipped through her recipe book. When she came to her recipe for Snowflake and Ice Cookies she began to smile. Everyone had loved them and she wanted to make them again. She glanced at the ingredients list and went to the pantry to gather the ingredients she needed. Then she stepped into the walk-in cooler to get salted butter and eggs. Once all the ingredients were arranged in order on the surface of the work station, she began to mix up the cookie dough. With every ingredient she used and set aside, Hannah thought of a clue that could possibly help her to identify Darcy's killer.

When Michelle had first told her about Darcy's murder, she'd mentioned how happy Lonnie was that his high school friends, Brian and Cassie, were back together again after they'd managed to weather the tragedy of two miscarriages and the death of their baby girl. Tears came to Hannah's eyes as she imagined how Cassie must have felt after finally carrying a baby full-term, delivering a healthy baby, and then losing that baby to SIDS. It must have been heartbreaking for Cassie and Brian, and Hannah hoped they'd received plenty of support and counseling from friends, family, and professionals. It was a pity that the tragedy had torn them apart for a while.

The moment Hannah thought of it, she washed her hands and called Lonnie on his cell phone. "I was just thinking about Cassie and Brian, and I was hoping that someone had referred them to a counselor when they lost the baby."

"Cassie went to a psychiatrist. Doc Knight referred her. Brian went with her for a while but when they split up, he stopped going."

"Do you think Brian got over it faster than Cassie?"

"I know he did." Lonnie's answer was immediate and definite. "He felt awful, of course, but he didn't take it quite as hard as Cassie. He got promoted at work and his new job was very demanding. He had to do some traveling, and he told me that being in a different city helped to distract him."

"How about Cassie? Did she go with Brian?"

"No, she stayed home for the final two months of her maternity leave."

"That must have been depressing!"

"Yeah. I think that's one of the reasons they broke up for a while. Brian thinks the only thing that got her through her depression was the shrink she saw three times a week. He said the pills helped, but he was glad when she didn't have to take them anymore."

"What kind of pills?"

"Oh, they tried all sorts of things until they found something that worked for Cassie."

"Cassie still takes pills?"

"I don't think so. When she came back to Brian, she was back to being the same old Cassie. She laughed again. They had fun again. And you can tell they love each other. Cassie even told Brian that they ought to try to have another baby."

When Hannah ended the call, she went back to work on her cookies. She prepared the cookie sheets and began to fill them with the cookies that had made such a big hit with everyone who'd tasted them. And all the while she was working, she thought about Darcy and the fact that she'd been pregnant.

When her Snowflake and Ice Cookies were ready to bake, Hannah slipped the cookie sheets inside her industrial oven, went to pour herself another cup of coffee, and took a seat at the work station.

As her cookies baked, Hannah's mind was buzzing with questions. Most of them fell into the category of *What if.* Kay Hollenkamp had said that she was glad Lonnie had volunteered to take Darcy home because it might have caused a problem with Cassie. And Lonnie had said Brian had hung out at the Double Eagle after Cassie had left him. Both Lonnie and Kay had said that Darcy seemed drunk, although she hadn't had that much to drink at the Double Eagle. When Cassie had taken her to the ladies' room, was it possible that Darcy had confided to Cassie that she was pregnant? Was Cassie jealous of the fact that Darcy was having a baby and Cassie wasn't?

Was all this far-fetched? Hannah knew it was, but since she hadn't yet interviewed Cassie and Brian, she decided she'd better do that as soon as possible. Cassie had gone back to her job at CostMart, and Hannah knew that their office employees were given a full hour off for lunch. One glance at the clock on the kitchen wall told her that it was a few minutes past eleven in the morning. There was no reason why she couldn't go to see Cassie at lunch and ask her some pertinent questions. Cassie could know something that could lead Hannah to the killer.

There was a knock at the door and Hannah rushed to answer it. Norman was here and she would run the idea past him. She wouldn't take Norman with her when she interviewed Cassie, since they'd be talking about personal things that Cassie might not want to mention in front of Norman. It was time for some *girl talk* with Cassie. Hannah would call and arrange to meet Cassie for lunch. And if the cookies she had in the oven right now turned out well, she'd even take Cassie a little care package to facilitate their talk.

Chapter
Twenty-six

Hannah pulled into the parking garage at CostMart at five minutes to noon. She parked where Cassie had told her to park, got out of her cookie truck, picked up the bakery box she'd filled with cookies, and walked toward the employee entrance. She was early, but it would give her time to gather her thoughts before Cassie came out.

Hannah's thoughts turned to Norman. He'd looked concerned when she'd made the phone call to Cassie inviting her to lunch, and she hadn't invited him to go along. Perhaps she should have explained her reticence. She thought Cassie might speak more freely if there wasn't a man present.

"Hi, Hannah!" a voice said, and Hannah whirled around.

"Hello, Cassie. Am I late?"

"No, I'm early, so I came out here to wait for you. I've been standing here for a couple of minutes and I saw you drive in. I guess you want to ask me about the night that Darcy was killed. Is that right?"

"That's right. Lonnie told me everything that he remembered, but I need a more complete picture. And he said that you weren't drinking that much."

"I wasn't. Did Lonnie tell you that he brought me a birthday cake?"

Hannah smiled. "Yes, and he said that it was your favorite."

"He's right. I just love your Coconut Layer Cake. I think it's the lemon icing that gets to me. I love lemon and coconut together. You really ought to try that in a cookie."

"Good idea! Thanks, Cassie. I'm always looking for new cookies to try."

"They should be soft and chewy. And maybe a little on the tart side? What do you think?"

"I think that sounds delicious." Hannah marshalled her thoughts again. She wasn't here to talk about new cookies with Cassie.

"Oh! Before I forget . . . thanks for the birthday card," Cassie said.

"You're welcome."

"I love the way everybody there signed it. That was really nice."

"I'm glad you noticed the card. Lonnie said it was tucked down in the cake box and he thought you hadn't seen it."

"I didn't until later, but I pulled it out and it's on my mantel. It's lined up with all the other cards I got."

Warning bells went off in Hannah's mind. Lonnie had told her he'd found the card left behind in the cake box. If that was true, how could it be on Cassie and Brian's mantel unless . . .

"I'm glad you found it in the cake box," Hannah said, doing her best to sound casual. "There should have been a business card in there, too."

"There was. I took it out the next morning when I had the last slice of cake for breakfast."

"I'm curious," Hannah said, "Was there a lot of frosting that stuck to the inside of the box?"

"No, Lisa or somebody lined the inside of the box with wax paper. I saved the box because it's pretty. I love your imprint."

"Well, I have another box for you, Cassie." Hannah opened the box and said, "Take one right now. I want to know if you like them. They're Snowflake and Ice Cookies. They have coconut and white chocolate."

"Yum," Cassie said, taking a cookie and biting into it. "I love the combination. These are delicious, Hannah."

As Cassie took another bite of her cookie, Hannah frowned. Things certainly were not going the way she'd planned. She knew she'd be much more comfortable if other employees were milling around, but here she was, alone in the parking garage with Cassie.

"What a shame!" Cassie said. "It's a real pity you won't be making these again. Of course, you won't be baking anything again, now that you *know*."

"Know what?" Hannah asked quickly, but she felt an icy shiver run through her. Cassie had suspected that she knew, and that wasn't good!

"You know what I'm talking about. You figured it out, didn't you, Hannah? But it won't do you any good! Nobody else is coming out here until one o'clock. There's an employee lunch meeting right now and everyone else is there. We're alone here, you and me. And soon it'll be just me."

Hannah's legs began to tremble. She had to keep Cassie talking. But the only person who knew she was here was Norman. And she'd told him she didn't need him to come with her!

"So what made you do it, Cassie?" she asked, hoping against hope that Norman would decide to check on her and drive in.

Cassie smiled and her eyes narrowed into slits. It reminded Hannah of the way a feline predator's eyes looked, determined, dangerously fixed and focused on the prey.

"Darcy told me," Cassie said. "What a fool! She didn't deserve to live!"

"Darcy told you she was pregnant?"

"Of course she did. She was proud of it." Cassie reached inside her pocket and drew out a small revolver. "She brought this on herself, you know."

"Why?" Hannah asked quickly, noticing that Cassie's finger was tightening on the trigger.

"Because *I'm* married to Brian! And *I'm* the only one who can have his baby!"

Hannah's mouth dropped open. Darcy was having *Brian's* baby?!

"Yes, Hannah, Brian confessed he slept with Darcy. And I added up the dates, Darcy was having *my* baby! *I* should have been having Brian's baby."

Hannah sent up a silent prayer that someone would enter the parking garage. And she knew she had to keep Cassie talking until someone else came. "Did you want Darcy to give you the baby?" she asked, hoping the question wouldn't enrage Cassie.

"No!"

"Why not?"

"Because the baby growing inside of Darcy was half *hers!*"

"That makes sense." An idea struck Hannah with startling clarity and she inched closer to the car parked next to her. It looked a lot like the car Andrea had told her not to touch in the DelRay parking lot, the one with the alarm that would set off all the other car alarms.

"Where do you think you're going?" Cassie asked. "You can't get away from me here. I've got you pinned down, Hannah. You're through meddling in other people's lives."

"I was just going to set this cookie box on the hood of a car," Hannah explained. "Do you want another cookie first?"

"I'll get one after you're gone," Cassie said, giving Hannah a twisted smile that didn't bode well for Hannah's future.

"Then I'd better set these down or the box will fall and the cookies will spill out all over this dirty floor."

That stopped Cassie for a moment, and then she nodded. "You're right and those cookies are too good to waste. Go ahead, but I'm watching you. One false move and you die."

As Hannah moved slowly toward the car, she caught movement out of the corner of her eye. Someone was at the far end of the parking garage. She didn't dare look to see who it was because that might tip Cassie off, but she could only hope that whoever it was had come to rescue her.

"I'm so sorry about your daughter, Cassie," Hannah said as she walked closer to the front of the car. "It must have been awful to have Brian's baby and then lose her."

"You don't know the half of it," Cassie said, and her

voice was trembling slightly. "Nothing like that has ever happened to a woman like you."

"Actually . . . it has. It's not exactly what you went through, but when Ross left me I thought for a while that I was pregnant. But I guess it can't compare to the heartbreak you felt."

"That's right. And it hurt all over again when I found out that Darcy was pregnant with Brian's baby. I wanted to die right then and there."

"I guess I really can't blame you for wanting to kill Darcy," Hannah said, hoping she sounded convincingly sympathetic. "It must have been horrible to learn that she was carrying the baby that should have been yours."

"Oh, it was. Maybe you *do* understand. I had to kill her. Part of me didn't want to do it, but I couldn't let her have Brian's baby. That baby should have been mine!"

"So you drugged her, and then you killed her?" Hannah asked, hoping that whoever had come in had overheard Cassie's confession.

"I didn't have to. She was drinking, Hannah! She was already staggering a little when she got up to go to dance with Denny. And everyone knows that when you're pregnant, you *shouldn't* drink."

"But why in heaven's name did you drug *Lonnie*?"

"Actually, I drugged both Lonnie *and* Brian!" Cassie explained. "I drugged Brian because I needed to get out of the house without him knowing I was leaving. And Lonnie because someone had to send the police investigation in the wrong direction. What better way to distract them than finding one of their own with the murder victim?"

Hannah's mind was reeling. Cassie was truly insane! And Cassie was perfectly capable of killing her, and she would, unless Hannah figured out a way to keep her talking. "I'm sorry you had to through all this, Cassie. I wish there was something I could do to help you."

"There is. You can stand still and say your prayers, because I have to make sure that Brian never knows what I did."

The moment was here and Hannah knew it. She dropped the box on the hood of the car and a scant second later, the car alarm went off. It was joined by another car alarm, and then another, as Hannah dropped to the ground and crawled to the rear of the car.

"Drop the gun, Cassie," a voice called out, and Hannah began to breathe again. It was Mike! Mike was here! She wasn't sure how, or why, but she was saved.

"Did you get it, Norman?" Mike asked.

"I got it." Norman ran around the back of the car and helped Hannah to her feet. "I started worrying about you, so when Mike showed up at The Cookie Jar we decided to come here together. And just in time! Are you all right?"

"Yes . . . now," Hannah answered in a voice that still shook from fright. "She was going to kill me!"

"We know. I recorded her whole confession." He slipped an arm around her shoulder and led her toward Mike, who had cuffed Cassie and was escorting her toward his cruiser.

"I'll take her to the station," Mike said, opening the back door and pushing Cassie in. "You drive Hannah back in her truck."

"Of course," Norman said, half-walking and half-carrying Hannah to her cookie truck. He opened the passenger door and helped her in. "Give me your keys. You're in no shape to drive."

"They're . . . in the ignition," Hannah told him. "I thought I might have to . . . to . . . I'm not sure what I thought."

"It doesn't matter now. You're safe." Norman got into the driver's seat and turned the key. But before he backed the truck out of the parking spot, he pulled Hannah toward him to hug her. "I want you to promise me that you'll never do something like this again. I love you, Hannah, and you've had too many close calls. From now on, when you think you might know who the killer is, you have to tell me. Will you promise me that?"

"I . . . I promise," Hannah said, and she meant it. At least for right now.

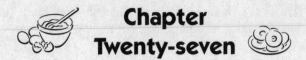

Chapter
Twenty-seven

Two days had passed since Cassie's arrest for the murder of Darcy Hicks. They had all decided to celebrate the fact that Lonnie was no longer a suspect, and they were gathered around a table at the Lake Eden Inn. Everyone was there including Delores and Doc, Andrea and Bill, Michelle and Lonnie, Lynne, Mike, and Norman. As usual, Hannah was seated between Mike and Norman.

"To Hannah!" Bill said, raising his glass of champagne. "If I were smart, I'd recruit her as a detective for the Winnetka County Sheriff's Department."

Everyone else at the table raised their glasses in a salute and Hannah laughed. "Thanks, but I'm just a baker. I'm not a detective."

"For someone who's not a detective, you do great work," Mike told her.

Hannah glowed under the unexpected praise. "Thank you, but I'd rather bake cookies. It's a lot less dangerous than catching murderers."

"Until the next case," Mike said under his breath, and everyone laughed, including Hannah.

"Are you tired, Hannah?" Norman asked as he led the way to his den.

"Yes, but not terribly." Hannah smiled. Norman was always so considerate. "How about you?"

"I'm fine. Would you like another glass of champagne? I have a split I can open for you."

Hannah thought about it for a moment and then she shook her head. "No, thanks. I had a glass at dinner, and now I'd rather have something non-alcoholic."

"Of course. How about some hot chocolate? It'll only take a few minutes to make."

"That would be great! Now that I think about it, hot chocolate is exactly what I need."

"Then I'll make some for both of us and be back in a minute or so. Lean back and relax, Hannah. You've had a busy week."

"You said it!" Hannah gave a little laugh and leaned back on Norman's comfortable leather couch. Just being with Norman was relaxing. There was no pressure, perhaps because Norman accepted her just the way she was, faults and all.

"I'm back," Norman announced, much sooner than Hannah had expected. "Let me know if you like this hot chocolate. It comes in pods and Florence just started carrying it at the Red Owl. She convinced me to try it because it's so convenient."

"It smells wonderful!" Hannah commented as she picked up the mug Norman had placed on the coffee table. She took a sip and then she began to smile. "I like it!"

"So do I. I tried it the second I got home from the store." Norman stopped and cleared his throat. "I really need to talk to you about something important, Hannah."

Hannah glanced at Norman. He looked very serious and warning bells went off in her mind. His expression reminded her of the time he'd told her that they couldn't see each other any longer, that he had to marry Doctor Bev for the sake of the child she'd told him was his.

"Hannah?"

Hannah took a deep, calming breath. "You can talk to me about anything, Norman. What is it?"

"I heard what you said to Cassie in the garage, that you thought you were pregnant after Ross left you. Did you mean that? Or were you just trying to get her to talk to stall for time?"

"Both," Hannah admitted. "I wanted to create a bond with her that might make her less likely to kill me. It didn't exactly work, but it did allow me to keep her talking."

"I understand. But did you really think you were pregnant?"

Hannah nodded. "Yes, that was the truth."

Norman put down his mug of hot chocolate and slipped his arm around her shoulders. "You could have told me, you know."

"Yes. And . . . maybe I should have. I wasn't thinking very clearly at the time."

"I'm here for you, no matter what," Norman said, pulling her a bit closer. "I love you and if you *are* pregnant, I want to help you with the baby. And I promise that I'll love your daughter or your son, just as much as I would if I were the father."

Tears came to Hannah's eyes. "That's . . ." She stopped speaking to swallow the lump that had formed in her throat. ". . . that's so wonderful! I love you, Norman. And I believe you."

Norman hugged her a little tighter. "Then tell me, Hannah. Are you pregnant?"

"No."

Norman gave a deep sigh. "I'm not sure if I'm disappointed for me or . . . relieved for you."

"That's exactly the way I felt when I Doc told me! He ran tests and he said that the only thing wrong with me was stress and I needed to get away for a while. That's the reason I flew to California with Mother to help Lynne pack."

"Really?" Norman looked absolutely dumbfounded. "And being in California with your *mother* was supposed to be non-stressful?"

That did it for Hannah. She began to laugh and Norman joined in. Finally, when she'd stopped laughing enough to speak again, she said, "I think maybe Doc was also trying to alleviate his *own* stress."

That sent them off on another round of laughter. They laughed so much that they woke the cats who were sleeping on the landing of the staircase to nowhere that Norman had built so that they could watch birds from the window near the ceiling.

"Now you've done it," Norman said to Hannah as Cuddles landed in his lap with a thud.

"Me?" Hannah gave a little gasp as Moishe landed in her lap. "You were laughing louder than I was."

They looked at each other as the cats settled down and

began to purr. The sound was soothing and Hannah felt a warm, comfortable feeling wash over her. Here she was with the cats she loved, safe in Norman's arms. Life didn't get any better than this.

She glanced at the recipe again, even though she'd made these cookies several hundred times in the past. She was standing by the work station at The Cookie Jar with a mixing bowl and her great-grandmother's wooden spoon in her hand.

"What should I get from the pantry, Mommy?"

Hannah glanced over at the little girl standing on the step-stool next to her. Everyone said she looked like a miniature version of Hannah with her curly red hair and happy smile. "You can get the chocolate chips and the corn flakes, honey."

"We're baking Chocolate Chip Crunch Cookies again?"

"Yes. They're still your favorites, aren't they?"

"I think so. I'll know after I taste one."

Hannah watched as her daughter jumped down, barely missing Moishe, who had been sitting at the base of the step-stool.

"Come on, Moishe," her daughter said, beckoning to the cat as she headed toward the pantry door. "If you help me find everything, I'll give you a little bite of my cookie when it's baked."

Once they had assembled all the ingredients, Hannah stirred up the cookie dough. She pushed the mixing bowl over to her daughter and handed her the wooden spoon.

"Great-great-grandma Elsa's spoon?" the little girl asked.

"That's right, honey."

"And she used it all her life to mix up yummy things?"

"Yes, she did." There was a yowl from the base of the step-stool and Hannah looked over at Moishe. "I think he's hungry, honey. Can you get his kitty treats and give him one?"

"Yes, I can."

The moment her daughter had gone off to get the fish-shaped, salmon-flavored treats that Moishe loved, Hannah reached over to give the bowl a final stir. The cookie dough was stiff and the wooden spoon was too large for her daughter's hand but she loved using it so much, Hannah didn't have the heart to buy her a child-size mixing spoon.

Less than thirty minutes later, mother and daughter were sitting at the work station. Hannah was drinking a cup of coffee and her daughter was sipping from a glass of milk. The kitchen was filled with the delicious aromas of chocolate and vanilla from the cookies that were cooling on the bakers rack. Both Hannah and her daughter laughed as Moishe gave a yowl.

"I think he wants to know if the cookies are cool enough to eat," Hannah said. "Would you like to go and see, honey?"

"Yes. Come on, Moishe. Let's go!"

Hannah smiled as she watched her daughter and Moishe race across the kitchen floor to the bakers rack. And then the kitchen faded, slowly dissolving into . . . Norman's master bedroom.

Hannah sat up and rubbed her eyes. A dream. It had all been nothing but a dream and now it was over. A soft paw reached out to touch her cheek and Hannah realized that tears were rolling down her face. She hadn't wanted the dream to end, but it had.

"It's all right, Moishe," she said, reaching out to stroke his soft fur. "Maybe someday it'll be real. Maybe someday."

Index of Recipes

Baking Conversion Chart

These conversions are approximate, but they'll work just fine for Hannah Swensen's recipes.

VOLUME

U.S.	Metric
½ teaspoon	2 milliliters
1 teaspoon	5 milliliters
1 Tablespoon	15 milliliters
¼ cup	50 milliliters
⅓ cup	75 milliliters
½ cup	125 milliliters
¾ cup	175 milliliters
1 cup	¼ liter

WEIGHT

U.S.	Metric
1 ounce	28 grams
1 pound	454 grams

OVEN TEMPERATURE

Degrees Fahrenheit	Degrees Centigrade	British (Regulo) Gas Mark
325 degrees F.	165 degrees C.	3
350 degrees F.	175 degrees C.	4
375 degrees F.	190 degrees C.	5

Note: Hannah's rectangular sheet cake pan, 9 inches by 13 inches, is approximately 23 centimeters by 32.5 centimeters.

Here's a special bonus recipe from *New York Times* bestselling author Joanne Fluke!

WHITE CHOCOLATE AND RAISIN WHIPPERSNAPPER COOKIES

Preheat oven to 350 degrees F., rack in the middle position.

2 cups white chocolate or vanilla baking chips *(I used Nestlé – the 11-ounce package)*

1 cup raisins

1 cup sweetened coconut flakes

1 box *(the kind that makes a 9-inch by 13-inch cake)* spice cake mix *(I used Duncan Hines)*

2 cups of original Cool Whip *(not low-fat Cool Whip)*

1 large egg, beaten *(just whip it up in a glass with a fork)*

½ cup powdered *(confectioners)* sugar *(for rolling the cookies—there's no need to sift unless it's got lumps)*

30 minutes before you're ready to bake, stick a teaspoon from your silverware drawer in a large freezer-safe mixing bowl. Place the bowl with the spoon in the freezer to chill.

Measure out 2 cups of white chocolate or vanilla baking chips.

If you have a food processor, attach the steel blade. If you don't, you'll have to do your chopping with a knife.

Put the white chocolate or vanilla chips in the bottom of the food processor bowl.

Put the raisins on top of the white chocolate chips.

Measure the sweetened coconut flakes. Make sure to press them down in the cup to fill it to the top.

Put the sweetened coconut flakes on top of the raisins.

Process the chips, raisins, and coconut flakes in an on-and-off motion with the steel blade. Continue to process until the chips and raisins are in pieces the size of coarse gravel.

Either spray a cookie sheet with Pam or another nonstick cooking spray, or line it with parchment paper and then spray that.

Remove the large mixing bowl from the freezer and add approximately half of the spice cake mix from the box.

In a separate bowl, measure out 2 cups of original Cool Whip.

Add the beaten egg to the Cool Whip. Using a rubber spatula, fold the egg into the Cool Whip. Be careful not to stir too much. Keep as much air in this mixture as possible.

Return to the large mixing bowl, the one that you chilled and now holds half of the spice cake mix.

Add the chopped white chocolate or vanilla chips, raisins, and the chopped sweetened coconut flakes to the large bowl with the cake mix. Mix them in thoroughly.

Add the contents of the smaller bowl to the large bowl. Using the rubber spatula again, fold in the Cool Whip and egg mixture. Try to do this gently to keep the air in the mixture.

Sprinkle the rest of the spice cake mix on top, and fold it in gently with the rubber spatula. Continue to fold until everything is well mixed.

Place the half-cup of powdered sugar in a shallow bowl. Dust your impeccably clean hands with powdered sugar.

Scoop out dough with your chilled spoon and place it in the bowl of powdered sugar, rolling it around with your fingers until it forms a small ball. The balls should be just a bit bigger than a walnut with its shell. Place it in the bowl of powdered sugar, and shape it into a ball with your fingers.

Form 12 dough balls, one at a time, for each cookie sheet.

Place the remaining cookie dough in the refrigerator to wait until your first sheet of cookies have baked and you're ready to bake another sheet. If you forget to do this and leave the bowl with the dough on the counter, it will be even stickier and more difficult to form into dough balls!

Bake your White Chocolate and Raisin Whippersnapper Cookies at 350 degrees F. for 15 minutes.

Remove your cookies from the oven and place the cookie sheet on a cold stovetop burner or a wire rack. Let the cookies cool on the cookie sheet for

4 minutes. These cookies will crumble if you take them off of the sheet too fast.

When 4 minutes have passed, remove the cookies from the sheet with a metal spatula and place them on a wire rack to complete cooling. If you used parchment paper, this is simple. Simply pull the paper off of the cookie sheet and onto the wire rack. The cookies can stay on the paper until they're cool.

Yield: 2 to 3 dozen soft and very tasty, insanely good cookies.

Spring has sprung in Lake Eden, Minnesota, but Hannah Swensen doesn't have time to stop and smell the roses— not with hot cross buns to make, treats to bake, and a sister to exonerate!

Hannah's up to her ears with Easter orders rushing in at The Cookie Jar, plus a festive meal to prepare for a dinner party at her mother's penthouse. But everything comes crashing to a halt when Hannah receives a panicked call from her sister Andrea—Mayor Richard Bascomb has been murdered . . . and Andrea is the prime suspect.

Even with his reputation for being a bully, Mayor Bascomb—or "Ricky Ticky," as Hannah's mother likes to call him—had been unusually testy in the days leading up to his death, leaving Hannah to wonder if he knew he was in danger. Meanwhile, folks with a motive for mayoral murder are popping up in Lake Eden. Was it a beleaguered colleague? A political rival? A jealous wife? Or a scorned mistress?

As orders pile up at The Cookie Jar—and children line up for Easter egg hunts—Hannah must spring into investigation mode and identify the real killer . . . before another murder happens!

Please turn the page for an exciting sneak peek of Joanne Fluke's newest Hannah Swensen mystery
TRIPLE CHOCOLATE CHEESECAKE MURDER coming soon wherever print and e-books are sold!

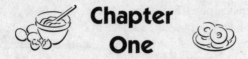

Chapter One

The chairs in Mayor Bascomb's outer office were uncomfortable and Hannah Swensen shifted her position. She'd brought the mayor's secretary, Terry Neilson, some sample cookies from The Cookie Jar, Hannah's bakery and coffee shop, and Terry was reaching for her third Vanilla Crunch cookie.

"These are great cookies, Hannah!" Terry told her, biting into the crunchy confection. "I'd better stop soon or Mayor Bascomb won't get any of these."

"Forget it, Andrea!" Mayor Bascomb's voice was so loud, they could hear it in the outer office. "Nothing you can say will change my mind. And if you keep it up, you're going to make me even madder! You and I both know that Bill was wrong to make that arrest!"

"Uh-oh!" Terry reacted to the angry words that they could hear, even though the mayor's office door was closed. "He's been in a horrid mood all week, and now he's on a real rant. I really hope your sister's got enough sense to leave before he says something really nasty."

Hannah sighed and shook her head. "Andrea won't leave. She's never walked away from a fight in her life. She's even more stubborn than Mayor Bascomb, especially when somebody insults her husband. And from what she told me, Bill was caught between a rock and a hard place. He had to arrest the mayor's nephew. The state trooper was standing right there, and Bill couldn't just let Bruce go the way he did the last two times."

Terry looked very apologetic. "I know. Bruce is a real menace on the road when he gets a snootful. I told the mayor that, but he never listens to reason when it comes to his brother's kid. He still thinks that Bill should have figured out a way to let Bruce go."

"But didn't the state trooper test Bruce for alcohol?"

"Yes, and Bruce's blood alcohol was twice as high as it should have been."

"I don't want to hear it, Andrea!" The mayor's angry voice interrupted their conversation. "My mind's made up, and your husband is history. He won't even get a job as a dogcatcher as long as I'm the mayor of Lake Eden!"

Both Hannah and Terry listened, but they couldn't hear Andrea's response. This made Hannah proud of her younger sister. So far, Andrea hadn't yelled back. The fact that they couldn't hear her meant that Andrea was still using a perfectly reasonable tone of voice, but Hannah knew that couldn't last forever. Eventually, Andrea would lose control and she'd give the mayor a piece of her mind!

"I'm impressed," Terry said admiringly. "Andrea's really keeping her cool."

"Yes, she is . . . so far. But she's always been very protective of her family. If Mayor Bascomb keeps this up, she'll snap."

"I almost wish she would. Nobody else has the nerve to tell him when he's being a you-know-what. Did Andrea tell you that Bill came in to talk to the mayor yesterday?"

Hannah nodded. "Yes, and she said the mayor refused to see Bill. That's one of the reasons Andrea came over here today. She promised me she'd be calm and reasonable, but she also said that she'd kick down his office door if he refused to see her."

"Do you think she actually would have done it?"

Hannah laughed. "Oh, yes. Maybe she wouldn't have succeeded. It looks like a pretty heavy door to me. But I know that Andrea would have given it her best shot. She's in mother-lion-protecting-her-cub mode."

"Enough!" Mayor Bascomb's voice was even louder than it had been before. "I've listened to your pathetic whining and sniveling for long enough. You're every bit as stupid as your husband!"

"Just one more thing, Mayor Bascomb. . ." Andrea's voice was louder and Hannah picked up her purse and Andrea's parka. "I think that'll do it."

"You mean Andrea's going to . . ."

"You bet," Hannah interrupted. "I know my sister and she can't take much more."

"You're the one who's pathetic!" Andrea's voice was almost as loud as Mayor Bascomb's had been. "You're nothing but a bully, and it's long past time that somebody stood up to you!"

"And you think that *you* can stand up to me, little lady?"

"I *know* I can! Bill's too much of a gentleman to take you on, but not me! Somebody's got to give you exactly what you deserve, you . . . you pig!"

Hannah jumped up from the chair. "Grab your coat, Terry! When Andrea charges in here, it's time for us all to get out of Dodge!"

"Right!" Terry grabbed her coat and purse and was pulling on her boots when they heard a sharp, stinging sound that was followed by a loud crash. "She slapped him?"

"That's what it sounded like to me. I think she slapped him right out of his chair!" Hannah hurried across the room and opened the door to the hallway. "Go out first, Terry. And stand out of the way. Andrea's so mad, she's going to explode out the door!"

Terry grabbed the plate of cookies that Hannah had brought and ran to the door. She had just stepped out, into the hallway, when Andrea came storming out of Mayor Bascomb's office. "Whoa!" Terry gasped, sheltering against the wall as Andrea raced past her. "Wait for us, Andrea!"

But Andrea didn't wait. She practically flew down the staircase and out into the street. By the time Hannah and Terry had managed to catch up with her, she was leaning against the old-fashioned, designer lamppost in front of the building, gasping for breath.

"Here, Andrea," Hannah, who had been holding her sister's parka, draped it around Andrea's shoulders. "Deep, calming breaths. It's okay. You're out of there now."

"I . . . I . . . I . . ."

"We heard," Hannah told her.

"I . . . slapped . . ."

"We know," Terry said.

"I . . . knocked . . . him . . ."

"You knocked him over in his chair," Hannah finished

the sentence for her. "Put your arms in your sleeves, Andrea. It's cold out here and you're overheated."

"Nasty . . . bully," Andrea managed to say. "I . . . I should have killed him!"

"A lot of people feel that way," Terry said.

"But . . . all I did was. . . was slap him!"

"Nobody else has ever done that before," Terry told her. "They might have felt like it, but they never had the courage to actually do it."

Once Andrea had calmed down enough to zip up her parka, they walked to their respective cars. "That was a really loud crash," Terry said, as she unlocked her car door and slid into the driver's seat. "I wonder if you broke his chair."

"Maybe," Andrea gave a weak little smile. "I hope I did, but after the things he said about Bill, I should have broken his *neck*!"

Connect with Us

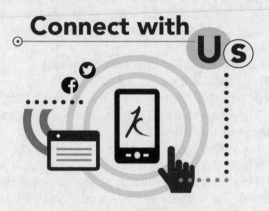

Visit us online at
KensingtonBooks.com
to read more from your favorite authors, see books
by series, view reading group guides, and more.

for sneak peeks, chances to win books and prize packs,
and to share your thoughts with other readers.

facebook.com/kensingtonpublishing
twitter.com/kensingtonbooks

Tell us what you think!

To share your thoughts, submit a review,
or sign up for our eNewsletters, please visit:
KensingtonBooks.com/TellUs.